HOUND
AND
KEY

OTHER BOOKS BY RHIANNON HELD

Silver
Tarnished
Reflected
Wolfsbane

HOUND
AND
KEY

Rhiannon Held

Printed in the United States of America

First Printing, 2016

ISBN 978-1-943545-02-5

Lantern Symbol by João Proença

Cover design by Kate Marshall
www.katemarshalldesigns.com

www.rhiannonheld.com

To Nana
A. Celia Sanderson
April 21, 1921–June 19, 2016
For how she created with her hands, with love,
and how she taught others to do the same

HOUND
AND
KEY

Prologue

In the before times
When the youngest of the gods was lost
Map found her waypoint
Hound followed her trail
Key opened the gates
Lantern lit their steps
And Breath brought her back to life

Around the time their shared appetizer was cleared away, Eric started cursing himself for not having told his date the truth about where he'd first seen her. Maybe not when he asked her out, but certainly before any of their food arrived. Listening to the ebb and swell of unvoiced laughter below the surface of her anecdotes, he already knew he wanted to ask her on a second date. He needed to admit the truth as soon as possible, no matter how awkward. No sense breaking the current conversation-al thread, though. "So you work for TendarisHerron?"

Patricia threaded a hand under her fine black hair to cup the side of her neck. "I guess you could say I'm scientist sup-port and official paperwork wrangler." She paused for laughter he was happy to provide. "I don't deal with our drug trials, but I make sure the scientists follow proper procedure and keep good notes in the research stages before then." She launched into a story about shaking down people for paperwork be-fore they left for the weekend. Eric caught himself reading her hands and the small lifts at the corners of her mouth, tracking the minutia of her mood to see if she was interested or bored, content or anxious.

He made himself stop. He was off duty. He didn't need to read her; he could simply enjoy her story. He listened while looking out the window instead. West facing, so for dinner they probably would need the shades unfurled, but now at lunch the expansive glass allowed spring light to flood in. A deck stretched away outside, green wildness below. Eric guessed they'd made lemonade out of mandated wetland-area lemons, but that didn't diminish the feeling of looking out over nature.

Maybe he could laugh off how he'd first seen her. *Funny thing, my boss is so worried about her boyfriend, your CEO, she has me photograph his female employees. Don't worry, though, I haven't found anything. My boss is just paranoid.* It didn't sound very humorous when he laid it out in his mind. It sounded like a stalker trying to cover his tracks.

"And you? You said you were an assistant?" Patricia sipped her water, tilted her head into her bracing hand.

"I've actually been friends with my boss since college." For a given value of friend. "So assistant's probably not quite the word, but I can't think of anything better. The duties end up being pretty eclectic. Scheduling a venue for one of her parties or chasing one of her guest's favored esoteric brand of whiskey all over town." Eric smiled to hide the glancing path his explanation took to the vicinity of the truth. He knew he was only piling on later awkwardness, but he couldn't help himself.

He had actually done both of those things once for Ariadne, but the bulk of his duties for her were the strange, semilegal ones he couldn't admit to anyone: the keys lifted, the people tailed, the long-distance photos snapped. Even if Patricia hadn't been the subject of one of those photos, he'd have had a hard time spinning his job to sound normal. He was reminded powerfully why he rarely dated anymore.

Patricia lifted her brows, teasing. "And the rest of the time? Unless she has a party every night of the week . . . "

Eric hadn't expected her to call him on the evasion. Another reason to want her to stick around: people got boring fast when you could read them and predict them too well. A woman who could surprise him—but now he'd missed his rhythm slightly. "Well, I—" The pause was getting too long. Shit. "You know Ariadne inherited her fortune, so she uses it to fund her hobby of genealogical research?"

Patricia sat back. There, the first flicker of awkwardness. "I heard that. When she first started her business partnership with TendarisHerron so we can use her data to help genetically tailor our treatments."

"'Business partnership.'" Eric exaggerated the air quotes

to try to recapture a note of humor, but it earned him only a smile, not a laugh.

Patricia looked down at the empty space before her on the tablecloth that awaited her entree plate and shook her head. "Anyway, I'm sorry, I didn't mean to pry about your work."

Eric spoke quickly, determined not to miss his moment this time. Damn Ariadne, not only for suspecting this innocent woman, but for indirectly spoiling his chances with her. Not that Ariadne could have spoiled anything if he hadn't agreed to work for her, of his own free will. "No, I'm sorry. I haven't had to explain it in a while, that's all. Honestly, I take care of everything organizational Ariadne doesn't feel like doing herself."

Patricia nodded but couldn't seem to find any particular response to that. Eric realized he needed to disclose something else important to him, and fast, even if it made her dismiss him for another reason. "My avocation is stage magic, though." Eric braced for her reaction. Would she be one of the people who considered his calling juvenile, or assumed it was all a con to fleece tourists on street corners?

Wonder of wonders, Patricia returned to her position leaning on her elbow and angled her body toward him. A very good sign. "Literally on a stage, you mean?"

"My hours with Ariadne are flexible, so I perform at renaissance faires and other summer festivals. You know how the local cheese or pickle fest will often have a stage for live music? Sometimes they invite other local acts."

"That's great." Warmth broke into her tone, paralleling a smile's spread across her lips. "Sawing pretty women in half?"

"Sawing my sister in half, if anyone," Eric said, dry. "But usually she's the audience plant instead. I do close-up magic, more intimate sleight-of-hand tricks than showy chains and water tank stuff." He made an ironic "ooh magical" twirled-fingers gesture with one hand to keep her attention while with the other he palmed a dried grain stalk, heavy with golden kernels at the top, from the table's small flower arrangement. At this point, even if they thought magic was silly, most people couldn't help but ask—

"Can you show me something here?" Patricia exhaled on a laughing note and leaned in to examine his apparently empty hands, presented palm up, then palm down.

Eric shifted his gaze to the side of her head, as if distracted from his coming trick. "Oh, here, you've got something caught . . . " He pulled the stalk from her hair, showed it to her, then tucked it behind her ear so she could wear it like a flower.

Patricia pushed his hands away, laughing, but he noticed that she didn't remove the stalk. Instead, she kept his hands trapped under hers on the tabletop. "Mr. Smooth."

Then she frowned. "Oh." Her tone dropped away, like she suddenly felt ill. "I—" Her pupils snapped open, black swallowing brown until she looked alien and blind.

"Patricia?" She didn't respond. What—?

Her pupils snapped down to pinpricks, and she slumped sideways in her chair, boneless. Eric lunged, bumping knees on the table in his rush, but couldn't reach her before she tumbled to the floor with the splayed indignity of unconsciousness or death. He knelt, shoved her chair aside, helped her onto her back. He searched her face for some reaction, shook her shoulders. She couldn't be—be—she had to just be unconscious. "Patricia?"

Someone gasped and chairs scraped across the whole room. It wasn't until someone behind him shouted, "Call 911!" that Eric realized he should have done that himself. All right. Check if she was breathing. He could do that. That CPR class had been a while back, but he had to do *something*.

She wasn't breathing. Start compressions. He had enough muscle memory to get his fingers laced, his body weight over his locked elbows. The resistance, the unexpectedly solid thud of a blow needed to get the chest down, he'd forgotten that, but he remembered it from the dummy now. He was doing the compressions correctly, then.

Counting. He was supposed to be counting compressions until he gave two breaths. He remembered that part: two. In a haze, Eric did another compression, checked her breathing. Nothing. She was so still. Another cycle. Keep going until the paramedics got here.

Eric kept going. Then between compressions and breaths, someone grabbed his shoulders, pulled him away. The world rushed back in: servers herding gawking diners away, beginning at the clear path they'd already carved for the EMTs and their gurney. A comfortingly uniformed man and woman already knelt over Patricia while a second man was the one who'd pulled Eric back.

"Sir? Are you her boyfriend?" he asked, tone kind. "What happened? Does she have any allergies, health problems you know of?"

Eric shook his head, kept shaking it until he finally found words again. "It's our first date. I don't know much about her at all. She was just talking normally, she wasn't even eating to choke on anything, then she fell—" He craned around the EMT. The others were busy over Patricia, models of efficient action, but something was missing about their body language. Some sense of—hope. "Will she—?"

The EMT grimaced, more than enough for an answer from someone of his training and experience. "We'll do our very best, sir."

Dead. She couldn't possibly be dead. She was young. She'd seemed healthy. Eric gave the EMT her full name, hardly heard anything else. There must not have been any other questions, though, because the EMT turned away and Eric found himself herded out of the way by the restaurant manager, toward the crowd of other diners.

Suddenly he couldn't bear the idea of joining the crowd in staring at her unmoving body. He pushed outward through the gawkers, movements getting increasingly rough. He needed air. You never expected someone to just *die* in front of you. What had even happened? "Heart attack" caught at his attention from the surrounding murmur of frightened conversation, though he lost the rest of the sentence in the muddle.

He reached the deck, clenched his hands around the nearest railing, new pressure-treated wood. She was too young for a heart attack. But that—that was familiar. Someone else he'd heard about recently had been too young. As a mental exercise to make his thoughts move in one direction, rather than spinning everywhere at once, Eric tracked the thought until he dragged up a name. It had been a young man whose keys he'd stolen. Part of the prep for getting close enough to lift someone's keys or tail them without being noticed was getting to know them, their daily routine, and what part an undistinguished man should briefly play in it. So when he'd recognized the name later in the news, he'd known how strange it truly was, how apparently healthy the man had been. Heart failure. Too young.

Now he'd found the connection, Eric couldn't get it out of his head. Two people whose lives he'd intersected, for his boss. Two people dead. He twisted to look over his shoulder into the dining room. He couldn't see Patricia through the crowd, but their energy was souring from hope into shock. The paramedics pushed into view, leaving through the front doors, but the body on the gurney was very still.

With shaking hands, Eric pulled out his phone and searched the Internet for every name he could remember that Ariadne had pointed him at, over the four years he'd worked for her.

Obituaries. Memorial notices. Every one. And he knew there were names he wasn't remembering. Eric shoved his phone away, like that would change the search results.

She'd told him his job was to help her compile her genealogical data even when sources were reluctant. That explanation had been lame enough to insult them both, so Eric had thought—that seemed like such a thin excuse now, but how could he have guessed something like this—he'd truly thought Ariadne had wanted to check up on her boyfriend and his employees. A few of the names had been directly connected to TendarisHerron, more had been people in the industry, regulators. So it had made a sort of sense on the surface, to assume the photos of female employees were to catch infidelity in progress, the other photos and keys to check for stolen trade secrets, either in a handoff or in people's apartments, but he hadn't *found* anything compromising. His photos, his sessions of tailing, showed only mundane activities, if no one was perfectly innocent. After his initial wariness, he'd justified the job to himself with that fact. If Ariadne wanted to dig up dirt on people with nothing to hide, Eric didn't mind the generous paycheck. Maybe it gave her a sense of control, to know she could find dirt when she wanted it.

He should have *guessed* that there had to be more to it. He longed to cling to the idea of failed surveillance and coincidental death, but the surveillance excuse made too little sense. Not that a hit list made any *more*.

This close, the greenery below the restaurant's deck lost its illusion and looked ragged, weedy, and swampy. So everyone he followed for Ariadne ended up dead. How? Patricia was too young and too obviously healthy for a real heart attack. Poison? No one had touched her, they'd shared the same appetizer, and their water had been poured from the same pitcher into crystal-clean glasses. He'd touched her chair. She hadn't visited the restroom . . .

Eric leaned forward until his forehead touched his hands so he didn't have to look at the weeds anymore. A conspiracy theorist could still posit a tasteless, odorless, invisible poison coating the inside of her water glass, but he doubted those kinds of poisons existed in reality. Nor did he see how she could have been exposed to something before arriving that would show no effect for hours, then kill in instants.

And that left . . . what?

Eric pushed himself up and forced himself to turn back to the dining room. Even with Patricia's body gone, a representative of officialdom might want to talk to him. He should stay findable. And someone official would inform her family, right? Should he—but he hardly even knew her. He didn't know anything about her family, or if she even had any she was close to. The contradiction of death so close to him, yet not touching him, made Eric's stomach twist, acid.

But it *had* touched him. He wasn't going to go back to his lame excuses and justifications. Something was going on here, and he was going to find out what the hell Ariadne was doing. And how.

And stop her.

1

Being late but not too late required careful calculation. Normally on a job, Eric was always early and included in his plans a point where he could watch and wait for his moment without being observed. But Ariadne wasn't stupid, and turning his skills back on her took more finesse. A month had passed after Patricia's death before Ariadne had given him his next assignment, and he'd spent every minute of it researching, thinking, planning, so he could play the next fifteen minutes perfectly.

He parked, off-kilter in his hurry, beside the garages at the side of the house where employees were supposed to pull their vehicles. The garages themselves had undoubtedly been intended for boats and ATVs and other rich adults' playthings, but Ariadne had filled them instead with her sleek luxury cars, inexplicably numerous flavors of transportation for someone who never drove herself.

Eric slammed his door and sprinted for the front of the house. Her chauffeur had opened the door of a silver BMW, and Eric was indeed late but not too late because Ariadne was striding toward it, not driving away out of reach.

"Got them." He raised his voice to carry across the remaining stretch of curved gravel drive and held up his hand, key ring over his middle finger and bunch of keys splayed over his palm. From here, she wouldn't be able to see he'd removed the house key, preventing a break-in and presumably neutering the worst harm the rest could do in another's possession. She'd said to have the keys to her by today, and so he had, though he hoped she wouldn't examine them herself or reflect that in the four years he'd worked for her, he'd never shaved a deadline so close before.

Ariadne paused with her hand on the car door. For once, with the car for scale, she looked as short as she really was, barely five feet tall. The recent daylight saving jump couldn't help her this late in the evening, so her skin was merely sandy in the splashed porch and window light from the house, without the ephemeral glow sunlight could give it, like sand heated not quite far enough for glass. Her black hair was loose around her shoulders, sumptuous. He supposed she was off to late dinner or drinks with her "business partner," Clive Herron, CEO of TendarisHerron. Eric always thought of him with his full title, since that was how news articles invariably referred to him when reporting how the local company had made it to the big leagues.

Ariadne was quiet for several beats, eyes on Eric's face, not on the keys as he would have expected. He didn't want her digging into his motives, even if he was certain all that showed on his face was the exertion of his sprint. He didn't look guilty, and besides, what could she possibly guess he'd be guilty about? The one brief footnote of a report on Patricia's death hadn't mentioned anyone eating with her at the restaurant.

Then Ariadne's lips curved. "Next time, don't be so late." She withdrew her phone from a highly fashionable clutch purse and ostentatiously checked the time. "It has to be done tonight. Get Hank to let you in at the cottages." She slid elegantly into the car and let her chauffer shut the door.

Eric returned the keys to his pocket and drew a deep breath to counteract both the panting and his relief. You could nudge, control as many elements in a situation as you could touch to remove other options, study past behavior until predictions zeroed in, but you could never be absolutely certain someone would make the choice you wanted them to. But she had. And now he had an in, tracking someone's lifted keys into the inner layer of Ariadne's empire. Or her web, perhaps, with Ariadne standing as a spider in the center of it all, attention on each thread-twitch.

He knew now that inner layer had to be something more than a server farm or office park space for more researchers. Something to do with *how* she accomplished all those deaths, because Eric had no doubt by now that she'd accomplished them. With any luck, the fact that the house key was gone wouldn't stop the process until after he got a few hints as to *why* people had had to die, as well.

Eric jogged back to his car. He watched his speed along the twisting roads among the houses—perhaps better called estates—along Lake Washington out of habit, but impatience got the better of him as he headed north on the freeway. After a month spent with the knowledge of what he'd been party to, he was so close to a few answers. Foolish, perhaps, but Ariadne could make tickets disappear as easily as sneezing if she was in the right mood and you could make a case for having acquired them in the line of duty.

And maybe he could do something with those answers when he got them. Eric couldn't plan any farther than that, not knowing what Ariadne hid at the cottages, but in the weeks since Patricia's death, he'd become increasingly certain that was what he needed to do to live with himself. Stop the deaths.

"Compound" would have been a better name than "cottages." Or "subdivision," maybe, tucked as it was among other raw, new developments in Woodinville. They all had coy names like "Evergreen Glen." Ariadne's cottages were only distinguished by being a gated community among open subdivisions that kept their own restrictions invisible as homeowners' association regulations.

Eric eased up to the gatehouse beside a ridiculous "Arbor Cottages" brick sign. He wouldn't be surprised if the locals assumed it was an Alzheimer's care facility, with walls and a name like that. The lights around the gatehouse were bright but aimed to pool close and not disrupt the soft darkness beyond among the houses, dotted only with standard suburban streetlights.

Eric rolled down his window to speak to the man on duty in the small booth, someone he didn't recognize. "Hank should be expecting me." Eric found the most obvious camera and faced it straight on. Hank knew him, after years of pleasantries over coffee as they passed each other outside Ariadne's home office, Hank giving security reports and Eric receiving assignments. Easier to let Hank identify him directly on a monitor now than to fuss with ID to make it up through the lower ranks to reach him. It wasn't like Eric had a badge for "hit list support."

He wondered idly how much Hank knew of the hit list. This plan—and frankly, good sense—didn't call for trying to drag the information out of him, though. This was the time for smooth smiles and playing along, Eric's real motives locked farther below the surface than usual.

The man in the booth listened to his walkie-talkie and punched the button so the steel gate, black paint not really succeeding in making it appear cast-iron, rolled aside with stately speed. Eric drove in at a similar speed and, as he'd expected, met Hank coming out of the nearest house. It was the one with the grandest landscaping and a water feature, undoubtedly built to serve as the sales office until it was sold last. The black man had a bit of a gut, but honest muscles showed in the bulk of his arms under the security uniform sleeves.

Hank waved Eric toward a visitor parking lot with a fence and gate worthy of a police impound lot. Eric tried to imagine why. To make sure anyone who entered and caused trouble had to escape on foot? Did they have people imprisoned here?

Hank strolled in after him. By the time Eric had parked and walked over to join him, Hank was waiting in the driver's seat of a golf cart. Eric weighed how well he knew Hank, then risked an honest opinion as he swung into the passenger seat. "You're shitting me."

Hank barked a laugh and scrubbed a hand over his buzzed-short hair. "Murder on the dignity, I know. But Key bribed someone into teaching her to drive about a year back and there's obviously nothing we can do to keep her out of any vehicle she wants to get into. So the best we can do is keep everything in sight of the gatehouse except things that aren't enough fun to tempt her to joyride."

Eric's mental brows rose at the unexpected flow of information. It was what he wanted, yes, to know what the hell was going on in here. That was exactly why he didn't trust it when it came too easy.

And Hank must know that as well. Eric cast him a sideways glance and let the merest trickle of his real thoughts onto his face. Hank barked with laughter again. "The Boss said if you're determined to stick your nose into a higher security clearance, as it were, I don't need to stop you. I'm well aware that if I decide I want out of this job before I'm literally too infirm to continue, my severance package is a personalized, untraceable heart attack. I assume you know the same, so I won't insult your intelligence."

Eric had to admit to himself he hadn't considered it in quite those terms, but maybe he should have. The same way he should have considered "illegal" and "invasion of privacy" in those terms way back when Ariadne had offered him the job.

And "complicit" and "murder" now. "I believe aneurism is also a common diagnosis." Patricia's death had been called an undiagnosed heart defect. Too young for a heart attack.

"Anyway, I don't mind my job. They're good kids, even if you could make the case for the Hound never having been much of a kid." The way Hank's expression softened made Eric wonder about opportunities for a family lost to long hours, safety paranoia, and living inside the compound simply because it saved on commuting.

Hank twisted in his seat to check a canvas grocery store bag of books was settled securely on the floor of the back seat, then set off at a brisk—for a golf cart—clip. "If you don't mind—" his tone suggested Eric better not, "we'll do the library run for the Hound before I take you to Key."

"Humanizing them?" Eric said. He didn't know who "they" were, other than kids with codenames, apparently, somehow connected to untraceable deaths. He wasn't sure what he'd been expecting, but kids sure hadn't been it. He'd been—still was—so angry at himself, he supposed he'd been hoping for a more righteous target to transfer the anger to.

"The opposite, in a way." Hank shook his head. "You'll see." He zoomed up the gently curving street. With no one parked on either side, it was ridiculously wide for only a golf cart. The March air hadn't been too bad to walk around in, but even at golf cart speeds, it bit hard.

They pulled up in the driveway of one of the neutrally painted houses, no different than any other. Hank snagged the bag of books and knocked perfunctorily on the front door before letting himself in. Another anonymous man in the same security uniform looked up from watching a game at low volume on a tablet at the kitchen table and nodded.

"Got a job?" A teen boy of fourteen or fifteen laid his arm over the back of the couch so he could twist to face them better. He'd gotten his height, but his face still showed obvious baby fat over what would probably be a strong jaw line eventually. He reminded Eric of a couple of his cousins at that age, in an undistinguished teen boy way, muddy brown eyes and golden brown hair.

"No job. New books." Hank thumped the bag of books on the kitchen table. The boy looked at them expressionlessly for a beat or two before closing the book on his lap with a snap. He set it on the coffee table, walked over, and unpacked the grocery bag into a single towering pile so carefully, Eric started to wonder if he had OCD.

But that wasn't it, either. When his pile of books shifted, glossy cover slipping on glossy cover, he didn't stop and straighten it. He apparently was simply so unexcited about the books that he didn't feel inclined to pause and examine or open any of them before he'd unloaded the whole bag.

They were all travel books, united only in that and their glossy pictures. The wine country of France settled on top of ghost tours of Chicago with no visible reaction from the boy. When the grocery bag was empty, the boy lifted the stack and turned for the hall. A beat late again, he spoke, uninflected. "I'll take these upstairs and read before bed." He sounded like he'd been taught he had to tell someone where he was going, but didn't understand that some destinations were unimportant or obvious.

When the boy was gone, Eric realized he was more than a little creeped out. Sullen silence and resistance to interaction, he would have understood, but this kid had been so . . . emotionless, Eric supposed.

"Quiet day?" Hank asked the guy at the kitchen table, who shrugged.

"He worked out for about two hours in the morning, spent some of the afternoon tracking a crow around the yards. Same old." He waited for further questions. When Hank nodded and headed for the front door instead, he turned the volume up on his game and went back to watching.

On the walk to the golf cart and the drive to the next house, Eric considered and discarded a number of possible comments. Definitely not particularly humanizing, as Hank had said, and with no clear connection to the deaths. Asking outright who the boy was felt beneath them both, so in the end Eric kept his mouth shut and waited to see what kind of kid had the code-name "Key."

"I'm surprised we haven't seen you out here before now." Hank's easy-going tone didn't even bother concealing that he was digging. "Rumor says you were sleeping with the boss, back in the day."

"Way back in the day." It was such a ridiculous situation, Eric's only real option was to laugh it off. "When we were in college and I was just a punk kid, undeclared because I still thought I might have an actual career in stage magic." Then he'd grown up, and she had gone on being the same focused, driven person she'd always been. She hadn't even needed to dump him; he'd seen the writing on the wall two years into the relationship.

And yet. Since she didn't have any living family, he'd stayed on as her emergency contact, and she'd helped him when his teen cousin got pregnant and he didn't know the first thing about adoption procedures. Somehow an ex relationship had become a surrogate family one, like when she asked him to be the executor for her will—but not so strong a relationship that she left him anything in that will. And then when he'd quit his office drone job to do his magic show full time and that crashed and burned, she'd offered him this job and proved to have no trouble with a relationship where she treated him like just another underling.

He'd gotten inured to just how weird the relationship really was over time, he supposed. Examined now, it was deeply dysfunctional. But none of that was Hank's business. Eric purposefully continued with a light tone. "I actually wondered if Ariadne was Mormon at first, given the obsession with genealogy. Asked her where her fancy underwear was."

Hank slapped his knee in appreciation and let out a laugh. "Listen to you with her first name and all. Living dangerously. Maybe you're getting a promotion."

Eric doubted it. The longer that "determined to stick your nose into a higher security clearance" floated at the back of his mind, the more it worried him. Ariadne had seen part of the way through his act—how far? What assumption of his motives was she operating on? Whatever it was, he needed to get as much information as possible in this visit, in case she moved against him soon. But he'd known that already.

"You'll want to leave your personal keys in the cart, by the way." Hank leaned over and tapped a small recessed shelf in the golf cart's dash, clearly meant for storing assorted small crap in lieu of a glove box. Eric dug them out without protest. It made no sense, but neither did a number of the security measures here. Being without his keys didn't seem likely to put Eric in any more danger than he already was.

They turned into another driveway in front of yet another house. Hank left the golf cart key in the ignition and led the way. The first sign of individuality was the welcome mat. It read, "Welcome, pardner," in old-timey script over a line drawing of a stagecoach. This time, after knocking and opening the door, Hank called ahead before going in. "Got a job, Key."

Inside the front hall, Eric felt a bit assaulted by the decorating scheme, or at least what he could see of it from oblique views into the first couple of rooms. It looked like one he privately thought of as "online shopping." No one piece of furniture or art was bad, necessarily, but no two items in the place matched, as if they had been purchased one by one without any means to gauge scale or blend with other items. They were also too new to be the "thrift shop and family hand-me-downs" style. The rooms were fairly cluttered, but at least that gave the house a comfortable feeling, like someone human lived here. He hadn't realized how stark the boy's house had been until he had this for contrast.

"A job or a target? I told Her Majesty I wasn't going to take another target so soon," a woman's voice called from farther inside the house. A moment later, the speaker stepped in stockinged feet into the hallway.

Her hair was . . . well, it was red. Eric supposed it would normally have been called fire engine red, but for him it instead evoked Clifford, favorite of his sister's story times when they were children. It was utterly the wrong color for the woman's skin tone, Middle Eastern like Ariadne's. He supposed in a way it matched her features, which were similarly too strong for conventional beauty. Having her hair back in a messy ponytail only accentuated them.

"You didn't say you were bringing someone new." The young woman—Key, Eric supposed he might as well call her for lack of anything else—lengthened her strides down the hall and stopped in front of him. Her expression held unapologetic evaluation, or possibly she was untrained in the social art of softening and hiding emotions. She looked a bit older than he might have expected for that kind of innocence, perhaps twenty-five or twenty-six.

"This is Eric Davis, Boss's assistant," Hank said. Eric suppressed a grimace at hearing the ill-fitting job title once more.

"So, Eric Davis, what's the key to your heart?" Key reached for his chest. Like any beginner, she was a bit clumsy with the rest of her body, which clued him to look hard at her hand. He caught a glimpse of the small object she was transferring from palm to fingertips to make it "appear" as she plucked it from thin air.

"Interesting." Key held the ornate brass key out on her palm. "I'd have expected something more modern." Hank leaned over and looked impressed.

"That came right out of your pocket." Eric made his voice a little strident to further tie up her attention and leaned to tap her front hip pocket. Probably not precisely where she'd gotten it, but that wasn't the point. He smoothly swiped the key with his other hand while she was distracted.

He transferred it hand to hand while she was staring at her empty palm in consternation, then flipped the key up right under her nose. He probably shouldn't play, but it was fun and she'd started it.

Standing right up close like that, he got an intimate view of the realization dawning in her expression. Far from being annoyed, her whole face lit up. Something in Eric lit up in response. Her body was nearly touching his in several places, and the curve at her waist looked just right to rest a hand on.

And she knew sleight of hand. Yow.

"Finding the keys to people's hearts was a trick all along?" Hank's easy-going face settled into a glare, and his hand went up to his own chest.

Eric remembered himself and hastily backed a step away from Key. What the hell was he doing, letting himself get distracted like that? He was here to investigate, not pick up women.

More immediately, should he out Key to Hank or not? He had no idea of the underlying currents. He did tuck the key away in his pocket, since "out of sight, out of mind" worked more often than people realized.

Hank didn't seem to need an answer from him, though. "We talked about this, Key. No misleading anyone about your powers."

"I believe what the Ice Queen said was 'for purposes of intimidation.'" Key made her air quotes into emphatic, jerky motions.

Hank sighed. Deeply, almost parentally. "If we can get this target taken care of without fuss, I won't say anything to her."

A muscle jumped in Key's jaw. To Eric's read, it was the tip of an iceberg of frustration and helplessness. "No deal. I told her no more targets for a while. But I suppose that doesn't matter." She held out her wrists pressed together, a classic "so arrest me" gesture. "And just so you know, never mind avoiding intimidation, someday I'd like a little credit for not running off to Canada or something every other week to make you all drag me back. You know Hound would enjoy it."

To Eric's surprise, Hank actually took her up on her gesture. He drew a zip tie from a bunch tucked into his belt beside his walkie-talkie holster and bound her wrists with a smooth, efficient movement.

"What I keep telling her is that when *she* acts up or refuses a target, one of *us* gets it from the Boss." Hank sighed like a parent with a wayward child, dropped his hands, and gestured in invitation from Eric to Key.

Eric checked Key's face for a reaction to being talked about like she wasn't there . . . and found no one at home. At least, not that he could see. A last flash or flicker of something flared as her tendons stood out, twisting against the tie, then died. It was like looking at the Hound's expression had been. "What . . . ?" Eric asked, unable to form a better question.

"It's a purely mechanical binding. She can't unlock it." Hank put one hand under the loop of plastic, one over, and for a moment it looked like he was simply clasping her wrists, fatherly. "But she tries so hard, it trips her into a kind of . . . focus state. Give her the target."

Eric took the lifted key ring out of his pocket, but held it tightly in a closed hand, undoubtedly imprinting zigzag lines into his skin. This wasn't anything like what he'd expected— even though he'd come into this thinking he didn't know what he expected. Not this. What was she going to even do with the keys? But this was what he'd wanted to find out. He couldn't choke now.

Key's gaze followed his movement, tracking normally. When he opened his fingers, her attention fastened onto the keys. Hank seemed to notice Eric's hesitation. He squeezed Key's wrists once and let go. "Don't worry; it's not hurting her. She's not human."

She could be human and an actress—she wouldn't even have to be particularly stellar, just competent. Only one way to tell. Eric nudged her hands ninety degrees until he could place the keys in her flat palm, and she clamshelled her other hand on top. "That's the target," he said, because it seemed like something formal was needed.

Key tilted her head slightly to the side, like something was interesting. Her already large pupils dilated even more, until the thin line of her iris was hardly visible, dark brown against black. "Done," she said calmly.

All thoughts of actresses, human, not human fled. Eric *knew.* The sight of Patricia's huge, black pupils was branded into his mind. Somehow these kids—kid and woman—were killing people.

As easy as that. Done. Removing the house key hadn't mattered. He'd just delivered another person to death. The weight on his conscience pressed in, making it hard to breathe for a second, but he shoved it back to its earlier position, merely looming. He was here to stop this. That hadn't changed.

Key twisted and opened her hands to let the key ring fall onto a decorative half-circle table along the wall, ironically probably designed as somewhere for a homeowner to drop their keys. Then she waited, passive. Hank glanced at Eric, but he must have read Eric's expression of iron control over shock as Eric being finished with Key. Hank took a utility tool off his belt and flipped open a blade. He popped it through the tie, cutting upward like he'd done it hundreds of times before.

"Can I talk to her?" Eric grimaced when Hank gave an "it's a free country" shrug. "Alone, I mean."

Key rubbed her wrists and shook her head once, again, like a dog shaking off anesthetic. By the time he could get a direct look at her eyes again, the pupils were normal. "I'll behave." He couldn't tell if it was an instinctive protest, like "Five more minutes," on waking disoriented, or if Key was reassuring her guard about leaving her alone with the newcomer.

Hank considered. "Don't promise to give her anything or teach her anything."

"I get to keep the keys, though." Key snatched the key ring she'd dumped so recently on the table, clearly meaning to get her nine-tenths of the law ready.

"She does," Hank said, relaxing fractionally. Eric wondered if Hank's read of Key, familiar as he was with her, told him that she wouldn't cause any more trouble tonight. "I'll head back to the gatehouse. Robert's stationed inside this house today, so just yell if you need anything." He hesitated on something more, facing Key's way, then didn't say anything. With a nod to Eric, he let himself out.

Eric and Key looked each other over in silence. "The zoo's open eleven to six p.m.," she said finally, tone sharp, and turned to walk back into the house. An inadvertent sock-slip step spoiled her air of self-possession. Eric counted to thirty under his breath as an interval for her to gather herself and feel more balanced, then followed.

2

In my youth, the elders told such tales.

Like how one day, in Dreamtime, the youngest of the gods wished to explore. She took up her dilly bag and spear and set out across the ocean in her canoe.

At the top of the stairs, Key paused with her hand on the doorknob of her TV room. *Unlocked.* That hadn't gone precisely well. She hated when people saw her nonhuman side too early. *Hated* it. It colored everything afterward.

But few enough new people visited their little walled city, she wanted to cultivate every one of them. The Ice Queen's assistant, of all people. Think of the information Key might be able to get out of him if she could win him over to her side.

And even if she couldn't get information, he was damn hot. Maybe it was the isolation talking—well, she knew it was—but the way his hands had moved in that trick . . .

Maybe he'd be safer for that than any of the guards, as well. It had taken a few months—glorious months—before She noticed that Key's first lover was always requesting the night shift, and She had Map target him. Map, not Hound, because Her Majesty knew Map would be sure to tell Key. The second guy she'd enticed even near her bed had been too tense to get it up and too frightened to stick around for anything else in the end. But if the assistant was only around for the space of one task, then gone again, no one should suspect him. And he wouldn't have anything to be frightened of.

Locked. Key frowned, switched the mechanism back. *Unlocked.* It didn't particularly matter, since the door was open, but it felt tidier. Whatever she tried to do with the newcomer, she probably didn't have much time to do it. If she could even trust him. Maybe he was Her Majesty's spy, sent to sniff out illicit lovers from a position on the ground or to report back if she propositioned him.

It all started with talking to him more, though. Feeling him out. Key left the door to lean for a view down the stairs into the hall, but she didn't see the guy following her yet. He'd said he wanted to talk to her, but was he waiting down there for her to finish her hissy fit? Should she go back down, or stay up here and play it cool?

Playing it cool got her further with the guards, at least. Key stepped into the TV room, leaving the door open and inviting. She could put her new keys away while she waited. She padded over and slid open one of her key baskets. She'd known she needed the shelf the moment she saw the picture online. The rows of baskets fit so precisely on each shelf, they were almost like drawers. Key unwound the ring from the keys and hefted the loose ones in her hand.

Storage unit. Ex's stuff. Maybe she'll still call to ask for it.

Car. Piece of shit. At least it's paid off.

Office. Juggling coffee. Might spill.

Supply closet. Always fucking blue pens. Why no black?

"Sounds like you must have hundreds of them." The new guy's voice made her jump. Here she was getting angry with Hank for zoning her out, and then she went and concentrated too hard on her powers herself. The office keys basket tipped in her hands, keys cascading out with a waterfall of heavy metal *tinks.* It wasn't as full as some of the other baskets, but he was probably right in his estimate.

"You startled me." Key knelt and stole a glance at his face. No disgust, at least. She gathered up as many office keys as her hand could hold.

Office. Hate t—Copier door. All o—File Cabinet. She could feel when she got to the ones at the bottom, whose target had been gone a long time, and that helped her relax. With the owner's emotions faded, she got a sharper picture of the lock it belonged to. *Old building. Fancy glass in the windows, marble on the stairs.* That one was rather sweet. She held it back and smoothed her thumb over the bow.

The new guy crouched next to her and scooped handfuls into the basket. The floor was quickly clear, leaving only the key in her hand. And suddenly the one she'd pretended came from his heart earlier. She hadn't seen him get it out, but he flipped it again, bow between his fingertips and blade suddenly pointing upward, like it had sprouted from his hand. "What's this one from?"

Key dropped the old building in the basket and took the key from Eric even though she already knew the answer. "A gate. Not as old as you might think, but old style. Kind of—" She traced the path of the curving metal bars she could see in her mind, but she didn't know if that helped Eric any. "Why ask about that?"

"You gave it to me." Eric smiled and pulled his hand back possessively, though she'd made no move for the key. "I was curious why that one in particular."

"People aren't very impressed if you tell them a Toyota key unlocks their heart." Key smiled back at him. He certainly gave off trustworthy vibes, but Key didn't really trust herself to read those correctly, what with her lack of practice. His casual black jacket hugged solid shoulders, and he had golden-brown hair. Not buzzed or gelled, but with just enough product to enhance the natural wave. Having watched Map experiment with taming his unruly curls, Key figured she knew from product even if she tended to fry her own hair with the bleaching for the dye, then give up in disgust and wear it back all the time. Eric's features were very even, almost tipping into average rather than attractive, but something about the pure interest in his expression transformed them.

"I'd imagine not." Eric touched one knee down to better balance himself. "Why hearts?"

This conversation definitely wasn't going as she'd imagined it would. Usually, if they'd been briefed on the basics of her and the other powers, new guards either bombarded her with questions or poisoned the silence with scrutiny, like wildlife biologists in a blind waiting for a particularly rare behavior to be exhibited. "Because it took me a long time to learn." A compromise with herself on trust: an answer, but no explanation of it.

Eric dusted one widespread hand against the other, banishing the key into thin air like a bit of fluff. He made a small questioning noise, as if asking if that's what she meant. Key wasn't fast enough to follow the key as he moved it, but she sensed it hidden against the bottom of his palm when he was done. "You're better at it than me, that's for sure."

"I've had longer, that's all." Eric shrugged.

Key plucked one—chemical supply cabinet padlock—from the basket and pretended to toss it up, catch it, and showed him the empty hand that didn't, in fact, catch. He laughed and it was as good as flirting. Better, even, than flirting with the guards, maybe as good as flirting on TV.

Her priorities were flipped, though. She wanted information more than she wanted sex, once she clamped down on the stupid flutter low in her stomach. Time to start initiating some topics herself, and watch his reactions. If he was Her spy, he would already know all this anyway. "Just so you're aware, I used to be human."

Eric settled his weight back, as if to listen even better. "Yeah?"

Key gestured vaguely toward the floor in indicate the scene below. "So you don't get the wrong impression from seeing me zoned out. I was born human. All of us powers were. Map, Hound, me, even Her Majesty. And Lantern." No reaction from Eric to the last name. Did that mean he didn't know who Lantern was, or he did and also knew to hide that information from Key?

"And you matured into your . . . power?" Eric seemed to have trouble with the word, which seemed like a good sign to Key. More likely he hadn't heard any of this before and so hadn't had time to get used to the idea and the vocabulary.

"I inherited mine. When the old Key died, I became the new one. I was probably about three or four at the time, because I don't remember it. If a power passes to a young child, they don't have any of that power's memories." That was a lie; she had a very few memories of her previous lives, but she certainly wasn't going to tell him that. "If a power passes to a baby, you get, well, Hound." She could tell Eric had met Hound, even before his exhalation of humor.

"And if it passes to an adult?" Eric's questions continued to be calm, patient. Key started to wonder again if she'd read him right. Shouldn't he be getting excited if this was new information?

"Map was around seven, I think. He has a few memories. And who knows about Her Majesty?" That got her raised eyebrows and she grimaced. Now was he playing purposely thick? "You know, 'the Boss.'" Key hated to allow Her the name, but—"Breath."

Key put away the office key basket and knelt up to get the reproduction basket to play with while she talked. Since those keys had been made for decorating and didn't open any real lock, she found them rather innocent and darling. She settled with the basket in her lap.

"Ariadne," he said, then cut himself off quickly. Key wondered if it was the first thing he'd said so far without thinking carefully. Calling the Ice Queen by her first name was awfully cozy. But Key *thought* she was right, that Her Majesty hadn't shared any information with him. Which would make him more trustworthy . . . and less useful.

Key dug a hand into her basket. "Do you even know the story of the powers?"

Eric switched to sitting cross-legged, probably thinking the story was going to be longer than it was. At least, it wasn't long how Key told it, as she'd first heard it from Lantern. She left the flourishes to Map because he occasionally remembered things.

"You think she tells anyone anything she doesn't have to?" Eric sighed, looked away, and seemed to decide on something. He looked back. "That's why I'm here."

Now or never. Key went with her gut because she didn't have anything better. "For information?" At his nod, she continued. "What do you have to barter for it?"

Eric spread his hands helplessly. "You seem to know much more than I do. What do you need?"

What Key *needed* were the memories of past Keys. Eric couldn't give her those. But maybe he could give her a path to finding Lantern. With Lantern, she could work on recovering her own memories. With memories, she would no longer be dependent on what Her Majesty chose to tell her, interspersed with as many lies as She wanted. And Key would know who she used to be, where she'd come from. Her roots. "It's less about what you know and more what you can find out from Her. But you need to hear the story to understand."

Eric dipped his head, prompting her. Key took a deep breath. Map was better at this. "So . . . the youngest of the gods, she was exploring and she got lost. Hurt, so she couldn't get back. So the gods sent the powers to find her because they didn't even know where to begin. But she'd left a drawing of where she wanted to go, so Map, he looked at it and led them to the destination, but she wasn't there."

Key checked Eric's expression. He had an actively listening air that was becoming familiar. "So Hound, he found where the youngest of the gods had walked. He touched her footstep and led them to a great palace built into the side of a mountain. But the palace gates were locked, so Key, she touched the lock and it opened for them." As she always did, Key tried to *remember,* feel the great, grand lock under her fingers, hear what it told her of the one who had built it, the one who had locked it. As always, she found nothing.

"And they went into the palace where it had been carved into the rock and it was so dark and deep, they could not see. So Lantern, she called the light and it came. And they could see the youngest of the gods. She had become so confused in the dark, she had fallen and was dead.

"So Breath said, 'She has no breath, no life in her. If only I had some, I could give it to her.' And Key was the bravest, and she said, take mine. And Breath did not wish to take the breath from her friend, but she did, and the youngest of the gods lived. And the youngest of the gods said, 'Fear not, Key lives again, as will all of you, from this time on. You must only find the person she has been reborn into.'"

It felt somewhat conceited to cast herself as the hero of the story, so Key withdrew her hand and stood to slot the reproduction key basket back in the shelf. "I don't remember that, as I've said. But Map has partial memories. I believe talking to someone with full memories will help trigger mine. Her Majesty isn't going to help anyone. That's why I need to find Lantern. She was reborn as an adult, so she has all her memories. And to find Lantern, I need your help. I think the Ice Queen knows where to start, even if She can't know precisely where Lantern is."

"Why?" At Key's blank look, Eric clarified. "Why would Ariadne know where Lantern is? Can you sense each other?" He was being so matter-of-fact about everything that Key abruptly found herself near relieved laughter. *Finally*, someone who didn't freak out because the powers weren't human.

"No, we can't sense each other. Except in a normal powers way, I guess." Key settled down cross-legged herself and chewed on her lip. This part wasn't anything She didn't know, but it was still hard for Key to talk about, because it was so personal. "Lantern snuck in and visited us when we were kids. That's how I first heard the story. But one of the guards must have seen and told Her, because She stormed in and She and Lantern had a screaming match." Key rubbed her temples with her fingers. She'd listened hard, but with little context at the time, the years had worn the substance of the words away all the more. "Mostly a lot of 'This isn't right, Breath!' And then Lantern had to run before the guards could grab her. I haven't seen her since."

Deep breath. "I'm sure She had Lantern followed. Her Majesty wants all the powers in one place. If Lantern isn't here, clearly Her Majesty hasn't found her yet, but She'd at least have

an idea where to start looking. I want you to get that for me."
Key stuck out her hand to formalize the deal.

Eric shook, with a kind of lopsided smile. "Fair enough.
But you haven't explained everything on your side yet. 'In a
normal powers way'? What does that mean? What can all of
you do? Besides . . . kill people."

That, for the first time, wasn't calm. Fair enough, Key supposed, since he wasn't looking at her when anger crept into
his tone. Maybe Hank had done her a favor by making it crys-
tal clear she wasn't doing any of this by choice, except for the
choice whether the coercion was implicit or explicit. "We call
it targeting. Cleaner that way." She allowed some of her morbid
humor through and even got a return of the lopsided smile for
the effort. "All of us, we can . . . know people, I guess you could
say. Through our particular means. And if you concentrate
hard, past knowing, that's targeting."

Key pulled a bottom basket out far enough to grab a key
at random. *Should have got the brakes checked before buying.*
What a lemon. "This key isn't owned by anyone right now, so I
can't know anything new, but it has a bit of a ghost of what the
owner used to be like, how they used the key." She slotted the
key back into the basket through the handle hole. "And I can
unlock anything."

"And the others?" Eric's attention followed the key like he
wanted to pick it up and examine it, but she assumed he realized nothing distinguished it from the hundreds of others.
"Map? Hound?"

"Hound reads people's trails and follows them. Like in the
story." Key stood. She was getting tired of story time. Eric's

questions had started out well, but they were heading into familiar territory now. "And if the story isn't clear in his case, you can ask Map yourself. He can decide what to tell you."

Eric started playing with the gate key again, making it vanish and reappear without apparent effort. Key stared at his hands with envy. "That's fair enough. You guys have been doing this all your lives, then? Living here, targeting for Ariadne?"

Key looked at her empty hands, flexed her fingers. "I've lived here as long as I remember. Me and Map, and then Hound. But all the targeting is new. She taught us how to do it in abstract, but we didn't have to use it until about four, five years ago, when our tutors left and more security showed up." She knew exactly where that key was. Her first. It was an office key, but it wasn't in the office key basket; it was tucked in her nightstand drawer.

She held up a hand for Eric to wait as she jogged to her bedroom, and he hadn't moved when she returned. "Maeve." She gave him a thin smile and held up the key. "I don't let myself linger much anymore, knowing them before I finish targeting. But she was my first." Even thinking about the woman, remembering the few seconds of footage the local news had shown of the memorial made her throat close up with the promise of tears.

Key spoke quickly to work the tightness out before it could grow. "I assume She didn't realize I'd see the memorial on TV, but it was so pretty, with all the knights from the faire she organized—" Key suddenly noticed Eric was pale, and she couldn't place when the blood had started to leave his face. Was he about to explode, accuse her of being a murderer? She tucked

Maeve's key into her pocket and crossed her arms. If he did, she'd call the guards on him. "What?"

"I knew a Maeve." Eric's voice wasn't strained, but it was definitely flat compared to before. The listening left his expression as his attention turned inward. "She'd promised to schedule me—the biggest ren faire in the Pacific Northwest, with multiple performances on multiple weekends. It was huge, for my career. In the confusion after she died, it fell through. A little over four years ago."

Then his face transformed again, all that stuffed downward as his listening returned to the surface. "Was it hard for all of you? Starting to target?"

Key felt vaguely like she should ask if it had been hard for *him*. They'd been talking so much about her feelings, and now he was clearly upset himself, but she wasn't exactly sure what the implications for his career were. And he had asked her. "Map doesn't talk about it. But he got a few jobs before I got my first, and it's not like he freaked out. Hound has to be close to his target, so he doesn't get many jobs even now."

Silence fell, like Eric was thinking really furiously, but he didn't come out with any more questions. Key started to get restless, and went to put Maeve's key back. Eric was standing when she returned. "Thank you for answering my questions," he said with a touch of formality.

She laughed tentatively. "If any more occur to you, I bet Lantern could answer *all* of them."

Eric exhaled on an answering laugh. "Well, not all. I do have one only Ariadne can answer, which is why she gets to be the boss. That's not in the story."

"Breath is the one who's supposed to find us, anytime we pass to someone new. That's what Map says, anyway." But there was a world of difference between finding and controlling, which was another reason she desperately needed an independent source of information, whether it was her own memories or not.

"Huh." Eric's eyes tracked on something invisible for a moment, thinking hard. "I'll certainly see what I can learn about Lantern." His gaze focused again. "Hound can't track her?"

Key was mildly impressed. He must have actually processed what she'd told him. "He can't track someone without finding a relatively recent point they passed. We don't have that for Lantern. Her only visit was years ago, before this Hound was even here. But once we find a recent point . . . "

Eric made a noise of understanding. "Can I come back and see you, even if I haven't found anything yet? And Map too? You might be surprised what you know that you don't realize is helpful."

Key hooked her thumbs in her hip pockets and tried to stand sexy. At least, it always collected stares when she used it on the guards. "I can't stop you. You have to convince Her." She leaned close to speak into his ear. "But . . . if it was up to me, I certainly wouldn't try."

"Good." Eric's hand moved, and Key thought he might be about to pull her closer. Instead, *gate key* slipped into her back pocket, and Eric turned away and slipped out of the room. She laughed.

3

Eric thought cleaning his place might calm him, but all he ended up doing was picking things up, getting lost in his thoughts, and putting them down again somewhere random. Clutter-wise, the whole process only made things worse.

He really should try to sleep, as it was well into the small hours already. The belief he'd found watching Key work came and went, like glimpses of a mark through the crowds at a fair. What had he seen her do? Dilate her eyes and make up some stories about keys. He certainly hadn't seen the Hound do anything other than act somewhat off. There was nothing in the news about the owner of the keys he'd taken, but there wouldn't be yet.

And Ariadne? She was . . . what, not human? Previously

human? She'd never seemed particularly inhuman to him. Mature and self-assured beyond her years, perhaps, but nothing more. If she had magic, couldn't she arrange her little empire herself, without using him to collect ways for her enemies to be killed by others? But she clearly did need him, if she'd killed to force him into working for her. Without the money he'd counted on from that ren faire, Ariadne's offer had seemed like a godsend.

And what was all this for? Something had changed four years ago. Perhaps something to do with TendarisHerron. When had she taken up with Clive? He couldn't remember. It might have been around that time. After the business partnership to use her data to help develop genetically tailored treatments was announced, the alleged sexual component to their relationship hadn't taken very long to filter into local gossip. Eric wondered what else, beyond money, Ariadne was getting out of the partnership. Successful genetically tailored treatments only benefited Clive.

Considering Ariadne's motives did nothing but raise questions, but Eric didn't see how he could stop the deaths without answering some of them. Since the other powers apparently had little choice in what they were doing, to stop them, Eric still needed to stop Ariadne. And it was difficult to stop people if you didn't know *why* they were doing something.

Eric picked up the empty glass he'd just set down on a shelf of the media console and forced himself to walk all the way to the kitchen sink without allowing any other thought. His phone beeped, and he strode over, picked it up, and swiped open the security system feed from the small camera over the door. Speak of the devil. Ariadne stared patiently ahead, completely ignoring the camera she undoubtedly knew was there, hair still perfect from earlier in the night.

What was she doing here? Eric couldn't imagine a situation in which her visit would be a good thing, and his adrenaline ramped up to a level that made sensations too sharp. How in the hell was he supposed to play this? When she'd sent him to the cottages, she'd known he'd meet at least one of her powers. She'd let it happen. That meant she had to approve, but then why was she here?

He'd have to play along as he went; there was nothing else for it. And start hiding his keys and avoiding cameras if she seemed angry. He slid his phone into his pocket and went to answer the door.

She didn't wait to be invited in, just walked forward like she owned the place, leaving him to tangle with her awkwardly or stand aside and hold the door. He chose the latter, as usual. Life went your way in the end more often when you picked your battles.

"So you've met my powers." Ariadne fetched up in his kitchen and leaned her hip against the edge of a countertop. "What do you think?"

Eric mimicked the confidence of her posture and leaned against the edge of the sink, ankles crossed and hands on either side of his hips. "What should I think?" Tennis match, he told himself. Blank face, bounce it back. He knew how to do this. No reason to freak out, outwardly at least.

"You've always struck me as pragmatic." Ariadne straightened from the counter and joined him, pushing into his personal space as she settled right next to him. He had to move his hand aside so it wasn't trapped between her ass and the sink, so when she was finished, she'd essentially put his arm around her. He hoped she couldn't sense his pulse picking up. Not from arousal—knowing what he knew now, he didn't really care for intimacy closer than a solid yard or two—but because she hadn't so much as alluded to their past sexual relationship in years. This had to be on purpose.

"The girl hit you hard, didn't she? Patricia?"

Eric clenched his jaw, and wondered if it would have been better if Ariadne had forgotten her name. Of course she wouldn't—even with a dedicated server room in her house for her genealogy research, she still seemed to keep a good fifty percent of it in her head. But then he could have dismissed her as evil more easily.

But she *killed* people. That was inherently evil enough. And him helping her. "Why her? She wasn't particularly important."

"The one who knows the filing system is the one who knows where the skeletons are buried." She reached across her body to pat his chest. "I should have warned you."

In the privacy of his mind, Eric scoffed. Like she regretted any of it. He noticed the words "I'm sorry" hadn't crossed her lips yet. "What's done is done." When had proverbial water around him had started slowly ratcheting up to boiling? When was the point he should have figured things out and tried to leave? And what good would leaving do, if Hank was correct about the severance package once you knew too much?

"You do good work." Ariadne dropped her hand and

straightened her body to gaze out over the kitchen island to the windows on the far side of the living room. "High-pressure work. High likelihood of burnout."

Eric tensed. Were they at the point of the severance package after all? Not while he still had skills to fight it. "Don't count me out just yet. Yes, you have a hit list, but I assume you have your reasons." He left that open-ended on the off chance she'd enlighten him, but was not surprised when she only smiled enigmatically. Let her feel that bit more in control of the situation, then. He'd find his own way there.

"I just wanted to get familiar with a different part of the process. A change is as good as a rest, after all." Really, he should have tried more subtly to lead her into coming up with the idea herself, but he didn't appear to have time.

"Oh?" Ariadne swung herself to face him, her hips pressed into his. Eric clenched his jaw and thought about how likely she was to order him killed soon until he was sure nothing would react to friction if she moved in the wrong way. "You have an urge to take up security?"

Eric summoned an image of Hank. He'd called them "good kids," and he was still around. Instinct told Eric that might be the way for him to play it as well. "The powers seem like good kids, but you can definitely tell something's off about them. If they ever went out in public, they'd stand out. But they don't have to. That's half my job, looking like I'm supposed to be there long enough to get close to the mark. I could teach them, give you the option to take them to targets." And didn't that last word taste bad on his tongue.

Ariadne flicked his chin. "How brotherly. It's adorable. Starting to feel the urge for a little nuclear family of your own, are you?"

Eric hardened his expression as if fighting against showing that weakness, and Ariadne smiled. Did she believe it? She looked as if she believed it. Wouldn't it make her life easier? Rather than losing his skill, she could channel it into being protective, as if that could make up for all the murders that had come before.

"All right. The coming struggle is too important for me to waste good talent. I'll give you a month to have something to show me. Work on Hound. He's the one I could use outside." Ariadne pecked his lips, but it was only camouflage to grab his crotch. "All the guards know that sleeping with Key is grounds for instant dismissal. Keep that in mind yourself. I know she's attractive, but if you can't control yourself, I'll be . . . displeased." There was just a touch too much pressure in her fingertips, promising hurt rather than fun. Eric stayed perfectly still.

"Yes'm," he said, a little breathless, and Ariadne laughed and climbed off him. Her manner snapped back to normal, and suddenly he might as well have been a potted plant for all her body language acknowledged him.

"I have to be very careful to protect them. When they're reborn so young, they have trouble hiding what they are. That's why they need me." Ariadne smiled at him, all surface, no eyes. "Need us. When the Hand of the Gods fights, we'll fight together."

Relief made Eric slightly light-headed, but he didn't want to seem out of character. He wasn't that much of a pushover. Time to prod. "Hand of the Gods?"

Ariadne held up her hand, fingers spread wide. She acted like she expected him to work it out on his own, but barely gave him time before she spoke. "Five powers."

Eric quickly counted them in his mind to match up with the story Key had told him. Breath, Key, Map, Hound, Lantern. "And you protect them now, because in forty years or so, when you're reborn, they'll protect you?"

Ariadne laughed, pleasant surface this time wrapped over knives. "Something like that. I suppose you can't really believe I have a power too, hmm?"

Eric turned to stack the dirty dishes in the sink more neatly. "I have to admit, having seen you naked on numerous occasions, I didn't notice anything then . . . " Sharper humor than he'd meant.

"Exhale for me." Ariadne didn't wait for him to respond. Her small hand at his back slammed him into the edge of the counter, and he lost his air in a gasping cough.

Ariadne's lungs filled where she was now pressed against his back. Eric's tried to do the same, but nothing happened. A beat passed of that being strange; then something smarter than his conscious mind, deep below it, hit the panic button.

Adrenaline flooded him and every muscle jerked into effort to correct the lack of oxygen that had stretched past the cushion that allowed a pause before an inhale. Chest jerked, hands instinctively came up to his throat, though there was no obstruction there. No air! Burning in his lungs, pain that screamed up into unbearable desperation, driven by unreasoning panic.

The tile backsplash behind the sink swam in Eric's vision, gray devouring it from around all the edges. Please, please. He had hardly enough conscious thought left for more than that begging, for which he had no voice.

Ariadne blew onto the side of his neck, exhalation becoming a recognizable sound only at the end. "Shhh."

Eric gasped in, then again. Tears prickled at the corners of his eyes from the violence of it and from remaining panic. Fuck.

Ariadne kissed the spot where she'd blown his life back to him. "You're so sweet." She pulled away, but Eric didn't turn to watch her go. He was too busy shaking, all over. He kept his attention firmly on the backsplash until he heard the front door shut.

Now he knew she must have believed his protectiveness, his professed view of the powers as kids. Otherwise he'd be dead right now. He still could be, very soon, and now he knew intimately what it might feel like.

No backing out of this now.

4

In my youth, the elders told such tales.

Like how when the seasons passed and the youngest of the gods did not return, the other gods grew worried. "We must send someone to find her," they said. They made searchers from clay, but they crumbled. They made searchers from wood, but they cracked. So they made five searchers from maize dough.

Key paced around her bedroom. She should at least try to sleep, she knew that, but then again, what did it matter if she was dozing off tomorrow? She stopped by the bed to get her pajamas from under her pillow, and ended up fingering her favorite padlock clipped over the headboard's metal bars instead.

Who was she kidding? Key slipped around the other side

of the bed, near the foot, and lifted the mattress off the box spring. She knew the feel of the slit she'd cut in the covering fabric, and she slid her hand in without looking. With her cheek on the mounded blankets, she grabbed the walkie-talkie hidden inside. Possibly the guards knew she and Map had lied when they'd claimed the handsets had been dropped out of a tree and slipped in the pond, respectively, when they were kids. But the guards hadn't done anything about it.

Key inspected the bumblebee yellow handset to make sure it was still charged. If only Her Majesty would have let them have phones, but Key supposed She figured phones were for calling people. Whom would she and Map have to call, besides each other? And maybe the police. But probably not. What would the police do with Hound?

She hoped Map would be in his room to hear his walkie-talkie, anyway. She doubted he'd be asleep. "Map?" She repeated it a couple times then drew it out as long as she could on a single breath.

"Christ, Key. What do you want?" His voice crackled over the handset and she smiled.

"Meet at the gazebo?" The connection wasn't great for conveying nuances of tone, but she must have sounded excited, because his exasperation faded.

"Give me five minutes to find my coat. It's going to be freaking freezing out there, you realize."

Key grimaced as she returned the walkie-talkie to its hiding place. She knew Map would be right about the temperature. But the gazebo was one of the few places they could actually talk in the compound. Their respective indoor guards would follow them, but the guards were only required to stay within sight. In the house, that meant in the same room, or at least a nearby room with a view of the exits. Outside, in the compound's manicured park, the guards could watch them from well out of earshot, and usually did, if only to swap war stories among themselves.

Key thudded downstairs, snagged her coat from a kitchen chair as she passed, and headed to the front door without speaking to her indoor guard. He'd follow regardless.

Unlocked. The not-quite-spring air hit her with a bracing slap as she stepped outside. No rain today, so no cloud cover to keep things warm tonight, or at least that's what her books said. Rather than zip up, she crossed her hands with the sides of her coat over each other and broke into a jog.

Map's house was closer to the park, so he'd beaten her there. She spotted his silhouette among the dark lines of the gazebo's posts as she arrived. The darkness made the swath of polite grass seem like it might actually contain mystery or adventure hidden in the corners, instead of a couple of pieces of play equipment for toddlers in a wood chip circle and the stupid gazebo. Every flower or bush was groomed to within an inch of its life by the landscaping service.

Maybe now it was spring and they'd be coming in more often, Map would be in a better mood. He tended to draw his lovers from that pool, rather than from among the guards. Key didn't know if that was simply because there were more women among the landscapers, or if the kinds of personalities that tended to become security guards weren't to his taste.

Because, of course, *he* was allowed to have sex, and no one died. Then again, doing it with the landscapers seemed to mean keeping it to fifteen minutes in the shed, which didn't appeal to Key enough to try it, though she'd considered it when she'd caught sight of some of the toned, tanned women. None of the few women among the guards had ever been the type to flirt with her.

When she reached the octagonal picnic table inside the gazebo, Key glanced to make sure Map's inside guard had not only joined hers, but the woman was gesturing and laughing. "A new guy showed up today," Key told Map. "Her Majesty's assistant, apparently. Eric Davis. And they actually let him see me work. Hank freaking zoned me out in front of him."

Map had opened his mouth, maybe to be exasperated with her lack of preamble, but snapped it closed when her words sank in. "Can you show me?" He ducked and grabbed a plastic tote of sidewalk chalk from under the table. It was maybe a little sad, Key reflected, how good they'd gotten at sharing information despite Her.

"I'll see what I can do. I didn't talk to him for very long." Key selected dark purple to provide the most contrast against the light concrete in their limited light. She knelt before a patch of concrete dusty with ghosts of past colors. Map could find people—or "know" them, as she'd phrased it to Eric—with a map of their face. Drawings were best, especially when the artist knew the subject, though photographs also worked less consistently. The point was to map out the important parts of someone's face and leave out the rest. A camera did that only by accident, so a lot of pictures he couldn't use. For targeting purposes, the Ice Queen usually got someone to take so many, at least one would work.

Key sketched the important lines of chin and forehead, then eyes, the whole face about two feet high. She hesitated over the face shape, rubbed out one of her lines with her free fingertips. She realized her tongue tip had sneaked out of the corner of her mouth and flicked a glance up to see if Map had noticed.

The nearest streetlight was behind her, catching him in the face, and for a moment she saw him anew in drawing terms. He had brown skin and black hair like her, but with tighter curls that made it look fluffy at the moment, lacking product to tame them into waves. He had a heavy line from the side of his face to the corner of his jaw but a delicate chin only rescued for masculinity by being squared-off at the bottom rather than pointed. He wore his beard in thin, neatly trimmed lines, though scruff currently had filled in around them somewhat. Manly scruff, she assumed.

"There." Key dropped the chalk back in the tote and examined her hands. With all her rubbing-out, both sets of fingertips were equally caked with dust. She got out of Map's way and went to clap them over the grass.

"South . . . east of us, right now?" Map frowned more deeply. If he couldn't get a good fix, it meant she hadn't seen enough of Eric Davis yet to capture him properly. Or she couldn't draw tonight.

"Restless. Upset about something." Map dragged a toe through the center of the drawing to kill its resonance for his power, and Key helped scuff the rest away so the guards wouldn't see it later. His gaze settled on her face as she flopped on the adjoining angled bench. "Wants to bone you."

Key felt her cheeks heat. "No way you're getting that kind of detail." He was at totally the wrong angle for her to kick his shin, but she tried anyway. He dodged easily.

"Mm." Map looked off into the night, thoughtful. "Still have a stock of condoms?"

Key covered her face with her hands. "Oh. My. God. Map!" She was pretty sure normal women didn't have this kind of conversation with their brothers, even if they were actually related and not just brought up together.

"Well? No one else is going to hassle you about this kind of thing. I guess I'm up." Map shifted in his seat to better enable his night-staring. Key realized he was just as uncomfortable as she was, which helped a little. "I don't think either of us want to see how She'd react if you got pregnant."

Key hugged herself and leaned over her knees. No, she didn't, really. "I still have some." Which was enough of that subject. "I made a deal with him to look up Lantern."

"Key!" Map's turn to sound shocked, now. "Are you crazy?"

He reached for her shoulders, but Key scooted down the bench and escaped to the other side of the table. "No, I'm tired of not having my memories, and only knowing what Her Majesty chooses to tell us! I just want to even the balance of power a little, find something out on my own, trigger my own memories. Find out where I . . . came from, you know?"

Map drew in a slow breath, held it. "Knowing the past isn't entirely what it's cracked up to be. You know who you are now, in this life. That's not a bad place to be."

Key crossed her arms and put another few strides between them. She stumbled when her foot hit the grass at the edge of the concrete pad unexpectedly. "Says the man with at least some memories."

Map didn't answer, which Key supposed was fair because she didn't know what she would have wanted to him to say. It wasn't his fault he'd been reborn into a slightly older body. She should be grateful she wasn't like Hound. Though if she'd been like Hound, she knew she wouldn't *care* so much.

She pulled out the only two memories she allowed herself to revisit on purpose. Sometimes her thoughts would link to a new memory and she'd grasp after it, but those two were the only ones she called up. After too many years of reliving them, they'd worn thin, worn to *nothing*, really, except memories of having the memories.

A woman had held her in her arms, singing. A tune Key couldn't *quite* hum, and words she couldn't remember or didn't understand. Another language? What woman other than her human mother would have held her like that? A nurse? She didn't know, and wasn't going to ask Her Majesty.

And she'd knelt, once, grinding something. Nuts? Seeds? Stone on stone with a smooth, sweeping movement forward Key had never used in this life. That had to be real, unless she'd seen it on TV and dreamed it later.

And almost as soon as she'd begun reliving the moments, they were done. That was all, a few breaths of time, a handful of sensations that lingered. She hated it. "Scheisse."

"Too much *Run, Lola, Run* for you." Map laughed as if trying to tease her out of it. He was right; she'd first heard the word in the movie, but she'd started using it because she liked the feel of saying it, not because she wanted to be Lola somehow.

She didn't join him in the laughter. "Not knowing is making me crazy, Map. I'm going to do this."

Map stood and kicked the chalk tote back under the table. "Don't hurt yourself." He shoved his hands in his windbreaker pockets and ambled off toward his own house. Key stayed where she was, feeling a little bereft. He must be angry if he wasn't going to say good night.

Sometimes she did wish she had keys to people's hearts.

5

Eric turned off the car in his younger sister's driveway and wondered if he was stupid for coming here. Her and her family's safety lay in not knowing anything, he assumed. After all, Ariadne didn't need to threaten loved ones; she could dispose of whomever had annoyed her and try again with their successor. As long as his sister didn't know anything, wasn't *involved*, she couldn't annoy Ariadne.

But would it look like he was telling his sister something now? Sharp spring sunlight invited him to step out of the car before the next cloud rolled over the sun, but he remained staring at the steering wheel. Ariadne knew he wasn't that stupid, he decided.

And he recognized he desperately needed this balancing.

Dwell too long in his own little world that had simultaneously expanded to include powers and contracted to hold him trapped, and the memory of what it had felt like to suffocate in clear air surged back up. Forget stopping Ariadne for abstract reasons of morality; now he was playing for his own personal safety.

He slammed the car door as if he could shut the thought away inside and strode up to the front door. Bricks from a defunct walkway from the sidewalk winked at him, red among the green grass and grass-shaped weeds, as his steps on the concrete around the garage converged with them at their destination. He knocked, and waited. His sister's husband must already have left for work. Diane herself would be awake, but probably still in her bedroom.

He knocked again. Footsteps thumped on the stairs inside, and the door popped open. "Learn to keep civilized hours," Diane grumbled. She wore jeans, but her feet were bare and the ratty school hoodie looked as though she'd pulled it on when she heard the door. She hadn't brushed the golden-brown mass of her hair yet either.

"So glad you're happy to see me." Eric grabbed her for a hug as he invited himself in. Diane hugged back, then pushed him away so she could shut the door.

"I'd be even happier if it was later." She jogged up the stairs, and Eric followed her to the invisible threshold of a view into her bedroom. He had no doubt it looked like a bomb had exploded, and he didn't want to know. "You get invited to do a show on short notice? I'm not sure I could fit in playing lovely assistant until at least next week." She thumped a dresser drawer shut where he couldn't see.

"No, nothing until next month, still." Eric answered on autopilot while the rest of his mind froze. The implications for his avocation hadn't hit him until just now. If he did, by some miracle, manage to stop Ariadne and disentangle himself from her safely, there went the high salary for ridiculously flexible hours that supported his stage magic habit. He'd have to start smashing it in around a nine to five again, and he knew how well that didn't work. Even as he felt like shouting at himself for even weighing that concern against stopping more deaths, he couldn't shake the sinking feeling.

Diane came out of her bedroom in a real shirt and snapped a hair elastic over her wrist before starting in with a brush. "Is everything okay? You didn't call before showing up. Not that I mind seeing you, of course, teasing aside. I was awake."

"I—" It took Eric a second to recall his excuse, crafted to slot into his larger plans. "You remember that box with your beading stuff or whatever you lost the key to a few months back?"

Diane fastened up her hair with a last swipe of her hand to make sure it was smooth. "Like a year ago, but yes. Why? Have you come over all handyman?" Her gaze on his face narrowed, and Eric was reminded forcibly that while he'd carefully trained his people-reading skills, he'd also had a seed of inherited talent his sister shared. "That's kind of a lame excuse for coming all the way over here."

Eric scrubbed at his jaw to stall. Perhaps he had come here unconsciously hoping she'd call him on any omissions. It certainly would have been safer to stay away entirely. He couldn't tell her everything, though. "I think I need to quit working for Ariadne. But I'm kind of . . . entangled, in her current project."

Diane's suspicion instantly transformed into sympathy. She murmured a reassurance and slotted her brush into a back pocket to give him another hug. "Having a third-life crisis in anticipation of turning thirty-three, are you? I know the hours are perfect, but it's not the only job with flexible hours in the city. It doesn't have to be a choice between working for your creepy ex and giving up magic entirely."

Eric returned the hug briefly, then stepped back, brows rising. That was an opinion Diane hadn't voiced before. He supposed he'd never invited it, seeming happy with his job. "You think she's creepy?"

"Kinda." Diane grimaced. "I know staying friends with your ex is a good thing, and she doesn't have any family of her own, but . . . eh. I've never liked her vibe." She grinned. "So I guess what I'm saying is, while you're finishing out this project or whatever, bitch about her all you like. Have you had breakfast?" She held out an arm toward the kitchen downstairs, in invitation.

"Yeah. I have to get to work, but I actually did want that jewelry box. One of the researchers . . . collects old keys. I thought she might have one that fits, or at least one she can jimmy into opening it." Eric looked away. Translating the supernatural elements of Ariadne's world into normal terms felt like tainting the normal world.

Diane set her hands on her hips. "That's . . . random. But okay." Her face suddenly lit up. "Are you interested in this woman? That's why you don't want to quit this minute? Is this an excuse to talk to her?" She laughed at whatever his expression was. "Oh my God, Eric, it is. Wait here, I'll get it." She jogged back into her bedroom.

Eric exhaled on a laugh while he waited. Not an excuse to talk to Key, no, but he hoped it should put her in a better mood since he couldn't offer any progress on his side of their deal yet.

Diane amazed him as always, because she entered ground zero and returned with exactly the box she wanted, which she'd last seen a year ago, in roughly five minutes. She presented it to him with great ceremony. It was simple wood except for the metal lock plate, large capacity, probably with layers of trays inside. He rattled it experimentally and stopped at her wince. He was mixing up the beads, he supposed.

"I think there are a couple finished necklaces in there. Nothing too valuable, or I would have taken it to a professional by now. If she gets it open, offer her one if she wants it."

Eric tucked the box under his arm and waited to see if Diane had any more teasing in her, but there was a reason he ate dinner with her and her husband a couple of times a month and saw their parents—well, their mother was the operative person in that equation—only two or three times a year at major holidays. Diane knew when to stop. "Thanks."

He gave her another one-armed hug in farewell and headed downstairs. Back to disentangling himself from Ariadne's world.

The woman on shift in the gatehouse when Eric arrived informed him that the Key and the Map were still sleeping, but the Hound was awake, which he found more than a little creepy. It didn't help when he found himself humming "Santa Claus Is Coming to Town" under his breath on the walk up through the compound. He'd declined the offer of a golf cart.

He thought it was interesting, how the powers' "the"s came and went. Hank had only used one for Hound, but the woman in the gatehouse had applied it to all of them.

The sun, as threatened, had been swallowed by the clouds, but the air was fresh with spring moisture. The subdivision could have been as friendly as his sister's, but it lacked any personal touches, the landscaping marching in lockstep from yard to yard.

As he walked, he laid out his next moves in his mind, checking them yet one more time for holes. Short term, he needed to get the powers out of Ariadne's control, that was pretty clear. Since they didn't target people—now *he* was doing it, *kill* people—on their own, getting them away from Ariadne's control would stop the deaths. And he hoped, as a side effect, would keep him from getting the severance package. She could clearly kill herself, but she also clearly wasn't choosing to. He doubted she'd go to the trouble of using someone else if she didn't have to, so perhaps she could kill only close by.

Then, once no more people were dying and he was safe, he could look into TendarisHerron, maybe even try to shake down the CEO himself, to find out what this was all for.

Hound might do what he was told, Eric wasn't sure, but if Key was any indication, she and Map would definitely need to be talked into anything. He hoped to get her the information she wanted about Lantern eventually, but that would take time, and he had the luxury of time only if Ariadne thought he was still working for her. He had no doubt his month would disappear if he didn't even talk to Hound. So he needed to make at least some kind of visible effort with Hound, right from the start.

And he hoped that would give him some insights into how to persuade Hound to play his part in the plan as well. Whatever that plan was. "Away from Ariadne" was pretty vague, but Eric didn't see that he could do any better before even meeting Map and getting a better idea of the powers' living situation.

Eric knocked, let himself into Hound's house, and went upstairs to introduce himself to the guard reading the newspaper on a couch in one of the bedrooms. His name was Guilherme, and while Eric didn't know anything about teams in the man's parents' native Brazil, he knew soccer well enough to converse companionably about the man's passion. Hound pounded in a tireless run on the treadmill on the other side of the room, ignoring them completely.

When the conversation lulled, Eric set the bead box on the floor, tucked against the side of the couch, and went to stand in Hound's field of view. "I need to talk to you."

Hound smoothly decreased the speed on the treadmill so he slowed to a stop without having to hop off. "About a job?" His voice and tone were completely expressionless, despite the at least mild interest his actions suggested.

"Sort of. The . . . Boss wants you able to track outside, without getting noticed. I know a little bit about blending in." Eric paused, unconsciously waiting for signs of either understanding or confusion to determine whether he offered more basic explanation, or details. Hound didn't give him either. "Look, get changed, and let's go downstairs and see if we can at least make a start."

"I run for an hour every morning." Hound reached for the treadmill controls.

Eric stepped around to intercept his hand. "The less you stand out, the more jobs the Boss will give you. It's that simple. I can make you not stand out."

Again, Eric felt himself searching for a reaction. He hadn't realized how much trying to influence people had a rhythm to it until half the music went silent. Hound stared at him for a couple of seconds, then got off the treadmill and disappeared into the hall. Eric followed after retrieving the bead box. Guilherme gave him a sympathetic smile. "Picking one thing and sticking with it until he's learned it is usually the best way with him. He'll get there." Eric nodded and headed downstairs to wait while Guilherme took his time getting to his feet. Apparently Hound wasn't much of a flight risk.

Downstairs, he left the box on the kitchen table and chose a seat in an armchair facing the couch. The house was clearly set up for a single person—only the couch faced the TV, like the owner would never have multiple friends over to watch together. Eric snagged a book from the coffee table and flipped through pictures of beautiful Turkish mosques while he waited.

Hound appeared, in T-shirt and jeans, and sat precisely on the couch, where any other teen might have flopped. He stared at Eric. To say he was expectant might have been a stretch, but he did give an impression of waiting.

Eric turned the open book around to show a two-page spread of sunlight streaming through small windows between colorful tiles. "Do you think it's beautiful?"

Hound stared. Finally, "Does it matter if it's beautiful?"

"Why do you read the books, then?" Eric pushed it onto Hound's lap, still open, trying to transfer his gaze there. Maybe where he looked would give some indication of any thoughts hidden under the surface. Or any proto-thoughts that Eric could seize and expand on.

Wonder of wonders, Hound actually drew a fingertip across the picture at floor-level. "I could track there."

"And tracking there would be better than tracking on the street outside?" Eric pointed vaguely in that direction.

"Different." Hound closed the book. Not with a snap—that would have required impatience—but with finality.

Eric closed his eyes briefly and pressed fingertips to them. All right. Eric would pick one new normal-human skill to focus on, as Guilherme had suggested. One thing to show Ariadne he was supposedly making progress in helping Hound blend in. "I walked up here. Why don't you follow that trail, so I can watch you work?" That might give him an idea what skill would be the easiest for Hound to achieve.

Hound stood and strode for the front door. Watching him move, Eric remembered he was a teen, with the particular awkward, lanky gait that went with that. It reminded him of seeing his cousin Kayla run after the ball in their softball game, the summer after she'd turned fourteen and shot up in height.

By the time Hound reached the driveway, his speed had bled away. Maybe Eric's trail wasn't different enough. He followed it much more precisely than Eric had remembered it, with every slight change of direction he'd made to get a better view between houses into yards. Guilherme ambled after them both.

Eric jogged to catch up and examined Hound's eyes as he

walked. The pupils weren't huge, but neither did they match the bright sunlight. Inside, it hadn't been noticeable because they'd been appropriate for the interior light level.

A few yards from where Hound would fetch up against the now-closed gate into the car lot, Eric put a hand on his arm to stop him. "Could you do that while in a vehicle? Or riding a bike, maybe?"

"Cars go past too many trails too fast." Hound waited, as if checking to see if he should go on, then turned to go home.

"And a bike? Can you ride?" They met Guilherme on the way back, and Eric appealed to him for the answer. He supposed the man wouldn't know if Hound had learned as a child and Guilherme had been hired since then, but he did seem more invested in his charge than some of the other guards had been.

Guilherme shook his head. "I believe the Map keeps his in the garage. The Key's only bike was child-sized, and we got rid of it. No one had the patience to teach Hound." Not only was his tone softer when referring to Hound, he omitted "the," Eric noticed.

"All right. Which house is Map's?" To Eric's surprise, Hound changed direction, so he followed. Hound cut across a postage stamp park trying to channel rural golden days with its white-painted wood gazebo just waiting for the Fourth of July band to arrive. Hound glanced at the gazebo, then kept on over the grass to a gate in the back fence of one of the houses fronting onto the park.

Hound looked ready to walk right in the back door and probably stop in front of Map himself, but Eric didn't like that scenario for meeting the man for the first time. Key had made it pretty clear that Map wasn't like Hound. That meant a personality that might be offended by first impressions, such as inviting himself into Map's private space too early in the morning.

Eric hooked a hand into Hound's elbow and towed him along the side of the house to the garage door. Guilherme, ever-faithfully trailing, spoke into his walkie-talkie, and a minute later, the door opened.

No vehicles inside, of course. The concrete and bare sheetrock looked even more industrial without the usual assortment of suburban clutter to soften them—no yard tools, no outdoor toys. Just an expensive mountain bike, a couple of bookshelves, and some kind of architect or drafting table with a multitude of long, flat drawers.

Eric turned to the guard. "Is Map up? I want to get his permission to borrow his bike."

Guilherme stared at him as if adding "the" to their name robbed people of the ability to own possessions. Or in a more sympathetic interpretation, maybe he was simply used to Hound, who undoubtedly didn't care who did what with his stuff. "His permission?"

The door into the house opened. "And the crime rate in this neighborhood is generally so low. What are you stealing from my garage?" A Latino man stepped down into the garage and winced against the bright sunlight outside.

Eric took advantage of the beat in which he could examine Map without the man returning the favor. He looked only a few years younger than Eric himself. He had somewhat delicate features that gave him a heartthrob actor air, and he was dressed in a way that whispered wealth because it was so crass to shout. At the moment, he wore a waistcoat and tie, with his shirt sleeves rolled up, like a stockbroker ready to get down to business. Eric wondered if the clothes were as much an effort to take control of *something* in his environment as Key's dyed hair probably was.

"Hound?" Map's tone was surprised, his gaze on the boy, now standing completely still beside the bike without apparent boredom. Then he found Eric and understanding visibly dawned. If Eric had needed confirmation someone was at home, the spread of the expression was definitely it.

In fact, he looked a lot like he'd heard about Eric from someone. The guards? Key?

"Strong jaw," Map commented inexplicably, and strode over to offer his hand to shake. "Map."

"Eric Davis." He checked Map's eyes, but they seemed completely normal. Map squeezed a little too firmly for Eric to believe his projected confidence, but his smile was pure corporate shark. "I'd like to borrow your bike for Hound to ride."

"Ha!" The syllable was explosive. "Good luck with that, chief."

Silently, Eric agreed, but he shrugged and didn't rise to the bait. He ignored Map as he wheeled the bike out onto the street and got Hound set up sitting on the seat, balanced with one foot on the ground. Too bad they didn't make training wheels for any bike that Hound would presently fit on.

Map wandered up to the edge of the shade cast in front of the garage and watched them both smugly, hands in the pockets of his slacks.

Eric explained the idea, got Hound to take the pedals through a revolution with one foot, hopping forward with the other. Then he balanced the bike from the handlebars while Hound got both his feet on the pedals.

Hound surged forward out of Eric's grip, pedaling as instructed. His front wheel sawed wildly back and forth, and he fell straight to one side, bike on top.

Well, hell. Eric pulled the bike off the kid, and by the time he'd set it to the side, kickstand down, Hound had sat up on his own. He considered the road rash down the side of his forearm and delicately started picking gravel out of the scrapes. Guilherme crouched beside him and gently asked a series of clinical questions about how much pain he was in.

No wonder Ariadne had laughed. Eric could appeal to Hound's sense of purpose long enough to get him to follow directions, but Eric couldn't ever make Hound act like a person if nothing gave him pleasure and nothing *hurt* him. Half the energy propelling a bike forward on your first ride was the fear of falling if you didn't.

Frustration formed a low, chemical-type burn in Eric's stomach. Ariadne and her *games*. His failure would probably be even more effective than his success at keeping her amused and distracted, but he hated feeling the touch of her manipulation in that failure.

Fine. He didn't want to hurt Hound further, and he'd harassed the boy enough for one day. This incident had been splashy enough to be reported back to Ariadne in great detail. Eric would let Hound go back to working out and get some coffee—there would be a security station with a pot or twelve somewhere—then take the box to Key.

Map flicked up the bike's kickstand. "I'll take this back," he told Hound. Guilherme was the one who nodded and escorted Hound away. Rather than return to his garage, Map headed for Eric, wheeling the bike along with him. "I could have told you that would happen."

Eric wanted to bristle, but he suppressed anything but a brief burst of irony in his tone. "Good for you." If he was going to take Ariadne's powers away, he needed to consider Map as well. He should at least be polite. "Ariadne wanted me to work with Hound, to teach him to blend in better with the outside world."

Map snorted and rubbed at the center of the bike's handlebars, perhaps checking if a spot was dirt or a chip in the paint. "Why are you really here?"

With frustration and fear lingering, Eric felt his patience eroding along with the effects of the coffee he'd drunk before coming out here. He really hadn't gotten much sleep last night. Rather than answering Map, he stared him down. What did the man expect him to say when he had no idea what would get back to Ariadne?

Map held his gaze long enough to satisfy his pride, Eric suspected, then dipped his eyes to the bike again. "Fair enough. Here's some free advice. If you can convince Key she doesn't *need* any more memories, that would be better for everyone and her in particular. She could be happy here, if she'd let that go."

His tone was light enough, but Eric was abruptly glad he'd watched his words. Was Map completely Ariadne's creature, or was he just afraid of rocking the boat? "You're happy here?" Happy killing people?

"Better to choose to be happy than to choose to be miserable." Map shrugged and wheeled the bike away. Eric watched him for a beat then resumed his path toward coffee. He could think about whether he trusted Map after he'd had caffeine.

When Eric arrived at Key's house, about half an hour later, he discovered Map had preceded him there. He hesitated in the hallway, bead box under his arm, and watched the man expertly flip an omelet in an undoubtedly expensive chef-endorsed pan. Key's guard was just visible in the living room, apparently listening rather than watching, since his sightline to the kitchen had to be blocked.

Map ignored Eric's arrival, but Key looked up from the Pop Tart she was eating at the table. When loose, her hair reached just below her shoulders, and softened her face a little. The color was still rather eye-searing.

She smiled, and he stopped thinking about her hair. He set the bead box down on the table across from her. "I wondered if you could help me with something. This belongs to my sister, and she lost the key. I don't know if you can just open it, or if you can make one of those keys you have upstairs fit . . . "

Key got up and came around to stand beside him in front of the box. "Give me something difficult next time." Her tone was delighted, though. She turned her fingers in front of the lock, and the box popped open. A key now protruded from the keyhole.

Eric would have sworn she hadn't used a trick for that, even if he was at the wrong angle to check her eyes. "You can make keys as well?"

"Of course." Key withdrew the key and handed it to him. "But if I just want something open, I don't bother."

While he was still looking at the newly created key, she clumsily tried to lift his phone from his pocket, and the difference between her skills and her power was night and day. He caught her wrist before she got the phone free. "Hey," he protested lightly.

"What? Maybe I was just groping you. Are you objecting to that?" Key let the phone go. Eric admitted to himself that he would love to see how this played out, and dropped her wrist so she could indeed grab his ass. She went for the phone again after, but this time he let her keep it. She'd worked hard enough for it.

"You and the praying mantis there should get a room," Map said, apparently without rancor, and set a plate with the omelet in front of Key's earlier place. He returned to set the pan in the sink then let himself out of the back door.

Key had jerked away, and Eric increased the distance between them a little more, feigning interest in the tray of beads revealed. That had been stupid of him. Key was so much *fun*, though. "Praying mantis?"

Key crossed her arms, shoulders hunched. "Map thinks it's his job to be all my older relatives rolled into one, just so you know. Ignore him." Eric waited to see if an actual answer might be forthcoming. A few more seconds, and she surrendered to his interrogative silence. "There was one of the guards, he and I . . . Her Majesty found out, and had Map target him." She blew out a sharp breath and stomped over to the omelet. "Anyway. He thinks he's funny but he's not."

"I have my own suspended death sentence regardless." Faced with that kind of admission from Key, Eric couldn't do anything but match it with honesty of his own. "I talked to Ariadne and offered to teach you guys how to blend in better. She picked Hound for my test case. I have a month, and I'm sure if I don't have some kind of results by then, she'll be . . . unhappy."

Key slowly sat down and poked at her omelet with a fork as she listened. When he finished, she seemed about to ask something, then glanced in the direction of where the guard lurked and cut herself a bite instead. Eric followed her look and nodded in endorsement of her choice. His position was no news to Ariadne—she'd put him in it—but if Key had been about to ask why he'd insinuated himself into the compound in the first place, he couldn't have answered.

After a few beats of pained silence, Key, who'd been holding his phone in her off hand under the table the whole time, finally brought it up and set it on the surface. She pushed it to him. "Here."

Eric glanced at the passcode screen her touch had woken. "Can't unlock that?"

"It's not—" Key spread her fingers, inarticulate for a second. "Actually a lock, if you think about it. There's nothing that latches or opens. It's just some electronic process that doesn't happen until you give it the right electrons."

Eric entered his code, phone angled so she couldn't watch, then pushed it back. "I'll admit I'm curious what you wanted it for." Of course, most things that came to mind, he presumed she wouldn't admit to with the guard right there.

"I just wanted to actually see one." Key touched an icon with a fingertip and jumped her hand back in surprise when the app opened. With great deliberation, she tried to scroll and scowled when nothing happened. "Who am I going to call? I don't know anyone."

"You've . . . never seen a cell phone before?" Eric could hardly conceive of it. Hadn't people even in Third World countries started adopting cell phones? He supposed it only made sense, if Ariadne wanted to control them.

"I watch commercials." Tone annoyed, Key punched buttons until she got a new screen and stared at that for a while before trying to scroll it. "I just haven't . . . touched one."

Eric suddenly realized he hadn't seen a computer anywhere, either. The guard with Hound had had one, but he'd bet the wireless was firmly locked—in a way Key couldn't open. "Here." He took his phone back and found a site full of lolcats. Short of porn, it was probably the fastest crash-course in Internet culture he could give her. At first, she mostly seemed pleased she could scroll, but then she exhaled in laughter.

For something to do while she read, Eric poked through the box's first tray of beads. This top level had a number of wood ones in different rich hues. He lifted it out to find glass ones of various shades underneath.

Key set the phone aside, the lure of interaction apparently stronger than the lure of technology. She nudged an oval red-toned wood bead with her fingertip. "These are fancy."

"They're some . . . " Eric searched his memory. Diane had told him about these, he could have sworn. Probably more than once. "South American rainforest wood. Fair trade and sustainably farmed."

Key picked up the bead with more interest. "It must be amazing to get to go to South America."

Eric lifted the last tray and found the promised finished necklaces in the bottom. He lifted one with wood beads only to discover when it unspooled that it was only a bracelet. Perfect. He pushed it across the table to Key. "Oh, she's never been there. They went to Germany for their honeymoon, but that's about it."

"Oh." Key examined the bracelet and tried to push it back. He stopped her with his hand over hers. "Have you been anywhere?"

"My sister said you should have something, as a reward for opening the box." Eric squeezed her hand, then pulled his away. She hesitated for a beat, another, like a feral cat considering food, then slipped the bracelet on, with murmured thanks.

"Anyway. I've been a few places." Back before he'd started trying to make a go of magic, he'd tended toward restlessness. "But I doubt I could paint a better picture than any of Hound's books." Key didn't even object to the evasion, just plucked at the beads around her wrist, which made him feel more guilty. "Where would you go?"

Key's face lit up, and she started eating again between the surprisingly detailed locations that poured out of her. Eric entered his active-listening mode, setting aside for later the thought that much more than Ariadne deserved to lose Key, Key deserved to get out of here.

6

In my youth, the elders told such tales.

Like how the five searchers began in the longhouse of the youngest of the gods. They lifted every tule mat, peered into every basket of smoked salmon, even stirred the cold ashes of the fire.

After breakfast was cleared, Key watched as Eric chased off her indoor guard. She almost couldn't believe it, even having watched it happen. Eric put on a guardish frown and joked with Robert about double shifts and bad coffee and suddenly Robert was agreeing that it made no sense for two people to watch the same power. He ambled off to the guard station, leaving the two of them alone.

Eric came halfway back from seeing him to the front door and frowned vaguely at the hallway walls. "Are you bugged?"

Almost immediately, he took another breath like he'd realized he might have to explain that to her. Key hurried so as not to lose her opportunity to prove she wasn't as ignorant as the whole embarrassing cell phone thing had suggested. "I don't think so. I mean, someone's watching us all the time. There are cameras around the gate and outside fence." Key huffed a laugh. "Map suggested Her Majesty doesn't use electronics because She can't intimidate them."

"I should have brought real equipment," Eric muttered, but brought out his cell phone and started sweeping it over the walls. "If there's feedback—"

"It means there's a live mic." Key trailed after him.

He paused at the entrance to the living room. "How much TV do you *watch?*"

"That was from a book." Frustration hit Key in a burst. Why was she trying to impress him? He'd probably been all over the world, and she couldn't hope to compete. She left him to his bug check and jogged upstairs. *Unlocked,* at her bedroom door. *Locked.* Then she left the door open anyway. She ached to keep talking to him far more than she did to show him up.

About ten minutes later, he swept the walls of her bedroom and sat down on the bed next to her. She'd pulled the burgundy coverlet over the sheets without entirely making the bed, so it was a little lumpy, but at least looked better from a distance.

She waited for him to start asking questions again, but he sat in silence, not looking at her. Finally she couldn't stand it any longer. "If you don't say something fast, I'm just going to kiss you."

Eric laughed. "I think praying mantises have better pick-up lines." He didn't stand up. And he knew the dangers, she'd warned him herself, so Key figured that was more than due diligence.

So she kissed him. She'd expected him to be like most of the others, quickly deep and pulling her to him, but he teased her with his tongue, sometimes light, sometimes a bit deeper than that, but hands down. She brought one of her own hands up to lace through the short hair at the back of his neck and hold him in tightly herself.

She finally pulled away. "Hold that thought." Good thing Map had reminded her to check her stash because she knew exactly where under her bed the box of condoms was. She straightened and tossed it onto the bed, then slowly pulled her shirt up and off, watching for his reaction. He grinned and dragged her closer with a fingertip in her waistband, behind her jeans button. With him sitting, and her standing between his knees, he popped her bra clasp, slid it off, and cupped her breasts, caressing, dragging his thumbs over her nipples before leaning to draw one between his lips.

A touch of teeth produced so sharp a sensation that it tipped from good into pain, and Key pushed his shoulder. "Not so—" He sat back immediately, and his thumb once more smoothed sharpness back to pleasure.

Key wondered if first times with a new person were always like this. He seemed to have more ideas of things to try than her, but both of them found that rhythm of trying, taking a false step, trying again, until the other person moaned. Around the time his shirt was off and she was down to her panties, straddled across his lap as he lay partially back on the bed, he slid his hands down to settle on her waist. The caress down her sides just freaking *tickled,* and she captured his hands and held them to the bed beside his shoulders. "Stop it," she teased.

He grinned up at her and waited. Next move: hers. She had him. What was she going to do with him?

Something connected in her mind with a feeling that was almost electric, instantly intensifying the sensations low in her body from simple warmth to lightning crackle. She did have him. Like when the guards tied her up to zone her out so she wouldn't object to targeting, only this time she was the one in control. *She* was. She tightened her grip on his wrists and leaned more of her weight on them.

Eric's expression shaded thoughtful. "I suppose you wouldn't have any real cuffs. Do you have any handcuffs? Have to be more careful with those, but they'll do in a pinch."

Key sat up quickly. What was she doing, even thinking of doing something like that to someone? She knew what it was like from the other side! "I couldn't . . . "

"Even if I ask you to?" Eric sat up, brushed a few stray strands of hair away from her lips, and kissed her again, slow and deep. "I don't mind."

Key joined the kiss again quickly as a promise, and hurried out of the room. She knew just where a pair was, with a bunch of padlocks inside her little safe in the next room. She pulled the open door wider, *unlocked—locked—locked—locked,* a whole chorus, and grabbed the handcuffs. *Unlocked.* Straight from the store, no particular person or emotion to find with them.

Eric was waiting where she'd left him. When he saw her, he scooted up to the headboard. She threaded the cuffs over a bar to hold his wrists on either side, and the way he just lifted his hands up, watching her, burst sensation between her legs all over again. She clicked the metal closed. *Locked.* "Not too tight?"

"That's fine." Eric settled into a comfortable position, propped against a pillow she tugged over for him, arms pulled not too far above his head. Key knelt up on the bed and looked him over again. The position of his arms exposed the smooth lines of muscles that hadn't been obvious before, coiled strength. She started at his navel and dragged her fingertips lower to unbutton then unzip his jeans. It was a little awkward, pulling them off for him, but all she had to do was look up at him, and she was just as ready as before. *Locked.*

Remembering what she'd learned from her first lover, Key teased him with careful touches when she'd freed his length and rolled on the condom. He grunted, wordless, which she took as a good sign. One final, brief false step as she guided him in, finding the right angle when he couldn't do it himself, but then he was in and they met, thrust against rolled hips.

She watched his wrists. *Locked.* Thrust. *Locked.* The rhythm kept driving her higher, and when she touched herself, she came, harder than she ever had before. *Unlocked.* Perhaps half unconsciously, he brought his freed hands down to hold her waist again, and she rode him to his own climax in a misty, flushed haze.

Unlocked.

7

After cleaning up, by common consent, they ended up back on the bed, half dressed, dozing, despite it hardly even being afternoon yet. Even had it been night, Eric didn't generally sleep well with someone else in the bed, and wouldn't have wanted to risk discovery by someone in the morning. Key pulled one of his hands over her abdomen when he spooned her and rubbed at the fading red mark the metal had left on his wrist like she was worried he'd been seriously injured. He wondered what being restrained was like for her if having it offered as a gift so amazed and shocked her.

"Ever considered robbing a bank?" He gently tugged his wrist out of her grip. He also wondered what she would do with the idea of actual BDSM—though she probably knew all about that from TV too. Or at least had absorbed the most common misconceptions available from the media.

"The alarms still go off. I suppose if I could grab money fast enough. And not get caught running away." Key finally settled, hand tucked against her side. "The Ice Queen took me to someone's house, once. I took an envelope out of the safe while She was talking to him in the next room." Her silence grew momentarily warmer, perhaps at a pleasant memory. "There was this huge staircase, and a chandelier—not like seeing it on screen at all. When you could actually stand there and look up and up . . . "

"You need to get out of here." Eric spoke without thinking, always a bad plan. Hell. Getting them out had been his goal since he'd realized what the powers were, but he had planned to introduce the idea much more carefully. Back when he'd hovered in that safe zone of knowing enough about Key to nudge her but not enough to empathize too much. And if he was going to blame the sex for tipping him into the wrong side of that zone, that was yet another reason he shouldn't have put himself in this position. Even if she knew sleight of hand as well as being attractive. But things had been piling up since he met her—Hound's travel books, her excitement at seeing a cell phone in person . . . her life here was pathetically circumscribed.

But that lack of experience with the outside world had a good chance of making her skittish about the idea of leaving, too bluntly stated. Now he'd stated it, about as bluntly as possible, so he'd better try to sell it. "All of you need to get out."

Key's attempted laugh came out as an awkward, gasped sound. "And go where? Live like some normal woman? I'm not normal." All her muscles seized up under his arm, like a reluctant skydiver clinging to the inside of the plane, shouting curses at the people who'd talked her into going up.

"Are you dangerous? Would you ki—target people if Ariadne didn't make you? If you're not dangerous, normalcy doesn't matter. Lack of it doesn't mean you shouldn't have a phone. And friends to call with it. And the right to sleep with whoever you want to."

Key pulled out from under his arm and sat on the edge of the bed, back to him. "Scheisse. You're pretty early with the 'so we can be together forever' stuff."

Shit indeed. Eric suddenly felt his own muscles seize up too. "Sometimes sex can be just sex, you know. That's all . . . I meant this to be." If he'd even thought that far, shame on him. But he knew love was nowhere involved.

Key picked at a loose thread on the hem of the sheet under her hand. "Friends with benefits." She sounded—as much as he could read her back—not actually unhappy with the term.

"Are you okay with that?" Better to be absolutely explicit, from here on out.

She tipped her head just enough to show a beginning curl of a smile in profile. "Suits me." She remained seated while he pushed up and started hunting for his pants. "I wonder if She doesn't care about Map's lovers because he can't get pregnant."

"Is he gay?" Eric had wondered about the strong jaw comment, but hadn't thought further than that. If he was, he wouldn't get anyone pregnant either.

"I don't think so. His lovers have all been women. That I know about. We haven't particularly talked about it." Key retrieved her own jeans. "Why?"

Eric frowned. "I wondered if he was flirting with me when we first met. Something about my jaw?"

"Oh!" Key shook her head. "No, he just talking about how

your features would translate into a drawing. A map." There was something more there, maybe something she was reticent about, but Eric didn't push. They'd probably discussed him between themselves. Drawn him?

"Huh." Eric patted his pockets, checking for all of his possessions. It's not that he really expected Key to have palmed something, but he didn't want to leave anything lying around to raise questions.

Silence fell briefly as she wiggled her jeans on. Eric watched appreciatively. "Have you found any trace of Lantern yet?" she asked suddenly. "I do know that I'd have to leave here to talk to her. Once we find her."

Eric blew out a frustrated breath. "When was I supposed to be finding this information? Last night, while I was busy being threatened by Ariadne? I need a bit more time than that."

A walkie-talkie noise crackled, and Eric started with panic before he realized it was so loud, the handset had to be in the room. Still barefoot, Key dived for the bed, lifted up the corner of the mattress, and groped for something.

She drew out a bright, child's walkie. "Map?"

"She's with Hound right now. Your guard would have warned you too if you hadn't freaking sent him away." Map's tone slipped past exasperation, but he stopped transmitting before it could reach anger.

Key hovered, looking worried, then remembered to hide the handset again. "Maybe . . . she's just got a job for Hound. That would make him happy."

"That's where I was supposed to be. She's checking up on me." Eric had no doubt. He strode to the vanity mirror to make sure nothing would give him away. He ran fingers through his hair and grabbed Key's arm before she could sit down and pull on her shoes. "Brush your hair. Right now, before anything else. Nothing gives it away like tousling."

Key glared at him, probably for his preemptory tone, but the expression faded when she saw herself in the mirror. She sat down and started brushing.

Eric used the time to think furiously. "She needs to catch us at *something*. I might be able to play it cool enough alone, I might not, but she wouldn't have come here if she didn't suspect something. We have to give it to her so she stops looking."

Key held out her hand. "Give me your phone again."

Not stupid, was Key. She hadn't even hesitated before coming up with that idea. Eric unlocked it and handed it over. "Go wild."

He made it to the foot of the stairs before the knock sounded. Before he reached for the knob, he took the time to correct his angle to having come from the first-floor hallway. The door opened under his hand, Hank a solid presence in the sunlight. He might have been trying to move a little slowly, but Ariadne was more than small and agile enough to duck under his arm and precede him into the house.

Her black hair was braided severely back today, and the sun kissed only a moment of glow onto her skin before she was into the indoor lighting. "Here alone? That doesn't look too good, does it, Eric?"

"The Key's upstairs. I think she got tired of me asking about how the Hound ticks and went to sulk." Eric imagined that he'd spent the whole morning speaking to someone who answered like Hound and set his jaw accordingly. If he really was doing the job he'd requested, he'd hate to have to break down and ask Ariadne anything. "Can *you* articulate how their emotions work? They certainly can't."

Ariadne's eyes narrowed and she completely ignored his question. "I thought perhaps I'd join you for lunch."

"Oh, is it that late?" Eric ostentatiously checked his pocket as if looking for his phone. "Fuck—" He patted his other pocket. "She must have—"

"Smiled sweetly at you indeed. Come." Ariadne got a good grip around a handful of his shirt and towed him toward the stairs. Humiliating that she didn't think he'd even resist in front of Hank—and even more so that he didn't. "Explain to me why I should let you near her when you hand her anything she asks for."

"I was watching everything she did until you showed up," Eric whined. The memory of what it had been like to be without breath made the tone fairly easy. Hank's silently watching presence made it harder.

Key arrived on the landing, as if summoned by the voices. Her hand was behind her back, and Eric winced internally. More believable to have hidden the phone somewhere in her room. Eric needed to distract Ariadne, fast. "Who's this Lantern person she's so obsessed with, the fifth one in the Hand? He's not here too?"

"She," Ariadne corrected automatically. Her attention fastened on Key with a snap and a slow, sharp smile spread across her lips. "Is that what she was looking up?"

Key stared at him, betrayal writ large across her face in a way she could never have acted. He suddenly wished he hadn't done it, no matter how strong the need to distract Ariadne. Key's hand fell to her side, and the phone almost slipped out of her suddenly weak grip.

"Well, inasmuch as when you Google 'Lantern' you get a bunch of random restaurants and newspapers as well as camping stores." Eric tried to put apology into his expression as Key approached him, but she just stared at him for a few seconds before offering out his phone and kneeing him soundly in the crotch when he took it.

Eric doubled over, and all he noticed over the pain was Ariadne's delighted laughter. When he could finally mostly breathe and move again, Key was gone, her bedroom's closed door a blank barrier between them.

Ariadne held out her hand like he was supposed to offer his arm like a gentleman. "Perhaps we should find ourselves lunch elsewhere today, hm?"

He offered her his arm.

8

In my youth, the elders told such tales.

Like how the first of the five searchers took up an uneven flat square of sticks, straight and curved, tied to crisscross each other at points of tiny shells. He studied the currents and islands of the stick chart. "I know where she has gone," Map said.

Key's indoor guard returned promptly after the others left, but lunch never materialized, as the catered meals tended not to— by simple oversight, of course—on days when she'd gotten into trouble. Breakfast wasn't catered, though, so the pantry was stocked with those items. When it got late enough it was obvious lunch wasn't coming, Key nursed her hatred of Eric over a bowl of raisin bran and tried not to think any deeper than that simple emotion.

As the afternoon dragged into evening, she picked up then set back down half the books on her shelves. Then she started off on a walk around the compound before deciding she didn't want to look at the same excruciatingly familiar houses and turning around.

She jumped to her feet with anticipation when the door opened around dinnertime purely for the distraction the food would offer. The low box, tray really, filled with food containers from the catering company was the same as always, but tonight it was the Ice Queen herself holding it. Key stood in the hallway and stared.

Her Majesty walked straight at Key as if she weren't there, forcing Key to move aside or get bumped into. She set the food on the kitchen table and speared Key with a sharp look. Key's stomach dropped away, and she smoothed her hair, but after a beat, she realized that Her Majesty was only registering her usual silent displeasure with her hair color. Well, that at least was tough cookies for Her.

"Sit," Her Majesty said, and Key sat. The Ice Queen had no hesitation in zoning out any of them who wouldn't listen to the lecture they had coming, so Key waited with clenched teeth to be chewed out. The smell of tomatoes and garlic from dinner teased her nose, but she ignored it rather than give in to hunger and prove that the lack of lunch had affected her.

Instead of starting right in, She tapped her fingers on the top of the takeout container stack. "Are you bored? Is that it? You want a tutor again?"

Key kept clenching her teeth until she wondered if she could make them crack. What kind of answer did Her Majesty even expect? She supposed she might as well be honest and see what happened. "It's not like there's much to do around here."

Her Majesty sighed and sat down herself, angling a chair that had been straight across the table closer to Key, so Her view wouldn't be blocked by the box. "You think Lantern and her lies are going to make you happier?" She waited, apparently seriously expecting an answer to that as well. Key held her ground this time. Her memories were none of Her business, and they were also one of the few things Key could keep that way.

Her Majesty finally continued. "Lantern has always had a hard time being happy herself, you know. Always sniping and complaining at the edges, trying to tear down what others have built." She set her hands on the table, palm up, as if inviting Key to see her point of view. "She wants everyone to be just as miserable as her, I suppose. I want her to come back as much as you do, so the Hand can be complete, but you notice that after she stopped by to sow her poison, she hasn't been seen since."

Key felt stunned. Did the Ice Queen expect her to buy a single word of that? She might have been a child when she met Lantern, but the worn, soft-focus memories held *affection,* as well as enthusiasm as Lantern told the story. Her Majesty was the one offering lies. Even if the truth came down to one woman's word measured against the other's, She had never given them any affection.

Ideas about youth and affection linked oddly in Key's head, and she suddenly found herself imagining Her Majesty with children of her own. "Did you get pregnant by mistake? Is that why you're so paranoid about me?" Key knew the question was a bad idea even before she asked it, but maybe a bad idea was a good distraction to keep Her from wondering why Key clung to the dream of finding Lantern.

The Ice Queen's lips thinned, and Key suppressed a flinch. That expression, from her earliest whole memories, had always promised a loss. A favorite toy, yet another privilege—only until she'd learned her lesson, of course. "Eric. Did he touch you?"

Key knew she'd been angry at Eric just a moment before—and she still was—but he didn't deserve to lose his life, especially not because of Key's blurted-out mistake. "Of course not. No matter what I offered. He's too afraid of you."

Her Majesty rubbed her lips like the expression promising so much pain was a few locks of windblown hair, easily tidied into something more pleasant. Even her tone was gentler when she next spoke. "No, I've never made that particular mistake, but I've seen plenty of other women make it. And other mistakes." She reached over the table and took Key's hands—actually *took her hands*, like she was a mother or an older sister or something. Key was too frozen with shock to pull away. The Ice Queen was a distant figure, handing out punishment from afar, not advice up close. Thus the name.

"There are so many men out there looking to manipulate you into sex." Her Majesty squeezed Key's hands. "Eric is a manipulator par excellence. A really good magician can make you see only what he wants you to see, and nothing of what he doesn't. Once he's gotten what he wants, only then will you start to see everything he was hiding from you."

Key swallowed and looked out the window into the backyard, at the box of takeout containers, anywhere but at the Ice Queen. Was that what had happened? The sex had been her idea, not his . . . but was that true? Had he manipulated her into thinking it was her own idea? So he could get back at Her Majesty?

Her thoughts must have shown on her face because She made a sympathetic noise. "You're young. Don't beat yourself up about it. You'll be on your guard against him now."

She suddenly smiled, and it transformed her face. "Not as young as I'd been thinking, though. You've grown up while I wasn't watching. Past teen experimentation to start thinking about something real." She shifted Her grip farther up Key's hands and stroked a thumb over the skin of her inner wrist. As tightly wound as Key was with confused attraction left over from Eric, the brush felt electric, jolting low in her body.

Key snatched her hands away. What—? This was the *Ice Queen*. What had happened to that distance?

But She was sitting back now, hands in Her lap, expression neutral. Key could only think that she'd imagined the meaning behind that touch. It was the only thing that made sense, so Key resolved to forget the moment.

"Old enough to understand this too, perhaps. The gods want their Hand back. They've threatened me for not meekly returning, and I'm sure they would threaten you too if they could reach you. I need all of you, even Lantern, with me if we're going to stay safe from them. This is bigger than any nice stories you might remember her telling you. The Hand has to pull together." Silence fell for a beat, then lecture, advice, warning, or . . . whatever the heck that had been done, Her Majesty stood up and let herself out.

Well, scheisse. The stuff about the gods was easy enough to

dismiss as another excuse from the old story for the Ice Queen to be in charge, but Eric was another matter. Maybe the Ice Queen was telling the truth about his motives.

Another glance out the window now she was actually paying attention told her it was far too cold to eat dinner in the gazebo, but Key grabbed a couple of the containers and dragged them out to the picnic table anyway. She sat straddling the bench and stared out through the occasional fat drips from drizzle gathering on the roof above her.

Scheisse. Her Majesty would never let anyone that close again. So Key had thrown away her chance to find someone else who could *tell* her something, help her find her memories, for an orgasm with David Copperfield. Great. Freaking great.

When Map arrived, he had his rain jacket on, but hood down. Moisture had beaded on his curls, and it slowly soaked in as he opened up the food and turned each container to face her. Key grabbed a piece of garlic bread and crunched through it. Maybe if she chewed loud enough, she could drown him out.

He didn't say anything, though. He stole the other piece of bread and watched the droplets with her. "Well?" she asked. He raised his eyebrows at her and crunched into his own bread. She couldn't believe he could resist a "you should have known better" of this caliber. "Did Hank not tell you what happened?"

"He had to. Seeing as I came out to see what the hell was going on, and Eric pulls away from walking back to the cars with Her to accost me and demand I carry his apology to you. So the logical question for me to ask Hank when She and Eric had driven away is, 'Apology for what?'"

"Screw him." Key pulled the container of spaghetti to her and dug in her fork.

Map dusted crumbs off his hands. "I'll leave that to you. Because—because—!" He cut off her growl of frustration before she found words. "When She'd gotten bored of listening to his flowery apologies and went ahead to the car, he told me what you really need to know is a little story about . . . "

Map sighed, and looked upward as if searching his memory for details he found completely irrelevant. "So there was this quaint little European town or something. And they had a ton of trouble with pickpockets going after the tourists, so they put up these warning signs in the worst areas. And thefts skyrocketed. Because people saw the signs and touched their most precious items to make sure they were still there. So the pickpockets just waited, watched, and went for where they touched. And if that was just some pickpocket flirtation I conveyed, I feel dirty now." Map pointedly dusted his clean hands again.

"Oh my god." Key's fingertips flew to her mouth as everything slotted into place. Bring something precious to someone's mind and they'd touch it, to make sure it was there. Like, say, information. "Scheisse, he's sneaky." And that piece of manipulation against the Ice Queen made so much more sense than one against Key. Key felt like the world had clicked back into alignment. Maybe she wasn't experienced enough to read Eric's motives if he tried to hide them, but all the external evidence was on the side of her original interpretation of events. Like, for example, the chances of Her Majesty killing him. "I think I still plan to be angry at him for another couple hours, though." He could have warned her about his sneaky little plan, after all.

At Map's increasingly annoyed look, Key laughed and explained properly how pickpocketing related to Lantern.

"So She checks her last lead on Lantern is still there. Then what?"

Key didn't really know the answer to that, so she started eating to give herself time to think. "Then we all go find Hound a point to track Lantern from, I guess."

Map snorted a ghost of a laugh. "Oh, I'm included in this little adventure now?"

Key twirled her fork in the pasta. "Eric thinks we should all leave. So She won't have anyone left to help drag the others back."

Map muttered a curse under his breath. "I hope you told him where to shove that idea."

"I don't know." The roll of pasta on her fork had gotten too big to chew politely, but she didn't lift it. "Hound and his stupid travel books—maybe he has the right idea. Maybe I don't want to be stuck in these same little houses my whole life, with Her telling me what to do because of scary gods."

"Yeah, you could travel to all those places if you were *rich* enough." Map's lip curled in a sneer, and he fought it down. "Look, Key. I'm sorry. He's the idiot, not you. But it's not . . . a bad life, here. Look at us." He gestured between them. "We could have been children starving on the evening news."

Key focused on his face. "That's oddly specific, Map." When he avoided her eyes, she knew she was right. "What do you know?" She growled, ready to work up to shouting if that's what it took, but he winced and gestured for her to stand down.

"I—" He stared into the drizzle, and a muscle jumped in his jaw, once, again. "I don't know anything about you. She just showed up with you one day, three years old and already a power. But I was seven, when She . . . "

Key waited, as still as she could, lest she break the moment, and he finally did start speaking again. At first, it was in another language, but he translated before she could ask. "So I remember the language. The town where I was born, in Mexico. How I lost my parents." He slammed his hand flat against the table, making Key feel like her heart spasmed then burst into overdrive from surprise. "I remember more than enough to stand by the choice I made."

Realization gripped her, swelling into an epiphany. The line She'd tried to feed Key, earlier, it would have been perfect for Map. *Trying to tear down what others had built.* Maybe She'd already used that line on him. Unlike Key, Map was happy here, in this safe little world that he and Her Majesty wouldn't want Lantern shaking up. Her Majesty had called Eric a manipulator, but look at the way She'd tried to manipulate Key. She'd led with Her last successful approach, then immediately abandoned it for another when it failed.

Key got up from the picnic table, awkwardly disentangling herself from the bench. She could hardly get enough breath to speak, she was so angry at Map. She'd fought free of the Ice Queen's manipulation, but Map was embracing it. "So *you* had a choice. Or you thought you did. Because it's not like She ever misleads anyone, now is it? That's great, freaking great. Maybe I should get my seven years on the outside, then, before I make a *choice.*"

Map stood too, more gracefully. "Eat your dinner. I'll leave." He brought up his hood this time, and headed off back to his house.

Key stayed standing for several minutes, fidgeting with the restless energy of her anger, now denied an outlet. She definitely needed to get out of this place, if only to understand the outside world like Map clearly considered he did. Even if it was pretty scary, thinking of all the things she would need to function. Credit cards and ID and all sorts of normal things.

And if Map didn't want to come . . . well, she could zone him out and drag him.

Key made herself sit down. Scheisse. She could hardly believe she'd even thought that. It wouldn't actually work, of course—Map zoned out when you drew a map of a real place on his skin, and it wasn't like he would stand there and let her do it.

How would she have felt if their situations had been reversed? If Her Majesty went to Map and said, we're moving to my volcano lair, convince Key to come, and Map tied her up? She'd have worse than kicked him in the balls, that was for sure.

Map was right. He'd made his choice, and if Key wanted him to respect her, she should respect him. So he could stay, and she'd just have to deal with it. Convince him to at least not target Eric, maybe. And if she and Eric took Hound with them, Her Majesty still wouldn't be able to track them. And Hound could see some of the places from his books.

Feeling a bit more resolved, if not precisely calm, Key dug into the pasta. She couldn't do anything to help Eric with getting the information on the outside, but she could ready things here. Lay the groundwork about a job coming soon with Hound, talk Map into a promise not to target Eric. Start thinking about how they could escape a compound built with her abilities in mind. But maybe Eric would have some ideas to help with that too.

Key ate her dinner and planned.

9

All in all, it was a shitty plan. Eric had composed shittier, on the fly, but it couldn't compare to what he would have done if he'd had time to think it over. Think it over before he'd set it in motion, that was. He had plenty of time to pick apart what he'd committed himself to while waiting at Ariadne's house.

So far, she'd reacted much as he'd hoped, though. Lunch had been a mere piece of rhetoric—Ariadne immediately drove back to her house, and Eric followed in his own car. By the time he arrived, she had disappeared into her private office, and her real assistant—she enforced the schedule with drag-onlike efficiency—fended him off. If he wanted to apologize or defend himself, he'd have to cool his heels for a good few hours.

So he sat in the researchers' break room with someone's

abandoned diet soda for lunch and thought about what could go wrong. From the drive, Ariadne's great sprawling house appeared to have two floors, but there was in fact a third set into the hillside, almost too grand for the term "daylight basement." That was mostly the province of the researchers, though the full-length windows and French doors facing the lake had clearly been designed for beach and dock access. The data servers lived in one of the windowless rooms against the hillside, and the break room had been created from what must have been intended as a minimalist kitchen for the downstairs bedrooms. No one used the stove, but the fridge was always packed full of random forgotten crap in various stages of sentience.

Now, if the cute little story he'd sent to Key proved true, Ariadne would come in and hassle one of her researchers to get her into the genealogy project computers. Ariadne didn't do computer security or data entry herself; she hired people to do it. Then she'd decide to snub Eric by leaving for dinner without talking to him. Then he could slip in, somehow talk the password out of the researcher, and check what files she'd accessed.

Or she could be so certain or so completely clueless about Lantern's location, she'd have no reason to log onto the computers. She could decide to chase down leads later and leave early for dinner. She could decide several hours was long enough for him to sweat and actually talk to him, and he'd have to figure out something to say. The computer could be locked down tight and the researcher unfriendly. Far, far too much of the plan depended on people acting the way he could only predict they might, not the way he nudged them to.

Heels sounded on the hardwood floor of the hallway, and

Eric melted back to the corner near the fridge, not visible from the door from most angles. Two pairs of footsteps. Ariadne?

" . . . send Carla to the archives with the scanner next week. Keep Tate on the transcriptions from the Pope and Talbot employment records."

Eric could just imagine the assistant taking notes on her phone, fingertips flying to keep up. "I've got to rip someone a new one and then check something in the database before I get changed. I'm running late; I hadn't planned to be shuttling back and forth to the cottages all fucking day."

Fuck. She did plan to talk to him. And after that kind of reaming, he couldn't very well stay at the house and sneak into the computer room after her. Hand very slightly unsteady with a burst of adrenaline, Eric rode the boost to new plan. He pulled out his phone and dialed Ariadne's, then pressed it to his chest so no hint of a doubled ring could reach her out in the hall.

Classical music sounded, then ended after enough time for Ariadne to pull out her phone, see who it was, and reject the call. She gave a disgusted exhalation. "Impatient, aren't we? Fine, he can wait until tomorrow. Don't tell him where I've gone this time either."

Her heels clicked faster down the hall, past the break room and away. Eric, still holding the phone to his chest, breathed a sigh of relief. Sometimes, his predictions about people turned out to be accurate. Ariadne had never done it to him before, but he'd listened sympathetically to more than one researcher who had waited well into the evening before they got confirmation that Ariadne had agreed to talk to them and then left for the night.

He could have chosen a more secure hiding place, but Ariadne had no interest in the break rooms used by her underlings, so when heels clicked past going the other direction about half an hour later, they didn't even pause. Eric waited until the timer on his phone had counted down a full minute, to make sure she'd gone upstairs and hadn't forgotten something, then ducked out into the hall.

He paused briefly at the computer room door, to summon casualness, then let himself in. At this time of the evening, only one researcher was left, one he'd met before, thank God. It wouldn't seem strange for him to initiate a conversation with her.

"Aiko?" He wiggled his fingers when she turned, and looked apologetic to suggest he hadn't wanted to startle her. "Ariadne isn't making you work overtime, is she? Don't you have classes?" Today, her hair was fastened up in—slipping out of—a quick ponytail. Approximately the lower two thirds were bleached light brown. The contrast reminded Eric of Key, and he wondered idly what she'd look like if she let her hair grow out substantially without renewing the dye.

"No classes today." Aiko's Japanese accent was strong, but her English was perfect. "She was actually just in here having me look something up. Sometimes I wonder if she even understands how to use the database herself, no matter how many times I show her."

"She's lucky to have you." Ariadne really was, in Eric's opinion. Most of the other researchers, of whatever age, though they did get a lot of students, just punched the clock, but he was always hearing about Aiko proposing procedural changes for greater efficiency and higher-quality data.

Eric wandered around the room, opening a couple of drawers as if in search of a highlighter. While he ruffled through the contents, he felt inside the walls for a sticky note with a password. No luck near the two other terminals. "You still should probably get home before she remembers something else, though."

"Working on it." Aiko was also assiduous enough that she closed every program and shut down the computer before she even started gathering her possessions into her shoulder bag. No entry to a computer that way. Maybe she had her password written on a note somewhere among her things, though. He couldn't imagine that a part-time researcher on an esoteric genealogy project would bother maintaining CIA-level security.

When everything else was stowed in her bag, Aiko scribbled a couple of notes in a black-and-white-cover student notebook, stuffed full of other papers and the bright tags of sticky notes. It seemed the most likely candidate for what Eric wanted.

"Have a good night," he said, tucking a random highlighter into his pocket to explain his rummaging. She slid her bag onto her shoulder and murmured a polite reply.

As she headed for the door, he leaned to the floor and came up with a database printout he'd stolen from beside another terminal. "Aiko? I think you dropped this." He handed it to her as cover while he smoothly extracted the notebook with the other hand.

"No, this is the family Carla's tracing." She handed it back, and Eric murmured an apology as he set the page back on the table, notebook unseen beneath.

Then she was gone. As smooth as he was in the midst of a touchy job, he felt now like he hadn't been breathing the whole time and was only now filling his lungs properly. He still might not have the password, though.

Time to find out. Eric opened the notebook at a random sticky tag. The majority of the notes were in English—though a little oddly angled, the cursive was better than any he'd seen in a long time—and did seem to be names and historical dates, as one would expect. Near the front, the notes changed to complex mathematical equations for a while, for some reason. From her classes maybe.

No sticky note, but Eric found the classic pairing of two words near the bottom of the inside front cover. The first included her name, and the second meant nothing to him. A transcribed Japanese word, he suspected.

Finally, he'd caught a break. He glanced around but decided to leave the room lights on, to avoid the telltale blue glow of a monitor left on in a dark room. He booted up Aiko's terminal and entered her password without incident.

The database wasn't particularly unintuitive, to his eyes, though it took him a good ten minutes to figure out how to get it to display recently accessed files, rather than prompting him to search for a name.

He checked the clock on his phone, then compared it to the computer clock to make sure his estimate of when Ariadne had been there lined up with the time stamps on the files. Only one, tagged *TH Dataset*. He opened it.

And it was just a rather mundane record of a woman named Laura Dixon in her forties. He paused to do the calculation properly: forty-three. The word "Lantern" appeared nowhere on the page.

But then it wouldn't, would it? Not with a bunch of random researchers' eyes all over it. Ariadne knew the name she needed. Eric took a photo of the whole page for later reading and one zoomed in on the address, just to be sure. Laura couldn't possibly be Lantern, or Ariadne would have captured the woman herself long since. But he'd bet Laura knew something about Lantern.

Even if she didn't, he would have gotten Key and the others out into the world long enough to find that out. He doubted Key would be eager to go back.

Eric shut down the computer and picked up the notebook, considering it. Aiko might well have a memory of putting it into her bag, so it would be stranger to find it still in the computer room than to find it on the ground as if it had slipped out somewhere by the garages, for example. And he still wanted to read through it properly to find the notes she'd scribbled while he was watching, in case they had something do with the record Ariadne had called up.

Eric tucked the notebook under his arm. He'd borrow it for a day or two. Time to go home and plan his next step with Key.

10

In my youth, the elders told such tales.

Like how the five searchers set off to follow the youngest of the gods, as they had been created to do. Map steered their course and as they sailed across the wine-dark sea, dawn, with her rosy fingers, painted their horizon.

Key was in her bedroom when someone knocked on the front door that morning. She stayed where she was, in case it was Her. Fortunately, she didn't have to hurriedly hide any evidence of packing, since she'd realized in the middle of the night she had no idea what to pack, and didn't own a suitcase anyway.

Two male voices downstairs. Key reached her doorway in time to see Eric handing his phone over to the guard on the landing, then allowing his pockets to be patted down. Key couldn't guess what other kinds of contraband they were worried about.

Eric casually stuck his hands into those pockets and ambled over to join her. The guard moved to hold up the hallway wall with his usual sightline into her room. At least he wouldn't be in there with them. That was something, at least.

"Morning." Eric nodded to her, completely calm, then went over to raise her blinds and examine the view from her window. Due to the angle, it mostly overlooked the backyard that adjoined her own. In the gap between two of the houses opposite, you could just see the swath of grass that surrounded the gazebo. Today was cloudy, but surfaces and leaves had dried after the drizzle last night.

"Ready to go?" Eric flicked her a brief glance before returning to his gaze out the window. Key didn't know how he could be so casual. She supposed he had to be, because the guard was watching their body language since he couldn't hear their words. She tried to stand as loosely as him, then remembered that without the message passed through Map, she should probably still be angry. She edged up to him so they could at least talk, but didn't try to hide her tension.

"Did you find something?" That was the important thing here, the only thing that partially excused his betrayal. Then again, maybe he hadn't, and she wouldn't have to leave. Key felt almost relieved for a second before Eric nodded.

"It's on my phone. I'll show you when we're out. It's just a name and an address. I doubt she's Lantern, but we can at least talk to her. See what she knows."

Key made sure her back faced the guard, then pressed her

thumb into her opposite palm, rubbing to remind herself to stay calm. After all this time, she might actually be able to get her memories triggered. But what if this woman didn't know anything about Lantern? Or what if they found Lantern and she wouldn't talk to them? "I don't have a suitcase." She winced. That sounded dumb.

Eric seemed about to answer; then his expression softened, and he gave her another glance. "Don't overthink it. Stick a toothbrush and some clean underwear and shirts in whatever bag you've got. We're not traveling to Antarctica; there will be stores. The harder part will be getting you guys out."

"I had an idea for that." Key didn't realize she was getting animated as she explained, until Eric put a hand on her shoulder. She stuffed her hands in her pockets immediately, to remind herself not to use them.

He dropped the touch as soon as she stilled, and in the silence after she'd finished describing her idea, Key tried to figure out how she felt about that. The feeling of hearing him tell Her Majesty about Key's secret dream, of hearing Her lies, was all tangled up in the warmth after the sex. Before those conversations, she would have said she definitely wanted to sleep with him again. Now she could only think of his casual expression as he mentioned Lantern, Her Majesty saying "manipulator," even as she wanted to lean into Eric's hand, extend his touch.

"Sounds reasonable to me," Eric said, with no sign of thoughts about the touch from his side. "I'll talk to Hound for a bit, while you get Map, and then I'll head for the gatehouse. We'll need to sell your story to your guard a little. Walk with me and follow my lead."

Key wanted to protest. What if his lead wasn't obvious and

she screwed this up? But he'd already turned away and walked out into the hall. "Hound likes hide-and-seek? Seriously? Wouldn't he automatically win?"

Key followed him out, touching the door as she passed. *Unlocked.* "We modified it a little. He's not, you know, homing in on you, so if you double back, you can sneak up behind him while he's still following the loop. That's how Map or I win." Key was halfway into the answer before she realized she'd just followed his lead perfectly. She didn't know how he did it, not just saying the right thing himself, but prompting the right thing in someone else. Manipulator.

No. Key decided right then that he was on her side, and she was going to stop thinking that way—the way She wanted Key to—until she had direct evidence that he was no longer with her.

Eric paused at the head of the stairs. "Well, I'll join you guys once you've started, then. See him in action." And he jogged down the stairs and let himself out.

Key returned to her room. *Unlocked.* She still had a backpack somewhere, she was sure of it. After some digging, she found it at the back of the closet, left over from her insistence on feeling like a real student when she could simply have left her books at the house where she and Map had their lessons. Fortunately she'd been old enough to choose one not covered with cartoon characters.

After putting in toothbrush, underwear, and shirts, as prompted, Key considered. She probably shouldn't—but she added the handcuffs and condoms. Only so the guards wouldn't find them if they searched her room.

In the kitchen, she stuffed a water bottle and bag of trail mix on top to justify the bag. She shrugged on her coat, slung the pack over one shoulder to look casual, and let herself out the back door.

The guards must have warned each other over the radios they were in for an annoying day, because Map met her at his door, impeccably dressed, brows high. "Hide-and-seek?"

Key knew what he was really asking. Both of them knew that they'd invented their variation on the game mostly to get a little privacy. Key could let them into any of the houses, and with three people to chase into and out of houses and through landscaping and back into houses again over a whole compound, the guards usually gathered centrally, set someone extra to watch the walls, and waited them out. As long as the other two showed themselves occasionally, the third could have as much as an hour of privacy curled up in a closet.

They couldn't have this argument in front of their guards, but Key figured they'd already had it last night. She didn't know what else she could say if his mind was made up. "Hound and I are going to, at least. If you don't want to . . . " Key looked at her shoes. *Unlocked,* was the door in Map's hand. Now she was here, she was having more trouble than she'd expected not begging him to come. "At least don't spoil the game?"

Map turned away, leaving the door ajar. Key hesitated, wondering whether to follow, but then he was back, coat on, bag of his own over his shoulder. "Maybe you can take care of yourself, but Hound can't," he said, biting the words off.

Key knew he thought he should take care of her as well, but she appreciated that he at least didn't say it. She grabbed his hand instead of thanks, and tugged him toward Hound's house.

Key glanced one more time at Eric leaning on the side of his wrist beside the open doorway of the gatehouse, chatting with the guy inside. She wished it hadn't turned sunny, but it wasn't like clouds would really have made them harder to see. "Okay, Hound, we have to be completely silent to get to the job." Map took his hand, and they all jogged for the chain-link gate to the parking lot, hugging the wall of the nearest house, then evergreen bushes, then the cinderblock wall around the whole complex the chain-link supplemented.

She gathered herself, throwing several more glances at Eric. The moment wasn't likely to get any better. She jogged the last few feet and opened the rolling gate just enough to slip through. *Unlocked.* Map pressed Hound through first, then followed, and Key rolled the gate back into place behind them. *Locked.* Step one.

"I'll go in the trunk." Touching the lock seized Key's attention with the emotional traces of the one it belonged to. *Locked. Where the hell had he put his cards? New venue, he had no idea if he'd have much of an audience. At least it wasn't raining.*

Map pulled her hand away as he passed on the way to one of the back doors. "That's probably for the best. You know you can always get out."

Unlocked. Unlocked. Key did the car doors before she did the trunk for herself. Climbing in wasn't hard, but then she had to find a good enough grip on the inside of the lid to close it so the latch caught. Locking didn't help with that.

Finally she got it, and there was silence and darkness. The carpet floor was scratchy, and she kept hitting her knees or the heels of her hands as she tried to shift to a more comfortable position. *Locked,* was the trunk latch now. *Locked.* Had the guards seen them climb in and were even now running over to drag them out? Did the lack of footsteps mean they weren't coming, or that she couldn't hear footsteps from in here?

Time stretched on and on until the car suddenly beeped, making Key jump and slam a knee into the wall. Freaking ow. A door opened, then shut. Eric had promised to throw his coat over whoever was crouched on the floor in the backseat, so that's what that must have been. Another moment, another door opening and shutting, then the car started up.

Key hugged herself and braced her feet on the wall. It didn't feel exactly stable in here. At least they were moving slowly for now. She tried to count turns, but she lost track the first time the car angled less than ninety degrees. She'd never paid that much attention to the minutia of the route between the parking lot and the gatehouse. They did slow and stop. Was Eric talking to the guard again? Was the trunk going to pop open any moment, before she could lock it on them? She hugged herself harder, as if that would slow her heart.

Then they pulled away, sped up, turned again. Had it worked? It had worked! *Locked,* the trunk still was.

11

Map's head lifted into view in the rearview mirror about ten minutes down the road from the cottages. Eric couldn't take his eyes off the road ahead and the road behind, where he was watching for following cars, for long enough to note anything about Map's expression. He didn't hear any clicks, though. "Seat belts."

Map growled under his breath, but Eric heard one click then another, and the next time he focused on the back seat, both Map and Hound were sitting up. "I want to get a bit more distance before I stop." Not that he had to justify himself to them—well, to Map, no one needed to justify anything to Hound—but he didn't like the idea of Key in the trunk for any distance himself.

When they entered Monroe, Eric turned away from the city center and drove until the road turned completely rural. He parked along the side of someone's generous, heavily vegetated yard, the house buried back in the trees. Better to chance letting someone out of the trunk here than in a hotel parking lot.

He popped the trunk from his seat, and Key was already climbing out when he made it around. She sat on the bumper and shrugged out of her backpack, leaving that inside. For half a second, she smiled at him, and he could see the high of a job completed in her face. Then the expression hid. She looked all around, a touch of fear appearing instead.

Eric offered her his hand, though she didn't need it to stand from the bumper. He glanced around, trying to see the world as she did, for maybe the first time, but he was too used to categorizing it as something normal. Just someone's yard, thickly growing Douglas firs keeping the ground clear of most things besides their shed needles. This house had a bright plastic tricycle abandoned up the driveway, and a split-rail fence along the road that was steadily falling to pieces.

Key stood up, but continued to cling to his hand while she looked around. "Like on TV," she said weakly, finally.

Eric murmured his agreement. Whatever got her through. Map got out of the car, but only to transfer to the passenger seat. Eric wondered at the dynamics, but Key didn't object. He handed her into her seat, and did not smile at all when Map reminded her to fasten her seat belt.

"Where are we going?" Map said, the moment Eric's door had shut.

"To a hotel, to lie low for a while." He pulled out his phone, lifted it as illustration. "Our lead's in Oregon, but there's no point heading there yet. If we've been unlucky and Ariadne suspects that's our destination, we need to allow time for her to check there and not find us."

Key unbuckled the seat belt she'd just buckled to sit forward and grab for his phone. "Show me the lead."

Eric held it out of her reach long to call up the picture of the computer record, then handed it over. Map still looked disgruntled. "Just some random hotel? That's your idea of a good hiding spot? Key can get us in anywhere."

"And then the alarms go off, or the owners come home. If there was a way we could know that someone was on vacation, that would be great, but otherwise . . . " Eric shrugged and touched the keys in the ignition, ready to start the car.

"Wait. I know a place." Map twisted to where Key was still reading the photo on the phone. Probably for the fourth or fifth time by now. "Does that thing have maps? I could find it again."

"And this magical place is . . . ?" Eric intercepted the phone on its way between the two powers. He did open the GPS app, but didn't hand it over. It needed a couple of seconds to find their current location anyway.

"When I was . . . " Map seemed like there was something he didn't want to admit to, but it was Key he glanced at, not Eric. "A child, we lived somewhere else for a while, before Key showed up. A cabin up near Darrington. Near the boundary of the national forest, I think. It'll be closed up now."

Eric let the phone fall to rest on his thigh. "You're suggesting we run away from Ariadne to her own cabin?" It sounded stupid on the surface, but often that was the point. He was curious how Map would spin it.

"She'd hardly look for us on her own property if we're supposed to be running away from her. We know the owners won't show up, and it's isolated. No nosy neighbors. Doesn't cost anything, so we won't run out of money while still trying to lie low."

"You never mentioned—" Key swallowed her objections with obvious difficulty. "Guess I'll get to see it now, anyway."

Eric centered the map on Darrington, then handed his phone over. Map made some good points. He'd withdrawn enough cash for a hotel for several days, but after that, they'd be vulnerable if Ariadne could convince her IT guy to track his cards. "If you need to zoom—" He made the gesture in the air with his fingertips.

Map touched the screen with more confidence than Key had—more illicit access to phones, perhaps—but then he froze and made a low, whimpered sound in his throat.

Eric waited a beat for an explanation that didn't come, then tried to take the phone back. Map hung on and twisted in his seat to take it out of reach.

"What—?" Eric appealed to Key.

"You should have seen him this one time a few years back. Someone sent an atlas by mistake with Hound's books, and Map got it and he just sat there for nearly a day, turning pages." Key leaned between them, weight on her hands on the two seat backs.

Map growled and made as if to push her back with a hand starfished over her face. She thumped back onto the back seat. "Shut up, Key," he said, embarrassment obvious.

Which had been the point, Eric abruptly realized. As much time as they'd spent together, growing up while locked in, they both probably knew how to manage each other's powers better than anyone. At first blush, the powers seemed no more than a supernatural version of a well-developed skill, but the more he saw of them, the more they seemed like an entire state of mind—sensory perceptions and patterns of thought.

"Here." Map held out the phone, zoomed in to a random spot in the woods, off some rural road too small to have a label even at that scale. "Head north."

Eric told his phone to map the route but turned the audible directions off. If he was getting turn-by-turn from Map, he didn't want the two fighting as they usually did when you pitted a local passenger against a GPS.

He opened his mouth as he buckled in and started the car, but Key beat him to it. "Seat belt," she said, exasperated, and buckled hers. He smiled as he pulled back onto the road.

12

In my youth, the elders told such tales.

*Like how as the five searchers sailed, a storm broke.
Rain was upon them for forty days and forty nights,
but Map held his course. When the rain cleared,
they saw a raven and knew that land must be near.*

Key figured out how to open her window on the freeway, but Eric talked her into leaving it closed until they turned off into slower speed zones. It wasn't as though she planned to hang her head out like a dog, but she didn't want even the slightly dusty distortion of the glass between her and seeing everything.

The woods were so much fresher in person, when you could smell them as well. They smelled like rain, Key thought. And they kept going, whatever direction she looked, except when trunks disappeared around a building or in a logged section. She liked it best when the trees came right to the ditch on either side of the two-lane road, because she felt embraced by them.

The cabin looked nothing like what she'd expected from the word. It was two stories, in a somewhat curved shape that cupped the front lawn. Huge windows extended up both stories in the center, making an angled jut of a front hall like the prow of a ship. It had logs on the walls, but they looked more like rounded siding than anything structural.

Eric bumped the car off into the brush a little short of one wing of the cabin. Less visible from the road, Key supposed. He told them to stay put, then stared at the house for a while before he got out and walked a long, loose circuit around it. Impatience simmered in her stomach, but she waited until he reappeared to open her door.

Blackberries tried to grab her shoes when she stepped out. Picking a way through them didn't help, so she finally crashed out to the gravel drive and hoped any that snagged would pull free.

Map stood where he was for a few minutes, while Eric pulled the shopping bags of food they'd grabbed at the grocery store from the trunk. Key wondered if Map was feeling like her, only he was too cool to gawk, but then she remembered he'd been here before. He was probably revisiting childhood memories. Scheisse.

She stomped up to the front door. *Locked. Unlocked.* Inside, everything was designed to look as if it were made out of logs as well, but stained very shiny. It was certainly different than anywhere at home—at her house. She left the door open for the others and went exploring.

One of the bedrooms had a huge bed, one that enfolded her with softness when she sat on the edge, making her laugh. When she'd worked her way back to the kitchen, she immediately joined Eric. He was slotting food into the stainless-steel monstrosity of a fridge, and even though she tried to sneak behind him, he clearly heard. "Hound said there were no recent trails from anything human entering the house. I tried to get him to define 'recent,' but he got bored and wandered off into the woods."

"He can't get lost," Key said, because Eric sounded worried about something. She wasn't quite sure why. They'd gotten a lead on Lantern, and they'd gotten away! She waited impatiently until his hands were free, then turned him around so she could kiss him. Free, free, free! Free to do things exactly like this, kissing someone just because she wanted to.

Eric nudged her, body pressed along hers, so the fridge door could swing shut behind them. He pushed the kiss deep, fast, only to pull back when she was wondering if that bed was too far away. At least they could save time by losing clothes along the way.

Then, with clear reluctance, he pulled completely away. For a moment, they didn't touch anywhere, but then he looped his arms around her lower back, warm but not particularly sensual. "We shouldn't annoy Map."

"I can lock the bedroom door," Key grumbled, but mostly to have something to say. Staying verbal was distracting, and her instincts calmed down a little. "All right. But *sometime . . .*"

"Tomorrow, we can figure out logistics." Eric laughed, seemingly just as frustrated as her, which made Key feel a bit better. He left her to open the fridge again and survey the contents. Maybe he wanted the cool air. He selected a beer and started rummaging in various drawers. For a bottle opener, she realized only after he found one and applied it to his cap.

Key got a beer of her own and rotated the bottle to follow the label design around the side. Hank had given her one on her twenty-first birthday, and she still remembered how gross it had tasted, but freedom was much less exciting if she didn't exercise her new privileges.

"You'll hate that." Map breezed between them and snagged the beer from Key and the bottle opener from Eric. He'd been offering it to her, and she hadn't noticed. "I'll take it off your hands for you."

Key kicked at his ankle, and he stepped nimbly aside. "You can acquire the taste if you want," Eric said. After a glance at Map, he offered her a swig from his own bottle. "Though you'll probably want to start with something lighter than this. I wasn't shopping with that in mind."

Key held up a hand in refusal, and turned back to the fridge. It wasn't like they didn't have plenty of soda. "No, he's right. I've tried it before. And wine. They were both . . . " She pulled a face. "I suppose the appeal must be mostly the getting drunk part."

Map popped his cap, and Eric opened the drawer again for him to drop the opener in. "I know Ariadne's no teetotaler. But she enforced a dry compound for you guys?"

Map swigged his beer. Key noticed that while both men

held their bottles with the utmost of nonchalance, Eric sipped
idly, while Map tossed his back. Probably still unconsciously
afraid of getting caught with it. "I suspect she was worried we
might decide getting drunk was a way to deal with any restlessness." Map's look at Key was pointed, and she ignored him just
as pointedly. She wasn't ashamed of being restless. She didn't
really see the point of being drunk, either, as portrayed in fic-
tion and on the news. It just made you do stupid things and
screw up your life.

She returned to the granite counter with her soda, only to
have Map slide over a glass. "Pour about half in there. I got you
a present." He bent, rustled around in the deflated plastic grocery bags, and came up with a larger bottle.

Eric laughed. "I wondered what you wanted that for. Vodka and 7-Up. I guess that's technically a mixed drink. Why
don't you let me pour?" He set his beer aside and tried to take
the vodka bottle from Map, who glared at him and hung onto
the neck.

"I know what I'm doing." Map regained control of the
bottle, but Key drew her glass of soda protectively against her
body. She might be with Eric on this one. If Map wasn't as experienced as he was pretending, she didn't want to find out by
getting sick.

"Do you?" Eric's expression remained mild.

"My friends would smuggle stuff in for me. I'm not completely ignorant."

"His lovers," Key corrected for Eric's benefit, helpfully.
Map deserved it, after the ignorance comment. Maybe he had
been getting drunk every day each summer, in the shed with

his landscaping chicks, but she doubted it. They'd had enough trouble finding a time to drink the half a bottle of wine someone had given him for Christmas one year, which was how she knew she didn't like it.

"That still means you'd be pouring for an adult male with some tolerance, not a woman with none. Look, I'll do it by the book." Eric returned to a drawer he'd opened earlier and pulled out a liquid measuring cup. "One and a half ounces is a standard drink."

"Give me that," Key said. Enough posturing. She wrested the vodka bottle from Map, and when she turned back, Eric had placed the measuring cup demurely on the counter, ready for her. She could read ounce lines as well as anyone, and this was her own liver. She was actually kind of excited to find out what might happen, in a looking out the window at the tree branch she was only eighty percent sure she could make the jump to sort of way. What would being drunk feel like?

She swirled the vodka with the soda once she'd poured it in and took a cautious sip. Not . . . too bad. Kind of weird, but still mostly just sweet like the soda would have been on its own.

Eric returned to his beer. He leaned his hip against the counter island with Key, while Map chose a patch beside the stove. A lull fell for a minute or two while they all drank. "Seems like Ariadne was harder on you than Map in a lot of ways," Eric commented idly.

"Got to protect the baby of the family." Map toasted Key ironically, and she growled at him. She supposed he was teasing, but it still seemed uncomfortably close to the truth for his behavior as well as Hers.

"Hound's younger than me." Key twisted to glance out the

nearest window, thinking of him rambling around out in the trees. She should go and join him later, maybe, rather than staying inside yet another house. "Not that he's ever going to drink. Or have sex."

"In abstract, he's the ideal teenager that way." Eric exhaled on an ironic note. "I'd bet you were a hell of a troublemaker yourself in that period, Map."

Key sneaked a dribble more vodka into her existing soda. Now she was used to the taste, she felt ready to up the concentration a little. "When Map was, what, nineteen? I couldn't discover all the details, but Her Majesty found out he had this whole side business with the guards, paid in contraband. Books we weren't supposed to have and pot, I think? Didn't smell like cigarettes. Anyway, they'd bring him missing persons cases, and if the photo was good enough, he'd solve it and the guard would call in the tip for the reward. The Ice Queen was *pissed*, and locked him in his house for like a month. I wasn't allowed to let him out, or she said she'd tie me to my bed."

All of that had flowed out a bit more precipitously than Key had expected, so she paused to reevaluate. Was she drunk? She felt warm, maybe a bit giggly. Eric did laugh, warm enough that it eased any tension Map's glower might have introduced to the kitchen. "Speaking of, Map. What does that mean, if the photo's good enough? Key said I should ask you if I wanted to know about your powers, but you don't have to answer if you don't want."

Map lifted his forefinger from the side of his beer. Tap, tap. Finally, he sighed. "Think of it like satellite photos. The process of drawing a real map, there's a whole lot of brainpower goes into what to put in, what to leave out, what to prioritize with labels or exaggerate in size. A satellite photo, sometimes it's good, sometimes it's not, based on the angle and lighting and what features happen to show well. It's chance. A good drawn portrait, that has the same inherent choices about what information to include. Photographs, sometimes someone's character shows up, sometimes it doesn't." He shrugged. "Some photographers seem to have learned how to lock into that a bit better, but photographs are never as good."

"When you're in a car with a zoom lens, you're lucky to get their full face, honestly." Eric shrugged, and Map straightened in surprise. Key was pretty surprised herself. She hadn't known Eric did that. Maybe he was being nice, since he knew something about Map now.

"So the assisting, or whatever, you did for Her Majesty, that was taking photographs?" Key mimed a camera in front of her face and giggled.

"Among other weird stuff I didn't understand at the time. Lifting keys. And nudging people into being in a certain place at a certain time. Might have been for Hound." As if suddenly restless, Eric set his half-full beer on the counter and scrubbed condensation from his palm onto the thigh of his jeans. "Mostly, it is—was—a way to earn money to fund my stage magic habit."

"Ever pull a rabbit out of a hat?" Key shook her head immediately, laughing. "Sorry. I'm sure you hate that question. You seriously have your own show? That's really cool."

Eric's tone turned melodic. "No rabbits, no cards, only the purest of prestidigitation to stun and amaze. And perhaps a lovely lady or two, though I think to take such beauty and saw it in half would be most rude." He bowed extravagantly. When he straightened, his tone returned to normal. "It's fairly intimate, nothing Vegas flashy. I take it to street fairs and events like that."

Key watched his face while he spoke. He looked so *happy.* "I want to see one of the shows. When—" When they weren't hiding out. After they'd found Lantern and Her Majesty decided to leave them alone. That wouldn't be too long, would it? She realized she wasn't too worried about it at the present moment. "When we don't have to worry about the Ice Queen anymore."

Eric shook his head, smile a little twisted. "Why do you call Ariadne the Ice Queen?"

Map rocked a step forward, smirking. "Come on, Eric. With all this talk about magic, you're forgetting the part of your real job where you 'assisted' Her in bed."

Eric froze. Key's head was too swimmy to do the same, but she leaned on the cool granite and focused on thinking. He'd slept with Her? Seriously? How did she feel about that? It was kind of gross, and she couldn't really wrap her head around it.

Then Eric laughed, not warmly this time. "Hank did *not* tell you that," he stated rather than asked.

Map shrugged extravagantly. "All the guards know."

Eric wiped his palm on his jeans again, though it must be dry by now. "I doubt that, given that Ariadne and I dated in college, nearly fifteen years ago, now. Rumors carry, but I'm sure that's a boring one by now, what with having absolutely nothing to renew it since." He relaxed back into his lean, smile returning suddenly. "Maybe I just have a thing for strong women."

He caught Key's eyes after he said it, and she felt like she'd blushed all over her body. Did he really think she was . . . ? That was pretty awesome. She supposed he was forgiven, then. Everyone did stupid things fifteen years ago.

Map mimed gagging. "Or maybe you just want to make Her jealous."

Eric crossed his arms and sighed. "Map, I have a little sister. She's married, but I'm sure she had sex before that. I suppose I had the luxury of not knowing any specifics, but I assure you: it's an idea you have to get used to."

Someone needed to distract both Map and Eric, Key decided. As soon as possible. "It's because She controls everyone from up in Her, like, tower of icicles. Ice Queen, I mean. She sweeps in to make your life worse and then sweeps out again."

"Given how much of a freaking fairy tale—in the worst sense—our lives already are." Map strode over and yanked the fridge open. "I'll start dinner." He slammed the package of steaks on the counter, and the pan onto the stove, but by the time he'd found salt and pepper, he seemed much happier, settling into the groove of his favorite hobby.

Eric circled out of his way and lingered in the doorway to the living room. Key picked up her drink to follow, but she had to pause and gather herself, making sure her head was steady. She laughed at how she must look to the others. "I guess I'm drunk."

"Not hardly, yet." Eric held out his hands to her, grinning, and she walked carefully over. "See? That was practically straight. You're just tipsy. This isn't a bad stage to stop at."

"Really?" Key got distracted again for a second, cataloging all her sensations. "I guess I can still talk fine."

Eric's grin shaded even warmer. "Repeat after me: she sells seashells . . . "

Key tried several times, before laughter at her own hopeless stumbles made her collapse into Eric's arms. Not that she was actually that out of breath and off balance, but it made a nice excuse. Eric didn't seem to mind, either.

"Let's get out of the chef's way." Eric led her to flop onto the couch. He'd left his beer behind, but she deigned to allow him to share her drink.

This part of freedom from the Ice Queen was just how she'd imagined it. Thank goodness they'd made it past the hard parts.

Conversation over dinner was polite enough, when there was any. The more normal Key started feeling, the more she wanted to wince in retrospect. Eric hadn't been kidding that the idea of someone sleeping with his little sister really annoyed Map, apparently. She was happy enough to pretend the conversation hadn't happened along with them, though, because at the moment she didn't feel like explaining how it was neither of their businesses. She'd lay the smackdown on them later if they hadn't learned their lessons and it came up again.

After they finished eating, Map pulled her away from slotting her plate into the dishwasher. "There's something you should see." He led her into the front hall. The floor was honey colored with the light from the front windows, and the moment Key followed that light back to its source, she saw why he'd brought her.

The sunset flamed in the angled windows, nestled between dark silhouettes of trees. Key sat on the steps of the grand staircase and watched the sun sink into red, then purple. Map sat beside her and didn't say anything when she leaned against his shoulder.

"I wonder how many regulations she ignored and neighbors she pissed off when she cut down all the trees for *that* view." Eric joined them, leaning against the bottom post of the staircase railing. Hound's fork and knife clinked every so often as he ate the food they'd saved for him. He'd shown up as they were finishing off the last of their own meal.

There must have been really interesting trails in the woods, though, because the back door, off the kitchen, opened and closed as Hound presumably went back out. "This is nice." Key winced. That sounded inane out loud. Map murmured agreement, though.

"Very picturesque." *Her* voice. Ariadne, Eric kept calling her. Key whipped her head around and there She was, strolling in from the kitchen. So perfect, black hair silky, figure trim, suit tailored, with two guards slightly behind her. Key knew she was a good seven inches taller than the Ice Queen, and still she felt like a child when Her Majesty wrapped Her authority around Herself like this. Defiantly, she changed that in her head. Ariadne. No queen, no majesty.

Key gathered her legs under her, ready to burst off the stair, to run—run somewhere. Not here. Not caught with Ariadne when she was truly angry. But Key wasn't a child anymore, and she didn't know if she could reach the front door in time anyway. And Eric was closer.

He, too, appeared ready to spring—at Her Majesty. Ariadne gestured and Hound came out from behind the guards. "Target him, sweetheart."

Eric rocked a step back—but he didn't know. How could he know? Hound targeted by touching an uncrossed trail, and Eric had been the last one to enter the hallway. Hound bent and Key burst off the stairs, swung around using the post, and got herself in front of Eric. She scuffed her feet to either side too, but Hound had already lifted his fingers and was straightening.

"Map, you said—" It started out plaintive, but Key knew the answer before she'd finished speaking. He'd made his choice, and now he'd imposed it on her too. He'd taken them somewhere he knew Ariadne would find them. Damn him to hell. But she didn't have time to be angry right now.

Eric's fingers tightened on her shoulders like he wanted to switch their places, put himself in front. But Key was the power, and Ariadne didn't care anything about anyone else. "I looked for cameras," he said, tone calm.

Ariadne snorted. "What good would they be if they were easy to find? The gods aren't stupid, when they decide to stop posturing and come for us in earnest."

"If you wanted to keep Key docile, you should have edited that little fable a little. Make up a name, pretend it's associated with that Lantern of hers, and she'll go wherever you want." Eric settled his hand on the back of Key's neck, possessive.

"You were supposed to let me lead her to failure and back to you, no longer restless."

Key didn't believe him. Maybe it was because he'd done this before—or was that all part of the same plan?—or maybe it was because she couldn't handle two simultaneous betrayals, his and Map's. She just wanted to get through this, keep Ariadne talking until they could figure out how to get away from her.

Ariadne held out a hand to her side without looking. "Guilherme. Your gun." Key finally looked at the blank-faced guards long enough to identify them, but neither would be allies. Guilherme was mostly assigned to Hound and tended to forget the rest of them had brains, and Robert didn't give a rat's butt about anyone who wasn't paying him.

Guilherme handed over his weapon immediately, and only then seemed to consider what he was doing. "Ma'am?"

Ariadne ignored him and pointed the gun at Key and Eric behind her. "I taught you half your games, Eric, or don't you remember? I'm in no mood. Key, Map, don't make me start all over again. We're going home."

"You don't have any new children ready," Map said. Key didn't turn because Ariadne had a *gun*. However much Key knew that she couldn't really die and maybe she'd even have her memories next time, she hadn't figured on how terribly much this body's instincts didn't want to *die*. It sounded like Map was still standing on the stairs, though. "If you did start over, who would you even breathe the powers into?"

Ariadne shrugged. The gun's barrel wobbled, but didn't leave them. "Even if I have to let you all jump naturally for one body, I'll find you again. I've done it before." Her expression pretended to soften. "But none of that's necessary."

"You've been—breathing us—" It all came together so quickly that Key had to think through it again, slowly, to make sure she hadn't gotten something wrong somewhere. Of course, Ariadne must have done something other than let the powers be reborn naturally, if she'd found Map before he was Map, if Map felt he'd had a choice, however false. And if she breathed the powers into whoever she chose—she chose the age.

Key had no memories because of her. Not just because she wouldn't give Key information, but because she'd *made* Key that way.

"Key," Ariadne . . . begged? But she couldn't be begging. "Map. I don't have time for this—*we* don't have time for this. The gods want their Hand back, to do their dirty work. I suppose they can't stand to leave any tools lying unused—by them. I need both of you, and I need Lantern, to stand against them. We can't take the chance that your powers will pass to someone the gods find first. But it's not just that. I want you by my side, Key. Like we used to be."

Key spat at her. "I'm not quietly going home with a murderer." She'd forgotten about Eric until his fingers dug even harder into her shoulders. She supposed he wanted her to pretend to play along like he'd done, but she couldn't. She couldn't. She glanced over to check Map's reaction, found his expression blank with tension.

"Still reading from the same self-righteous script." Ariadne's shoulders went down, and her second hand came up to the gun. "Last chance, Key."

Scheisse. They were outgunned and outnumbered—but did Hound really count for Ariadne's side? Hound wasn't on anyone's side. But if Ariadne gave him one order and Key gave him another, whom would he listen to, the Ice Queen, or someone he'd grown up with?

Key decided to find out. At very least, it would be a distraction, and she knew Ariadne would never hurt Hound, not when, as Eric had said, Hound was never any trouble. "Hound, take the gun away from her!"

Hound stepped right in front of Ariadne. Her expression darkened and she hissed a curse. Robert drew his weapon, but didn't seem to know where to point it. Hound put his hand on the barrel of Ariadne's gun and tugged.

"Hound, stay out of this." Ariadne snarled over top of Key's wordless sound of denial. Handling a gun that way wasn't safe. Even she knew that, having seen them only on TV. Hound needed to—

Ariadne yanked a last time, and the gun went off.

The sound, the shock—Key felt like she'd missed a few moments, but her heart was racing as if she'd spent two lifetimes in those seconds. The next thing she knew, Hound was looking calmly down at the blood pumping down his leg, wicking from an ugly stain around the hole punched in his shirt over his stomach. He touched the hole, experimentally. Guilherme crossed the space between them in one step and caught him as he folded up. He eased Hound down to lie on the floor, and a puddle spread out from his side, like water from a trickling hose onto summer pavement, creating little ripples.

"Fuck! Out of the way, I need his last breath." Ariadne knelt beside Guilherme. She seemed to remember the gun only when the side hit the floor under her hand. She shoved it aside, and it skittered across the hardwood.

Key was closest, closer than Eric. She picked up the gun, pointed it at Ariadne. It was heavier than she'd expected, she was probably holding it wrong, and she was shaking—

"Get down, ma'am!" Robert hit Ariadne from the side, knocking them both sprawling. He twisted and fired at Key, probably more at the ceiling than anything because he was still tumbling.

Key shrieked and ran. Someone was *shooting* at her. She was going to *die*. Eric ran with her, but she couldn't see Map. *Unlocked.* They made it out the front door, and she dared a look back, scanning for Map. No sign, so he must have made it into the opposite wing of the cabin, out that side door. Well, screw him. He could stay with the woman who gave him *choices* and see if she gave him a choice not to get shot.

Key pressed the gun onto the ground, then curled her fingers up and away, rather than dropping it. She didn't want it to go off. Robert didn't fire again from inside either, but Key could hear overlapping voices. The most strident was Ariadne berating Robert, her voice at the level of a shriek. "Let me up! If he dies without me there, I'll kill you—"

"Ma'am, you're still in danger—"

"Hound, I'm going to press on the wound, like this. You're losing a lot of blood—"

Key straightened and let her next steps take her into a run, grabbing Eric's hand on the way. Map could take care of himself. They were almost to the car when Eric gasped and stumbled heavily into her side. Her heart couldn't speed up any more, but dawning horror made her feel woozy as Key realized he must have been hit by one of the shots. Or a ricochet.

Key pulled Eric's arm awkwardly over her shoulder, got them moving again. Any minute, Robert might be coming after them, but Eric remained a heavy dragging weight on her. Shock. Eric must be in shock. Key tried to remember what she knew about shock, but nothing came. She'd just have to go with "treat by getting the hell away from the people with the guns."

She bumped them into the car, and he stayed leaning there. She'd . . . she'd have to drive. She knew how. Mostly. She glanced behind them, but no one was following yet. Maybe Ariadne was still busy trying to get Hound's last breath—was Hound really *dead?*—but Key needed to focus on Eric, who wasn't dead yet. She needed to find where he'd been hit and get pressure on it.

"Where are you hurt?" No answer. He just lay there against the car. "Eric?"

She checked his back, his legs, his sides—no tears in his clothes, no blood. She tugged on his arm and got him to flop with his back on the car instead. Nothing. Scheisse, where the hell was he hit? It must be somewhere bad, if he wasn't responding.

She checked his face again, up into his hairline, which was when she saw his eyes. Black. All pupil, no color left.

She put her hands to his cheeks, thumbs at the corners of his eyes, and angled his head so she could be sure it wasn't a trick of the light. Maybe shock did that to normal people, but this time was different, she knew. Somehow, she *knew.*

"Eric? Oh, Eric." She hadn't realized how near tears she was until she heard her own voice. Deep breath. "Hound, you need to get in the passenger seat."

Eric focused on her with black eyes, imprecisely, then pushed away from the car and walked around to the correct side, let himself in, and buckled his seat belt.

Key pressed the side of her fist under her nose, to keep the tears where they were, contained. She had too much to do. She knew a power wasn't supposed to pass simply to the nearest human, but it had to pass some way, and it appeared this time it had.

Time to drive them out of here, and deal with it.

13

Map, heading southeast, crossed.

Key, heading southeast, crossed.

Old; Ariadne, heading northeast.

"And a bike? Can you ride?" the new man asked. His trail spoke of concern, restlessness, but he had no jobs to give. The question was unimportant, so Hound didn't make himself answer.

Bird, starling. Hopping, then flying. Heading north.

Key was . . . saying something? Eric should—

Key, trail close enough to target. Very upset. Upset, upset.

Hound stood so he could touch the uncrossed, targetable trails of both Key and Map at the same time. Key was upset; Map was resigned. "He's always going to be like that. It's how he was reborn." What they were saying about him was unimportant, so

Hound didn't comment. The trails here were simple.

Map, climbing out of the car. Touched the door, touched the handle. Older: Map climbing in, touched the handle, touched the door, touched the dash.

Eric tried to—

"Perhaps they'd teach us how to build one of those, once we are no longer strangers." Map shaded his eyes against the sunlight to track where the sled—though Hound didn't know that word then—slid so smoothly along the snow. Hound smiled, and squinted instead at the tracks it left. Not only was this new land beautiful, it had interesting trails indeed.

Car trail, old. Ariadne. Their own back trail. Bird, heading s—squirrel head—Key, recros—

The car he was riding in wove alarmingly, and Eric instinctively pressed a foot to a brake that wasn't there. A breath, another, and his thoughts actually went where he told them to. What did he last remember? Ariadne had accidentally shot Hound. Key had used the gun to get them outside—

Breath let herself and two guards in through the back door while Hound ate. When he looked up, she pressed a finger to her lips and gestured for him to precede her. This was obviously a job, so Hound placed his cutlery down neatly and stood. All three of the most recent trails went where Breath was directing him.

The sound of Eric's own moan brought him back this time. Muscle memory, unaffected by the wild swings of his thoughts, told that the car was drifting in its lane. Key. Key was driving. "Watch the road!"

Key did the opposite, of course. She sobbed a breath and turned her head to him. "Eric?" He lunged to correct the wheel so they didn't slam into the trees at the end of a tight curve.

"You'll kill us if you don't pay attention. I thought you could drive." Eric stared at the road until at least their current situation straightened itself out in his mind. They were driving away from Ariadne. They needed a destination, and really needed for him to be the one driving to it. But was he any safer than Key? "My mind keeps—drifting. Was I drugged?" When could Ariadne possibly have drugged him? Something in the air?

Key gave a harsh bark of laughter and stared hard at the road. She was seated bolt upright, back inches from the more comfortably inclined seat, and her hands were strangling either side of the wheel. "The Hound is dead. Long live the Hound."

"This is not the time for fucking literary references." Eric instantly regretted his hissed tone, but he could barely hang on—

Key let her scraper still, stretched hide barely touched. "Just because you find a trail, Hound, doesn't mean you should follow it. Sure, we ate well tonight, but you could have been killed." Hound turned away from their camp, anger simmering. Easy for her to say on a full belly from the kill Hound had made.

"Eric?" Key sounded like she'd been saying the name enough times for it to start to lose its meaning.

All right. Basics, not daydreams or hallucinations. Who, what, where, why? He was Eric Davis. He was in a car with a woman with supernatural powers. They were trying to escape his boss's—former boss, he presumed at this point—cabin, before she killed them. "Where are we going, Key?"

Key sniffed like she was near tears. "I don't know. We have to stop somewhere, so you can adjust. And I have no idea how long that takes, because I was too young to remember. Map might know, but he's probably on Her side, and now he's gone anyway." She looked at him, then swiftly back to the road before he could protest. "You're Hound now. It's not supposed to pass to the closest person; it's supposed to be a relative or something. I swear that's what Map said, but he never wanted to talk about it except when he slipped a couple times, and I never had enough time with Lantern to find out anything much . . . "

Eric ignored most of that. He was having enough trouble tracking right now, and she was talking too fast, like people did when they were upset. The first part was hard enough to think about. "I—"

"I know this is a lot to understand." A young man, a stranger, though he spoke the trade tongue, rubbed Hound's back as he retched beside the small trickle of a stream he'd been trying to drink from. He'd wandered so far, in the grip of the visions, he didn't remember when last he'd eaten. "I'm Map. I know you're remembering being someone else right now." The stranger leaned closer to check Hound's face, and the thick rope of his black braid slid forward over his shoulder. "It will get better, I promise. The trails will become just another sense, and the memories, they won't bother you unless something specifically reminds you of a moment in a past life."

Hound lifted his head to look the stranger in the face properly. Map. He . . . remembered that. That kink to his nose. The handsome, weathered darkness to his skin. "The visions . . . "

"The visions fade." Map straightened and drew him up-right by both hands. "We've walked this trail before together. You might remember that."

Eric gritted his teeth as they fishtailed through an intersection on a yellow light. "Key. Stop and let me drive."

"Not when you keep zoning out," Key said, but their speed did diminish slightly. Eric eyed the parade of car dealerships along this stretch of the highway, but nothing seemed familiar.

"Cars go past too many trails too fast," Eric quoted, with a brief mic-echo feeling of having both said it and heard it. "It smooths everything together. I'll be fine." Some part of him could hardly believe he was accepting this, but what else could he do? He *remembered* that it was true.

Key bit her lip, but at the next intersection, she turned off. "Swerved" might have been a better verb. They finally halted in a parking lot in front of a small storefront whose sign was too faded to read, its threatening towing notices being eaten by blackberries crawling over the fence from the next property. Key was too white knuckled to remember to put the car into park and turn off the engine for a full thirty seconds.

Eric started to shake as he unbuckled his seat belt. There were more trails here than there had been at the cabin, at least of humans. He made it out into the air, but stood within the car door and kept hold of the top in case he started to fall. He didn't feel dizzy, but he didn't feel stable, either.

The trails weren't visible, and he couldn't touch them, but he didn't have the—have the *words*, for what they were. Layer upon layer, all saying things without being audible. Like a computer visualization, false color for something the human brain wasn't naturally designed to process.

It helped to think of them as glowing blue, Eric found. Like unseen traces revealed on a forensic show. They felt like water, with slightly more resistance than air. He reached to one, which was laid along the ground, and also floating at waist level above it, both and neither.

"Fuck," Eric hissed.

"Call it whatever you like. See it however you like. It is what it is. If you understand only part of what it is, so be it. Diminish it until you can hold it in your mind all at once. Then begin to study the parts that don't fit, until you expand it again."

Eric jerked himself out of the memory before he registered more than the fact that it was a woman speaking. Key was beside him, without his having noticed her move. "I told you," she said, concern straining her tone to something almost inaudible.

"It will be better when we're moving." Hurting so much, and none of it physical, Eric only wanted to be alone, where no one could see, but he forced himself to say the next words anyway. "Help me walk over there?" Key pulled his arm across her shoulders instantly. He didn't need her to carry his weight, but having her there, a warm presence moving in the direction he needed to go, was more helpful than he'd predicted.

Everywhere blue. And none of it helpfully time stamped. No wonder Hound had said "recent" was the best he could do. And what was he supposed to call the teen? Eric was Hound now, apparently. As well. Instead.

"My name's still Eric." He didn't know why it was suddenly so crucial, but Key nodded as she stopped beside the open driver's door.

"If I remembered my name, I'd still be using it." Her tone was sad, and Eric should—should say *something* about that, but he couldn't at the moment.

All right. Driving. Eric knew how to do that. The motions were all physical, a little below the level of thought, and he got the car started and turned around. Where were they going? The cash he'd withdrawn was in his bag, back at the cabin. He couldn't go home.

Eric jackrabbited forward out of the parking lot. Some example of good driving he was. He would have to drive a ways until he recognized where they were anyway.

Blue blended together until it only distorted his view ahead slightly, like heat shimmer. But they'd run out of gas long before he was back to normal, if that was even an option, ever again. They had to go somewhere.

"My sister." They shouldn't, he knew. But he couldn't think, and at least he knew she would always help as much as she could. And Ariadne would have to delay to find Diane's address, if she thought of it, which should give them time to leave again.

And he couldn't think of anywhere else. Literally.

14

In my youth, the elders told such tales.

Like how the five searchers sailed their junk into port, and walked among the rice fields. They called out to the workers: had a young woman passed, traveling alone, dressed perhaps as a scholar? And the workers nodded, and pointed where she had gone.

Eric was right, he could drive, but he didn't talk much. Or at all, really. Key stopped watching him directly after a while because she got the sense it was annoying him, but she couldn't help stealing glances in her peripheral vision.

He had all his memories. Or he would. Key knew she shouldn't be glad, knew she should empathize with what Eric was going through, but he'd have all his *memories.* All that information about all of them, without Ariadne controlling it. And maybe after Key talked to him, some of her own memories would trigger.

But not if Ariadne caught up to them. She'd kill Eric so she could breathe Hound into a child, as Map had said.

Eventually, they turned off big, fast roads, streaming with cars, onto more familiar, small streets between houses. The houses were familiar but different, so many different shapes and colors that flowed between neighborhoods. One street was all tall, thin houses, like in books, in dark brown and red, and the next was flatter ones, all with the same siding in pastel colors.

Key assumed they couldn't stay long with this sister of his, but she didn't have any better idea herself. No connections of her own, outside of the other powers. And since Ariadne hadn't been able to catch them at the car, Key figured She wouldn't have been able to get to Her own vehicle in time to trail them anywhere. She'd have to search, probably at Eric's place first.

Eric pulled into the driveway, turned off the car, then stared at a point at the top of the steering wheel. Key shoved his shoulder. "She's *your* sister. You need to talk to her." Sudden panic made her shrill. She had no idea how to talk to new people outside of the safe confines of the cottages.

He moved with the shove, unresisting, and frowned slightly at the garage door in front of them instead. Key clenched her hands in fists on her knees, then got out, *unlocked,* and came around to open his door. No choice but to do her best.

"Hound, come inside with me," she said, and pulled his arm across her shoulders again. *Locked.* He was walking fine at the moment, completely zoned out, but she hoped he'd come back to himself somewhere along the—she glanced over to measure the distance—whole ten feet to the front door. He'd better work fast.

The front yard of the sister's house had more grass and trees and fewer bushes than Key's did. She thought it looked nicer to play in, more free form and shaded for the kids—if the sister had kids. She hoped the sister didn't have kids. The only child she remembered meeting was the former Hound, and he didn't count.

Locked. Key knocked politely, *unlocked,* and let herself in. Eric came passively, and stared blankly in the general direction of the floor.

"Don? Did you forget something?" The woman who arrived from deeper in the house didn't really look much like Eric on the surface. Her hair was closer to golden than brown, maybe with a little help; Key couldn't tell from a distance. Of the two, she was probably the more attractive, which was saying something, since Eric was no slouch. The sister's face was rounder, but when Key looked close enough, she finally found what tied them together, with a snap of belonging: both carried their height in long legs.

"Eric? I never gave you a key, did I?" The sister's frown deepened, fast, started to seem angry. "What happened? Are you all right? Who's she?" She crossed to them in two steps and started looking Eric over, probably for injuries, much as Key had earlier.

"I'm his friend." Key suddenly thought she should make up a normal name for herself, but at that moment, every female name she'd ever heard deserted her. Maybe the sister wouldn't notice for now. "He's kind of . . . sick, I guess. He just needs to rest somewhere safe for a while."

The sister glared at her with frank suspicion, and Key realized after a beat that it was partly focused on her bright red hair. "You two come from a rave or something? I can't imagine Eric ever attending one, but—" She lifted his chin to look at his eyes, and her own widened in reaction. "You slip him some drugs? Is that what happened? Eric would *never* take anything by choice."

"No, I didn't do anything!" Key tried to hang on to Eric's arm, but the sister came up on Eric's other side and pulled him away. Scheisse, she needed Eric to explain himself. "Look, I'm a power, and now he is too, because the last one got killed, and it passed. I know it sounds weird—"

"I know it sounds like gibberish. Get out and sober up." The sister pivoted under Eric's arm and tried to yank the door open. *Locked.* She frowned, pulled away from Eric enough to get better angle to turn the inside mechanism. Key gritted her teeth and held it. *Locked, locked.*

"I'm Key." She flexed one hand to bleed off her frustration and let her hold go. *Unlocked.* "I'd be happy to demonstrate on anything else you have handy."

The sister lifted her hand off the door lock, then touched it again, delicately. She seemed to be stepping back from throwing Key bodily out the door, at least. "So you're one of his . . . magician friends, then?" Key didn't get it until the sister made a gesture of fanning a handful of cards, holding them out.

Apparently magician friends were more acceptable than rave friends. Key nodded because it seemed like progress in kind of vaguely the right direction. "His boss was the one that did this to him, not me."

"Well." The sister considered her again, lips thin. "There's no need for showing off to me with tricks. I grew up with Eric's shenanigans, so I've seen it all." She gathered Eric against her side, the same way Key had brought him to the door, and headed back into the house. "Come in, I guess."

Key followed, feeling kind of useless. She was another power, she should be able to help him, but he could probably remember a hundred times more than she had to tell him. At least she didn't see any evidence of kids. The house was pretty tidy, with light wood furniture, and lots of plant photography on the walls.

Eric seemed to wake a bit when his sister left him seated on a bar stool at the kitchen counter. He tracked on the sound of water as she filled a glass at the sink. "Diane?"

Key sprinted to the other side of the counter to put herself square in his view before he zoned out again. "Eric, you have to explain to her. She's not going to believe me."

Eric growled and scrubbed the heel of his hand against one eye. "I'm trying, Key. It was easier to stay in the moment in the car."

"Maybe we should take you to the hospital." Diane slid the full water glass across the counter and crossed her arms.

"That's not going to help." Key couldn't help a growl of her own when Eric decided to stare down into the glass rather than lift it. "Come on. If you want me to keep calling you Eric, act like it! You can zone out for days at a time if we can find somewhere safe." She knew chewing him out wouldn't do any good, but she supposed it made her feel better. Not much, though.

Telling Eric to act like himself and Diane's comment about magician friends met in her mind and mixed. Key picked up an advertisement card for a local restaurant from a pile of mail on the end of the counter, checked it was only addressed to "resident," and tore off about a third. She crumpled it until it was tight and fairly round, about the size of a cherry tomato. "Look. Which hand?" She showed him the ball in one, closed it, turned it over, and tapped her fists together. She opened the second. Not there. She opened the first. Not there either.

Eric reached across to readjust her wrists. "Your angle's wrong. I can see it if I look." He stole the ball and demonstrated seamlessly. In another situation, Key would have asked him to keep doing the move all night, just so she could watch.

"All right." Eric look a deep breath, and kept his hands moving as he spoke. Key offered out hers, so he could use them as props, disappearing the paper ball after he'd placed it safely in one of her palms, only to draw it out of the other. "Diane, I'm sorry. I'm putting you in some danger, being here, even considering telling you anything."

Diane's crossed arms turned into something more like hugging herself. "If my brother's getting dragged into some-thing dangerous and asks for my help, I'm giving it to him. Never doubt it."

Eric dipped his chin in acknowledgment, though he didn't look away from the paper ball. "I guess the first thing to get straight is, this isn't a trick. It's not part of an act. It's not special effects." He made a noise of frustration on the heels of her scoff. "Not what I'm doing this second with my hands; that's a trick, yes. Key, can you—?" He blew out an irritated breath. "God, I'm sorry, Diane. We left your bead box at her house."

Key made a second paper ball of her own. She'd forgotten about that too. What with Eric running out after having slept

with her. "She didn't believe me when I showed her my power."
She wondered how much of every conversation over the next
few days was going to be a retread because he was zoned out
the first time. It was frustrating enough at the moment. "You're
harder to fake, Hound." She leaned into the name, bleeding off
some of the frustration, and regretted it the very next second.

To make up for it, she pushed herself into Diane's attention
again. "Here," she said, thrusting the second paper ball at her.
"If you want to see something that you'll be able to believe isn't
a trick, go hide that somewhere. Wander aimlessly along the
way, lots of zigzags."

"I am not going to play your stupid—!" Something in Eric's
face made Diane cut off. Key looked again and tried to quantify
it for herself, because she definitely saw it too. He wasn't hag-
gard, precisely, or pale, but something had retreated from his
eyes as if hiding from a world crumbling around him.

Diane took the paper ball and strode off into the living
room, not zigzagging yet. Key wanted to follow her to remind
her, but if she did, Diane might think she was signaling Eric
as he traced her path. Instead, she stayed in the kitchen and
fidgeted, uselessly.

In Eric's hands, the first ball appeared, disappeared, appeared again. Key didn't have any words to offer, so she circled around and leaned against his back, a hug without arms.
He didn't pull away. "I just hope I can actually do what you're
pitching me for," he said.

"Just follow her trail to where she hid it. It'll be recent, and
uncrossed. Easy-peasy." Key put more confidence into her tone
than she really felt. What did she know about how long it took

to learn your power? She'd had hers literally as long as she could remember. "You might be able to feel her a little, too. Since it's uncrossed." Key pressed her lips together. Scheisse. Maybe she shouldn't have brought that up, since— "Just don't concentrate too hard on that feel, or you might end up targeting her."

"Targeting?" Diane strode back into the kitchen, coiled her hair into a loose tail to make it stay behind her shoulders, and leaned on the counter. "I'm ready to see this nontrick, then."

Eric turned into Key, grabbed her wrists too tight. "I could—target—?" His pupils were normal for the moment, but his eyes were wide.

Key didn't know where Diane's exact trail was, but she dragged her foot in a long arc between Eric and his sister, and he relaxed slightly. Diane snorted. "So targeting is bad, then?"

"You have no idea." Eric stood. He had to let go of one of Key's wrists to walk, but he kept the other one. Key writhed her wrist until they were at least holding hands instead. She could see Diane noticing. Pointedly noticing, even. Or maybe Key was just paranoid. Eric didn't seem to want to let go in any case.

As Key had expected, Diane's trail as paced by Eric didn't waver much at first, but then it made a couple of arcs back, as she probably peered around corners to make sure she wasn't being followed. Eric touched the banister only twice as he went up the stairs, idle touches. Key checked covertly. That seemed to finally make an impression on Diane.

They entered some kind of home office, with two computer stations, and Eric glowered at the bookshelf for a beat or two before he touched a couple of books at his sister's eye level, then pulled one out on the shelf above to grab the paper ball from behind. He drew in a shuddering breath, pupils wavering, but braced his feet and seemed to stay with them.

Diane rubbed the side of her upper arm. "That was . . . reasonably creepy." When Eric offered her the ball, she winced back like it was infectious. "So you're suggesting you've spontaneously developed . . . what? ESP?"

"That's slightly closer—and less confusing—than calling it magic, in the absence of elf ears," Eric joked raggedly.

Key peered at Diane. She wasn't actually sure the sister believed them. But at least she was pretending she did, so the conversation could advance. "The powers are from a fable from long, long ago, and we've been reborn ever since." She glanced at Eric, and when he didn't object, she launched into the story and any other details about the powers she could think of. Diane listened with the same dubious patience she'd started showing after Eric found what she'd hidden.

"And why you?" Diane gestured down the whole of Eric. "I thought reincarnation happened at birth. You were just at the wrong place at the right time?"

Eric frowned into intermediate distance. Not like he was zoned out, but like someone accessing a buried piece of information—or a memory. Key was suddenly so envious, she wanted to hit him. Just that easy, huh? Scheisse. "You remember Kayla?"

Diane gave an incredulous laugh. "How could I forget?" She waited for a beat, clearly expecting something else to be said, and frowned at her brother when he missed his cue.

When she turned to Key, Key realized Eric had been supposed to enlighten his own friend, not leave it to Diane. "She was our crackhead cousin."

"Who got pregnant." Eric ignored his sister, still lost in his memories or thoughts.

Diane glared at Key. Maybe she wasn't supposed to hear personal details. But after a glance at their linked hands, Diane gave in and added a few more. "When she was—what, sixteen? She did get pregnant, and Eric moved off campus to let her live with him while he was at college. I was no older than her, but he and I basically covered her entire rent so his roommates wouldn't kick her out. And forced her to stay sober until she'd given birth and adopted the baby out. Then she ran off again because we were 'so mean.'"

Key had to admit, she had no idea what the point of this was either. She'd have thought Eric would be spouting random facts from Hound's ancient history, not his own.

"Ariadne helped me with the adoption." Eric's hand tightened, just having to say her name. "That was when we were first dating. There were so many forms, and Kayla certainly wasn't doing them. So she helped me fill them in—dropped them off, even. And there was a couple there, at the birth, to accept the baby, but . . . "

"Fourteen years ago?" Key's mouth blurted that out while the rest of her mind was still grappling with what she now understood. "Relatives. Scheisse."

"If you're going to come here and ask me for help, you can't just talk to each other!" Diane rocked forward to push into both their personal spaces. "Explain. I suppose it was fourteen years ago, so Kayla's baby would be a teen. Did you meet him or something?"

"Powers pass to relatives naturally. But Ariadne put Hound into Eric's—second cousin? And then it passed to him when she killed him." Key could see in Diane's face that what she said hadn't really helped, but she didn't know how to speak to someone normal about the powers. She'd never had to do it before. The tutors who didn't know what she was, she'd never discussed anything important with.

"Cousin once removed." Eric managed a shaky laugh when they both looked at him. "A lot of years spent with the geneal-ogy researchers."

Diane held up one finger for them to wait, and focus. "So your boss. Secretly adopted Kayla's baby herself. And killed him?" Her voice got shrill by the end. "Fuck. Can you call the police? Your boss can't go around *murdering* people."

Eric laughed, this time like a wrenching sob. "You have no idea. You have no fucking idea."

"Wait." Key held up a finger of her own. If they started listing Ariadne's crimes, they'd be here all night, and she'd be showing up personally. "Why would she kill Hound with you standing right there, if she knew he was your cousin? She didn't look like she expected you to get the powers."

"I never told her Kayla was related to me, just that she was a friend of my sister's." Eric drew in a deep breath, paused, but the change of topic meant he didn't fall prey to another harsh laugh. "Kayla wanted an adoption that was closed tight, and it

seemed like the fewer people who knew any connection between us, the better."

"Thank God she won't ever know what happened to him."
Diane scrubbed at her eyes, whether because she was exhausted
taking it all in, or holding back tears, Key couldn't tell. "Okay.
So it's sounding like your boss is secretly some kind of badass
bitch with other crimes under her belt?"

"You don't believe us; I don't think the police will." Key
glowered at the carpet. Thinking of Hound as someone with
a mother, cousins—she'd been keeping grief at bay by thinking about how the old Hound at least hadn't really cared either
way, but now she could feel emotions starting to strangle her
so she couldn't breathe.

"She'll have called someone in to clean up by now." Eric's
harsh laughter returned. "Ariadne has people for everything."

"So what now?" Diane turned away from them to straight-
en books on the shelf, even ones not disarranged by their earlier hunt. "You can't sic the police on her, and she's angry with
you . . . for getting this power when she didn't expect you to?"
She waited while Eric murmured agreement.

"We need somewhere to go, and I don't—have anywhere,
and he at least had here, even though we need to leave soon,
because She'll think to look here eventually. We have a lead to
find Lantern, and then Lantern can help us figure out how to
stay out of Her control. But until Eric's more settled, we need
somewhere safe to stay." And Key needed to not sound so pathetically desperate. Maybe her emotions were nothing to Eric's
right now, but she still needed time alone. As soon as possible.

"Sweetie." Diane's whole posture softened, and she turned
around to pull them both into a single hug. Eric was stiff for
a moment, possibly too distracted to realize he was being

hugged, before embracing Diane with a familiarity Key could only envy. She definitely felt like the odd one out here.

"Key can just walk into absolutely anywhere she wants, barring alarms. But most places are going to have alarms or, you know, owners." Eric pressed the side of his cheek to Diane's hair. Key tried to disengage to leave them to it, but he wouldn't let go of her. She wouldn't argue, she decided.

"So that's how you got in here." The annoyance in Diane's voice was fleeting, or at least she hid it better after a moment. "Look for For Sale signs. Especially ones that say foreclosure. Then the old owners will definitely be gone. If you make sure you're not followed and then find a place just by getting lost and driving down random streets, she can't really track you, can she?"

"I should have thought of that myself." Eric let a breath of relief trickle out, and with that, they lost him again.

This time, Key did pull out of the hug. "He'll be better again once he's driving." Was that to convince Diane, or herself?

Diane tugged at her brother's arm, waved her hand in front of his face, measuring his reaction. He tracked her movement, but his eyes were completely zoned out. "You can't possibly let him drive like this. Don't you have your license?"

"Well, no. I know how to drive, but doing it on real roads is harder than I expected." Further defensiveness bubbled up in Key's mind, but she didn't let it out. The sister was probably suspicious enough as it was. She didn't need to make it worse by exposing how ignorant of daily life and— Well, fine, she'd admit it to herself, scared she was.

Diane examined her with an unreadable expression, then started towing her brother for the door out of the office. "So you're one of these powers too? That's how you guys met?"

"Yeah." Key felt uncomfortable, like Diane had asked that for a reason, and she wasn't sure what it was. Was this a question about their relationship? Should she admit they'd slept together or not? "I guess he wanted to figure out what was going on, and he found us."

"You seem pretty good at not—" Diane gestured to her brother. "Doing that, like he is." Diane considered the stairs with some trepidation, so Key stepped in.

"Hound, would you go and sit at the kitchen counter again? We'll join you."

Eric stepped around his sister and jogged down the stairs. Diane stared after him, lips slightly parted for a beat before she summoned words. "That's open to abuse."

"I assume that was Ariadne's goal, when she made the last Hound. He was just that, all the time." Key gestured where Eric had disappeared from view; then her words choked off as she understood the real point of Diane's comment. "He knows how to put me in the same state! I didn't mean to—I know what it's like, I'd never—he knows—" But did he? Key resolved not to give him a single order more until she'd at least talked to him about it when he was himself.

"No." Diane put a firm hand on Key's shoulder. "No, I don't think you're an abuser when it's clear to me you're as terrified as he probably should be." Her lips started to form words she seemed to discard; then she decided on different ones. "I want to understand, and I want to help."

She had to decide, Key realized. Pretend to be normal, and keep trying to persuade Diane to let them leave, or actually admit to what was scaring her so badly. "I can act . . . almost

normal, yeah. But I haven't actually been outside the neighborhood where Ariadne raised us my whole life, until today, and
now Hound's dead, and I don't actually remember anything
from when I was a child and got my power, so I can't help him
with that either."

"Oh." The distracted air with which Diane spoke suggested
she was still coming to terms with what Key had revealed. "I
would have said you're not going too badly, on the power part.
You got him here, got him talking."

Key took a deep breath. Right. A good reminder not to
wallow. Maybe it was a sibling thing, like Map might have—
but she wasn't thinking about Map right now, or she'd really be
wallowing. "And we know where we're going, now." Next step
in not wallowing was to continue admitting what she needed help with. "I don't know what we'll need. Food, obviously,
but . . . " And she'd never bought anything for herself in a real
store, either. She'd only watched Eric do it for the first time today, and now she couldn't count on him. What if she did something wrong, and everyone noticed?

"We have an air mattress we can lend you, but you'll probably want to get sleeping bags if you're crashing in a foreclosed
house." Diane squeezed Key's shoulder briefly. "My husband's
not going to be home for another couple hours. Why don't I
follow you guys to the store? Once you're supplied, I'll come
home and you guys can take off. I won't have any idea where
you end up."

Key considered the idea, trying not to rely on TV too
much, but even using that standard, she couldn't see any way
Ariadne could find them using Diane as long as she wasn't

lurking when they left for the store. They'd have to check for that, but otherwise . . . "Thank you."

"It's the least I can do when you guys are dealing with ESP and murders." Diane winced, and led the way down the stairs. Key wondered if maybe she was more than a little scared herself and hiding it better. It made her feel better not to be alone in the emotion.

Though, of course, that didn't make any of them any safer.

15

In my youth, the elders told such tales.

Like how Map consulted the drawing upon the palm leaf and pointed to the ground. "The map leads here and no further, but the youngest of the gods is not here. Look, elephants have trampled away her footprints."

Eric dragged himself out of the world of blue that was a house that had been shown regularly—how many people could possibly tramp through one property before someone bought it?—after an unknown interval to find Key trying to use the foot pump on the air mattress. She seemed to be making no progress, and when he joined her, he found she hadn't pushed the tube in far enough to open the value, and she'd literally been accomplishing nothing for the past however long.

He took over pumping—he wasn't sure, but he thought she'd brought in most of their supplies, so he deserved to work a little—and looked around the room to try to see it without blue. The house appeared to have been built in the '20s or '30s, peeling paint on rotting siding suggesting why it hadn't sold. But it had the big yard of as-yet-undivided lots of that time period, and plenty of overgrown bushes to diffuse any light from the windows. Inside, the carpet was worn, but the walls were cleanly painted. Key had set out the mattress and supplies in the den rather than a bedroom. The window there was more than shadowed, it was *devoured* by a bush, and they had access to both the kitchen with remaining avocado-colored appliances and a bathroom without windows. At least they could turn the lights on in there.

Apparently Hound hadn't been in this kind of house before, because no memories tried to suck Eric under. He capped the valve and flopped back on the mattress to test. Then something did try to suck him under, but it wasn't memories; it was simple exhaustion. He recognized the particular muscles-fine/brain-toast combination from final exams, back in the day.

Key sat on the edge of the mattress much more delicately, feet tucked to the side on the floor. "This looks big enough for two people."

Eric rolled his head a few degrees to face her, and she climbed onto the mattress to lean on her hands, on either side of his waist. He got a great view up her cleavage and wasn't in any doubt what she was offering. "I mean, if you want . . . " After her initial burst of confidence, hesitation bled in.

"You'd be helping me by providing a distraction." He kept his voice low and warm, and she rewarded him with a great smile. Remembering that she hadn't liked anything too hard on her nipple before, Eric cupped her breast with his hand under her shirt, but over her bra. His mind might be tired, but he could let his body take point on this one.

She leaned into his touch, then sat up to free her hands and fuss with her hair so it didn't get in the way when she leaned down and kissed him. Eric concentrated on the sensation. Just him and—

Hound trailed fingers down her lover's chest. She knew the deep, rich, red-earth hue that enclosed his every muscle intimately, and still she found herself coming back to his chest, his arms, wanting to trace each. Map grinned, with just a splash of arrogance like the spice of garam masala. He knew she loved him all too well, but so, too, did he love her.

He leaned down to nip at the side of her neck, breathing in her scent from the black fan of her hair on the pillows. She parted her legs, climb having reached a height where she wanted him, wanted him now. He entered her in one smooth stroke, so much familiar between them, but still heady, euphoric in these bodies. Hound hooked her leg over his hip, arching up to meet him, urging him deeper—

Eric shoved. Off! Off of him. He wasn't—wasn't—

A thump and Key's gasp of rage grounded him. He'd pushed her not only away from him but right off the bed, so she landed on her ass. An air mattress was only about six inches high, but he could see in her black expression the shock had been the worst part.

"What was that for?" Key shoved at his shoulder, then again when he didn't react enough to satisfy her anger. Her blows were at the wrong angle, but he could still feel the flailing strength behind them. "I *asked.* If you'd said no, I wouldn't have touched—"

Eric considered trying to catch her wrists, but judged it better to instead bring up his arms to block the blows before any threatened his face. "Key, I'm sorry. No one ever said—Hound was a *woman.*" He probably shouldn't have said it like than in front of another woman, but the feeling of wrongness was too raw.

"Why wouldn't he—she be? Sometimes." Some of Key's anger drained away, though. She stopped hitting him. "So you remembered—"

Eric ran his hands down his body—clothed this time, that was another grounding detail—and reminded himself of every familiar line and muscle beneath fabric, the same ones he'd known for thirty-two years. Definitely not going to tell her about Map. "Fucking as a woman." Maybe he'd unconsciously hoped the crudeness would help distance him, but it didn't.

"But you're a man." Key smiled with encouraging humor. "I can assure you of that." She knelt up and reached for the button on his jeans.

Even the implication of a blowjob wasn't enough to stir anything. Eric knew himself well enough to be able to tell that his hard-on was well and truly gone, probably for the whole night. "I can't, not tonight. I want to, but—" He didn't even want to name what filled his thoughts, and bring the memories even closer.

The next step presented itself to him on autopilot, and he tried to sound properly enthusiastic when all he wanted to do was curl up and sleep and not think a goddamn other thought that came from fucking powers. "We don't have to stop, though. Let me do something for you."

"Let's cuddle." Key got to her feet and circled around the mattress, stripping efficiently rather than sensually. When she was down to panties, she pulled her shirt back on without her bra, and dragged one of the two sleeping bags over to join him on the mattress.

Normally, Eric would have wondered whether he was supposed to argue her out of the consolation prize, but Key sounded like she actually wanted that as an end in and of itself.

But then, when would she have ever had much of a chance to cuddle properly, with Ariadne and her murderous tendencies breathing down her neck? Eric shoved reluctantly to his feet to lose enough clothing to sleep himself, then pulled her to him. He didn't sleep well with someone else in the bed, or at all with someone else all over him, but she wanted to be held, and at least he could do that. To be honest with himself, he probably didn't have much chance of sleep anyway.

Key dropped off fairly quickly and rolled away to burrito herself in the sleeping bag in unconscious stages. Eric stared at a poorly mended nail hole on the wall and dared the memories to appear. He was Eric. He was good at sleight of hand, and had had egregiously terrible taste in girlfriends in college. Maybe he was Eric who could now see trails, but that didn't mean he was any less Eric.

"I consider myself the same person," Breath said. *Lantern frowned, clearly disagreeing but always slow to put her thoughts into words. "Yes, I remember having a different name—"*

"Eric." He breathed it low enough that Key didn't stir. "Eric." He ran the words into each other in a chant that eventually became indistinguishable from an exhaled breath. He didn't need new memories. He'd simply refuse to let them through, hold up a wall against them.

His thoughts finally began to drift, near sleep, but he held on to that wall.

Eric.

16

In my youth, the elders told such tales.

Like how the second searcher said, "Though the snow is fresh, I can see her trail." And Hound ran with the dogs of their sled team, showing them where to go, out across the sea ice.

Key wasn't sure if Eric was that exhausted, or if he hadn't gotten off to sleep for a long time, but he remained a sprawled lump the entire morning, while she woke, got up, apologetically spread the sleeping bag back over him, and rummaged in their supplies for something to eat. A couple of granola bars later, she decided she was thoroughly bored and it was sunny enough outside for her to risk moving around the house and using other lights. She'd bought a romance novel at the store, less out of preference for the genre and more because all of were romances, but she didn't want to use it up the first day if Eric was going to spend all his time sleeping or being a jackass who tossed her out of bed.

She'd also bought black hair dye, because fashion was stupid when you stood out in a crowd of people. With a last glance at lump-Eric, Key collected the dye and a towel and headed for the stairs since the downstairs bathroom had no shower.

She couldn't believe how everything in the entire house creaked. Maybe she was just oversensitive, thinking of waking someone, but the floor creaked and the stairs creaked and she could have sworn the banister creaked when she touched it. Old houses were weird. When she found the bathroom, *unlocked,* the knob was elegantly molded metal, but it wobbled where it connected to the wood. It took her a couple of seconds to figure out how to turn it without just wiggling it up and down.

Waiting for the dye to finish was pretty boring too, so Key wrapped up in the towel and creaked around the upper floor, looking for other locks. She didn't find any except on other doors, but she did find a dresser built half into the wall, so the drawers extended twice as far back as it looked like they should, under the eaves.

When she had rinsed out all the dye, she wandered to stand in front of the mirror to towel her hair dry. The steam retreated from the bottom of the mirror first, leaving an upper oval frame like on an old sepia photograph. On an impulse, Key wrapped the towel to cover her hair, like a headscarf.

Of course, it wasn't quite right, because she didn't know how to arrange it. For a moment, though, in a steamy mirror, she looked like maybe she belonged. Somewhere likely to be on the evening news, as Map had said.

She wondered if Ariadne had gone to the Middle East and rescued—or stole—a child who would grow up learning the name of her birth country when it was invaded, and not even realizing.

Key yanked off the towel. Stupid. Ariadne could have falsely adopted a child of U.S. citizens in Cleveland, for all she knew.

When she arrived downstairs, dressed, Eric was at least sitting on the edge of the mattress, eyes open. When she diverged from her original path to check his pupils, he growled something and flailed a gesture for her to go away. Seemed like a good sign.

"I didn't use up all the hot water." When Eric only grunted in response, Key got an apple and went to explore the ground floor. If he stayed lucid after breakfast, maybe she could ask him about what he was remembering. Even imagining all the different things he might know made her stomach flutter.

She made herself stay quiet, though, while he ate breakfast after showering, chugging diet cola instead of coffee while he stood at the kitchen counter. When his bagel was nothing but crumbs, she sidled up to the counter and picked at a chipped corner of the faux-stone laminate surface. "Maybe we don't even need to find Lantern now."

Eric scrubbed at his jaw like he'd noticed he'd missed a spot shaving, though he looked fine to her. He seemed possibly suspicious. "Why's that?"

Key would have thought he'd be relieved, not suspicious, though maybe from the outside this seemed like a fast turn-around from her earlier insistence. "We just have to wait for you to remember everything." When he started to protest, she cut him off. "Which might be a while, I know. I can be patient."

Eric leaned his weight on stiff arms on the edge of the counter. "What did you ever expect to get out of Lantern? I've never really had the time to ask. It's all very well saying 'information' or 'what she knows,' but to what purpose?"

"My memories." Key couldn't keep the frustration out of her tone. "You should know. Everything you're getting, about your power, your past lives—I want that. I've never had it. I know who I am now, but I have no idea where I am from, who my ancestors were, any of that."

"And then what?" Eric closed his eyes briefly, expression pained. "You go home to Ariadne and cuddle your memories happily for the rest of your life?"

Key glanced around at the unfamiliar dimensions of the empty room. Being in a house again made it a little easier to think, made her realize how naive she'd been to think she could adapt immediately to life outside Ariadne's little neighborhood. But even if it scared the crap out of her, she didn't want to go back. "No. You were right, back there. I need my own life."

Eric fanned his fingers out, closed them around the counter again. "And Ariadne's not going to let us do that, unless we stop her. And to do that, we probably need to figure out what she's up to with a pharmaceutical company, and why she started killing people four years ago. And what the hell gods have to do with anything, other than general religious delusions added to her controlling and murderous tendencies."

Key shook her head. That stuff at the cabin hadn't made any immediate sense to her either. "She said something like that to me yesterday. It was the first I'd heard of it. But I assume she's referring to the story. The gods made the powers to find the youngest of the gods."

"Five powers. The Hand of the Gods." It was Eric's turn to shake his head. "Isn't the story just metaphor?"

There were no locks nearby, but Key made a key-turning motion to illustrate. "The powers are real. Why wouldn't the rest be?"

Eric glowered at the counter for a while, thinking. Maybe checking his memories? She could only hope. "So some group of unknown people, somewhere, want to control us at some point, maybe, and Ariadne, very close, wants to control us now, definitely. I think we have to prioritize our threats. Even if the gods are real, that doesn't mean she's not taking their names in vain for reasons of her own."

"We can find answers to all of that in your memories." Key smiled, pleased he'd led so neatly to her next point, but his expression suggested the same thing had occurred to him, and he was just waiting for her to get it over with. She stopped smiling. All right, fine. "Who the gods are. What to do about Ariadne. She might have a weakness, or if we get good enough with our own powers, it's mutually assured destruction, right?"

Eric sighed and straightened. "All very good points, if the memories worked like that." He shook his head. "They just kind of . . . pop up. Linked to something else I'm thinking about, like forgetting an item on your to-do list until you see the object you were holding when you first made the mental note."

Key already knew that was how memories worked, thank you. "That's why you think about defeating Ariadne. Why you think about the gods."

"And the memories aren't coming at all now." Eric started tidying away the breakfast food like that was the end of the conversation.

Key stared at him. "What's that supposed to mean? This is important. Try harder!"

Eric whirled on her. "I am not your—" He jabbed a finger at her, and his tone, controlled until then, rose. "Fucking encyclopedia! I am so glad you've got a use for this power that has been inflicted on me, but I'm not here to sacrifice my self-identity to provide it."

Key gritted her teeth. Okay, that had been the wrong thing to say, but there was no need to yell. Or use that kind of language. "I didn't mean . . . none of this has to happen right away, anyway. It would make you safer too, wouldn't it? I'm not just trying to do it for myself."

"Aren't you? I think we both know someone else who likes to use whatever tools she has to hand. Maybe you learned from the best."

Key couldn't—she just—she was so incandescently angry that she was shaking and she wanted to hit Eric, *hit* him until he took it back. She was nothing like Ariadne, nothing at all. She wanted to scream at him. What, she didn't even know, so she made herself turn around. Turn around, walk out of the kitchen and up the stairs. Stop in one of the bedrooms and breathe, shaking. Screw—fuck. Fuck him. He wasn't the only one who could swear.

She sat down and set her cheek against the open bedroom door. It swung inward until it reached the wall, and she scooted with it so she could lean. *Unlocked. Locked. Unlockedlockedunlockedlocked . . .*

She let herself stay halfway zoned out for who knows how long. Eventually, though, she sighed and got up. She shouldn't have pushed Eric. He was right; he wasn't there to be useful. Realistically, she needed to plan her actions without any thought of his memories. Then he could come into them in his own time . . . or not.

When she came out onto the landing, Eric was seated on the stairs. Neutral territory, she realized after a moment. He was reading, waiting for her. She descended and sat beside him. The step was wide enough for them both, but her hip brushed his.

He shut the notebook he was reading and pressed it between his palms between his knees. "You're nothing like her. I'm sorry."

"And I shouldn't have treated you like you're just your power. I'm sorry too." Key brushed ineffectually at dust along the side of her thigh.

"Talking to Lantern clearly has the possibility of doing me some good as well." Eric grimaced, but at the floor downstairs, not at her. After that sideways glance to check his expression, she stared down too. "We might as well start for Oregon today. The name we have is just a lead, after all. Who knows where we'll be going after that."

"Okay." Key sandwiched her hands between her knees, mirroring his posture without a notebook. "It'll be an adventure." She'd aimed for the enthusiasm about traveling she remembered from childhood, but the humor turned ironic instead. "You know, if I'm stupid again, just force me to go and buy my own bagel at the store." So many strangers, all watching, so many rules that you didn't see on TV about how to talk to the checker and where to put your card . . .

"Add us together, I think we might approximate nine-tenths of a well-adjusted person who can go to Oregon." Eric set his notebook on his knees, leaving his hands more relaxed, and actually looked at her. "You should be flattered, that I forget all the things you haven't had direct experience with."

"Well, abstract knowledge helps you fake it, but doesn't make it less stressful." In the silence, Key's mind circled around to the beginning of the conversation, and she decided the rest of her explanation was important for him to know, even if it was kind of an excuse rather than an apology. "I also want to say . . . it's not a weird idea to think Ariadne kind of warped us, raising us, but she didn't actually raise us."

Key met Eric's eyes, so she could make sure he understood. "I mean, we saw her on and off. But she wasn't really even like a relative. More like the wealthy patron of the orphanage who wanted to check on our teachers and clapped because it was expected, after we did a few tricks for her."

"Given that we're . . . supposed to be peers, in a way, I'm not surprised. Maybe she was planning on different behavior once you were all adults." Eric stopped, frown ironic, for no reason Key could determine until he mouthed a word: "we."

She almost asked if he'd figured that out from the memories, but she pressed her lips together and controlled herself.

Patient. She'd said she could be patient, and this was clearly a situation in which she needed to exhibit that patience.

"Your hair looks nice like that," Eric said, and reached over to touch one now black lock on her shoulder.

"Thanks." Key rolled her shoulders. What else did you say to compliments? With Map, she punched his arm because he was usually making fun of her. "It had sort of outlived the original point long enough, I'm not entirely sure I remember what that point was. To piss Ariadne off, if nothing else."

She'd had enough of talking about her messed-up childhood, though. "What's that?" She tapped the notebook. "I brought it in because it was mixed in with all the groceries in the car, but I wasn't sure what it was for."

"I lifted it from one of Ariadne's researchers." Eric opened the notebook on his knees and flipped around. "I thought I'd see if Laura Dixon showed up, or anything else useful, but it's just notes on appointments and different families and historical sources. No Dixon of any kind." He smoothed a page flat. "That, and math."

"Can I see?" When he didn't object, Key took the notebook, searching her memory of school lessons. "Well, it's some kind of equation about a population, anyway. Like disease transmission?" When Eric looked at her funny, she stuck out her tongue. "Our tutors went up to college level, you know. I loved math, because it was so straightforward, and didn't have suspicious holes like history always did."

She pointed to the page. "I think she must have been working on it for a class. It doesn't seem like it went anywhere. Look, here's her dataset, and the equation results don't match." She flipped pages. "Variable: distance in kilometers. Variable: genetic consanguinity."

Her tone must have lifted a bit, because Eric jumped in to explain. Maybe proving himself when she'd showed him up with the math. "It's a numerical representation of how close relatives are. Siblings would be 0.5, for example. I guess something rubbed off on me, after being around Ariadne's project so much."

Bringing Ariadne's name into it must have prompted the same thought in both of their minds, because they spoke over each other. Eric nodded for Key to go first. "She's trying to figure out how powers pass! Distance, closeness of relationship . . . " She looked down. "Only that can't only be it, because the equation doesn't work. There has to be some missing variable."

"Maybe Aiko was trying it out before Ariadne passed it on to a mathematician." Eric turned a page while the notebook was still on Key's lap. "She's never afraid to hire an expert, but she wouldn't want anyone to be able to tell what it was really for. I bet she was waiting to see if Aiko asked awkward questions."

"While Aiko just plays with a problem with a premade dataset for class." Key touched the page where, buried among all the other scribbling, a due date was written. She turned to the next page, but the math had ended, and it was devoted to appointments, addresses, and phone numbers.

Eric jerked the notebook from her. "Wait." He ran his finger under a line, reading it out loud as if to convince himself he wasn't misreading more than to share it with her. "'Call Patricia, set up meeting about TH dataset.'" He looked up at Key, as if that should be a revelation to her, and continued when she looked blank. "Laura Dixon. She was in the TH dataset.

TendarisHerron. They do things with genetics. The transmission equation, her work with the CEO and the lab—it's all to find Lantern. She must be using their genetic samples to try to find who Lantern is now, based on her relatives."

Key smoothed a lock of hair over her shoulder, trying to make the black shade stop surprising her in her peripheral vision. Maybe Eric was right; they didn't need his memories for figuring out Ariadne's plans. The way he was putting things together did make sense. But that left her without a stronger excuse to buttress her wish he'd find personal things in the memories.

"I won't be surprised if the recent spate of deaths has something to do with finding Lantern too, however tangentially. Many of them had at least a tenuous connection to TendarisHerron when I was first investigating." Eric closed the notebook and smoothed the back cover. "We have to go to the lab. See if we can find out anything there."

Key tried to lay their travel plans out in her mind, but she didn't know enough to estimate times and distances. "After Oregon?"

"Before. The lab's down outside of Bellevue. It wouldn't make sense to go to Oregon and then come back." Eric cut off her protest before she got it out by squeezing her hand. "Laura Dixon can't be Lantern. It's not like we're putting off finding Lantern herself. We'd still have a next step after Oregon. And the more we know about Ariadne's motives, the better."

"What if Ariadne finds us there?" Key tried to look like he hadn't hit her first, automatic objection right on the head, and drew her hand away.

Eric set the notebook aside on the step above them. "She'd

have less reason to look there than she would in Oregon. She knows we're interested in Lantern. She doesn't know I've put anything together about her boyfriend and his lab." Eric scrubbed at his eyes with the heels of his palms. "It's her hold on Map we have to worry about anyway, when it comes to her finding us."

"He won't necessarily *help* her." Key wished she sounded confident about that. She wished she *felt* confident about that. Or even believed it in some part of herself other than the small, hurting core that felt like his sister. "Maybe he didn't know about the cameras."

"Key . . . " Eric started his objection, but didn't remove his hands from his face, and after a minute, she realized he probably wasn't going to finish it.

She finished it for him. "It would be a logical assumption, though, given the number of them at the cottages. Maybe he was conflicted? Taking us somewhere we *might* be seen isn't the same as calling her up." If he was conflicted, did she feel any better about him?

After a few beats of silence, Eric dropped his hands and sighed. "We can't do anything about it, either way. We'll have to hope you're right and he won't actively track us for her." He reached for the notebook and stopped with his hand arrested just above the carpet beside it instead. Key supposed, as a gesture, it looked strange enough, but she'd seen Hound—the old Hound—do it often enough. He was touching her uncrossed trail.

"How do you not target someone, then?" Eric's voice came out a little strangled.

"Don't concentrate so hard you choke, essentially." Key realized she probably sounded awfully cavalier, so she hurried to reassure. "I only mentioned it last night because you were so out of it. I'm not worried now. You'll feel what you're doing and stop in time. Trust me." She tried to convey her own trust of him by sitting still rather than trying to get her trail crossed, but his twisted expression didn't lift.

"Look. You have to at least try it so you know how it feels. That'll make you more comfortable about where the line is, right?" Key plucked at his pocket, but the angle was wrong and she couldn't get her fingers in. "Give me your keys. We can mutually assured destruction ourselves for maximum safety. I'll squeeze if you're doing something dangerous."

Eric knocked her hand away automatically, and held his protectively over the pocket for a beat of worried silence before stretching out his leg to get at the keys himself. Key expected more hesitation when he had them in hand, but he offered them right over.

Probably going to die when Ariadne found them. Didn't he deserve it? Not just complicit in murder, a potential murderer himself now.

Key clutched the keys to her stomach, metal pressing into her skin, as if she could cut their connection to Eric as easily as crossing a trail. Things didn't work that way for her, though. Someone's keys had to be in another's possession for far more than a few seconds to lose their connection. He looked so *calm* on the surface. Or maybe the shocking intensity of emotion was because she'd only touched people through their keys at a great distance before now. Map had never had any keys, and the guards hid theirs. "Okay then," she said, when her voice was steady, though she couldn't avoid a touch of irony.

"What?" Eric searched her face.

He didn't understand any of this magic. Too dangerous. Was ignorance or knowledge worse?

"You've got a lot for me to read. Go ahead and concentrate on me. You should get a sense of who I am, maybe some emotions." Key waited, and while she did get a sense of effort from him, it was too scattered, more focused on determining whether it was focused than on the task at hand. She thought he might have it once, but he brought his hand back to his lap before she could be sure.

Key tossed him his keys back. Maybe if she was a good teacher, she'd insist, but she was tired of reading him so intimately. She had no idea what to do with what she'd read. Should she address it out loud? Or was that rude?

Eric saved her from the decision. He squinted at the sunbeam sneaking onto the hall floor from the front windows in the living room, some of the few without bushes. "I think we have time to get some fresh air, but then we should pack the car and get on the road."

Key wondered if he intended to distract her from his failure to even half try to target, or if he hoped to settle his emotions before he had to drive. Either way, she agreed with the idea of the latter, and reached the front door before she remembered. "But we're not supposed to be here. What if someone sees us?"

"They'll see people acting like they're supposed to be there, so they'll assume they're supposed to be there." Eric smiled and seemed to relax for some reason. "The world is far too full of unfamiliar variables to be suspicious of every single thing you didn't expect." He opened the door and gestured for her to precede him. "We're a young couple who just bought the house, and now we're going to go for a walk. We have no idea why anyone would be looking at us, so we're not watching for anyone."

That sounded nice in abstract, but Key wasn't an actress. She wasn't going to be like him and just refuse to try, though. That got her through the door. *Unlocked.* Even outside, it was a lot like being at home, she reminded herself. Just lots of houses. And lots of cars parked along the street. That wasn't like being at home.

"Just taking a walk," Eric murmured beside her ear, so she must have tensed up. He turned around and hid his hand on the knob with his body. They'd already removed and hid inside something Eric called the "realtor's lockbox" on their arrival. "And I'm just locking up because we obviously have a key because we have every reason to be here. Would you?"

Locked. Once Key started walking, it did get easier to keep going. The sidewalks here were wider than at home. And the cars were all so individual and different, seen at rest rather than in streams on the road. She got one driveway ahead before she noticed Eric was slowing down. There were a lot of trails here, of course. She slowed until he caught up and took his hand. Nine-tenths of a well-adjusted person together, taking a walk.

The weather really was beautiful, if cold, and every yard had something completely different, whether it was a raised bed or a plastic castle playset or varieties of flowers and bushes and trees she'd never seen before. Eric looked mostly at the ground, but she had to tug him less and less as they went along. By the time they turned back, he glanced up every so often and actually cracked a smile.

Key smiled back, automatically, but still had to ask. "What?" She hoped she didn't look humorous, gawking at a normal neighborhood and cars and such.

"I have . . . " Eric spread his free hand wide and his smile grew even as he stumbled over the exact words. "Real magic, I guess. Magical powers. That's . . . pretty fucking cool. It just struck me."

Key had to laugh. She certainly hadn't considered powers from that perspective before. Maybe she should try. "Remind me of that every so often, would you?"

"Promise." Eric's steps were looser and longer on the way back to the house, so Key had to skip a bit every few steps to keep up. Time to pack and get on the road.

17

In my youth, the elders told such tales.

Like how the four other searchers followed Hound through the lushness of the jungle, great canopy above, vine-draped trunks around them. A jaguar leaped at them from a branch above, but Hound had tracked where it, too, had passed, and shot it with a poison-tipped arrow.

The TendarisHerron lab building was three stories, one more new, red brick building with plenty of shiny glass among other red-brick, shiny-glass office buildings in a light industrial park. Eric had also taken photos at their corporate office space downtown before, one floor in a high-rise filled with other high-profile companies, but at this time of the morning, Clive

Herron, CEO of—Eric made himself stop mockingly using the news article title even in his own mind—Clive was usually here. Eric had decided on the way over to go all the way to the top, if they could reach him, and shake down the man who probably knew exactly what was going on. Or as much as Ariadne had told him, at least.

This location had been the easiest of the two to scout, and he'd even been here recently, for the photo that had doomed Patricia. He concentrated on the irony of Ariadne's job coming full circle to help him work against her, rather than on all the trails.

Most of them were layered into streams rather than tangled, at least. They left the various parking spaces and converged, root system–like, on the front door. He got out of the car, which was probably a mistake, because then anyone going in and out of the building would notice if he just stood there and stared. Part of him was desperate to stall and run over plans in his mind, but he knew the layout already. Better they were here for as little time as possible in case Ariadne took it into her head to visit her business partner.

Time to enter show mode. Whatever came, he'd roll with it, based on trained instinct rather than planning. Eric strode for the front door, and Key tagged along behind.

It didn't have much of a foyer—an elevator to one side, and a seating area with a potted plant, a few chairs, and a reception desk to the other. Semiabstract depictions of chemical bonds and double helixes shimmered from pieces of art etched into metal. Between the elevator and desk, a wide hall led down into the building, with offices and workspaces opening off it.

Eric strode up to the desk, where the young woman only belatedly looked up from her computer screen. Not the tightest security, but he suspected the really important samples and data were on the floors above, protected by a key-card-operated elevator as well as the internal door locks. And a security guard would be around somewhere, within easy calling distance.

"We're here for an appointment with Mr. Herron. He told us to come right in." Eric smiled at the receptionist, very polite, but like he was doing her a favor by telling her when he really didn't have to. He watched her face, which, thank God, was wonderfully expressive. She glanced down the hall and frowned when she didn't see an open door or CEO emerging to meet his guests. She opened her scheduling program on the computer. "Are you sure—?"

"It was pretty last minute." Eric shrugged. "If he's busy, I'll come back and do things properly." He offered her another smile, apologetic for not following process. Smiles and apologies were key. Everyone liked to have their inconvenience—and thus their importance—acknowledged, even if the acknowledger then continued right on inconveniencing them.

Without waiting for permission, he strode for the hallway. The blue trails stayed mostly in one stream here, too, carrying him along. Clive's would be among them somewhere, but he didn't need that, which was a good thing, because he didn't think he could have sorted them out without stopping and zoning out in the middle of the hallway. The angle of the receptionist's glance to check for an open door had covered two of them, and the second door down in the hallway had more space on either side than any of the other doors, making the room beyond the largest. He'd lay money that was Clive's, even without a nameplate.

"Key," Eric murmured, shortening his next few steps so she came even with, then passed him. "Open this one and make it look like it was unlocked all along, would you? Then follow my lead."

She had all kinds of tells, slowing down, and glancing over at him for verification or perhaps moral support, but she turned the handle smoothly, and the card reader above it didn't protest. The receptionist didn't call out, so they must have chosen the right door, playing into what she expected: the boss had left his door unlocked for the last-minute appointment to let themselves in, exactly as they had said.

Clive was at his computer, glancing between it and the cell phone in his hand, giving the absurd impression that he was answering two e-mails simultaneously. He looked up at the sound of the door opening. "What—?" As Eric had hoped, his first impulse was not to demand who they were, which might lead immediately to his calling security, but to assume, like the receptionist, that since they'd gotten in, they must have permission to be here.

"We're with Ariadne." Eric strode in and stood with his legs slightly apart, hands in pockets, to psychologically take up as much space in the office as possible. Clive set his phone down and shoved his chair back. Seen up close, he was different than Eric had expected. In press photos, his silvered hair and snappy clothes drew the eye, but in person he exuded the kind of frenetic energy that Eric associated with much younger entrepreneurs. He had that scrawny look, like he forgot to eat or sleep while holding everything within his company together personally.

"But she never sends anyone here—" Clive's initial fear transformed into wariness. "I talked to her just last night." He started to reach for his landline phone, probably for the intercom.

"Wait!" Eric barked the word with enough force that Clive froze. Eric's performance instincts might be writing checks his intellect couldn't cash, but every instinct shouted one play at him. Clive's initial fear told Eric that Ariadne had probably given Clive the welcoming near-death experience.

"Don't confuse 'with' Ariadne for 'employed by' or even 'possessed of the same goals as.'" He held out his hand in a vaguely threatening gesture he would have used to emphasize a trick on stage just before the reveal. He let the trails in the office fill up his vision, blue sharpening with the information about Clive and the receptionist and several other employees, and not Ariadne, as Clive had said. Eric couldn't lose himself, but he needed Clive to see in his eyes that he had magic, like Ariadne. It would be even better if Key could do it too, but that was a complicated lead to follow without any warning. That was the trouble with performing with an assistant.

Clive slumped in his office chair, frenetic energy bleeding away to leave his face a little gray. Eric blinked a beat too long, trying to focus on his face and not his trail. Come on, come on. He was losing his timing.

"What do you want? Are you going to threaten to kill me

as well?" Clive asked. "She never misses an opportunity to re-mind me that she saved my life, and she can take that gift right back."

"No!" Key pitched in, finally. The need to keep the encoun-ter on the path he'd selected snapped Eric out of his battle with the trails. Eric hoped Key's expression wasn't too shocked. He was concentrating too hard on reading Clive to check.

"Death is not a solution we like to turn to so . . . quickly, as Ariadne does." Eric smiled, making it sharklike. "We came to appeal to your intelligence. There's no reason for Ariadne to know that we were here, that you told us anything, unless you're the one to reveal it to her."

"I'll tell you what I told her." Clive flapped a hand and stood to pace. Eric braced while trying to make it look as though he wasn't, but that's all Clive did: pace behind his desk. His energy returned twice as strong. "The virus isn't ready. And I don't know when it will be. The incubation period is far too short. People will show symptoms and possibly even die before they have a chance to spread it very far, and the CDC won't figure the strain out fast enough to gather people for treatment."

Eric's stomach fell away. He'd never imagined Ariadne was engineering a virus—but it didn't make *sense*. There must be something he was missing here. How did random deaths make Ariadne any safer from her boogeyman gods? "She had you make a virus." Eric tried to state it, like they were already well aware of that, but his inflection lifted a touch at the end any-way.

Clive paused, facing them again. "Yes. After she was sure I knew my life was in her hands." He closed his eyes for a beat, and Eric curled his lip mentally. Clive wasn't only a victim here.

There was something about the sexual component to their re-lationship—Eric had no doubt now that there was one—that he did not object to at all. He supposed it was hypocritical of him to blame any man for sleeping with Ariadne, but . . .

"The virus is influenza based, designed to only activate in someone of the bloodline she gave me. The incubation period was supposed to allow time for the strain to be identified and the sufferers to be brought to central locations for treatment. Then Ariadne could sort through them to find the person she wants." Clive was back to his pacing, back to pure victim. "It's not designed to be lethal, I assure you. I have no idea who she's after."

"Lantern," Key said, voice flat. Clive showed no hint of rec-ognition.

"And she paid you well for this virus? More than enough to develop it and also keep the company afloat no matter what else you did?" Having seen one crack in the "poor victim," Eric sounded for others without sympathy.

"Well . . . " Clive straightened his cuffs. That was enough for Eric. No one ever started a real denial with "well." They used "well" to start their explanation of the extenuating cir-cumstances supposed to justify their actions.

He didn't give Clive time to finish his excuses. "Were you aware of all the people she was killing to smooth your path? I assume that's what it was for—regulators who might have no-ticed something suspicious, employees who might have talk-ed . . . like Patricia?"

Clive shook his head violently. "I *told* her, I would take care of Patricia; she didn't need to— Once we're finished, we'll need fudge the paperwork, bury the time and materials spent on this project, but we're not at that point yet. I was just going to fire her so we could 'lose' the records, anyway."

Eric snorted. Again, a niggling feeling of hypocrisy couldn't squash his growing anger. He hadn't questioned Ariadne much either. But the deaths hadn't been staring him in the face in quite the same way as they had Clive. "So the other deaths were all right?"

"I didn't know that's what she was—"

Eric supposed he had asked, but he suddenly didn't want to hear the excuse, even if it was true. He held up his hand to stop the man. Clive could have been that willfully blind, he supposed, putting all his energy into his company and his research and not questioning when both sailed along a bit too smoothly.

Clive switched tacks. "What do you want me to do about it now? You forget she has *me* over a barrel. What was I supposed to do? What's done is done."

Eric rocked a step forward, to reassert his control of the situation, and Clive winced back. "You just said the current virus could kill people."

Clive held up his hands, pacifying. "It has that potential, but we can't know for sure. She doesn't have any of the samples in her possession right now, anyway. Maybe she won't release it yet after all." It had been a long time since Eric had heard someone who sounded less like they believed their own words.

"You have a concrete reason to believe she wants to release it soon?" Eric let his tightly controlled anger seep into his tone.

"Well, she was asking about how to choose a release location." His tone developed a whine. "She's so angry about whatever it was that she lost, she's completely irrational." He tried an awkward laugh. "More than usual." The humor faded into hollow silence as he seemed to realize that the powers in front of him might well be as irrational as Ariadne was.

Eric glanced at Key, a beat before he realized he was showing tells just as much as the receptionist had. Key was the lost thing, he'd bet. "And you're going to do everything you can to stall her when she asks you to hand it over, aren't you?"

"I—" Clive looked around the room, everywhere except at him and Key. Apparently no answers jumped out at him. "I'm not sure I'd be very good at stalling." He tried to smile. "I mean, I'll try. Don't want anyone else hurt. But honestly you'd be better off talking her out of it yourselves."

"Oh, we'll be working to stop her directly," Key said intensely. Eric touched her back to catch her attention before he headed for the door. They had the information they needed, it was time to beat a strategic retreat. Even if Clive did tell Ariadne about their visit, she still wouldn't have a lead on their location if they left quickly enough. Any lead she wouldn't have had already, of course, since her influence on Map and knowledge of Oregon were unknown.

And he could tell that pushing Clive into a stronger promise to develop a moral spine and use it wouldn't help anything. "If you think about telling Ariadne about us, remember that the easiest way for us to thwart her is to dispose of you," he said by way of farewell. He ushered Key out the door immediately to lend finality to the threat.

Outside, in the lull after being essentially on stage, the trails surged up in Eric's vision, making it impossible for him to see the carpet. The public hallway had a lot more of them, old and new, than there had been in the private office. He drew a deep breath. "Key? Lead the way?"

Key didn't move. "He said she doesn't have the virus yet. If we steal it now, destroy it ourselves—" Her tone was too soft to carry to the receptionist, but Eric didn't want to spend too long here in visible—and in Key's case, slightly guilty-looking—conference.

"Alarms," he murmured, just as soft. "Guards. The security on their actual lab facilities will be ten times what it is on these offices. That kind of thing takes planning. We need to leave now, so we don't look suspicious. We'll come back later, all right? Maybe at night. First we need to warn Laura Dixon, in case she's in danger."

"Oh." Key dropped her chin in acknowledgment. To her credit, she remembered his earlier request to lead the way without his having to repeat it. She turned to take his hand, but he squeezed her shoulder, moving his hand up from where he'd kept a touch on her back. Hand in hand didn't fit the image he'd presented to the receptionist.

She turned back, he heard Clive's office door lock click tidily back shut, and she did lead the way, back through the stream of trails. As Eric relaxed a little, relying on her, they subsided some, allowing his thoughts to stretch beyond the immediacy of their next move. Ariadne *really* wanted Lantern. She must really fear what would happen if she didn't get the full Hand under her control.

Eric, on the other hand, feared what would happen if she *did*.

18

They came upon a palace worthy of a tsar, built into a great mountain. Around the palace stood a fence of human bones. Atop each post was a skull, and the third searcher spoke to one. "You must open for us." And when Key touched it, a gate of bones opened.

—Traditional folktale, first recorded late eighteenth century

Once they'd cleared the well-signed bend and swoop of I-5 through Portland, Eric made Key stop exploring his phone and leave the GPS to its work. They'd have to leave the freeway sometime before Salem, or at least that was his memory of the overview map when he'd inputted the address before setting off.

The hours had ground down his sharp impatience to find Laura, warn her, leaving it an aching distraction at the back of his mind. The miles blended together, mild traffic in the middle of a workday and no actual rain to slow anyone down. Outside of the city, it was all gray skies and alternating trees, malls, and light industrial parks. And car dealerships. Highly traveled areas were washed slightly blue, like those streams of movement were being seen in summer twilight away from modern lights.

Key hadn't spoken much the whole way, but now he noticed her body language tightening up, arms crossed over her chest and shoulders angled down as if she wanted to curl up and didn't realize it.

"It shouldn't be that much longer now," Eric said, breaking the silence layered over low music from the radio. She glanced toward him with a jerk. "We'll warn Laura, and then we can plan how to get the samples when I don't have to pay attention to the road."

"I know." Key nodded, but her body language didn't ease. Clearly something more was bothering her. Was being out of the compound hitting her hard again? Probably time to switch the radio from music to some kind of program with words to focus on, but Eric automatically checked first. "You okay?" No point trying to fix the problem with distraction if it was the kind of thing that needed talking out.

"Yeah, fine." Key straightened her shoulders pointedly. A beat of silence, filled with the soft rumble of classic rock, then— "I just . . ."

Something she did need to voice, then. He hoped actively listening would be enough, because God knew he didn't have any wisdom to address his own problems, never mind anyone else's. He let her gather her words without further prompting.

"I was thinking about whether Hound would be impressed by any of this, since he has those books of places all over the world, but of course he's—you're—kind of here, and I don't know if I even actually miss him."

Eric made a prompting noise this time. Clearly that last part was the key one.

"We weren't ever close. You couldn't be close to him; there was nothing there to be close to. But he was one of us, you know? I haven't cried or anything. I just don't know . . . how I should feel." Her shoulders curled down again.

He had memories about grief, especially grief among the powers. Eric could *feel* it, like the hovering weight of a certainty that there was a task you were supposed to be doing, right now, that you'd forgotten. Eric gritted his teeth and told the memories to go fuck themselves. He wasn't going to reach out and resolve that weight. "There's no right way to grieve. I've lost a few friends, and the process was different every time. And not like on TV, any of them." That last seemed ill advised when he reviewed the phrasing in his mind, but Key didn't object to it.

"So I'm . . . grieving?" Key's voice cracked with something Eric couldn't identify until he stepped away from an unconscious assumption it would be sadness or anger, related to her grief. She sounded *relieved,* which about killed Eric. He supposed he'd been spot on. With her screwed-up, circumscribed life, all she would have seen was people sobbing on camera.

"Yes. And you'll feel—all kinds of stuff. The only connection among all of it is that you'll feel each really strongly. But the part where everything's so strong, it does end." Next, he might have mentioned something about remembering the person who'd died, so they'd live on through memories, but of course Hound did, literally, live on in Eric.

Fuck.

Silence settled under the chatter of a commercial on the radio, and Eric punched the seek button to find more music. Key's thoughts must have turned in the same direction, though. "Do you—did you—remember anything from him?" She hardly gave him time to answer before she backpedaled. "I mean, I was just curious. You don't have to look for it."

Better to answer, Eric decided, than to leave her silently wondering, and him imagining her silently wondering. "I got a couple memories at the beginning. It was more like the memory of watching a movie. No emotions, just things he'd seen."

"Oh." Key smoothed her palms over her thighs, once, twice. "Thanks." Silence again, still curled up, but he hoped she was finding her way to grieve. Eric stopped the radio on a classical station and thought his own thoughts about Kayla and how she wouldn't ever know what had happened to her son, to allow her to grieve. If she would feel the need to grieve. He wasn't even sure of that.

The house the address led them to looked no different than any of the neighborhood's other houses in the cloudy, late-afternoon light. At the outskirts of a small town, the lots were big, but the houses were all one story. The one Eric and Key were currently loitering beside had a yard stuffed with pinwheels, concrete birdbaths, and twee statuary being eaten by the undergrowth. Someone's trail looped around and through it, so apparently the owner did enjoy it. Laura Dixon's yard, next door, was comparatively restrained, mostly neatly trimmed lawn except for planting beds filled with flowers along the house and in a circle around a central maple.

"Ariadne hasn't been here. At least for however long I can see." Eric squinted at Laura Dixon's front path again, then looked down at his phone, him showing something to Key being their ostensible reason for standing on the sidewalk. Assuming he wasn't completely missing something because he didn't know what he was doing. At least they knew Ariadne couldn't have come in the back, because the two of them had looped the block and he hadn't found a trace anywhere.

Probably.

Key gave him a thin smile. "I suspect it's not nearly so hard as you're making it. She's not here now; she hasn't been here recently. She probably hasn't even realized we know about Laura yet."

"Laura's not here at the moment either." Eric pointed to the driveway. "At least, a woman on her own left in her car from the garage. I'm going to take a chance and say that's probably Laura herself." Which was honestly a good thing. This time he wanted to prepare before talking to her. He didn't have even half the mental energy left he'd need to ride the situation on a performance high as he'd done with Clive.

Of course, he'd had plenty of planning time on the drive down, and he'd lacked the mental energy to use that either. He nudged Key into an easy stroll away from Laura's house again. Maybe if he worked on his plan out loud, he'd be able to concentrate on it. "We need to figure out what the hell we're going to say to her. If we try to go in with a story that's too simple, she'll smell a rat, because the information we need isn't simple, and I don't think even I can play nonsuspicious at the moment. Maybe admit that Ariadne's involved, to explain the hinky element, and set ourselves up in opposition to it. Makes us seem like honest allies."

"Why can't we just explain about the virus and then ask her where Lantern is?" Key's sheer naiveté tempted Eric to stop and stare at her, but he knew she didn't deserve that. She hadn't had a chance to get it knocked out of her in the real world. "We told the Herron guy the truth."

"Because if we start talking about the powers to someone who hasn't seen real, tangible proof of them—maybe even repeatedly—we're going to sound crazy. And if Ms. Dixon thinks she's let a couple of crazy people into her house, she'll politely show us the door and call the cops if we refuse to go. We can still warn her without being completely up front about the details."

"But if she knows about Lantern, she already knows about powers." Key crossed her arms, apparently planning to stick to her guns.

"We don't know she knows about Lantern. It seems likely she's a relative of hers, but we don't know how close. You always want to go in with the story that keeps someone talking. Then you can decide to admit to the truth or not later. Go in with the truth, and if the door's shut in your face, that's it." Eric walked another two steps before he realized Key had paused. Speaking of choosing the wrong tack to start with, apparently he should have been trying to persuade her into this.

"So you're talking about . . . working up to it?" Key still seemed dubious, but apparently any persuading happened in her own head because she nodded once and started walking again.

"Yeah. I'll read her reactions when she hears the cover story." Eric outlined one as it came to him, and though Key merely looked blank, hearing it out loud helped him spot a couple of holes on his own. "And if she does react, then we'll have somewhere to work from when we do bring up Lantern and the virus."

Key nodded again, and they walked in silence for a while. The uppermost trail spooling out in front of them was their own, strengthening with repetition, almost reassuring in a way. A residential neighborhood was certainly easier to think straight in than a city. Then they were back at Laura's house. Eric could *feel* it happen, feel his concentration on details slipping into OCD-like ritual, but he had so little control over anything right now. "I want to check the trails at her front door," he said, and they turned up the worn and intermittently white-graveled path through the center of the yard.

A dog had run all over the yard, and at the door, Eric found a number of different children's trails, and the adult woman's again, but no one he recognized. Of course. But he'd just wanted to check.

A car turned into the driveway, and Eric twisted around guiltily. Hell. He was already making rookie mistakes. Key didn't look guilty, but Key wasn't carrying the weight of talking them both through this. Laura pulled the car into the garage, then slipped out along its side rather than going into the house. "Can I help you two?"

They were on. Time to charm. Eric strode forward confidently, offering his hand to shake. "Ms. Laura Dixon?" She was aging gracefully with expressive wrinkles around her eyes and a peppering of gray in her dark brown hair, concentrated in her part. Her jaw was squared off, but greater-than-average height lengthened any sense of angles out of her body.

She took his hand with a grace of movement that made Eric suspect she worked with her hands somehow. "That's me. Are you here about piano lessons?"

"No, I—" Eric offered her an apologetic smile. "It's a bit complicated. My name is Eric Davis. This is Kyna."

"Give me a moment." Laura pointed to the front door. "And you can come in." She strode back into the garage, and the door shut behind her. As promised, however, the front door opened a minute later.

The inside of the house was something of a shock. A baby grand filled the entire front room, and the rest of the furniture complemented its gleaming blackness. The walls were covered with performance photographs of Laura, the framing of the shots suggesting the locations were immensely famous concert halls that the photographer expected viewers to recognize. Eric supposed after all the neighbors' houses and especially garden statues, he'd been expecting knitted afghans and ceramic knickknacks.

A medium-sized dog bolted in from the back of the house, tail whirling. It had the gray over black and brown coloration of a cattle dog, but a more indefinable mutt body type. Key plastered herself to Eric's side, hands pulled well up out of biting distance, clearly petrified. Eric offered his hand for sniffing in case that might settle the dog a little, but it preferred to continue bounding in ecstatic circles around and around them. Blue tangled up into complicated skeins, because the dog didn't ever repeat a path and there was trail after trail underneath that.

"Ivan, no jumping!" Laura said, apparently reading Key's body language. Eric wanted to say something reassuring, but there were so many trails. *Dog, heading north—dog, heading east-northeast, dog, heading—dog, heading—*

"Ivan." Laura got a firm grip on his collar and dragged him away as he finally loosed a couple of frustrated barks. A final bark sounded, muffled by an intervening door, probably one of the bedrooms, then she reappeared. When Eric could finally look at her face rather than the blue she was leaving, she seemed suspicious. Why was being afraid of dogs suspicious? Key hadn't been excessive with her fear, though he suspected that only due to personality—or possibly training. She wouldn't have had a childhood where throwing a tantrum or making a scene would have been a good idea.

"Have a seat," Laura invited, suspicious or not. The den was similarly sleek to the front room, and notably lacked any kind of TV, the conversational arc of the seating focused on the gas fireplace instead. She held out a hand to the couch, then fussed around behind them for a moment, turning on a small fan. "I hope you don't mind. It gets so stuffy in here."

It didn't feel stuffy at all to Eric, but he was definitely in no position to object. He murmured agreement and chose his seat on the couch so he wasn't in the direct path of the chill breeze. Key flopped down and scooted into his side almost immediately when the air hit her. Laura took a love seat across from them.

"Thank you again for speaking with us, Ms. Dixon. This is going to sound strange, I know, but I used to work for a woman named Ariadne Respiros." Eric paused for a rhetorical beat to check her reactions, but also to mentally slap his forehead. He hadn't realized the dumb joke of her name until now. Laura didn't show a clear reaction to the name, unfortunately.

"She has been constructing a private genealogy database for many years, but it wasn't until recently that I realized she'd been using it for rather . . . unethical purposes. We think she's been using it to track transmission of genetic diseases, but without informing any of the people she's spoken to of her real purpose. We think she might have visited you and asked for a DNA sample. We wondered—do you have any female relatives she seemed to be specifically searching for information on? If they are at risk for the disease, we'd like to contact them."

"I can't say I'm close to any of my relatives. I was raised by my mother, and she committed suicide close to twenty years ago now." Laura showed no particular emotion, but Eric recognized what she was doing—in making him feel like he'd pushed her into a painful admission in a socially unacceptable way, she was trying to force him to back off from further questions. She could have easily said she had no living relatives, or that her mother had "passed on." Mentioning the suicide was purposeful. But Eric recognized both that trick, and the fact that she hadn't answered about Ariadne.

"I'm so sorry." Eric dipped his head in sympathy. No need to leave the social acceptability game yet. Had the mother been a targeted death? He needed to know more. "You must really miss her."

Key fidgeted, which Eric realized a moment later was a warning sign. "How did she die?"

Eric slipped a hand down to pinch her arm where it was hidden between their two bodies, making her start. She must have been thinking along similar lines as him, but she lacked finesse in following up on it. "Kyna, I'm sure Ms. Dixon doesn't want to talk about . . . " And she especially wouldn't want to talk about it when approached directly like that. You had to work sideways up to upsetting topics, and then if you were lucky, people would open up and what you needed would pour out.

"Pills. She was well prepared, apparently." Laura stood suddenly and went over to an end table with a small drawer underneath that Eric hadn't noticed until she pulled it out. "To save you, I suppose."

It was probably time to abandon the cover story, but Eric's mouth continued on autopilot in the absence of instructions he was too confused to give. "What are you talking about?"

"Which ones are you, then?" Laura held up a sheet of paper, cheap enough to have yellowed slightly, though it didn't otherwise look excessively old. It was thin enough for a drawing to show through from the other side, no words, but the light was wrong to make out what the drawing depicted.

"I'm Key." She paid Eric back by flexing her fingernails into the meat of his arm. He could read the message well enough: "told you so" with a side of "don't you dare pinch me again."

"Plausible." Laura angled the paper toward Eric next. For comparison, he realized. "And Map."

"Hound." Not that he liked making that identification, but that was more a matter of his own mind than their approach for talking information out of her. He held out his hand for the page. She hesitated, then shrugged and handed it over.

Line drawings, as he'd expected. Ariadne, as a close a likeness as if it had been drawn yesterday; a girl maybe eight years old; and a boy, maybe twelve or thirteen. To him, the children just looked like children, and he caught himself holding up the drawing exactly as Laura had, to compare Key with the girl directly. A diagonal slash of charcoal right through the girl's face made the task more difficult. It didn't really obscure much, but it broke up the drawing and made it hard to see the person as a whole.

Key was craning her neck, so he handed the drawing on. "Someone didn't like you much," he warned, lifting his thumb to tap near the slash. He'd have understood that impulse with Ariadne, but not Key, especially so young.

"No." Key pushed away his hand and pulled the drawing close, precious. "That's to make sure Map can't use it to target." She turned her gaze to Laura. "Lantern drew this?" She barely waited for a nod before rushing on. "I remember—I never knew when it happened because her visit wasn't connected to anything, but this seems the right age . . . "

"To save them?" Eric prompted Laura, when Key trailed off and didn't pick up again for several breaths.

"To save more children from being raised by Breath, Mom always said." She held up a forestalling hand. "Before you start the interrogation, I didn't know much. She was very quiet about her abilities, and she only explained about the children she was trying to save when we moved out here and she started trying to get access to them." Laura gestured generally in front of her face. "Saw her eyes go black often enough. Like yours." She nodded to Eric.

Which is why she'd gotten suspicious, when the dog had thrown him off balance. Eric gritted his teeth. So much for his illusion that he was in control of himself.

"Nearly twenty years." Key looked like she really needed to

hug something but didn't dare crumple the drawing, so Eric slid his hand over hers for her to cling to. "I never knew how long ago, but she visited, talked to us. And then she never came back. She killed herself because Ariadne found out and she had to start again, with a face Ariadne wouldn't know."

"Yes." Laura tugged the drawing away from her, smoothed it even though it wasn't bent, and put it ritually back into the drawer. Tears had risen in Key's eyes, but Laura looked balanced in her old grief.

"I'm sorry," Eric said. Empathy with the two of them made his muscles tight.

"In her note—" Now, some huskiness entered Laura's voice. "She said this was her battle, not mine, and if anyone ever came looking, there was no reason for me to help them. But . . . " She looked at the drawer. Eric wondered if she was thinking of the children pictured inside it. Finding out their situations, even as adults, he'd certainly been quick enough to commit to interfering. Even if he'd had his own selfish reasons as well.

Laura blew out a breath. "So if one of you is secretly Breath, so be it. Now you know I know."

"Ariadne still looks like that." Eric's turn to nod to the drawer. "It was eerily accurate, actually. But I understand why you wouldn't want to take our word for that."

"It's certainly what she looked like a few months later when she showed up about her genealogy research. She didn't say anything about DNA, but my house was broken into a few years back. If you told me she had a sample, I wouldn't be shocked." Laura rocked her weight and crossed to stand in front of the love seat again but didn't sit. "You sound just like her, you know."

"I did work for her. Before I—" Eric stumbled over the words, cursed silently for a few seconds. Why was it so very hard? "Became Hound."

"We can prove it." Key clenched Eric's hand for a last beat then dropped it and stood up. "That we're Key and Hound, not Breath. Just let us show you, and then you won't have to worry and you can tell us where Lantern is."

"Sweetheart . . . " Laura flexed elegant fingers, helplessly. "Even if you do prove it, I can't tell you what I don't know. To me, she's dead, and has stayed dead. That's how it has to be, I guess." More pain showed this time, less worn down than the grief, perhaps because the sense of betrayal had been so large and cutting in the beginning.

"No, we'll prove it." Key might not even have heard Laura. She strode for the front door and presumably the lock there.

Eric held back with Laura for a moment. "Sorry. I think she imprinted on your mother a little."

"Can't say I blame her." Laura didn't move, glancing from Eric, to the hallway, and back. It took him several seconds of awkward silence to realize she wanted him to move first. Whatever she said about trusting them with her knowledge, it appeared she didn't want to get into a possible Breath's reach.

Eric led the way to the front door, which Key unlocked and relocked several times. Key stared expectantly at Laura, even after the woman had shaken her head. It took a verbal denial before anger seeped into Key's expression instead.

"Now your turn. Prove you're not Lantern, hiding from us!" Key stepped right up to Laura. The woman's brows rose in surprise, but after Key's demonstration, she allowed the closeness. "You're her nearest relative. It could have passed to you!"

"But I knew her. It never passes to someone who knew the old incarnation well." Laura seemed sincerely surprised Key didn't know that.

Eric stepped forward and grabbed Key's shoulders to pull her back when she started to reach out to Laura, maybe to shake the admission out of her. "Key. Remember the missing variable in the equation? She's telling the truth."

"But she—she has to know—" Key twisted to face Eric, expression begging him to somehow warp reality and make this not a dead end in the search. Honestly, he wished he could. He hugged her, because that was all he had. She clung back, but was still all tension in his arms.

"I . . . " Laura's lips thinned with indecision, though the tension didn't make it into her hands, thumbs hooked into her pockets. Eric watched Laura's face, and squeezed Key tightly when he felt her gather herself to break free and return to her earlier shaking idea. Laura needed to get there herself, without any kind of persuasion.

"Sometimes I send something to her old e-mail address. She died when e-mail was still a new thing, you know? She was delighted by it. Anyway, I've never once gotten a reply." Her teeth closed over her lower lip for a beat; then she seemed to find her peace with her decision and finished in a rush. "But it never bounces, either. I don't know if free services delete accounts that go unused for a certain period of time, or what. But . . . "

"Eric!" Key twisted away from Eric. Ignoring her implied demand for speed, he calmly took out his phone and nodded to Laura when he had his address book open. Since Key might well explode if he didn't, once he had a new e-mail open and the keyboard pulled up, he handed it over to let her peck out letters in painful, untrained slow motion.

That left him and Laura sharing a look, rueful on her side. It damped Eric's frustration a little to see her acknowledge how likely this was to be false hope. "Maybe there's information you don't realize you know that could help us." He'd almost said "actually help us," but Key wasn't listening anyway. "Your mother told you not to get too close to Breath, correct?"

"And the fan." Laura brightened fractionally at being able to offer something concrete. As soon as she said it, Eric wondered why he hadn't made the connection before. She'd set the fan up so she was downwind, keeping her air out of Breath's reach. Clever. "Scribe Map, scatter Hound, blind Lantern, bind Key, and blow Breath." Laura gave it a lilting rhythm, like a children's chant.

"To zone us out," Key said, low. She looked up from the phone, as drawn by the information as Laura was in giving it. So, so much pain from ignorance to be found around the powers, Eric reflected.

"Mom called it pure state." Laura shrugged, half smiled. "I don't have it at my fingertips, but I could pull together what little I know about my maternal relatives, if you want, send it to you in a few days. If you have an equation, maybe you could work from there."

"Thank you." Eric supposed he was somewhat eager himself to find Lantern and put some of his burden on other shoulders, because he rattled off his e-mail too quickly and had to wait for Laura to get her phone out before he repeated it more slowly.

"If she doesn't answer us before then. Here, you do this."

Key thrust Eric's phone back at him. "I'm terrible at typing."

Eric accepted it, but saved the e-mail as a draft without reading it yet. "Let me get Laura's contact info as well, first." He entered both her e-mail and phone number as she gave them.

And now something he absolutely didn't want to forget. "Ariadne . . . " He tried to think of a phrasing that didn't sound overdramatic, to make Laura discount the very real threat. "Got someone to make a virus keyed to your DNA so she could find Lantern among the sick. I'll try to call if you're in immediate danger, but for the near future, you might want to avoid crowds, wash your hands, and run to the hospital if you feel even a hint of flu."

Laura's eyebrows rose, but she absorbed that without any particular resistance. "Suppose Mom bought me a couple quiet decades," she said. "Not to be sneezed at." Near the end, her tone did turn bitter, but Eric didn't think it was directed at him.

Eric returned Key's draft to the screen, but ended up lowering the phone as he prodded his overtired mind. Was he forgetting anything? There was something else they didn't know enough about. "Did your mother ever mention the gods?" Key's impatience pushed her up onto her toes, but she confined herself to a grumble under her breath and didn't otherwise interfere.

Laura exhaled on a note that never matured into a laugh. "In a proverb sort of way. Never make a deal with them, you'll always come off the worse. Even if there are no hidden terms, they rarely have anything to offer that's worth what they'll ask of you. She didn't tell me to watch out for them like she did the powers, though. She seemed to think they weren't interested enough in her to bother to show up."

Eric nodded. "Is there anything else you can think of,

about your mother's powers? How she used them, or what she thought about any of the rest of . . . us?"

Another shake of Laura's head, even as she spoke. "I was an adult when she . . . left, but she told me less as I got older. When I was a child, it was easy to . . . accept the story of it, let it flow over me. Breath was evil; the rest of the characters were imprisoned. I wish I had nuance to offer you. I know that's what you want."

"You gave us something to try, at least. Thank you." Key burst out of the door, clipping off the end of her thanks, perhaps correctly predicting that Eric would return to the e-mail draft once they were done talking and outside.

Eric lingered, feeling something more was needed, but having no smooth social ritual he could make fit. "If she does reply, do you want us to ask her to contact you, when this has all shaken out?"

Laura grimaced. "Let me think about that and get back to you." She didn't seem to know how to finish the encounter either, so they nodded to each other, and Eric waded through the dog's trails to let himself out. At least one of Ariadne's possible victims had been warned, but now they needed to come up with a way to save the rest.

19

The stone door blocking the cave swung wide, and revealed great dunes of sand within. When they walked among them, a sultan's treasure revealed itself, great jewels twinkling among the grains. But the five searchers were not tempted, and touched nothing but sand with the soles of their boots.

—Traditional folktale, first recorded tenth century

Twilight was falling as they reached a greater density of buildings that Eric called the outskirts of Portland, and by the time they'd bought takeout and found a house for sale that fit their specifications, it was fully dark. She'd thought Eric believed they had no chance with Lantern's e-mail, especially when, after correcting her typos, all he added to her probably slightly incoherent description of their situation and impassioned plea for assistance was, *Key needs you. —Hound.* But when they'd brought in their supplies, she caught him sending the house's address to the same e-mail, so he must believe at least a little. Hope just a little, as Key did. Though she hoped less, the longer they went without a reply to the original message. How often did Lantern check that e-mail, even if she did maintain it?

The house was much more like the ones at home, newer, and beigely personality-less without the furniture and possessions real owners would have added. The beige carpet was a flattish, nubbly kind that was very cushioned under bare feet, though, which was nice, given that in the bedroom they'd chosen for its blinds and obstructed windows, they could sit on either it or the sleeping bags on the empty air mattress to eat.

Eric showed every sign of wanting to finish eating in morose silence before they started their planning session, but Key didn't let him. "I know without you saying it that you think we should act like Lantern isn't going to reply very quickly, if at all. And doing something to stop the virus is too urgent to wait. Do we have to go back to the lab to steal the samples at night? Clearly we can't go tonight, and that means we'd have to wait a whole day."

"Night means we're not trying to dodge a whole lab full of employees who know we don't belong." Eric lifted the takeout container to catch juice from salsa dripping out of his steak taco as he took a bite, chewed, then sighed. "I think this needs to be said. Why shouldn't we try to take care of Ariadne directly? Her security's always been focused on her properties and her possessions—" He gave Key a thin smile without meeting her eyes, probably trying to make that more of a joke than a sharp truth. "Than on her person. It wouldn't be impossible to shoot her from beyond the range of her powers."

Key stared at him. How could he possibly suggest—? "But then when she's reborn, she's still after us, still able to go collect and release the virus, only we don't know what she looks like! How does that help us stay away from her, or stop her doing anything?"

"We'd probably have been arrested for murder by then anyway. Shooting's not like an untraceable powers death." Eric finally looked at her properly.

Key supposed she was too shocked to listen to Eric's words at first, because it was only when she registered his apologetic expression that she reviewed them in her mind. He'd been playing devil's advocate. "It wouldn't help anything," she asserted, firmly, and he nodded.

"Honestly, I think you're right about destroying the samples. It would be nice to do it from outside, but I'm sure their fire-suppression system is state of the art, and I don't know about you, but I don't have access to explosives or the skill to make my own." Eric's hands lowered, food forgotten. The effort for him to plan in his current exhausted state was visible. Maybe he'd been right to try to finish eating first, Key realized guiltily.

"Plus, you can never be sure no one's in the building to get hurt. Our best course might be to try to outrun the alarms, after all." Eric frowned into intermediate distance.

Key nudged one of his hands up so he bit into his taco again. "I was thinking about the guards. You'd be able to see how many there were, what their routes were, wouldn't you? Do they really have set routes, like on TV? At home—at the compound, they mostly followed us, or guarded the gate."

"Not quite that set, but they often have approximate rounds. I could definitely do something with that." Eric's concentration eased up enough that he kept on eating, and Key went back to her own food, flushed a little with pride that she'd come up with a usable idea. "We could talk our way in during the day tomorrow, get a look at where the locked doors are, and where the security guard routes pass. Then we'll be better able to plan to actually go in tomorrow night."

"Good!" Key sat up straighter in anticipation, until she caught Eric giving her a dry look. All right, her enthusiasm probably was naive, but it felt so good to be not only out of Ariadne's control, but actively thwarting her. "Ariadne would never expect me to be able to do something like this."

"Embark on a life of crime?" Eric relaxed another few degrees, even smiling to underscore his humor.

Key finished off her taco and started licking her fingers. "Work against her, I mean. I doubt she's ever considered that Map or I could stop her from doing something. We're just her possessions, like you said."

"I wonder why." Eric finished his last taco and licked his fingers as well, more efficiently. "Why is she so obsessed with controlling all of you guys? Yes, she stepped up her search for Lantern and launched the virus plan when she was threatened by the gods, but Lantern's suicide was long before that. Ariadne was looking for her back then, just not as hard."

Key gave in and actually used a napkin, so her hands would be safe to clasp around her knees when she drew them up. "Supposedly it was her job to find us and take care of us because we were reborn into children and she was already an adult. But if she put us there . . . " Whichever way she tried to turn the idea, she still couldn't come to terms with it.

"I suppose she *was* protecting you," Eric muttered, gaze a point up near the ceiling. "For a given value of 'protection.' I mean, why else be so Victorian schoolmistress about your lives? If she just wants you guys locked up, targeting for her, it would make much more sense to give you whatever you wanted to keep you content. But until recently she wasn't making you target, and she didn't allow you any vices to pass the time."

"I read a series of books about some British kids in a boarding school when I was a kid. Like, set historically. It felt really familiar. I think Hank must have 'forgotten' to include them on some kind of list when he got them from the library, though, because nothing set in boarding schools showed up after that." Key looked at her knees, and didn't mention the notebook filled with her creative and unique story with an identical plot but different names. Real names, of course, changing every time her taste in what her real name should have been did. Which was often. "Maybe powers are supposed to teach each other when one's an adult, and another's a child, but she doesn't know how to do it properly."

"Or the last time she passed to someone, the memories drove her completely nuts and she's clinging to a half-remembered sense of what to do." Eric's laugh lacked real humor. "Not that I'd have called her anything but a sociopath. Who the fuck knows, though."

Key shifted her knees down, impulse to lean over and comfort Eric after the "going nuts" comment fizzling out when she

couldn't quite figure out how. After all, she did want him to remember, and she didn't think he'd go crazy when all the powers
had passed successfully many times before.

In any case, he took a deep breath, forced his shoulders
down, and picked up the next taco. "It doesn't really matter,
anyway. Tomorrow evening, we'll do the recon, and get the virus away from her so she can't do any more damage for the
moment. Then we can look for Lantern properly."

Key picked up a square of pepper from her own puddle of
leaked salsa in the bottom of the takeout box and ate it absently. "You can practice differentiating trails around here tonight,
too." She didn't say anything about remembering, but maybe
she didn't say it a bit too hard, because Eric gave her a sardonic
look.

"Any memories I get, I'll tell you about immediately." He
fussed around with getting rice and beans from the shared container of them for a few moments. "Do you know what all the
things were in that list Laura recited, for pure states? I didn't
bother making her clarify, because you seemed to."

"Well, I know us three, and Lantern and Breath seemed
pretty straightforward." Key returned to her own tacos. "It's always seemed to me to be kind of . . . either overwhelming us
with too much information to process, or with an impossible
task, so we zone out trying. I mean, you know mine." It felt
weird for a moment, to bluntly state her vulnerability, but she
pushed the feeling aside. "Bind with something impossible to
unlock. Map, I can see how you wouldn't get that one immediately from scribing. You draw a map on his skin. And scatter—" Eric leaned forward, apparently without realizing it.

Key freed a hand to flick all her fingers outward. "A bunch of chaotic trails all at once, in a small space. The old Hound, if he got caught in a flock of birds, he'd freeze up completely, and you had to drag him free."

"I won't schedule any trips to Grand Central Station in the near future, then." Eric leaned back and kept eating as though pretending he hadn't ever been interested. "So if something goes wrong and we run into her, we just have to draw Ariadne outside and hope it's a windy day." His sarcasm ended up sounding awfully bitter.

Key nodded, but talking about facing Ariadne directly made her think of the old Hound. She saw him again, lying on the floor of cabin, and her throat closed up. "Once we've found Lantern, we'll be able to face her better."

"You're right. No sense borrowing trouble," Eric said, his smile of reassurance thin but present. He didn't pester her further when she got up and went to find her romance novel. Now they had their plan, she wanted to read over the last of dinner and distract herself from feeling about the old Hound, not talk about Ariadne more.

The two of them shared the bed that night without anything more interesting happening, and ended up time shifted again. Key vaguely sensed that Eric was restless for a long time before he worked up the exhaustion to sleep. She hoped his restlessness was not because he was cold, because when she woke before him, she was wrapped in her sleeping bag as well as half of his. She straightened his over him before she sneaked off for breakfast. He needed the rest for tonight more than they needed to get on the road to the lab immediately.

The orange she selected had an extra-thick skin, so Key had to dig in her nails and really pry to get it even started. As she peeled, she thought about Laura. In retrospect, accusing her of being Lantern seemed especially stupid. Why would Lantern be hiding from them? But she'd been so *angry* at Laura, anger she was only now starting to realize had been from another cause.

Laura had gotten to have Lantern as her mother for half her life. It didn't feel fair, way down in the small part of Key that didn't care that she knew better than that. Key had wanted someone like that so badly—*needed* someone like that as a child, and all she had was a memory of a memory, as with everything else.

The light tap on the kitchen window about stopped Key's heart. She dropped to the floor beside the counter, so no one could see her through the window, but then she couldn't see who it was either. She hadn't turned on any lights this morning, but the kitchen didn't have blinds on the small window over the sink, just a dowel, probably meant to hold some miniature curtain.

The tap didn't come again, and Key's brain ground into motion. Why would Ariadne tap politely on the window? Why would anyone? Wouldn't they knock on the door or just kick it down if they were cops and here to arrest her and Eric for trespassing? Maybe it had been a branch, or a bird.

She gripped the edge of the counter and drew herself up until she could see out. Map lifted his fingertips in a sardonic wave.

Key thumped back to her knees on the floor. Scheisse. How was Map here? Was Ariadne with him? She'd have thought if Map was feeding her information, he would have told her and stepped back, letting Ariadne arrive first. By having the guards kick down the door, of course. But whatever his motives, if Map had found them, the damage was done. What good would making him stand outside do?

Realizing her only other options were to cower on the floor or walk around like he wasn't there until he went away decided Key. She pushed to her feet and went to the back door. *Unlocked.* When she opened it, he walked up, completely unhurried, hands in the pockets of his immaculate dark jeans. He was alone as far as she could see. The only false note that distinguished this from an arrival at her house on a normal day was the way his black curls were smushed on one side as though he'd slept on them and not redone his product.

"Don't look so damn smug." Key almost slammed the door behind him, but that might wake Eric, and boy, did she not want to deal with both men at once right now. She shut it carefully instead. *Locked.* "How did you find us?"

"Hank's got some undiscovered art talent." Map pulled a folded square of plain paper from his waistcoat pocket and offered it. Key supposed it was a sign of trust or a peace offering or something Eric would have been able to analyze more precisely. That didn't stop her tearing it in half before she even looked at it. She fitted the halves back together to examine herself, pen lines catching the darkness of her hair better than Lantern's pencil sketch had.

She tore it again into quarters and dropped the pieces on the counter. "And is Her Majesty right behind you?"

"Is your boyfriend upstairs sleeping off all your fun?" Map blocked where she feinted a punch at his shoulder, but missed the real one to his stomach. They hadn't scuffled properly since they were both children, but the old skills came right back. She hadn't hit that hard, but he still had to wheeze for a moment, and he dropped the sardonic act.

"Key, I was worried about you. She might have found you. Killed you too." Map crossed his arms over his stomach and didn't move them until he'd said his piece and she didn't strike again.

"You're the one who directed us to a house full of her cameras!" Key left her hands clenched. Looking at Map's face, the distrust she'd talked herself into was slipping away. This was *Map*. He wouldn't have directed them into Ariadne's power, even if he hadn't wanted to leave home.

"I was a child last time I was there, Key." Map spread his hands. "Maybe I should have expected it, but even if you have cameras installed, why would you be watching the feeds from an empty house? Unless you're as paranoid as Her, apparently. I've done nothing to help Her, all right?" He waited until she nodded reluctantly at the floor, then blew out a breath. His ironic tone returned. "Your boyfriend *is* here, isn't he?"

"Eric helped me escape. Anything else he is to me is none of your business." It hit Key, like a return blow to her own stomach, that Map didn't know that Eric was Hound. And even if she thought maybe she could still trust him, she couldn't tell him. About Eric being Hound, or their plans to destroy Ariadne's virus.

"All right." Map initiated the hug, and she grabbed him tightly, hands bunching the fabric at the back of his waistcoat. "You got some upsetting news yesterday. Is that related so I can't ask about it either?"

He must have been targeting her through the drawing at the moment when they'd found out about the virus. Or when she'd been so envious of Laura having had Lantern at all. Only one of those things was safe to tell him about. "Our lead on Lantern didn't give us anything solid."

Map rested his cheek on her hair. "I'm sorry." She snorted, and his chest vibrated in an awkward laugh. "No, I am. We're committed to this now. I'm not going back to Her, and letting Her make me hurt you. When She killed Hound, I ran for it, same as you and Eric. But now we can work together, find Hound and Lantern both."

"And ditch Eric?" Key said. It came out more ironic than she'd intended. If only Map knew. "I don't know what it was like for you getting down here, but I've been leaning pretty heavily on his knowledge of the outside. He was trying to explain to me last night, how you tip at restaurants, but not if you pick up the food, but you do if they deliver it to you—" Key waved her hand. "It's impossible to keep track."

Map tensed. "It's not *that* hard to figure out. I'm sure we'll be fine, with a little practice."

Key pulled away to check his face. "I bet you drove straight down here, didn't you? You haven't even bought anything in a real store." She twisted to check on her half-peeled orange. The bag of bagels they'd bought was still unopened. "You must be starving."

"I . . . " Map seemed to be struggling with his dignity, then gave in. "Hitchhiked home to get that drawing, and Hank let me steal some sandwiches as well as borrow a car. I wouldn't say no to breakfast, though."

Water sounded somewhere above them and Map froze. Key felt a little tense herself. Time to play mediator, now Eric was awake. "Map, just let me—"

Map put a finger to his lips. "Get rid of him," he whispered, then faded back into the den as Eric's footsteps came down the stairs and reached the hallway to the kitchen.

"Key?" Eric stopped the moment he saw the back door, then strode forward to verify the trail, Key supposed. She expected him to bark at her for letting Map in, and readied her defense, but he only glanced at her and grimaced in resignation. "Map! Get out here."

"How the hell did you know?" Map glared immediately at Key when he appeared in the doorway to the den. She held up her hands. She hadn't mimed anything. This was Map's own fault.

Eric, presumably unconsciously, traced his trail to him. It was straightforward enough, except it turned aside briefly in front of Key, and Eric took a whole step in the wrong direction before he caught himself. He tried to make up for it by striding the last few feet across the kitchen more quickly, but Map's eyes widened. He'd seen.

"No." He drew the syllable out in pure disbelief. "You're kidding me. You have to be freaking kidding me."

Eric's lip lifted in a silent snarl, and he clenched his hands into fists. "I'd have thought you'd be pleased, to have information to run back to Ariadne with. Two birds for her stone."

"No one's working with Ariadne. All right?" Key interposed herself between the men and shouted when they didn't seem to pay attention. "No one!"

Eric growled and turned away. He noticed the torn drawing on the counter, picked up one quarter, then tossed it down in disgust. "You draw this?"

"Map can't draw for himself. It doesn't work that way." As sick as Key had been of talking about powers last night, she was glad of it now. Maybe they could work their way back to civility. "You can't see your own trail."

"You really are Hound?" Map's tone of—was it wonder?—brought Key around. While she hadn't been looking at him, his face had transformed, lighting up. A smile broke, spread, and he stepped around Key, grasped Eric's shoulders, and kissed him.

20

The great mead-hall through which they passed was empty, benches tumbled, beakers spilled, but long before the youngest of the gods had passed there. Her footprints passed through the dust of great heroes long dead.

—Traditional epic story, ninth century

The moment Eric processed what Map intended—too late to stop him, because he could hardly believe it until it was actually happening—he brought up his hands, but then the memories had him.

Hound pulled back from the kiss. She wasn't sure—but Map was smiling, with a knowing, pleased quality that told her she'd been right to wait. He'd not only grown into himself, but found a normal girl to learn himself for the first time in this body. "You waited long enough," he said, grinning, and slid his hands along the sides of her neck, setting the many heavy hoops of her earrings swinging.

"You passed to a boy, not a man." Hound laughed, because this was her Map back with her, the four years apart while he came of age falling away as if they had never been. She drank in the warm, earth color of his skin, as if he'd been newly molded by the gods for her, and traced the unfamiliar shape of his full lips with her own and her tongue. "Even *I* was taller than you, remember?"

Map laughed, and yanked her to him, strong hands on her waist. She wasn't taller now, and he bent his head to join a new kiss properly.

The kiss was different than any Eric had experienced before as himself, the bristle of Map's neatly trimmed beard under a hand that had come up automatically to Map's jaw. But just as passionate and heady as any he could remember without magical assistance, deep and—

Eric planted his hands on Map's chest and shoved. No! He was Eric, no matter what memories took over his mind, and he was straight. He was not *dealing* with this right now.

Map remained where he'd been shoved, confusion stealing over his expression. "Hound—"

"Don't touch me!" Eric found his hands clenching, and he took a step backward instead. He solved problems with words, not violence. That was part of being Eric as well. "I'm not gay—"

Map backed up a corresponding step, hands lifted soothingly. Eric found the assumption in his expression that a little soothing would be all it took absolutely infuriating. "I'm not either. I'm sorry. I thought you would have remembered. I never should have done that without warning. I just didn't think. I've waited so long . . . "

"How much do you remember yourself that you've never told me, Map?" Key's voice tried to layer humor on top of frustration of her own, only half effective. "You and Hound . . . ?"

"What, you waited and stayed away from a Hound without enough free will to consent?" A snarl leaked into Eric's voice. "Let's arrange a parade! Map wins a gold star for basic-fucking-morality."

Then he saw the barb hit home in both Map's and Key's faces, and instantly regretted it. What the hell was he doing? He'd been propositioned by gay men before—though admittedly not kissed without warning—but he'd been able to be tactful with them. But everything was so tangled up with the memories and his identity, now. "I'm sorry. You didn't deserve that."

Map shook off his shock faster than Key, who'd taken his hand and was still staring at Eric with wide eyes. Map's gaze searched his face more carefully. "*Do* you remember?"

Eric clenched his jaw. "It doesn't matter. You're in love with Hound, not me."

"You remember." Map's face lit up at "love," and Eric cursed his choice of word. "Take all the time you need. I won't push."

"You're not listening." Eric jerked his hand in a slicing gesture, but Map didn't seem to notice that either. "I don't need time. I'm more than Hound; I'm Eric, and I'm straight."

Nothing seemed to rock Map's certainty now. "I told you, so am I. But this kind of love, the love of so many lives before, transcends all that. But I've waited this long; I don't mind waiting a little longer." Under the certainty flickered desperate longing. Eric noticed it when Key's face flooded with sympathy.

She strengthened her support with a hand on Map's wrist over their clasped hands. "You could have told me." She winced. "I mean, yes, I wish you hadn't kept that from me, but that's not what I mean. I wish you'd told me so you didn't have go through that . . . wanting, alone, you know? We're in this together."

Map gently disentangled his hand and shook his head at Key. "It's all right now."

"No, Map." Maybe if Eric repeated the man's name with enough emphasis, he'd start to pay attention. "It's not a matter of remembering or not. It's never going to happen. Period. Full stop."

"It's not a matter of remembering here." Map tapped his temple. "It's a matter of feeling it here." He settled a hand over his heart. Of course he did. Eric's performer instincts muttered that it was all a bit too much, but of course it would be, if Map had had all that time to construct a grand love affair in his mind. Eric could see honest intensity beneath.

Eric didn't see what else he could say to make Map understand. The grinding frustration of it—he always found another approach to try, when it came to convincing someone—combined with annoyance at the brush of smugness to Map's phrasing, trembled on the edge of real rage. They were both trapped in their situations, he and Map. Was Map inherently more worthy of sympathy? Any minute, Eric would give in and say something he really regretted.

Fortunately someone knocked at the front door in the moment of charged silence. Or perhaps that was unfortunately, depending on who it was. An angry real estate agent, looking for the lock box? He presumed Ariadne wouldn't bother knocking.

Eric froze, grabbed Key's wrist when she moved to answer. "If whoever it is sees movement through the windows, they could call the police to report squatters," he said, low.

A voice, heavily muffled on the other side of the door. "Key? Hound?"

"Lantern!" Key jerked away from Eric, conclusion apparently achieved in one Superman-worthy leap while Eric traced it more carefully. Who else would have this address, know to call them that? They were going to find out, anyway. He followed on Key's heels, Map close behind him.

The person on the other side of the door looked to be in her—his?—their, anyway, midthirties. They had their hands in their pockets, waiting for an answer with every evidence of patience and relaxation. They wore skinny jeans and a baggy flannel, but veered away from hipster at the last second by lacking facial hair, clunky glasses, or a knit cap over their short, blond hair. "Key! You've grown so much," they said, brows rising.

"You're here!" Key's laugh of joy laced itself into the rest of her speech as well. She threw her arms around Lantern—Eric presumed it had to be Lantern—and clung for a beat. "You're so different. Are you a man or a woman?"

"Key, don't—" Eric swallowed the rest of his words. He shouldn't really say anything when the same question was at the forefront of his own mind. If he warned her about being rude, he couldn't tell her what she should have said instead.

"Male pronouns are fine. That's what my physiology says this time around, but spend enough time as both, the differences between stop seeming nearly so stark as people make them out to be." Lantern shrugged. "Shall we move off the doorstep?" He shifted Key to his side and slung an arm around her shoulders to escort her in. Eric shut the door for them.

"Now your body language firms up," Lantern said with a laugh as he looked Eric's stance up and down. "Once you know you're relating to a man." Eric winced, but Lantern waved it away before Eric could form an apology. "Just giving you shit."

Lantern held out his other arm in invitation to Map, who accepted without hesitation. "And look at you too, Map. Both of you, adults."

Eric rocked a step back as subtly as he could. To give them privacy for their reunion, or to make sure he wasn't pulled into it as Hound? He supposed Key and Map hadn't met this Lantern any more than this Lantern had met this Hound, so Eric wasn't truly the odd one out. But Lantern looked to have incorporated his power into his identity—and why not, he'd had nearly twenty years of grace—in a way that Eric wasn't sure he ever would, or wanted to. Lantern must have been in his teens when the power passed to him, perhaps that made the process easier than for someone Eric's age.

"And Hound." Lantern offered him a smile Eric looked away from. "Sometime after I last saw the others, Breath made you pure state, didn't she? When did you pass? Is that how you all got out?"

"Something like that." Eric supposed that story would have to be told, but maybe one of the others could tell it instead of him.

Key squeezed her arms tightly for a second longer, tucking her cheek against Lantern's shoulder, then pulled away. She held herself straight, surprisingly focused now. "We need your help so she doesn't just drag us back, though. Or hurt anyone trying."

Lantern pressed a fraternal kiss into Map's hair, then let him go too. "We can leave immediately. Now we're together, there's no way for her to track us, so we'll be safe until loneliness brings Breath to her senses."

And nothing in this life was ever that simple. Find Lantern, find all the solutions to their problems. Right. He'd been listening to Key too much, though he supposed Key had achieved at least part of what she wanted, in embracing a revered figure from her childhood. "Didn't you read the e-mail? She's planning to release a virus that will target anyone genetically related to you—while it's still lethal. Who knows how many people could die? We have to stop her."

Lantern laced fingers through his hair at one temple, losing his ease for the first time since he'd arrived. "Stop her how? The powers of the Hand don't move against each other, Hound. We work together. That's how we're made."

Helpful as usual, Map looked thoughtful and nodded, but Key stepped into the breach while Eric was still gaping at Lantern and voiced his exact thoughts before he could assemble them. "And what exactly has Ariadne been doing all this time, imprisoning us, denying us our memories, breathing us into children when she feels like it?"

"Breath . . . " Lantern growled under his breath, frustration in his expression composed more of confusion than anger. "She's gone astray, but before now, she's always had at least one of us under her control. Now we're together, none of us pure state, we can talk some sense into her. United is how we're meant to be."

"You think she'll hesitate to kill any one of us when we get into her range?" Eric tapped his temple. "Maybe I'm glad I've been able to keep the memories at bay, if the past blocks out all the hard truths of the present. Killing her seems likely to only make things worse, yes, but there's a whole hell of a lot of territory between 'kill her' and 'run for it' that gets this virus out of her hands and keeps others from dying!"

"Hound." Lantern held out his hands to him. "Breath has been playing this game for centuries. She's not going to start killing indiscriminately in search of us now."

Eric crossed his arms over his chest to emphasize his repudiation of Lantern's gesture. "Maybe she has, but now apparently the gods are in the mix. She wants us together to oppose them, and so far as I can tell, she's getting increasingly desperate." Strange as it was to think of Ariadne, smiling her ice-water-in-her-veins smile in his memory, as desperate. "Key and I had a two-person plan, and if she's willing, I'm still going to go through with it, with or without your help."

Key nodded and crossed her arms too, though the motion turned more to hugging herself at the end. "I agree with him." Hurt seeped into her face. "Is that why you never came back, Lantern? Doing nothing to stop her had worked so well for the past however long—centuries, apparently—that you decided to do more nothing?" Tears rose at the bottom of her eyes, but didn't break free. "The child without her memories you left behind didn't have the luxury of that perspective."

"Key." Lantern's face crumpled and he pulled her into another hug, with her crossed arms sandwiched between them. "When I passed, it was to someone young enough I couldn't do much on my own, but I should have tried harder. I can't change that, but we can still go now, all of us, and we never need to be separated again."

"That's right. Hound, come with us." Map held out his hands, the gesture similar on the surface to the one Lantern had recently made, but Eric could sense the undercurrents beneath. Go with them and give in to Map's version of the sharp longing to belong Key had displayed with her obsession with Lantern and memories. Map's version, that focused instead on the remembered love between the two of them.

Go with them, give in, and lose a little bit more Eric each step of the way.

But that wasn't the point. He hoped if giving in to Hound stopped Ariadne, he'd do that instead, but in this case, it most certainly did not. He took out his phone, unlocked it, and tossed it into Map's hands. Fortunately, Map caught it instinctively. "Leave your number, would you, Lantern? So we can get hold of you two after we've dealt with the virus." It seemed a safe assumption that Map was taking Lantern up on his offer, though it hadn't been explicitly stated.

Eric jogged up the stairs, leaving Key to make her farewells. She surprised him, though, because after the briefest of murmured good-byes, her footsteps followed his up the stairs. Not long after, the front door opened and shut. Lantern had left them no worse off, at least, Eric supposed.

21

Hound led the other four searchers past grand staircases, past chandeliers and tapestries, to the cellars of the castle. There, on the steps to the deep stone below, a single glass slipper. The youngest of the gods, always hurrying on her way to adventure, had lost it there.

—Traditional folktale, first recorded early eighteenth century

Key wasted a lot of hot water in the shower after hurriedly finishing her interrupted breakfast, passing time to give Eric space and also thinking her own thoughts. Of course Lantern wouldn't be the same as she'd built him up in her mind, based on a child's logic. And Key could still have asked for him to share some of his memories before he left, but the fact that he had chosen to leave, yes, it did hurt, in a chest tightening to not quite allow enough air way. He'd left her and Map years ago, left Laura too, whatever his good reasons, and now he still had reasons—though they seemed pretty lame to Key—and was still leaving. Key abruptly felt a surge of fellow feeling with Laura.

So she and Eric would do this, destroy the virus, then she would call Lantern, and they could talk about memories for as long as Lantern would put up with it. That was a bright spot, at least; after feeling his arms around her, Key had no doubt he'd indulge her. It had been like greeting another adoptive brother, as Map was. Key had waited long enough for memories already; she could wait a little longer.

Her fingers were getting pruney, even in the shower, which was an accomplishment, so Key finally shut off the water. She didn't even think when she toweled off, hung up the towel to dry, and walked into the bedroom where she'd dumped her clothes on the airbed. The guards had always stayed out of her room when they'd heard the water running.

But this was Eric's room at the moment too, and he froze in the doorway when she walked in. Key flushed and at least crossed her arms. Of all the times—he must think the worst of her motives. "I'm not trying to suggest anything!" She hurried to get the words out before he stormed away, angry and hurt again. "I'm sure after that kiss, you don't want to even think about—"

Eric pressed his fingertips to his temples. "I don't know *what* to think, no. And you? How would you feel in my place, about all this fated-love stuff?"

Key was pretty sure she already knew the answer to that, but she gave it careful consideration for a second or two anyway, making sure to choose the right words. "I know about wanting a connection to how our lives as powers used to be, but I also get not wanting to just be what the memories say you are. All I have is this life, who I am without memories." She lifted one hand and pressed it, spread wide, just under her throat. "And I have to believe that's just as good."

"Thanks." Eric crossed his arms too and leaned against the door frame with an appearance of ease that was almost believable. "Anyway, at the moment, I'd love to indulge in some straightforward sex, but I can't really face being tied up right now."

There was another layer there, and Key looked his face over carefully and tried to read it. He wanted to be Eric, not Hound, in bed. That was easy enough to guess after their last failed attempt at sex, without today's confrontation. She figured it was more than just not sleeping with Hound he wanted, though. What had he said? *I'm Eric, I'm straight.* So maybe he wanted to be stereotypically masculine, in control.

"Tying up isn't necessary." Key let her arms fall and waited for him. He prowled closer, seemingly indulging his curiosity and confusion rather than initiating anything. She edged both of them back a little, until they were nearly up against the wall the bedroom shared with the bathroom. "I want you, Eric."

He pressed closer and when she smiled encouragement, she felt the tipping point when he eagerly accepted what she'd offered. His arms fenced her on either side, and he pushed her into the wall with his kiss, his whole body. Key had just room to get one hand down, fingers between her legs, and that was just about perfect.

He wasn't tied up now, but he could have been. Chains. A collar around his neck and he'd been in her control, but the chain to his collar had been too long and he'd lunged, and now he had her, trapped against the wall. If he had been actually chained up, she'd have begged him to let her go and not meant it, but now she just murmured his name, rising intonation as he kissed, bit at the side of her neck. "Eric."

And she'd have felt the lock at his neck, and he'd have ordered her to release it, like he wasn't the one chained up. And she'd have held that grip on the lock close, close until her grinding, driving, climbing need overcame it and she popped the lock and the collar fell away and he grinned at her.

Eric tugged her, pulled them away from the wall together, and she tumbled to the bed, laughing, as he pulled off his clothes, dug out a condom. When he was ready, she pulled him down onto her, into her, one gentle entry to find the angle before he was thrusting roughly, insistent, no pause because she was already dripping wet. His weight on her, holding her close, down, and she was climbing, thinking of popped locks and how at this moment he was hers, chained or not.

And she was his because he'd picked her. Eric, not Hound.

When they'd packed what little there was to pack, they ended up back in the kitchen for a second breakfast—or maybe brunch—consisting of the leftovers they didn't want to have to carry with them. It reminded Key a lot of home, where guards were always lurking, but not always available to be chattered at. Eric was being pretty taciturn, and she wasn't sure what subjects would be safe. They'd already said all that could be said about stealing the virus, before they scouted the lab, and she didn't particularly feel like dwelling on the opportunity she'd had to let walk out with Lantern.

The morning's sun had turned intermittent, flickering in and out through the windows, running from scudding clouds they couldn't see. Key wished the house had TV, since she generally turned that on when a guard lurked too badly. Even if some of their attention wasn't drawn off her, she could watch TV and not care.

The back door shuddered with a solid bang. Then a thud on the next strike as the wood splintered, soaking up some of the noise. Men appeared in the doorway, silent and focused.

Key didn't look at individual faces, but she knew the uniform intimately. Part of her tried to freeze, too programmed to do what the guards from home told her. They never hurt her, or Map, or Hound, but the guards could immobilize or zone any of them so easily. You couldn't do a thing about it.

But now she could. Key ran. Eric was inside the kitchen counter, corralled on three sides by counter and walls, but she was outside the counter and freer. She sprinted for the archway to the front room, but one guard was right behind her. He grabbed her arm, dragged her in, got an arm across her body from behind.

"Hudson. You're on Davis." Hank's voice, but Key couldn't see him in the chaos. How many guards were there? Another was coming around to join the one who had her, and they'd have her zoned out in a minute. She'd roughhoused with Map often enough as kids; she just needed to remind herself to use those skills. She went limp, all dead weight, and her guard couldn't shift his grip before she was free. New direction to run now, stumbling to her feet as she launched herself that way. Hank was near the back door, having arrived last, but not directly in front of it. If she was just fast enough, she could brush past—

Someone's foot tangled with her stride, whose she didn't even know, and she tumbled. A hand under one armpit got her up, and this time the guard's grip went to her arm and twisted it behind her back, tight and then tighter. Ow, ow, ow—Key paused in her struggles because she simply had to from the sheer physical shock of the pain.

Matt Hudson—she'd probably recognize everyone, if she looked hard enough—had his gun out, trained on Eric as Matt stepped carefully around the counter. Eric stood still. Blankly still, Key noted with panic. Scheisse. She must have helped scatter him, running one direction then another in the small space with three, four other people. Two guards holding her, Matt on Eric, and Hank watching everything with his most closed expression.

"Eric!" She screamed it, again. If he didn't snap out of it, they might even shoot him. One of the men on her shoved her into walking. She tried kicking out, the moment her arm wasn't twisted quite so badly, but the second guy efficiently scooped up her ankles until the two of them were carrying her suspended. She twisted, writhed, but this was what her instincts had known from the start: she was simply physically outnumbered. And there was nothing here to unlock.

22

All was darkness, in the tomb, and the searchers could not go on for fear the floor would fall away beneath them. The fourth searcher said, "I will bring us light," and Lantern filled the tunnel with a warm glow. The searchers saw that no treasures remained in the tomb, only a sarcophagus. The youngest of the gods lay within.

—Story from papyrus fragment, dated to twelfth century BCE

"Eric!" Key's voice. Eric's mind slogged through heavy syrup. He—there was something—

There was a man in a security guard uniform beside him, left hand going to Eric's shoulder as he holstered his weapon with the right. Getting ready to grab a zip tie, Eric presumed. Since he was standing here as responsively as a mannequin, no threat. By instinct, he stayed that way for now. Almost faster than conscious thought, Eric assessed what he could get to. There, on the side of the man's belt, a Taser.

All right. Eric didn't bother with any other distraction and relied on speed to lift the Taser and shove it into the guard's side. When the man gasped, convulsed, Eric stepped back and fired the Taser properly. The guard grunted and folded, head clunking against the counter edge as he went down. Eric dropped the Taser and grabbed the man's gun, brought it up trained on an empty room.

Eric lowered the gun, still in a braced grip that didn't feel nearly as comfortable as it should have. Too damn long since he was at the range. Where was Key? He didn't dare try to read the snarl of blue trails in front of him again. They must already have her. He ran for the back door, half open with its furry edge of splinters. Why wasn't there any noise? They were in a residential neighborhood; she should be screaming her head off to get the police called. But would she even think of that, having grown up in a compound staffed by people like these very guards?

Trails straightened out in the backyard around to the side gate, and he saw the nose of a car pulled right up on the grass beside the garage, back doors just shutting. Hank stood inside the open driver's door. For a moment, their eyes met, and Eric brought up the gun. "We're leaving. Get her secured," Hank barked, and threw himself into the vehicle. Eric should have—but he couldn't see completely into the back seat at his angle, and he didn't want to shoot anywhere near Key's direction.

And the car peeled out, thrashing the grass to leave two bare strips, and roared away. Eric lowered the gun. Fuck. He jogged down the trail to the street, but he could hardly follow them on foot, all the way to the freeway and probably back to Washington. And he couldn't see the trail while driving . . .

But he was holding a gun in a residential neighborhood. And he'd left the other guard unwatched behind him. Eric whirled, but no one was sneaking up on him. He kept his grip on the gun, ready to raise it at any moment as he jogged inside, but the guard was still out cold. Suddenly worried, Eric crouched to check the man's pulse and breathing, ready for any change in body language that would indicate the man was faking. He seemed legitimately unconscious, a goose egg rising on one temple but no blood. Good enough. He could stay here and wake up or get scraped up by his colleagues without Eric having another death on his conscience.

Eric ejected the gun's magazine and the bullet from the chamber, then dropped the gun itself beside the crumpled guard. More trouble than it was worth, with his rusty training and habit of zoning out. He'd ditch the ammo in a Dumpster somewhere.

He made it as far as the stairs to grab their stuff before taking off, when the reaction set in. He leaned a hand against the wall, foot on the bottom step. No memories about guns pressed in, for whatever reason. Small mercies.

So they'd taken Key. Would they hurt her? It seemed unlikely, after Ariadne had taken care of the powers for years, but then again, she'd seemed willing in person and in memory to start again on new children. He supposed it depended on how much time she felt she had before the gods arrived. The security guards' orders had clearly been to collect them, not dispose of them. Was that simply to get Key into Ariadne's hands so she could transfer Key to another body?

And what was he going to do about it, whatever Ariadne's motives? If he called Lantern for help, would Lantern agree, or just renew his sales pitch for Eric to join them on the run and let Key take care of herself? Eric couldn't face another useless argument, he decided, especially given the delay it would create. The guards still had to get Key back to Ariadne, in another state, but Eric needed all the time he could get to track them. Somehow.

He hoped Ariadne would take some time to make her decision about what to do about Key, too. That had memories behind it, and, defenses gone, Eric took a deep breath and let them come.

Hound heard the wailing of the baby first. That noise was common enough in the city, but they were camped on the plains once more. Alone in camp, no livestock, no humans, just the powers and their tents. The wailing came from behind Breath and Key's tent, and Hound strode to investigate. No recent trails led there other than their own.

Breath cradled the child, black hair pulled free of bindings and tumbling around her shoulders and near the tiny, balled, brown fists. She smiled, misty, lean features softened by a satisfaction Hound associated more with fathers, who had watched the pain of birth, not borne it.

Then Hound saw Key. Her black hair, more delicately waved, was similarly disarranged, flung across the dry, scrubby grass along with one arm. She lay open eyed and far too still. *Their* sort of still. But Breath—Breath could not have—

Hound leaned down, touched Breath's trail. Her love for Key blazed strong as ever, no grief to be found. But it was focused differently, on that baby. "Breath, what did you *do?*"

"She didn't want to live forever with me. I've given her time to reconsider." Breath looked up at Hound, and through her trail, she felt so certain. No hint of the madness in her words.

"You killed Key." Hound could only repeat it. She didn't understand. How could Breath do this?

"I have not. I've only passed her on to another, without stupid games of chance and proximity. I could do it for all of you. That's my gift." Breath twisted her neck in an elegant movement to remove her hair from her face and stepped over to Hound, as if to show off the babe.

The breath twisted away from Hound, a malicious snake in her own chest, one that no longer took orders from her. Run. She had to run from this madness—

More memories crowded in, linking among each other, fractured—*tight chest muscles, fighting for air, Breath's voice, "Hush, Hound, it's all right." Growing quieter—*

—*gasping, choking, his own fingers plucking at his neck,*

*Breath glowering at him, "Why do you always run, all of you?
You don't understand—"*

*"I've found an older child. It will work this time; don't worry."
Breath holding her hand and patting it, while gray stars ate up
her vision—*

Eric sobbed in a breath, a full breath, and forced his body
into movement. He needed to save Key from one more needless
death at Breath's hands. Lantern's relatives, yes, them too, but it
was Key who filled his mind. No matter how big the breaths he
pulled in, his chest still felt crushed under some unseen weight.

He grabbed their bags, made it to the car, pulled out onto
the street, before the desperate energy of those memories left
him and he started shaking worse than before. Crawling along,
he followed the path of Hank's car until they turned onto an
artery. Eric turned with it, hoping he could follow it anyway,
but an SUV came up behind, screeched down to his speed, and
honked at him until he sped up. The trails dispersed and slid
away from him, and he pulled over on the next side street, sobbing breaths returning.

All right. He had to think. Think. Had Ariadne traced their
location using their visit to Diane, despite their precautions?
He needed to check on his sister. He turned off the car's engine
and fumbled out his phone.

She answered on the second ring. "Is everything all right?
Are we safe to be using our own phones?"

"She got Key. I don't think it matters anymore. Are *you* all
right? Did Ariadne come sniffing around?" Eric clenched one
hand around the steering wheel. Think, and keep thinking.

"Everything's been completely quiet around here. Eric,
what does that mean, 'got'? Is Key dead?" Diane's tone thinned

with stress.

"Kidnapped. I suppose she can't really die, anyway. Any of us. Technically." Death or not, it was all in how you thought about it. He suspected Lantern would be on the side of figuring they couldn't die because the powers couldn't, and Breath clearly was too. Ariadne clearly was too. Eric finally realized that it was her face he'd seen in these latest memories, Ariadne's as if she'd been standing before him in the twenty-first century. Maybe he was finally assimilating the memories if his mind was swapping in elements from his knowledge, as it did in dreams.

"So now my brother's immortal? I guess that's . . . comforting." Diane didn't sound particularly comforted.

"Hound is. Eric isn't." So simple, to state it that way. If only he could state the line between Hound and Eric so simply. Which one of those names should he have replaced with "I"? I'm immortal; Eric isn't. Hound is immortal; I'm not.

"Can you rescue Key? Do you need help?"

"I can follow them, except I need to be still to find the trail, and they'll be on the fucking freeway." Frustration reached up and strangled Eric as efficiently as Breath had in the memories. "Why am I so useless? I can hardly walk a hundred yards on my own with this *shit* in my head, without Key holding my hand. Like some kind of crutch." And Map and Lantern would be happy to prop him up in her stead, prop him up and help him walk away and abandon her.

Calm. Think, keep thinking. "You're immortal in no sense, so better you stay clear. I can do this. I just have to figure out . . . how. Breath has her power, but so do I. If I can get to her to face me one on one, no one else needs to get hurt. Me against Breath, until I can release Key."

Eric looked up, finally registering the world enough to note the speed at which the clouds crossed the watery blue of the sky ahead of him. When he looked hard, he found branches tossing at the tops of the taller evergreens suffered to keep growing at the edges of the residential lots. If the wind stuck around, and he drew her outside into it, it would at least help.

"Me against Breath *and* her guards." The moment the thought occurred to him, he spoke it out loud, trying to think it through that way. "I could target them, I suppose, even though I haven't ever done it before. I don't want it to come to that, though. I know Hank, at least. I'll have some purchase if I try to talk him out of the fight."

All right. People. People had angles of approach, buttons to push. He was used to thinking of those. He could do this. "Now I just need to get there. If I could find their turns—pull over at every exit or intersection, I suppose, get my direction. It'll take forever, but it'll get me there."

"Shall I go do the dishes and pop back in later? You seem perfectly capable of holding down both sides of the conversation yourself, so I might as well get some chores done." Diane's humor might have been stretched a little thin, but her warmth was genuine enough.

Eric laughed too, and the sound flushed some of the fog from his thoughts. He didn't need a crutch. He was still enough himself to do what needed to be done. He'd better warn Laura Dixon now, since his and Key's plan to neutralize the virus had been officially preempted. He'd call, then get on the road. "Love you."

"Love you too. Be careful. I don't buy this immortality bullshit." Diane shaped her good-bye from a final laugh, and they closed the call before she could freak out too, perhaps. What must it be like for her, to find out her brother was suddenly in danger from causes that didn't make any sense, and that she probably barely believed?

No worse than being in the danger.

23

*The youngest of the gods lay composed so sweetly
upon the stone bier, skin pale as death. The perfect
bow of her lips, the delicate shells of her ears, all
were drained of the warmth of love and life. Perhaps she had swooned, called out, before fate so
cruelly ripped her future from her.*

—*The Tomb*, 1811

Hank should have zoned Key out, but he hadn't. She couldn't
escape at the moment anyway, wedged between two guards in
the back of the car, legs either tangled with knees high and feet
on the center console, or spread wide with shoes uncomfortably intimate with the guards' in their foot wells.

He'd been the one who zip tied her hands, efficient movements after the guards had set her on her feet, and before they'd

shoved her into the car. But he'd left it loose around her wrists, enough to roll and twist one hand out, then the other; it must be, because she was still aware. She watched slightly familiar freeway scenery scroll by in reverse through spray kicked up by cars even though it wasn't presently raining. They were heading back up north to Washington, but she doubted they were going home. To the cabin? To wherever Ariadne lived?

And Hank had done it on purpose. He'd crimped the plastic loop below, to keep it mostly lying along her skin on top. As soon as she could, she'd settled her wrists into her lap, to keep the crimp hidden. Why? If Hank was on her side, Eric's side, why was he directing the team dragging her home, maybe to the old Hound's fate?

She'd better not waste the opportunity, though. She tried not to look around too much, stare out the windows too often, but it was hard. She wanted to know where they were taking her, and she was no Map. She had to rely on street signs for cities she didn't know, names that slipped away quickly in their unfamiliarity. And whom would she tell, even if she did figure out their destination? Powers didn't come with telepathy.

With too much time to think, Key's mind circled around to the virus. They couldn't destroy the samples now. Could she stop Ariadne somehow in person? Distract her, keep her attention on Key, so she didn't leave to collect the samples from the lab or to release them? Escaping seemed like it would be fairly distracting, and Key already planned to be working on that anyway.

She was certain Eric would try to track her, of course. He'd run after them—she'd caught a glimpse of him through the windshield before they sped away—so that meant he'd managed to pull himself out of being zoned out all on his own, and gotten away from Matt for a while at least. But she wasn't sure if he could make it alone without zoning out. And even if he called Lantern, Key was even less sure Lantern would want to oppose Ariadne so directly, so Key might as well act as if she were on her own in this.

The longer she pretended to be zoned out, the more the guards relaxed beside her. Manuel and Ethan were their names, Manuel the hulking one who made her feel like he could probably crush her shoulder like a raw egg whenever he touched her. It showed how frightened and focused on running she'd been that she hadn't recognized him immediately in the house. Ethan was newish, which had made his name harder to remember, even now she had time—too much time—to sit and think about it. Guards came and went, and if they weren't friendly, she didn't bother learning much about them.

Hank turned the radio on so it hopped steadily from station to station, and every time Manuel or Ethan requested they stop, the other guard mocked his taste in music. Key supposed they actually had cause to act like she was a piece of furniture and talk right over her; she was supposed to be zoned out. At home, some guards did the same thing without nearly the excuse. Key couldn't see his face, but Hank's next punch of the button seemed harder than necessary. The radio stayed on a discussion of some sports team's chances in the next game.

Sweat pooled in a line along the side of either thigh, where she was pressed against the guards' legs, and dripped down the small of her back. Neither guard suffered from body odor, but one or the other had a muskily male scent that really turned her off. The wrong antibodies, she supposed, or whatever that half-remembered science program had said.

With no road signs for a while, Key started to wonder whether Hound would have said anything about being crowded. She'd never been zoned out so long she'd gotten this uncomfortable before. She didn't even really remember much from when she'd been zoned out—as Eric had said about the old Hound's memories, just events without thoughts or emotions.

The old Hound definitely had told everyone when he needed to pee, though, if he'd been ordered to stay put and no one had remembered to add an exception for the bathroom. The minute that occurred to Key, her bladder whined at her, and she couldn't get it out of her head. Forget making a break for it. They probably had hours ahead of them, traveling across the state, and with nothing else to think about, she felt ready to burst.

"I have to use the bathroom." Key channeled Hound from her memory, that blend of expressionless and urgent that he used for all of his physical needs, because he left them until they were desperate.

"Seriously?" Ethan scoffed.

"She's a vegetable right now, not a robot. If you leave her too long, she'll probably wet herself." Manuel seemed philosophical about the whole thing, but Ethan immediately tried to edge away from her as if the danger were immediate. There was nowhere to edge, so he settled right back against her, but at least the momentary separation between their hips cooled her skin a little.

Key wanted to hit them so badly. With Manuel, it would probably be like hitting a brick wall, and it would break her cover, but man, did she want to. Even a short time in the outside world had made it seem almost natural to think of herself as a person, not a power, and now she never wanted to be called a vegetable again.

"We'll have to find somewhere to pull over. Anywhere public, we'll either have to cut her loose, in which case she'll make a scene, or explain why we're dragging around a young woman who's visibly tied up." Hank's voice silenced a presumably annoyed retort from Ethan to Manuel.

Make a scene. She should make a scene, Key realized. If she were being a normal person, she would scream for the police. Scheisse, she hadn't even thought of doing that at the house.

Was Hank trying to secretly suggest that she do that very thing? Or was the loose binding a trap? But trapping her into what? They'd already captured her, she wasn't sure how things could get worse until they arrived and maybe Ariadne killed her like she had Hound then released the virus, which she'd been trying not to think about, because she was going to escape before then.

"Throw a jacket over her hands," Ethan said, tone slightly smug. "Go in the separate handicapped restroom with her."

Manuel saved Hank the trouble of answering. "What jacket?" Key mentally cheered him on. That had been a dumb suggestion. They were all in uniform long-sleeved shirts, and she wasn't wearing a jacket since they'd grabbed her from indoors. A beat later, she wondered why she was cheering any of the guards on. None of them apparently had any problem with putting themselves in a situation where they had to discuss hiding bindings.

Hank pulled off the freeway, and passed what Key supposed was a mall. It had the huge parking lot and big store signs straight out of commercials. The big gray square at one end of a long line of gray had no sign, just areas of darker paint in the approximate shape of letters. Hank turned down a road right after it.

They pulled up at the back of the gray square, but there was no one around to make a scene to. Just the back of the store, the strip of road, and a patch of weedy vegetation over broken rocks and concrete leading up to a wall she presumed delineated the whole back of the mall. The store had a couple of doors off platforms up way too high to be useful, Key would have thought. They even needed stairs up to them.

"I'll take her. You two cover the approaches." Hank shut off the engine and didn't get out until the guards had pulled Key to her feet. It smelled terrible, like nothing she could identify. She wondered if Eric could have, if this were the kind of smell a normal person would have encountered before. Garbage, wet from the recent drizzle, maybe? There were bottles and wrappers here and there, sandy bits of broken glass underfoot.

Hank set his hand under her elbow and guided her to where the jut of the staircase to the platforms added cover. A breeze tossed her hair across her face, leaving a couple of strands caught on her lips. She spat them out and tossed her hair back as much as she could without hands.

The other two men sauntered over to the center of the alley between building and wall, one looking left and the other right.

One of them must have also decided to take advantage of the stop because liquid splashed.

Key drew a deep breath. There were people in that mall, in the parking lot and other stores. How far would a scream carry?

"Don't." Hank clasped her wrists with both his hands for a moment, then popped the button on her jeans. "I'm giving you time to think." The words ran together, as if he worried the longer he spoke, the more danger there would be of the others hearing. He raised his voice for their benefit. "Eyes front."

With efficient, clinical movements, Hank pulled down her pants, his eyes firmly on a point in the vicinity of her shoulder. Hank had seen her running nude in the sprinkler when she was five or six, as Key recalled, so she wasn't particularly worried about his eyes except that he wasn't turning his back so she could rush him and run. He stood firmly in her path, and the other two guards were there anyway.

"Not even tempted to peek?" Ethan sounded like he'd wandered a bit closer to them, even if he was still facing his assigned direction. Key crouched, grateful that she couldn't see him because that meant he probably couldn't see her. She'd had creepier guards, but they hadn't lasted more than a day or two past the first time she mentioned to Hank they made her uncomfortable. Either they stayed and never gave her an improper look again or they disappeared. If Map had targeted them, he didn't mention it to her.

"Jesus fucking Christ, man. The boss will literally kill you." Manuel's tone was low, but intense. "Not, 'literally,' I'm exaggerating to sound like a hard-ass. Literally, like *literally*. She will *have you killed.*"

Which would have been comforting, in a way, Key supposed, if Ariadne didn't also kill men Key had invited to look. She straightened, and silently let Hank resettle her jeans. It was an awfully big building, and she couldn't see anyone else, so she doubted anyone would hear her scream. And if she ran, two guys would be in her way, whatever direction she chose.

And how stupid was it that Hank said "don't," and she didn't? But Hank had taught her and Map to ride their bikes, to play catch, to Rollerblade. He'd been to every single one of her birthday parties. That she could remember. When he said don't, she didn't, and tried to think, as he'd suggested.

Back in the car, sports scores droning on, Key thought as hard as she could. But it was those birthday parties she found herself thinking of. She'd been envious of Laura for her childhood with a mother, but didn't Key have family of her own, after all? A brother, a father figure? Shouldn't that be enough?

It should, but it wasn't, entirely. She was still rootless, unconnected. Even with her steps toward becoming normal, her power was too big a part of her to ignore. It might be nice to know about her birth parents, yes, her human ancestors, but what tore her up was the hole where anything about the past Keys should be. Her power was what was rootless.

But that was thinking far longer term than Key could allow herself at the moment. She could think of roots once they'd taken care of Ariadne's virus.

Once Key got free.

She'd missed her chance to escape along the way. Now she'd have to deal with whatever Ariadne had planned. She hadn't started shooting immediately, at the cabin, after all. Maybe that was a hopeful sign. Key would certainly listen to anything Ariadne wanted to say, agree with nearly anything she had to, now. Keep her ears open for any mentions of the virus. It seemed like the kind of plan Eric might make, with his careful decisions about when to say what to whom and his skill at listening.

Which was as close to a positive thing as Key could find in all her thinking, right now.

Key watched the scenery go by until her eyes ached with the weight of several disturbed nights in a row. They'd left the freeway north of Seattle, and Key sort of assumed they were heading generally east because west was the Sound, as she recalled from the state map in one of Hound's books, and east was also home. Former home.

The roads got smaller and smaller until they were on dirt, trundling between fields and dots of widely separated houses covering a plain that ended in hills on either side. "River floodplain" bubbled up from very old school lessons. It was very different being on, rather than reading about, one. Hank drove slower and frowned at prominent houses more than street signs, as though he had been given directions based on landmarks.

They turned and headed for the hills, and a building with a curved roof resolved itself against the hillside. It looked almost like a shed, with corrugated metal siding, but too big for that. It was twice as tall as necessary for the car, measurable when

Hank parked with the car's nose right in front of the line of recessed panels across the front of the building. A really fancy garage? But where was the house to go with it?

"You two go and make sure everything's in order inside. Then open the door, and I'll pull in," Hank said. The other two men grunted, climbed out of the car, and after some examination of the building, walked around to the side. A normal door became visible as they opened it, then shut it again.

Key kept her wrists low and started twisting off the zip tie. It wasn't quite as loose as she'd initially assumed, at least when it came to trying not to cut off the circulation across the heel of her hand. Now was her chance to start running properly, no one standing in her way.

Something clicked in the doors, and Hank sighed. "The child-proof locks are on. You could still unlock them your way, but I have the button up here to lock them again. Do we really need to play that game?"

Key rolled the zip tie the rest of the way off and dropped the damned thing on the floor. She was tired of taking Hank's word, so she scooted over to the door. *Unlocked.* It clicked over, clicked right back. *Unlocked.* She did it with her hand on the handle this time, but she still wasn't fast enough. Click-click. All her frustration boiled over. If he *was* like family, surely he should have done more. "Why are you helping me only to not help me?"

Hank sighed again and angled the rearview mirror so she caught his deep brown eyes framed by his frowning brow. "Get away from *us,* we'll only catch you, or be killed. Then the next person in line catches you. But if you get away from *the Boss,* I don't know. Maybe you can convince her to give up the chase. At the very least, you'll probably get a good head start again while she organizes us. I thought you deserved time to think out your approach."

"You're all heart." That was a straight quote from a cop show, even an imitation of the tone, and Key saw it hit the way she'd hoped. Eric had done more in two days to directly help her than Hank had done in two decades.

Hank dropped his eyes from the mirror. "The Boss has a lot to answer for. You may not understand, with half your world built on TV shows, but taking a solitary stand against evil doesn't always mean your allies swoop in and rescue you at the last possible second. Usually it means you're dead and someone else follows orders anyway. To gather enough support to *fight* evil, to make a difference, sometimes you have to wait, and work quietly on the inside."

Key smacked the door handle, like that would help anything. She wasn't sure about evil. Was Ariadne evil? Even when considering that Ariadne might kill Laura and unknowing humans in her quest for Lantern, she hadn't used that word in her mind. She'd grown up thinking of Her just as *Her*, capitalized, the source of restrictions and tests. And later, targets. Did that make Key evil too, or at the very least as bad as Hank, targeting all those people? She hadn't been zoned out for all of them, or even most, but she'd always known that she could be, so what was the point of refusing?

"So what do I do, Hank?" She hadn't meant it to come out that pathetic and young. She'd meant it to be a challenge, to make him back up all that stuff about allies and working quietly. She scooted across the back seat so she was at the right angle to see his profile between the seats.

Hank scrubbed his eyes, ended with a hand run along his head. "I don't know, Key. This is young man's work. I'm sure your young man will try to help you."

Of course he would. If he could. Even knowing he might not make it, the idea of him fighting with everything he had to reach her grounded Key, gave her a warm core of strength to draw on.

With a whirring, machinery sound, the panels in the building's front wall started sliding to the side, each slotting neatly behind the next. She was looking at a sideways garage door, Key realized. She should have guessed when Hank had talked about pulling the car in, but she'd never seen a garage like this before.

Hank's profile hardened back to the man who'd directed her kidnappers at the house, and he drove the car slowly into a huge space. It had swallowed up another few cars already, but still felt empty. Big steel truss beams held up the roof. At least, that's what Key thought they were called. Only when she felt the glass cold against her cheek as she tried to see upward through the car window did she realize she was gawking. She was kidnapped, not on a sightseeing tour.

Hank opened his door, stood inside it. "She's unbound. Shut the doors." Key couldn't find any other guards just at the moment, with her limited ranges of view, but the garage door started whirring its way back shut. Hank had the button for child-proofing the back doors, but maybe she could climb between the seats, up to the passenger door—

Manuel opened the farther back door and got a meaty hand over the back of her waistband as she pushed between the two front seats. She dug her fingers into whatever she could reach as he dragged her inexorably back, but she knew this game. It was a delaying tactic, a way to end up with a bunch of sore fingers and bruises, nothing more. That, and a way to prove a point. That's probably why she was doing it now, proving she was no freaking vegetable.

Manuel grunted as she kicked at his chest, and he leaned in farther to pry her nearest set of fingers from the seat. "Always the hard way when you're awake," he growled under his breath, with a couple more curses. Key writhed and kicked, but he wrestled her out of the car anyway.

Rather than wait for Ethan, he bent, rammed his shoulder into her stomach, and stood with her slung over his shoulder. Key declined to uselessly hit his back with her fists, like she was a toddler drawing out a tantrum. She got a good grip on his shirt instead, steadying herself so she could see as much as possible of where they were going. She got only a slight angled improvement on upside down, enough to see metal walls and dusty concrete floor.

"Here, please." Ariadne's voice. Key tensed, twisted, but with Manuel's body in the way, Ariadne might as well have been invisible. Manuel grunted acknowledgment, turned to something Key also couldn't see and was wild to be able to, and dumped her down onto her butt.

Into a cage. A freaking *cage*. Manuel slammed the door shut with a ringing sound that made it clear the bars were real metal, and he methodically zipped ties down the length of the two bars that met at the edge of the door. Key pushed to her knees to throw her weight against the door, but it didn't help.

By then Manuel had fastened a dozen or more ties and the door wasn't going anywhere.

"Thank you." Ariadne was now fully in view, the fluorescent lights in the garage bringing out the yellow tones in what was usually the warm brown of her skin. Rather than carefully styled, the black waves of her hair were back in a simple ponytail. Functional. Good for all the work of caging people up.

Key scooted into the center of the cage so Ariadne would have to work harder to reach her and darted a few glances to assess her situation. There was plenty of room to stand up in the square cage, but not enough to lie flat. Maybe curled up. She didn't test them yet, but the bars looked close enough together that she'd hang up on her upper arm if she put hand through. One patch of bars was even closer together, like a little door at waist level at the edge of the main door. The floor was wood, and the only other thing inside was a ceramic bowl thing she recognized from an antiques show as a chamber pot.

And the cage was on wheels. Ariadne grabbed one bar and started towing. It took a jolt for it to get going, but then it rolled quite smoothly. It was like she'd gotten it from some prop house, built to contain a bunch of imprisoned Muppets and smoothly twirl them through the choreography of the big song number. It was so *ridiculous*. Key scooted over to the corner and felt along the bars, the welds between them. Prop or not, it felt depressingly well constructed. Key's movement disturbed Ariadne's gait, but she kept on rolling without comment.

The wheels clunked from one surface to another, and Key looked up. The open bars gave her a good view of the ceiling, much lower now, and built of concrete. Everywhere was concrete in this new area, in fact: floor, walls, ceilings, and squat posts down the center of the room. Like a bunker, though movie sound effects nowhere near captured the dead distortion of sound inside it.

Key spoke partially to push back at the deadness swallowing up the rumble of the cage wheels. "Like in the story. Built into the mountain." As they got deeper into the bunker room, it smelled more and more like stony damp. "Why are you remaking the story?" In the story, Key had died. By *choice,* to save someone. But maybe Ariadne didn't care about that.

Ariadne stopped towing and maneuvered the cage neatly against a pillar nearly as wide as the cage's wall. "I didn't build this. But when it was auctioned to cover the owner's debts, I saw a certain . . . poetry it in." She pressed a hand to the pillar. "I sold his little planes and made it a little more comfortable in here. Useful for so much more than just storage."

"So you're not storing me?" Key countered. It felt wrong, to be flippant with Her Majesty, of the restrictions and targets, but she didn't want to seem cowed, either.

Ariadne drew her fingertips down the edge of the door, bumping over each band of plastic zip tie. "I want to have a conversation with you, and this seemed like the only way to keep you as a full participant."

Key stood properly and backed to lean against the rear bars, against the concrete. "Or you could have just talked to me, without kidnapping me."

"You'd have never stayed to listen." Ariadne sighed, and pulled her hand back. "Let me get us some privacy." She strode off to the garage part of the building again. It took Key several seconds to realize that her shoes were sensible and functional too, which was why Key subliminally missed the click of her heels.

The metal roof bounced the sound of Ariadne's voice, but then the concrete walls ate it, so Key couldn't catch any of the words. Half a dozen guards filed out of the normal-sized door, to patrol outside, Key supposed.

She walked back to Key without hurrying. Key watched her from the back of the cage. She didn't look evil right now. She looked more approachable than usual, really. "Are you hungry?" she asked as she arrived.

The answer to that was "very," when Key stopped to think about it. She felt frustratingly suggestible, desperately needing whatever came to her attention, whether it was the bathroom or a meal. But it was probably more an indication of how worried she was about her situation, that she pushed everything aside until it fought its way back in.

"Had to leave my cook at home, I'm afraid." Ariadne crossed to a kitchenette setup along the wall: sink, full-sized fridge, range, microwave on the countertop. Had that been a joke? Key wasn't sure what to think about Ariadne making jokes.

Ariadne took a square box from the fridge's freezer and freed the pizza from cardboard and plastic before sliding it into the oven. That was about as much cooking as Key ever did for herself, especially when Map would usually do it for her. Key hadn't been able to spot the toppings, but the smell of sausage slowly drifted out as they spoke.

"Does someone live here?" Key found herself hoping that someone did, because otherwise the kitchen didn't speak well of how long Ariadne was planning to keep her here.

"As far as the gods know, no one could, which is the point." Ariadne leaned on the counter and gestured around. "It's a place to disappear to. I'd hoped not to have to use it until I had all of you together, since too much in and out compromises security, but there's nothing for it now."

Lucky Key, to get to test it out. It was a really good thing, it appeared, that Hound was tracking her, not unpowered Eric. "Why did you have to use it now, then?"

"I don't have time to chase all of you if you keep scattering to the winds." Ariadne paced closer. "It made me realize I need to stop playing around. I can keep you all here until you *understand* the danger from the gods, and then we'll be safe here, because no one will know about it except the people here with us." She glanced back over her shoulder. "That's why I had you take care of all the workers who made it livable."

Key twisted her fingers around a bar just behind her hip, trying to find the tightest position and not react. "I didn't." She had no idea if she had or not. Her stomach clenched around a lump of nausea. Shouldn't she at least have tried to remember all her targets? But that might have driven her crazy. Ariadne was obviously deeply insane, to talk so calmly about how it was necessary.

"Didn't you? My memory isn't what it was. You see how well you do after multiple centuries." Ariadne rubbed the side of her nose, as if trying to remember if her first bike had been red or blue. So outrageously calm about all this. "You're right. I think it was Map. Yes, he waited until they were driving together, made it a car accident. Very neat."

"I don't understand the danger, though." Key flexed her fingers, but ended up clenching them again immediately. She'd rather talk about that subject than get into more details about Map's poor targets. "Why do the gods want us? Why now?"

"To use us." Ariadne's calm gave way briefly to anger. "To unlock, to track. They made us because they couldn't find the youngest of the gods themselves, after all. They aren't going to let such useful tools go to waste. The youngest of the gods helped us stay hidden from them for centuries, but I suppose they found a way around her. Or encountered some problem she could not refuse to solve. It doesn't matter. We are more than tools, to be used and discarded at will. We have wills of our own to refuse with."

Key didn't have an answer for that, because it had hit her like a slap: Ariadne had not the slightest conception of the irony of the fact that she wanted to control the powers . . . to make sure the gods couldn't control her.

Ariadne sighed, anger dissipating—or at least retreating deeper—and let the subject drop. She fussed around with plates until the oven dinged and she pulled the pizza out. She put two very generous slices on a place and picked up a pair of scissors with her other hand. She neatly snipped the two ties over the mini door and opened it to hand the plate through. Key took it with one hand so as not to warn her and grabbed for the scissors with the other.

Ariadne held them up and away without surprise, and took them miles, *continents*, away to a drawer in the kitchen. Then she refastened the mini door with one tie. "I'm not going to hurt you, Key. You just have to listen."

Key took her pizza to eat sitting with her back against the pillar. Sausage, olives, and onion. Her baleful look must have made it through Ariadne's crazy, because Ariadne laughed lightly, exasperated. "When you've eaten, then." She slipped off deeper into the bunker, somewhere Key couldn't see with the pillar in the way.

24

The fifth searcher holstered her six-shooter, for it was plain to see that whatever varmint had perpetrated this terrible deed had skedaddled long since. "I could give her back her life," said Breath. "If I only had one to give her, but it ain't like folks leave that kinda thing lying around."

—*The Search Across the West, 1872*

If Eric had paid attention, he would have noticed the doubled trail on the road leading away from the freeway, turning off but also coming back. But he'd been so relieved, after hours of excruciating search up the freeway, to find a trail leading off, that he'd sailed down it and not even glanced at the other side of the road.

And now he was here, trail out from behind the abandoned store just as clear as the trail in. Helpless anger made his steps along the service road, following the trail anyway, almost a run. What the hell had they wanted back here? There *was* nothing back here. And it smelled like piss.

Eric stopped short, hissed a curse at his own stupidity. That's why they'd stopped. And he'd just wasted yet more time, tracing a pit stop. He kicked savagely at the cinderblock wall to the side of one of the loading bays, which obviously did nothing more than make his toe ache.

Crows had been all over this little patch of abandoned real estate, and squirrels, and raccoons, and kids, and a couple of older adults, possibly homeless, and— The moment he stopped concentrating on Key's trail, the rest of the lines surged up, electric blue and beating with the throb of a burgeoning headache. Fuck, he still could hardly control this, and it was only getting worse.

He looked up, because bird trails were at least more diffuse, and the clouds decided to clear at that moment and send sunlight in a shaft like an icepick into his skull. He squeezed his eyes shut instantly. He thought for a moment he must have looked right at the sun, but now in darkness, he could feel the slant of warmth from an entirely different direction, low in the sky as it obviously would be so late in a spring afternoon. The spaghetti of trails vibrated against his eyelids in an afterimage, but still blue rather than the opposing color it should have been.

He stumbled back to the car and opened the door wide so he could collapse into the front seat, feet on the ground. He leaned the side of his forehead against the seat's headrest, but each throb settled behind his eyes, one after another, without diminishing.

Was it pride, keeping him from calling Lantern for help? It was all very well to say Lantern would refuse, but Eric hadn't even asked. Besides, even if Lantern refused to move against Ariadne, maybe he could offer Eric advice, something to help him bring his power under control.

So if it was pride that made him hesitate, now was the time to crush it to pieces. Eric found the entry Lantern had made in his address book and stared at it for a while. Even his phone was lightly brushed with the blue of other people's touch.

No, he was wasting time. Either he did this or got back on the road. Eric pushed the call button, brought it his ear, and closed his eyes as it rang.

"Hound?" Lantern answered after three rings. Even in one word, he sounded absolutely centered, an almost absurd juxtaposition with Eric's current situation and mental state.

"No, Eric." How to explain most concisely? He should have thought of that before starting the call. "Ariadne's guards took Key. I'm tracking them, but I'm not sure I can hold it together long enough to get there. I know you don't want to oppose Breath, but knowing I'm going to do it anyway, is there anything you can tell me? Something I'm missing about how to . . . filter all of this?"

Silence. Good, bad? Eric desperately wished he had Lantern here to read his body language, but that would also have involved opening his eyes again. "You know, I just realized you never answered me about when you passed," Lantern said finally. Not accusing, but patient, waiting for Eric to respond to the implied question in his own time.

"Couple days ago." Eric bit it out. "Doesn't change the fact that I have to track Key."

"No, but you shouldn't have to do it alone. Even if you'd been a power for years. Where are you? Would you be willing to wait for us to get there?"

Sarcasm gathered on Eric's tongue. Now Lantern was willing to act, now it was sweet, naive yet perceptive Key who was in danger, rather than undefined strangers or semistrangers. But he suspected that was pride again, prompting him to point out how he'd been right and Lantern had been wrong, all along. That wouldn't get Key rescued either. Instead, he gave Lantern the name of the mall, waited as silence fell again, probably while Lantern used his phone to check a map.

"About an hour," Lantern said, when his voice returned. Eric grunted assent. That wouldn't make so much difference in the time Ariadne would already have with Key to make it worth stumbling through on his own. "Hang in there, Hound."

Eric couldn't correct him again because he was already off the line. So. Now he waited. Maybe he could kick the headache, though that had eased at least a little while he'd had his eyes closed. Too bad lying down in a dark room was out of the question.

Dark—Eric felt like smacking his forehead to emphasize the stupidity this time. He'd seen the former Hound walking around with dilated eyes, wondered if the sunlight hurt them, and now he was sitting here whining about a headache like a moron. He shifted straight in the seat and brought down the driver's sun visor to uncover the small mirror there.

His pupils seemed on the large side of normal, but the moment he relaxed his focus through the windshield and allowed the trails beyond to fill his attention, then focused back, he caught the black circles spread wide. He needed sunglasses. Eric rummaged in the center console, digging down through archaeological layers of gas receipts and other crap, and suddenly realized that this patch of the car was blessedly free of blue.

But then, it was his car, and he couldn't remember the last time he'd lent it to anyone. Key had said he couldn't see his own trail, so much of the driver's seat was clean, only a brush of blue from Key when she'd driven them away from the cabin. Wonderfully clean. He wondered if any of the past Hounds had gone into the wilderness to live as hermits. Though there would still be animal trails, of course.

It didn't matter, anyway. He wasn't about to start examining memories to satisfy idle curiosity. His fingertips found the plastic length of an earpiece, and he pulled the sunglasses out and slid them on. The headache didn't disappear immediately, but the throbbing eased over the space of a minute or so. It left him feeling a little light-headed and not just from relief. When he got back out of the car experimentally, his head swam and he ended up leaning against the top of the open door.

Well, he had his choice of causes. Stress, lack of sleep. He would need to go longer than this on the late breakfast he'd had before having problems, but not having drunk anything since coffee with breakfast might be the more applicable state. He had no idea what kind of demands powers put on him physically. Key had never mentioned it, and it wasn't like she was sleeping sixteen hours a day or thin as a rail, using hers.

He should at least get some water at the mall's food court or something, since he was waiting for the others anyway. He considered moving the car, but decided walking would be safer in his current state, and followed the access road around and set off across the swaths of parking toward the main mall entrance.

He made it as far as one of a line of big concrete spheres placed to keep cars off the pedestrian courtyard before he felt like hyperventilating. Whether it would zone him out or not, he couldn't make himself go any closer. The mall looked like a B-movie plant monster had grown inside it, bulging blue tendrils out of every door.

He brought out his phone in a shaking hand as camouflage for standing still, but no one gave him a second glance. Of course, he was simply a man in sunglasses lingering near a pick-up point. Which was worth remembering. Ariadne and her guards didn't know he was Hound, and if he wore the sunglasses, he might have a chance in hell of keeping it that way.

That was a logical thought, and Eric tried to stay on that track. Water would do him good and he couldn't keep running from the trails, but neither did it seem like the smart course was to attack the problem head-on and end up zoned out.

He'd pushed the memories back to a safe distance, at least. That was one success. Through what, a sort of . . . mental block through meditation on the edge of sleep? As absurd as concentrating on not thinking of something was, he knew that it was a skill that could be learned in therapy. Could he do the same with the trails? Learn to block them out of his vision like people's brains erased their blind spots?

If he didn't, how would he ever do a magic show again?

Eric wished he hadn't thought of that, because it made him the opposite of logical. He couldn't give it up. Cut back, without the money Ariadne was paying him, maybe, but not *give it up*. He couldn't. But he didn't see how he could keep doing it, not with a summer fair's crowd, full of people scattering on every side. Even if he did make it up to the stage without getting zoned out, how could he look out at the crowd, read them, play to them, if he could hardly see them properly?

Deep breath. Eric cut off that train of thought, as practice. It was simply more motivation to find a way to block most of the trails out. Targeting, at least, he'd never learned, so he wouldn't have to unlearn any impulses to use it.

Eric edged over until his leg pressed into the cold, solid curve of one of the concrete spheres and closed his eyes. He tried to center himself in the moment, hearing the rumble of engines and crunch of tires and the chug of a distant diesel probably from a delivery truck, feeling chill air on his skin, not seeing anything. He was Eric. His perceptions were under his control. He needed to see trails right now to track Key, but anything else, he wasn't going to think about. He didn't even want to target, and if he never did, maybe he could keep control of this.

All right. Eric opened his eyes and jogged back into the parking lot a ways for a better angle on the mall's outside storefronts. Those should be easier for him to enter; he could get water from a coffeeshop. When Lantern arrived, he'd be rested and ready to go, maybe even with a plan.

Eric considered moving the car once more when he'd pulled himself together, but the unused service road beside the empty storefront seemed a better place to talk than even a quiet section of an active parking lot. His text to that effect must have been received, because just about an hour after his conversation with Lantern, a sleek silver hybrid pulled in and slowed to a stop at a reassuring distance. Even so, Eric waited for Lantern to step out before he did himself. Paranoia, maybe, but he'd hold on to the control of himself he had, at this point.

Then Lantern strode over and was hugging him. Eric considered resistance, but even if his emotions were born of some tiny leak of memories, the gesture offered a comfort that reached deep, and he needed that at the moment. "Please tell me we were never in love," he said, trying to play off the way his arms had come up around Lantern's back in turn.

"I promise, though we do come from a time where male affection was permissible," Lantern said with a light laugh, and let Eric go when he pulled reluctantly away. Modern social mores aside, worries about wasting time still applied.

Map climbed out of the car's back seat, looking very much like he wished he was the one doing the hugging when it came to Eric. In hurriedly avoiding his gaze, Eric almost missed the woman who'd been in the passenger seat until the solid thud of her door shutting provided an echo for Map's.

What the hell was this? They were certainly out of Hand members. "Who's she?" Eric's voice came out more strident than he'd meant. He examined her minutely, but she looked normal enough, of East Indian descent and wearing jeans and a breezy white top. The only note to set her apart from a dozen young woman he'd just seen in the mall was the intricacy of the braided crown her thick hair had been caught up into.

Lantern winced apologetically. "I thought it better to contact her if the gods were involved. She's the Youngest."

"The one you saved." The woman's voice was soft but utterly musical. She came over but stopped before her closeness became challenging. At some kind of speaking look from Lantern, Map stayed with the car. "I had not realized my siblings had contacted Breath, for which I apologize. My debt to you all deserves a better discharging than that."

Eric eyed Lantern. "And we trust her?"

That earned him a frown. "Don't you remember—?"

Eric cut him off with a raised hand. "Assume I don't remember anything. What does that mean, being a god? All-powerful magic?" If all this time they'd been stumbling around, there had been a woman who could stop Ariadne with a wave of her hand . . .

The Youngest shook her head. "Our magic is powerful, but rarely concrete in its effects. That's why the Hand was originally needed. And why some among my siblings think to prod Breath into reassembling you, whether through following their orders or attempting to oppose them." She spread her hands, and did not look young at all. "But I owe you a debt, and have enough influence to buy you time so you may face them from a place of strength. I will assure Breath of this."

"I think Ariadne's problems run deeper than that." But there was no need to be rude. They well might need the Youngest's help with the gods when the rest of this was resolved. "Thank you."

The Youngest's lips lifted at one corner like she'd guessed at Eric's thoughts. "And if you must kill Breath—"

"No one's killing anyone." Lantern gestured in invitation back to his car. "If I drive, will you be able to track them?"

Eric remained stubbornly by his own vehicle. "You can drive, but my car's cleaner. Of trails." He drew a breath, expecting to have to justify that, but no one objected. Then again, two of the three of them were probably more familiar with his power than he was, so he shouldn't be surprised. "But the guards—wherever Ariadne's holed up, I'm sure there are plenty around—know me as one of her employees, so I should probably drive the last leg, so we can see how far we can talk our way in."

"That's reasonable." Lantern stepped up and opened Eric's own passenger door for him. "We can figure out more detail on the way."

Eric shot him a look, but let it pass and climbed in. Having Key's touches and trail cradling him on the seat and door handle and center console was almost comforting, in a way. He'd have her back soon enough. How could they fail, with one of the gods on their side?

If only she could actually do anything, that rallying thought would be much more effective.

25

*Key fingered the controls for the broken stasis field.
"We've run and rerun the scans. We have no other choice if we're to save her." She powered down
her visor, set it aside so it wouldn't break if she fell.
"Take mine."*

—*A Future Lost,* 1964

Key slid her empty plate out sideways between the bars, like a
letter through a mail-slot. It reminded her of her childhood,
when she'd mailed letters to no one through the outgoing slots
of the clusters of unused mailboxes around the neighborhood.
She settled the plate on the concrete as quietly as she could
manage. Ariadne wasn't far, but she couldn't see through the
pillar any more than Key could, so maybe Key had time to try
something.

Key sat on the bottom of the cage and threaded her foot out. If she could get her legs out and pull or push herself along, like rolling her office chair . . . but she stuck before the knee. She could touch the floor with her toe, but she couldn't rock her leg with enough leverage to pull or push. She switched to kneeling and tried her hand next. There, she could flatten her palm at the right angle, but she couldn't get enough grip. She could push away from the pillar, of course, but that would get her only about a foot of progress unless she could combine it with some other method.

Footsteps, and Key immediately touched her fingertips to the edge of her plate. Just setting it down. That's all she was doing, honest. Ariadne silently retrieved the plate and set it in the sink.

"Can I have something to drink?" Next plan: get a glass and break it later, when Ariadne was at least somewhat out of earshot. Broken glass should be plenty sharp enough to saw through the plastic. Same with a soda can; the aluminum was thin, but maybe she could fold together a decent edge.

Ariadne filled a glass at the sink and collected the scissors again. Key evaluated the glass out of the corner of her eye while she stared obviously at the scissors. The glass was a little thick, but, with luck, not too sturdy.

This time, Ariadne didn't refasten the little door. Key tossed half the water back, set the glass negligently aside to finish later, and investigated the door's diameter. Ariadne undoubtedly expected Key to try something, so she wanted to make it appear she was focused on the physical dimensions of the cage. She could get her arm out to her shoulder, but that didn't help anything, especially at waist height.

The large hangar door whirred into life, and Ariadne smiled briefly as if pleased with someone's timing. She strode away and Key withdrew her arm and craned her neck to see who had arrived. Ariadne hadn't bothered with the guards going in and out.

A car door slammed, and conversation carried indistinctly to Key. She got a good look at Ariadne's visitor about the same time their words resolved as the pair approached the bunker. The man with her was silver haired, thin, walking with jerky steps: Clive. He carried a small cooler, deceptively prosaic in its outward appearance. It reminded her of a TV show where the detective had tracked a stolen donated organ, and Key had thought the cooler looked like it should have held someone's lunch instead. Key's fingers tightened around the nearest bar. Far from stalling, he'd brought the virus right to Ariadne? No, no, no. Scheisse.

"That's the sample?" Ariadne was asking. She reached for the cooler, but Clive stopped walking and clutched it to his chest.

"Yes." He took a deep breath, fingers relaxing slightly as he channeled that desperation into words that were probably supposed to seem logical, casual. "Maybe you're right, maybe it's better to have one sample stored off site in case the lab's compromised—security in anonymity rather than alarm systems and all that—but that's only in the short term. You don't have the facilities to keep it over the long term. Wouldn't a different off-site location be better?"

Ariadne reached a hand to Clive's shoulder, which he apparently thought was safe enough. Key was not surprised, though, when Ariadne caressed down his arm, ending at his hand, then she had the cooler in her own grasp. No struggle, no threats, it was just under her control. "The short term is long enough."

A need to lunge, to grab, to smash, surged across Key's muscles. The virus was *right there*, if she only could get to it. If she could reach, snatch it away—but she couldn't smash it, of course. That would only release it, not destroy it. She pressed against the bars anyway, trying to impress their immovability deep into her mind, to the part that was urging her to batter down the metal.

"You're not going to—" Clive's fingers clenched around each other, without the cooler to separate them. "It's not *ready*, Ariadne. I told you, the incubation period . . . And the mortality will likely be too high." Despite everything, he seemed shocked. Key wondered if he'd gotten used to the idea of the virus's release as a far-future hypothetical, never to actually arrive.

"Fine." Ariadne shrugged. "If Lantern doesn't wish to die herself, or lose all of her new family, she can turn herself in. It works well enough that way, to get her to come back." She went over and nestled the cooler lovingly in the kitchenette fridge.

Key waved at Clive emphatically until the movement finally caught his attention. *Stop her,* she mouthed, several times. He shook his head. No, he didn't know what she wanted him to do, or no, he didn't want to do that? Jackass.

When Ariadne returned to him, Clive gave her a sickly smile. "Well, I'll, uh, leave you to it. Whatever you feel needs to be done."

"Ethan!" Ariadne snapped, voice pitched to carry beyond the dead acoustics to leave no corner of the building where Ethan could claim not to have heard her summons. She continued in a more conversational tone. "You're not going anywhere. That's the point of a bolt hole. You'll stay here until I have the whole Hand together, and we're finally safe."

Clive opened his mouth, but nothing came out for several seconds. "But—I have *work* to do!" After everything, that seemed to summon a little fire in him. "I'm sorry, but that's impossible." He turned firmly away, but Ariadne caught his arm, and suddenly he fell against her.

Had she killed him? Key was at the wrong angle to see if he was still breathing. Not that Key would mourn him in particular, but Ariadne being in a mood to kill quickly and easily was a very bad thing.

When Ethan approached, Ariadne shoved Clive at him like a sack of potatoes. "Tie him up. I didn't take a lot; he'll wake up soon. I might need him later, so he can continue to be our guest for now."

Ethan accepted the burden easily—Clive couldn't have been heavy if Ariadne had been supporting him—and nodded to acknowledge Ariadne's orders without comment. Even if he wasn't heavy, he was unwieldy, and once Ethan had Clive over his shoulder, he paused a moment to balance him more precisely.

"And gag him," Ariadne added, as Ethan left.

Key supposed since she couldn't reach the virus, she was down to stalling verbally. If only Eric were here, he would have been really good at it. "You're really going to release the virus when it's not ready? Why not wait? If it's lethal, the CDC might come up with a cure fast enough Lantern can keep hiding." Were cures really that easy? Key had no idea. They were always ready at the end of a two-hour movie.

Ariadne shook her head and absently brushed off her shoulder where Clive had leaned. "If it's the humans you're worried about, don't. Lantern won't let anyone get hurt." She snagged a chair on her way back to the cage. "I didn't want to use it yet either, but Eric stealing you away has made me realize that I can't count on pulling Lantern in slowly. I need to be quick."

Before the rest of us escape again, Key finished silently for herself. The worst part was, she knew how wrong Ariadne was. Should Key tell her that Lantern would likely run and count on Ariadne's plans being merely a bluff? Would Ariadne believe her, or if she did, would the knowledge that Key had been in contact with Lantern only enrage her? Even if it was the correct play, Key couldn't bring herself to give up the secret pleasure of Ariadne being completely unaware Key had reached Lantern despite all Ariadne's efforts.

As Ariadne approached, Key retreated to a seated position on the floor of the cage, back against the pillar. Ariadne placed her chair so the clear space of the open mini door allowed their line of eye contact. Key looked at her once, then away. Now was clearly the time when she was supposed to listen to the insane self-justifications in earnest. At least every moment Ariadne was here, talking to her, the virus sat unused in the fridge.

Key could also feel the water glass's presence out of her range of vision like the psychic weight when one of the guards stared at her from behind. Later. She was ignoring it right now.

"I've missed you over the years, Key." Ariadne looked into space, slightly upward. Maybe into memory. She sounded so sincere, Key found herself listening despite herself.

She got her mental feet back under her quickly enough, though. "You knew where I was. Better than anyone. I think you were about the only person in the world in a position to do something *about* missing me."

Ariadne shook her head. "I told you before, you grew up while I wasn't looking. Sometimes time gets away from me. When you were a child, I couldn't have you thinking of me like a relative. I had to stay away.

"I love you, Key." Ariadne leaned forward and hooked her fingers on the bottom of the mini door's opening, as if hanging on against the tide of her emotion. Then her grip relaxed, and she dropped her head, exhaled a laugh. "Not like a mother."

"Like Map and Hound," Key said, because she could not think of a single other thing to say in the face of that. That moment when Ariadne had stroked her wrist had been real, then. Key didn't know how she felt, never mind how to put those feelings into words. She pressed her hand to her mouth a beat later—she'd meant to keep Eric a secret—but then, she hadn't said Eric, had she? Map could have told her about his memories with Hound at any time.

"Oh, he remembers that, does he? Next we can find a nice, older girl for Hound to be, maybe." Ariadne slowly flexed the fingers hooked on the bars. "They took their time, did those two. Shy, perhaps. Or fearing to be hurt when we didn't even know what our lives would be like, after. You and I, we must have found ourselves in the course of the Story. No one has memories of the Story, of course, only after. So I only know, as long as I've been me, I've loved you, Key."

"Please—" Key held out a hand, like it could block the words. Even if she put her hands over her ears, she doubted she could fail to hear so close to Ariadne. "Stop saying that."

"But I have to. Before the gods interfered, I only wanted to raise you so we'd have a chance to start again. One stupid argument between us, and everything went wrong. But now we can start over. You're not a pure-state child; you're you." Ariadne smiled, small and sweet. "You look so much like you used to. The children start so young, I never know how they'll grow up, but you look like *yourself*."

Key leaned forward. She couldn't help it. "I do?" She looked at her hands, wished she had a mirror, even though she knew what she looked like. But she wanted to look at herself with that knowledge in mind, fix that image instead as how she once looked.

"You do." Ariadne smoothed a lock of her own hair escaping from the tail away from her temple with a knuckle. "Especially now you're back to your natural color."

That touch drew Key's gaze, and while she couldn't look at herself with her new knowledge, she could look at Ariadne. Was she imagining an alluring quality now to the dark brows and high cheekbones that had seemed authoritarian through a child's eyes? Key traced pointed chin to elegant neck to curve of collarbone.

"But you're always beautiful." Ariadne unhooked her fingers from the bars and slid her arm into the small door's space, palm up, an invitation. "You're the only one I've ever loved, the only one I've ever wanted."

"Tell me about us, how we used to be." Key didn't even need Lantern's memories, if Ariadne would open up to her instead. She was clearly more than comfortable with her memories, not like Eric. Imagine how many memories such a strong emotion as love would trigger for her, too. Her chest felt tight with suppressed excitement just thinking about it. She touched Ariadne's hand, squeezed to encourage her.

"I'd rather just be now." Ariadne smiled, lopsided, and drew Key forward onto her knees so she was facing Ariadne directly through the door opening. "Do you remember this?"

She ghosted her free fingertips from Key's earlobe around the corner of her jaw, tilted her chin up, and kissed her. Her lips were soft, undemanding, drawing Key in deeper with their sweetness rather than forcing it on her. It was a nice kiss, as alluring as Ariadne herself, but when Key let herself be drawn in, she found nothing but more niceness beneath. No memory, no echo of a memory. No love, not even the fear of Ariadne's wrath or Map's love that had spiced Eric's touch.

Key shifted back, lightening the kiss before breaking it, and Ariadne's touch turned desperate, as if that had been hidden beneath all long. Her fingers curled around the side of Key's neck, hard enough to hurt. The kiss felt suddenly like a binding, meant to rob her of her will.

Key jerked away, unbalanced weight sending her back onto her ass. "I don't remember anything about you."

"It doesn't *matter*." Ariadne's smile didn't show her desperation, but her tone was edged. "We'll make new memories."

Key clenched her hand into a fist on the boards, opened

it carefully, and set it down again. She could barely articulate the bone-deep importance of memories to herself, but the very depth of that importance pushed her to try. "I have no *foundation*. I suppose I know who I am in this life, some of what my powers do, have a few people worthy of being called family, but it doesn't *connect* to anything. I don't have my memories, I don't know where I came from, I don't know anything about past Keys or the past all of the powers share. I just want to *remember*, have even a few of my memories triggered. You don't understand how much I need it because you already have it!" By the end, she was almost shouting.

Ariadne's dark brows rose, but only to a refined angle. "Key, any memories you haven't discovered by now don't exist, until your next lifetime."

"No!" Key thumped her fist on the boards. "I have a few memories. I only remembered them when they related to something. I just need something to relate the others to."

Ariadne's expression settled into something pleasant with perhaps a hint of humoring Key. "What do you remember?"

"Grinding." Key knelt up to mime the movement.

"After we found those farmers, perhaps," Ariadne mused, gaze going unfocused. "Or earlier, when we would gather those seeds. Or maybe when we'd joined the city . . . "

So basically, it could have been any time. Key's frustration bubbled up, and she knew that wasn't good enough, not right now. "And a song. My mother was holding me, and singing." She threw that at Ariadne, not even sure what she was trying to prove. Ariadne hadn't said Key didn't have memories, simply that she wasn't going to find any new ones.

Ariadne tilted her head, silent, and Key realized she was waiting to hear the song. The words escaped her as always, so she hummed, added a nonsense syllable here and there.

Ariadne beamed and picked up the thread of the song from Key, her voice husky and rich on the foreign words. "When I first found this body for you, I sang that to you to get you to sleep on the journey home. I didn't know you were listening."

Where Key's chest was tight before, now she couldn't breathe, not at all. No. No! She'd thought perhaps that memory could have been from when she was a child, before she was Key, but whether it was from before or after being Key, it had been *hers*. She'd clung to it, held it close when she had nothing else about herself, and it was a *lie*. Empty and hollow as the rest of the life Ariadne had trapped her into. Everything about her was Ariadne's, not her own.

She kicked the bars in front of Ariadne, but with only the thud of the rubber of her shoe against the metal, that wasn't enough for her anger. She slammed her shoulders back so the bars clanged against the concrete. It hurt, but she welcomed that at the moment.

Ariadne stood and brushed off her knees, though she hadn't done anything to get them dirty. "I don't particularly see why that's worthy of a tantrum."

Key paused before using the first reply that occurred to her, determined not to prove Ariadne's barb true by sounding childish. In the end, she couldn't think of anything better, but she delivered it in the iciest tone she could manage. "You wouldn't understand."

Ariadne gave a bark of laughter, just as icy in its irony.

"I can't say I ever have, Key." She slipped off into the bunker, where Key couldn't see.

Key listened to her fading footsteps, as they got to their farthest reach and stopped when Ariadne settled somewhere else. Maybe she had a real bed down here, while Key was stuck in the cage. She didn't dare break the drinking glass yet, to do something about that, not until Ariadne had had time to get distracted or fall asleep.

As long as it wasn't releasing the virus that distracted her. Not only had Key let her hope tempt her into listening to Ariadne, she'd let her anger push her into driving Ariadne away, when Key should have kept her close and away from the virus. Scheisse.

Key curled up tight and ended up on her side on the floor, back against one wall and feet against another because she felt like she needed pressure to keep all her misery contained, compressed into a heavy lump near her chest.

Was that all it took? A nice smile and a profession of love, to make Key forget all the targets—no, she needed to face it— all the *people* Ariadne had forced them to kill? The others who might die if Ariadne released the virus? Worse—the thought burst into Key's mind with a suddenness like pain—if Lantern was still close, she might catch it and die herself. Die, pass to a relative, and still be in danger if the virus kept spreading.

The ripples in the also-spreading pool of blood under Hound flashed into her mind, and she couldn't get them out until she was panting with imminent tears. Ariadne might still do the same thing to her, because she wasn't playing along, loving her and joining her united Hand to face the gods' alleged threat. How many times had Ariadne killed her and made sure her powers passed to a child before? This time, she looked like the old Key. What about the other times? Had any of those girls argued too much?

Remembered too much?

And was memory worth it? Map had some of his, and all they'd helped him do was construct a fantasy of love with Hound, the same as she'd done with her fantasy of memories to be triggered someday. She could hope Ariadne had been lying, but something told her that Lantern would tell her the same, that Key had no more memories to be triggered, no matter what she did.

It was freedom she and Map had both needed, though they hadn't known it. Hadn't really known what freedom was, to want it. But now she knew. And she had her self-identity, and her constructed family, and Eric and Map and Lantern. She didn't need her fantasy of memories. She needed freedom, to keep holding on to those things she did have.

Key uncurled by degrees, testing that misery didn't rush back to swallow her once more. She could see the fridge from here, cooler still safe inside. She'd see if Ariadne took it out. And with Ariadne gone and the water glass in her cage, she had the first step to freedom in her hands. Time to use it.

Throwing the water glass seemed likely to make the loudest noise and tapping seemed like it might endanger her hands. When Key had listened hard for Ariadne for at least five minutes, she climbed to her feet and wedged the glass sideways, base under the sole of her shoe. With the other shoe, she stomped on the top edge. Nothing. She adjusted the angle and tried again. On the third attempt, it *crunched,* side caving in. The noise seemed so loud, Key could have sworn it echoed.

Rather than listen for footsteps, she scrabbled for the glass as quickly as possible. If she could clean it up before anyone arrived—

Among various tiny shards and dust, a section of the side stood out. It was flat at the top along the original rim and curved at the bottom. With the rim, it should even be safe to hold.

Key set the rest of the glass inside the chamber pot and brushed the dust onto the floor between the cage and pillar with her toe. She held her chosen shard concealed against one wrist, as if ready for a magic trick. No one arrived to investigate the noise. She counted her own heart rate, until she could no longer hear it in her ears. Then she attacked the lowest zip tie. When she was free, she could grab the cooler and run, solving both problems at once.

The tie parted very, very slowly. She could feel the slash in the plastic with her thumb, finally see it as it grew deeper, but she had to saw and saw to get even that far. When it was a bare plastic cobweb from being cut, Key set down her shard, leaned her forehead on the bars, and let her frustration hiss out in a breath without words. This was going to take a while. She would have to leave them nearly cut, so no change would be visible until she was ready to go. Frustration made her reach with her power, searching for that indescribable feeling of knowing a lock was there, but it slid away with nothing.

Key picked up the shard, got a firm grip, and kept sawing.

26

With heavy hearts, they spied Key stilled, life fled.
Four searchers bowed their heads at such grave cost.
Gods' youth drew breath and lived, but Key was dead.
Thought Breath: the searchers found, and finding, lost.

—"Five Explorers," 1599, in *Lesser-Known Eliza-
bethan Plays,* 1992

Eric switched places with Lantern when the trail turned onto a
nearly empty two-lane road. Even if Ariadne's hideout was still
miles away, there was no reason for Eric not to start driving
now he could go at the slower speed he needed. It was long
dark by now, and they'd left regular street lights behind. Stars
pricked from between the clouds, and hills loomed as silhouettes on either side of him. Farmland surrounded them, trees
scattered too far off the roads for them to track the presence or

absence of wind. Well, Lantern and Map planned to stay well back when they drew Ariadne outside in any case, so wind was simply a bonus.

The lack of light didn't make any difference to the appearance of the trail, though. If anything, it glowed brighter with fewer colors to distract from it. Eric turned onto a gravel road and crunched along, lining the trail up with the belly of the car.

The spread of his high beams showed him a car pulled diagonally across the road ahead of him. Pretty effectively, too, because the ditches on either side were too deep to ford and take off overland, even had he wanted to piss off a farmer by smashing crops. The driver's door opened, and a Latino man climbed out, muscles straining at the upper arms of his uniform shirt. Eric didn't recognize him, but the uniform was the one Ariadne's people used.

So he was at the right place. Now he just had to talk his way past the watchdogs. Eric stopped short, rolled the window down, left his lights on, and climbed out. He hoped the guard wouldn't notice there were others in the car with the lights blinding him. With the window open, they'd be able to hear, and both Lantern and Map had solemnly sworn to stay out of things until guns actually came out, even if it seemed the conversation was going badly. There was, after all, a zone that sounded like "going badly" to outsiders, where things could still be saved with a little skill. The Youngest had seemed inclined to strict noninterference in general.

Eric shoved his hands in his pockets, aggressively casual. "I'm here to see Ariadne." As Eric approached, the guard didn't noticeably brace himself for trouble, but he probably didn't need to. He looked pretty grounded by nature. Eric had left his sunglasses in the car, since anyone's eyes would be dilated in this darkness, if the guard could even see them properly. "What's the problem?" The wind was enough to stir Eric's hair, but came and went capriciously.

The man gave a bark of laughter. "You've got fucking balls on you. What did you do with Hudson?"

Hell. Had this guy been there at the house, for the grab? Eric hadn't seen anyone properly except for the guy he'd taken out, and Hank, getting away. So that had been exactly the wrong way to play this. At least he didn't have a bullet between the eyes yet. That was something. And the guard was focused on him, ignoring the car, so that was something else. "I incapacitated him briefly. Hasn't he called in yet?" He could see from the slight hardening of the guard's expression that Hudson hadn't.

Eric wondered briefly if Hudson had instead decided to walk away from a job that wasn't worth it anymore. Eric should really have done that himself. Four years ago.

But then Key and the others would still be imprisoned and Ariadne would still be poised to kill on a larger scale to trap Lantern. So if he had it to do over, he figured he'd stay that time too.

Gaze fixed on Eric, the guard lifted his walkie. "This is Manuel. Davis has shown up," he said. To Hank, perhaps, if he was still directing this rodeo. Eric had never yet seen Ariadne hold a walkie-talkie in her own manicured fingertips.

"Hell. I'm coming out there. Keep him here." The crackling voice sounded like Hank, as much as timbre carried over that kind of connection.

Eric settled his weight back on his heels. He'd have liked to lean on the car, but he was keeping attention off it. He hoped the others weren't getting impatient inside. He made sure to make no sudden movements that might suggest to the guy that Eric would need active keeping-here measures. In the painfully awkward lull, trails ate away at the edges of his attention. He had a direct one to Manuel, and it gnawed with particularly sharp teeth. Instinct told him if he just concentrated, he could—but Eric didn't care what he could do if he concentrated. "You know she doesn't pay you enough to get caught up in this."

The guard snorted. "Caught up in what?"

"Hank knows." Eric tipped his chin to indicate the quickly approaching car. The headlights stabbed his eyes mercilessly before he remembered to look away. He focused on Manuel instead, now with two afterimage dots superimposed on him as Eric's eyes slowly readjusted.

Hank's car was just as much blocked as Eric's was, so he pulled up with a skidding crunch, got out, and jogged around to join the other guard. "Dammit, Eric, you could have walked away from this. She's not going to hurt Key."

"No." Eric crossed his arms. "No, I couldn't have. She won't harm Key right up to the point she decides to kill her, like she did Hound. And then she'll go right back to killing people in search of Lantern. Did you know she created a virus to make anyone who might be related to Lantern sick, to flush her out?" Eric supposed abstract death might not reach them, but did Hank or the guards who hadn't been at the cabin know about Hound? If they didn't, it was time they did. But would Hank care, or was the old Hound too hard to care about?

No, they hadn't known. Eric read that much in their tightening expressions—but Hank had *guessed*. Eric would lay money on that. Manuel slid him a look and seemed to catch that implication too. "You believe him about Hound?"

Hank sliced the air with a frustrated gesture. "We had no orders about picking him up, nothing about a hand-off or meeting with the guys who joined her up there, not a single mention of him. You know how she micromanages. That's not proof, but . . . " He sighed, and pulled out his gun. "We do have orders to bring you in, Eric. And you didn't walk away."

At the sight of the gun, adrenaline went from making Eric's senses sharp to making his hands shake. The too-fast beat of his heart in his ears hadn't really calmed since Key had been taken; he was used to that. Eric's thoughts tumbled fast, like going over a waterfall in a barrel. Wherever you tumbled, you were going in one direction. Lantern and Map had only Tasers, and if things went completely south and they stepped in now, they might well have to resort to Lantern's targeting. Of any of the Hand, he was the most dangerous, as he needed only line of sight, since he was based on light. Eric didn't want them to resort to killing the guards any more than Lantern did, though, so damned if he'd *let* things go south.

Manuel hadn't liked the news of Hound. Maybe with the right push, he could be convinced to remove himself from the situation. Eric needed *information,* though. Something to base his words on, rather than cold-read stabs in the dark. The pressure of the direct trail to the man closed in on him, and he—he had to.

But having decided to do it, it was like that time with Key all over again. The more he concentrated, the less instinct guided him. The feel of it slid away from him, and he scrabbled after it. He wasn't sure he even wanted to do this, but in thinking he'd held back out of choice rather than rank incompetence, maybe he'd been fooling himself. It was worse than any cold reading he'd ever done.

But in a cold reading, you kept trying, as long as the person was still there, throwing out one thing, then its opposite. Something stuck. Something gave you an in—

Family at home. New baby soon, needed the money, best paycheck he'd had in years, but weird. Getting weirder all the time. Didn't know whether to believe this creepy bastard—

Family. Yes, the family was good. Eric could work with that. He just needed more specifics. *Didn't know what the creepy bastard was doing now, but he felt—felt panic—*

Manuel gasped and staggered back into the blocking car, babbling pleas, curses. "No." He shook his head violently, expression stripped down to raw fear. "Not worth it." He threw himself into the car, and Hank had to jump to the side as Manuel straightened it and sped away down the road. His tires spun on the gravel before getting real traction, and a rock stung Eric's cheek.

"Son of a bitch." Hank drew the words out, his realization in the syllables. Eric heard him as if from a distance. He'd almost killed Manuel. He'd *told* Key he wouldn't be able to stop, and he'd felt the panic as Manuel's life started to be crushed out of him. He knew that primal terror intimately, from when Ariadne had taken his air, centuries ago, it seemed now. And now he'd done the same thing to someone else. He put out a hand to his car, but with the door shut, all the metal was rounded, no place to cling. This was why he needed to avoid targeting, push it out of his mind. In the passenger seat, Lantern mouthed something at him, expression concerned. Eric couldn't figure out what it was, so he shook his head.

"You sorry son of a bitch. You're a wreck, aren't you?" Hank's tone was a strange mixture of disgust and . . . sympathy?

"A son of a bitch who can kill you." Eric tried to smile confidently, while the blue lines pressed in on them because he had no energy to hold them back, not when he was halfway to shaking apart.

"I haven't been this far from the hangar in hours. My uncrossed trail goes only that way." Hank pointed behind himself, up the road. "Don't insult my intelligence. I probably know more about Hound than you do."

"No one's killing anyone." Lantern folded out of the car on lean legs and stood inside his open door. Map tumbled out a second later, probable nervousness robbing him of grace. Hank pointed the gun automatically at Lantern, professionally braced in his stance, but at the sight of Map, he hesitated, lowered the weapon, and finally holstered it.

Hank blew out a breath, paced a few steps to center himself in the road, but not one inch closer to Eric. "I suppose this is Lantern? Guess if you're Hound, that explains how the hell you found us. I could hardly believe it when Manuel called it in. Even Map doesn't know where this place is."

"I could have found it had I needed to. I would have come to rescue Key even if I'd been alone." Map bristled, frustration visible even in the uncertain light between headlight beams.

Hank laughed, a single explosive sound. "Would you? You escape, you're your own man for the first time in your adult life. What do you do? You come straight home."

Eric sensed Hank's focus drifting away from all of them, his justification directed inwards. "And so I had to give you what she told me to. If you'd just *stayed away*, but of course none of you can ever do that."

"Give Map . . . ?" Eric wasn't sure he'd heard right at first.

"The drawing of Key the Boss made. The car, with the GPS tracker." Hank refocused on Map. "And off you drove, not even a split second of suspicion." Hank gestured at the car's path. "I can't help any of you if you insist on continuing to walk. Into. Her. Arms!"

Map whirled like he planned to punch whatever his fist impacted first, but wrestled control of himself before subjecting his knuckles to the metal of the car door. He flattened a palm against the window instead as he cursed under his breath.

Eric leaned more of his weight on the car while mentally kicking himself. He should have detected that fishy odor to Map's situation when the man first told Eric and Key about it. He couldn't afford to miss things like that. "Helping us," he repeated Hank. "Only by a generous definition."

Hank squared his shoulders belligerently, and Eric suddenly remembered the strength under the mild veneer. "Do not start with me too, boy. You've been busy since you swanned in, but you took your time noticing they even existed. How long have you known the Boss?"

"I'm here now." Mostly to see what Hank would do, Eric took a step away from the car and for the building. All he could see of it was a lit square of an open garage door and the curved line of its roof against the dark hill. Hank blocked his way. "You know her body count. Yes, I didn't discover it for too long, but now I know the full extent, I have to at least try to do something about it. Ariadne can't be allowed to keep slaughtering whoever stands between her and her obsession."

"And yet it's such a nice stand to take, when it means rescuing the hot chick you're banging." Hank sneered at Eric's expression of surprise. "Every couple thinks they're so very discreet."

Eric cast a worried glance at Lantern, but couldn't read any reaction, positive or negative, in the sharp relief of the headlights on Lantern's face. "This has nothing to do with Key—" Eric couldn't lie that smoothly at the moment. "This has everything to do with Key and nothing to do with banging her. She deserves a better life than what she has with Ariadne. Her and Map both." That was true, and he hoped Hank could read that. Sex was sex, but the friends part had become so much more important than the "with benefits," sometime when he wasn't looking. He cared about her too much not to fight for her.

"The kids can't survive on their own. Sorry, Map, but it's true." Hank spoke over Map's inarticulate denial and crossed his arms, apparently settling into his stance now he'd chosen one. "Do you think I haven't considered leaving the barn door open, metaphorically, hundreds of times over the years? But then they'd be wandering, lost, and I'd be dead, no good to any of them."

Eric rocked back and looked over at Lantern once more. Could Lantern target Hank sort of . . . halfway, as Eric had with Manuel, only with better control? Eric could hardly ask in front of Hank, though. Keep talking. "If she didn't have the other powers, she couldn't touch you."

Silence for several beats, intense. "What?" Hank said, low.

Of course. Of course, why would Hank know? Eric hadn't known, Key hadn't known. And Ariadne probably tenderly encouraged her creepy reputation to grow. Eric heard the same realization in Lantern's low, sardonic laugh. "You know she's a power?" Eric said.

"Yes. She . . . well, you know." Hank nodded where Manuel had sped away. "To me, when I took on a certain level of responsibility."

"I didn't mean to." Fucking useless excuse. Eric left it. "She has to be close to you. She needs the others to work at a distance. And even close, blow . . . " He couldn't find the exact words for a moment, but then the first came to him, and the rest followed, tumbling over each other. "Scribe Map, scatter Hound, blind Lantern, bind Key, and blow Breath." Maybe he shouldn't have handed Hank the other weaknesses, but he already knew several of them. Wasn't it better to spread that information around? Normal people should have some sort of defense against powers. "You can go, and be safe. If we win this, they'll have both Lantern and me to lean on."

Hank took one step toward his car, another, climbed in. Eric thought he wasn't going to say anything, but after he started his engine, he paused to open his window, and low words reached them. "I'm sorry, Map. Tell Key that too."

Eric pressed up against his own car, out of the way, and didn't offer a farewell of his own. Neither he nor Hank could throw stones, but he somehow knew Hank would not be following them. Hank's turn to walk away.

Lantern settled a hand on Eric's shoulder. "If you can manage an encounter that well when you're a few days out from your power passing, you must be a force to be reckoned with when you're on your game. Color me impressed. Our chances of getting through this with a minimum of violence are starting to look pretty good."

Eric shook his head and vaguely pushed away the touch. What Lantern couldn't see was how thin his control over himself was stretched on the inside, hemmed in on all sides by blue lines. At least they were far enough from the building ahead that they shouldn't be audible. There was enough time to catch his breath. "I don't really know any of the guards besides Hank well enough to repeat that trick. And there will be a lot of them. Personal levers don't function in aggregate, and sometimes don't even work on a single person if they know too many others are watching and judging them."

He pressed his hands flat over his eyes. When he opened them, Map had edged up solicitously, but fortunately Lantern still stood between the two of them. With only one car left, none of them were in direct headlight beams, and Map's black curls faded out to cut a soft silhouette against the sky's light pollution and scattered stars. "Speaking of a lot of people, Lantern, I didn't realize I could sort of . . . stop short of fully targeting and still be effective. Is it something you can do?"

"Nope." Lantern shoved his hands in his pockets, briefly looking hipster once more to match the flippant tone. Then he grimaced in sincere frustration, and the resemblance passed. Eric recognized the impulse toward gallows humor. "Of all of us, I'm the worst for that. I'm doing light by way of electricity in people's brains, and brains and electricity both are very unforgiving. If we had the time for recon, much better we hold a little sketching class for Map's benefit than have me try to stop short of anything."

Or Hound could do it using their trails, if he'd pull himself together and stop stalling, Lantern didn't say. Eric thought it on his behalf. "And my control's shit." All right. Back in the car. They'd put off more than a general plan until they could see the lay of the land, and right now it was about as laid out as they could hope for. Eric spoke to Lantern and Map through the open doors. "Map, once we're a little closer, I'll get out and walk in, and you should drive. You'll want to get out first and de-mand to speak to Ariadne anyway, for the maximum amount of confusion since they know you, and if you're the driver, they won't necessarily expect anyone else. Then, once there's enough chaos that Ariadne comes to investigate, Lantern can reveal himself to keep her focused on you guys."

Lantern ceded the passenger seat to Map with a gallant gesture. When Map was seated, he glanced over at Eric, his ear-lier anger at having his helplessness in the real world pointed out still stark across his features. For a beat, Eric expected Map to lash out at him too—fated love giving way to his original asshole-tinged protectiveness of Key—but Map only nodded with a jerk of his head.

"I'll follow you, Hound," the Youngest said from the back seat, which actually made Eric start. He'd like to blame it on some kind of talent she had for blending into the background, but he was sure it was his fault, not hers.

Eric took a beat for thought, as calm as he could manage. No other tweaks for the plan occurred to him. Time to go, then.

27

Goddess rose and smiled
Your rewards: to be never gone
Like Key, flowers from bulbs

—*Journey: An Exploration of Contemporary Haiku*, 2003

Key didn't notice Ethan until suddenly he was jogging for the cage. She was on her feet, sawing at one of the higher ties, and didn't have time to get the glass shard out of view. Scheisse. When she stumbled back, folding the shard against her wrist, that only brought her closer into reach on the other side of the cage.

"What have you got?" he demanded, apparently rhetorical because he was already reaching through the little door for her.

He got a grip on her shirt first, then her upper arm, transferring finally down to her wrist.

Ethan hissed something under his breath, and they wrestled over the shard. Sweat made her fingers squeak along the surface, and when she adjusted her grip, skin pressed into sharp edges. The moment she felt it, she let go, but Ethan still scraped the edge along the inside of her first knuckles as he jerked it triumphantly out of her hand.

Key shrieked, more out of pure frustration than pain, though it did sting. She instinctively brought her hand up to suck at the cuts. When the sting had faded to something bearable, she examined her hand. Not deep, but still seeping enough that discontinuous lines of bright red welled up on the skin she'd just cleaned.

"What the hell is going on here?" Ariadne strode up, apparently summoned by Key's shriek. Ethan brandished the shard at her and started to explain, but Ariadne brushed right past him. "Please?" she asked Key, tone gentle once more. She held out her hands to take Key's.

Key lifted her hand for Ariadne to see from well back. "I'm fine."

"Ethan!" Now Ariadne rounded on him. "You never hurt Key. Those are my orders. Under no circumstances." Her tone turned sharper than even the glass in his hands. "Do you understand?"

Ethan looked mulish, but he gave a nod and restrained himself from any verbal reply. Key found her sympathy, frustratingly, straying his way. When "keep Key from escaping" conflicted with the other order, which was he supposed to choose?

"Get me a bowl of hot water, a washcloth, and soap." Ariadne paused a beat, then smiled. Ethan didn't visibly quail, but Key would have in his place. "Then you can make it up to me by being useful, I think."

"Yes, ma'am." On the way past the other side of the cage, Ethan dipped his hand through the bars and extracted the rest of the broken glass from the chamber pot. Key clenched her teeth. She hadn't really thought he'd miss making that connection, but somehow she'd hoped.

Ariadne collected a handful of new zip ties and calmly felt over each of the existing ones, zipping in a new one where she felt Key's cuts. So that escape attempt was well and truly a failure.

All right. Key forced herself to relax her jaw. She was back to keeping Ariadne talking, but Key didn't know how to initiate a conversation in this situation. The silence between them grew more and more painful until the sound of the garage door opening, across the hangar, made Key jump. She leaned into the bars, but beyond watching a car pull out, she couldn't see anything in the small square of darkness beyond.

Ariadne didn't even glance that way. "Look, Key, I shouldn't have tried to hide our argument from you." She hooked her fingers over a crossbar again, standing this time. Her frown had softened into old pain. Key felt the tug at her sympathy again. Ariadne was trying, that expression said. She'd failed, long ago and recently, but she really was trying.

Key didn't care. Ariadne's failures weren't balanced by any-thing so small as "trying." Not for a long time yet even if she started succeeding at her reparations. Like, for instance, letting Key out of the cage.

"You shouldn't have tried to hide anything from me. That's not love." Key examined the cuts on her hand again. They'd stopped bleeding.

Ariadne brightened, as if Key had instead said, "tell me ev-erything, and I'll love you," which she hadn't, at all, but Key assumed Ariadne was pretty good at hearing what she wanted to hear. "You didn't want me to use my power," Ariadne said, words coming out a little quick.

That sounded too nonsensical to be true, so Key stared at her hand and didn't answer. Ariadne waited a beat, then sighed. She rested her cheek against the bars, gaze going into middle distance. "As it was meant to be used. This . . . cycling, losing ourselves every generation, it doesn't make *sense*. And you were right." Ariadne rushed into that admission, like she was so very proud of herself for making it. "Taking a whole life isn't fair, but it doesn't have to be like that. I can take pieces. Small pieces. Small pieces from dozens of people. That's why I never realized it until we started spending time in the cit-ies. We'd always wandered before then, even when other tribes were settling down. Kept moving, traveled as far as we could, picked up bodies across the world. But the cities got too hard to avoid . . . and inside there were so many other humans . . . " Her eyes closed briefly in recollection.

"Taking pieces? To do what?" Key had intended to let Ari-adne talk without either interrupting or encouraging her, but the pause was stretching long, and she had to know. Taking pieces of people's lives—like targeting?—and doing what with them?

"To stay young." Ariadne's lips curved gently, and she opened her eyes. "I told you, Key, we don't have to let ourselves die over and over. I can take it for myself, and I can take it for all of you. Just the smallest piece of life. The human never misses it. I did it to Clive, to keep him quiet for a while, but I can prove it to you now, where you can see."

She stepped away from the cage to see back into the bunker. "Hurry up," she snapped, switch in tone instant. Ethan jogged up and offered a steaming mixing bowl of water with the washcloth floating in it, and a hand-soap dispenser, maybe from the bathroom. The bowl was plastic, Key noted, then made herself stop. They wouldn't let her try the same trick twice, and the bowl looked too big to fit through the cage's small door anyway.

Ariadne took the bowl and dispenser without thanks and set them on the floor beside the cage. "Now." She slid her hand into the angle of Ethan's elbow and smiled up at him, an almost humorous picture with their relative heights. Ethan looked wary, but didn't pull away.

"No, Ariadne, you don't need to—" Key raised her voice, repeated the words again, quickly, but Ariadne ignored her.

Ariadne pivoted to face Ethan, leaving her back to Key. "Just a little piece." She muttered it to herself, like someone concentrating on a task. Ethan's chest, sinking on an exhale, quivered, a second of hyperventilation, then his eyelids sank and he folded down like a doll without internal supports. Ariadne stepped out of the way this time.

"Stop it!" Key slammed into the side of the cage facing them and got her arm out as far as possible. Knees bent, Ethan hit at hip, shoulder, then head, she hoped not hard enough to cause serious damage.

"He's sleeping it off. If you do it in bed after sex, they never notice." She laughed, a spontaneous bubbling up of sound that matched the brightness of her eyes. "You don't understand how it *feels*, Key."

Key was glad of that. Ariadne shifted the bowl of water closer to the cage's small door, wrung out the washcloth, and soaped it. Key allowed her to access the cuts this time because she was still a little in shock, staring at Ethan's unmoving body. She thought she could see his chest rise, but she wasn't sure. She supposed she'd watched Ariadne do the same thing to Clive, but this was different. Now she knew that Ariadne had taken a piece of his *life*.

The sting of soap snapped her out of it. Ariadne delicately cleaned the cuts, then brought the bowl up for Key to rinse her own hand. "How old are you? This body," Key asked. It was hard for her to squeeze the words out, she was so desperate for the answer. How many "small pieces" had she taken? Key shook the water off her fingers, then wiped her hand on her jeans. Ariadne's face looked no different. Strong. Alluring. Human enough.

Ariadne looked up and to the side, clearly calculating. For a long time. A scarily long time. "I swear, I'm losing some years somewhere." She shook her head, her gaze focused again, and she laughed. "I'm sure you weren't asking for that kind of precision. Six or seven hundred, anyway."

Key heard the words, ran them through her mind. And again. She was missing their meaning somehow, because what she'd always thought they'd meant before now was impossible. "You . . . "

Ariadne's smile twisted bitter. "You didn't want me to do it for you, didn't want me to do it even for myself. That was our argument." She settled the bowl of water against her hip as if she'd forgotten it. "I don't want to lose you over and over, Key. Don't you see? This way, we can always be together."

Key swallowed. She wanted to cower against the opposite corner, beat herself against the bars. *Centuries,* and all of that madness focused on Key. She opened her mouth, didn't know what she was going to say until she said it, except that she had to fill the silence somehow. "This is why you kept me from having memories?"

"I wanted you to have time to consider. I know I said the wrong things, made you angry . . . " Ariadne lifted her free hand, let it fall, gesture uncompleted. "I killed someone and tried to give those years to you, and you wouldn't take them. But I don't have to kill anyone now."

Except when they build your house, Key thought. *Or work at a lab, or have the bad taste to be related to a man you want to control as well.* Key nodded like she was actually considering the idea.

"And I didn't know, when I put you into that baby after the argument, that you'd be a pure-state child, instead of yourself. I just wanted you to be yourself, but not to remember the argument until I'd had time to explain." Ariadne smiled, like it was so neat, so understandable.

"How . . . many times have you tried to explain before?" If Ariadne had been trying to create her perfect, docile, unquestioning—yet still herself—Key for all of those centuries since she figured out the secret of ceasing to die . . . And maybe she'd be trying still, if not for a threat from the gods, that had made her kill too widely. And hire Eric.

Ariadne's expression hardened. "That doesn't matter now."

She'd tried many times, Key suspected. How *dare* she, and call it love? The words burned in her mind with the heat of her anger, struggling to get free—*I can never love you on those terms. No matter how many times you try again.*

And she swallowed them. This time, she'd seen the outside world. This time, she'd become intimately familiar with her own and Ariadne's abilities to kill. She had no doubt that Ariadne *would* kill Key, if Key denounced her. The past times, lacking that knowledge, had she denounced Ariadne immediately, not realizing what the consequences would be? Key suspected so. The denouncing impulse cooled, giving way to thoughts not just of the virus, but of Eric. He needed her to stay alive. He was far too new to his powers, and she'd bet his pride would never let him listen to Map or Lantern. She couldn't leave him to stumble along three-quarters zoned out, trying to hide it from the others.

And *Eric* wouldn't denounce Ariadne. He'd think of just the right way to stretch the truth, get her to let down her guard. "It's a lot to take in," Key said. She hoped that was neutral enough to stall.

Ariadne seemed to sense some sort of reservation, because she stepped over to set the bowl of water in the kitchenette sink, then stopped by Ethan on her way back. She got a good grip with both hands on his wrist and dragged him over to the cage. She lifted his arm and threaded his hand between the bars, though it couldn't get far with the size of even his forearms. "I'm not lying, Key."

It took Key a beat to realize that she was supposed to be checking his pulse. She leaned down and found it after a fair amount of fumbling. She didn't know how strong it was supposed to be normally, but she could feel it.

"See? Not dead." Ariadne laughed again and dragged Ethan off in the direction of the hangar, though she gave up before she reached it and tossed his arm negligently over his chest. As well as the bruises from falling, he was going to have a heck of a sore shoulder, Key suspected. Ariadne dusted her hands and left him sprawled there. On her way back, she beamed at Key. "When one of the other two comes back, I'll transfer it to you."

Now was the time for saying just the right thing. Key swallowed and tried to ignore growing nausea. "Not yet, Breath. I need time to get used to the idea. I didn't agree with it at first, and now I need more than—" She mimed checking an invisible watch. "A few minutes to think it over."

"Okay." Ariadne angled her path toward the chair she'd been using earlier, like she was planning to sit there and watch Key think, creepily. Before she arrived, arguing voices drew her attention to the front of the hangar, where the garage door had been left open. Running footsteps too. Something was happening, but it sure didn't sound to Key like it was a something with any kind of organization to it. The argument grew louder. Was it Eric? She had to think he was smarter than driving right up and stirring up the guards like a kicked anthill.

Ariadne whirled around. "You'd think once, just once, I could find some security to hire who can find their asses with both hands and pointers from both Map and Hound."

Ethan groaned. Yes! If Ariadne was too distracted—and she was. She strode for the hangar. Key let whoever it was take care of themselves and pushed the cage away from the pillar with all her strength, toward Ethan.

She called his name, low and intense, then louder. "Wake up. Wake *up*." He could let her out of here. He'd probably be eager to do it, even if he understood only half of what Ariadne had just done to him. He had the bruises to prove it.

Key reached an arm for him, though she was far short. "Ethan! Wake up!"

Ethan groaned. One hand went to his face, while the other touched the concrete, either bracing himself or trying to figure out by touch where he was. Rather than sit up, he rolled to his side, got both palms on the floor.

"Don't try to get up. Just listen." Key kept the words low, but Ethan did turn his head, focus woozily on her. "The Boss drained some of your life force. You have to let me out of here."

Ethan pushed himself up and huffed a laugh. "That's a new one. What really happened?" He rolled his shoulders and twisted his forearms, probably feeling out his bruises.

All right. That clearly wasn't the right tack. Maybe Key should focus on Ethan instead of herself, tap into his self-preservation. Everyone had self-preservation, after all. "She used magic on you. How else do you think she knocked you out with a touch? She'll be back to finish the job any minute." She glanced toward the hangar, but she couldn't see anyone.

Ethan touched his chest and his hand rose and fell as he seemed to feel out his lungs as he had his muscles for bruises. He must remember *something*, then.

"She stole your breath. You know she did. She's dangerous." Relief washed through Key, fresh adrenaline on top of stale. He believed her; she could see it in the dawning horror on his face. She reached out to him again. "Do you have a knife? Give it to me. We need to get out of here."

28

Lack of Hank's guiding authority must have hit the remaining guards harder than Eric had even dared hope. Far from having to sneak around in search of some unlocked side door on what he now saw was a hangar, he walked straight in through the open garage door when consternation at seeing Map had drawn the guards into a knot, arguing. Probably about whether they were allowed to take him down. Even when internally, his self-confidence felt built on eroding sand, Eric walked like he absolutely had a right to be there, more right than he'd had to be anywhere in his entire life, and it must have worked. Even if they saw him in their peripheral vision, his manner and the vague familiarity of his face ensured that no one turned.

No sign of Ariadne among the knot of guards, or approaching it, but Eric couldn't waste this opportunity. He'd wait somewhere inside for her to pass by. There *was* nowhere sheltered from sight to wait, however, at least not immediately in the open, echoing expanse of steel-roofed space that swallowed up the few vehicles inside it. Eric hurried across and sidestepped as soon as he reached a concrete pillar where the roof lowered. If the Youngest was still following him, she was on her own. He didn't catch sight of any movement when he glanced back, however.

In the pause, he slipped on his sunglasses. Familiarity with his face would cease to help him if one of the guards recognized him as a power. He might look like a tool for wearing sunglasses at night, but that was an additional advantage if it made anyone underestimate him subliminally.

The lights dimmed, though tangled trail-blue did not. Among the mass was Key's. That was the important part, but he'd lost the thread of it in his hurry to cross the empty space and had to cast about again. No, he needed to be smarter than that, he should look for Ariadne's trail first, figure out where she was. When Eric looked in the wrong direction, toward the center of the doorway where most of the guards had converged, he had to breathe through it as his mind faded out and only eased back when he fought for each inch of progress. He had no fucking time to be scattered now.

"Oh, look who's here." Ariadne was heading straight for him from deeper inside the hangar, shadows he couldn't penetrate with the glasses on. As she neared her walk smoothed, feet lining up, hips slightly circling. The harsh fluorescent lights matched no catwalk Eric had ever seen, but she conjured her own in sneakers and messy ponytail.

"You're trying to hide your tells. That's *adorable*." Ariadne stopped in front of him and tapped beside her own eye to indicate his sunglasses.

He should have planned better for this, should have *expected* Ariadne wouldn't go running immediately toward the big, obvious distraction. Eric eased back to at least make sure he could keep out of her range. Was the Youngest here by now? No, he couldn't so much as glance aside in search of her; Ariadne would jump on that. Besides, who was to say the Youngest would suddenly feel inclined to break the apparent policy of nonintervention she'd held to so far?

Ariadne treated him to a shark's smile. "So you're the one Map's out there providing a distraction for. I knew if it was really him, he must be playing a part in a plan someone else handed to him."

"He'd be much better able to think for himself if you hadn't imprisoned him his entire life." Eric spouted the rhetoric on autopilot and eased back again. Maybe he could make it outside, to the wind. Then she could sic her guards on him, of course, but he'd have Map and Lantern on his side. Maybe.

Ariadne did follow, keeping him in either unconsciously controlled conversational range or at the edge of consciously controlled powers range. He didn't care which, as long as she kept at it until they were outside. He wished he had more time. More time before she got bored with talking at the edge of her range and closed it, more time before hovering memories swamped him. He hadn't realized it would be this bad. It had been bad enough with Map and their remembered love, but Hound had apparently had plenty of strong feelings about Breath, all summoned to the surface of his mind now. Breath had killed her, when once they'd been friends.

"You're not the first would-be rescuer I've encountered." Ariadne's smile, if possible, turned even sharper. "You all tend to . . . lack perspective. This isn't a fight you'll win."

"Just let Key go, and we'll leave you alone." Eeeease back.

This time, Ariadne didn't follow. Instead, she laughed suddenly. "No. That's not going to happen. But I do have a use for you. Hold that thought." She turned and disappeared into the shadows at the back of the hangar. Her trail spooled out behind her. Uncrossed, right back to him. If he just—just concentrated.

Breath leaned into her lover on the other side of the group's fire, brushed golden hair away from her ear to whisper into it. Key laughed, bright against Breath's low, husky tones, and blushed. "Breath, be nice, they—"

No! No memories. And Ariadne was coming back, dragging something behind her. Eric risked a quick lift of his sunglasses. Key in a *cage?* Seriously? Better than tying her to a chair, he supposed, with bonus Bond villain points. Christ.

Eric dropped his glasses back. "You are the most genuinely fucked-up person I know." All right. New plan. Maybe he could get past Ariadne and free Key. He feinted one way, tried to step around Ariadne the other.

She moved the correct direction to block his path to the cage. "She can have all of your years. You're too much trouble to keep around." Tightness gripped his lungs and grew rapidly into burning.

When Ariadne approached, Ethan shot her a calculating glance, then folded back down to his earlier flopped pose, eyes closed. Key thought she might burst with the words she held back. "No!" she wanted to shout. "Help me!" But her argument for self-preservation had worked too well, and now he was saving himself.

And it worked. Ariadne ignored him completely and strode over to drag the cage toward the hangar. She didn't seem to notice Key's desperate glower at Ethan as they left him behind.

They reached Eric and before he could get to Key, he started fighting for breath. Key was certain he had some kind of plan, sunglasses and all, but that plan wasn't *working* and now Ariadne was killing him. She scratched at the few weakened ties, managed to snap one, but that was moot with its replacement beside it. Unlock, unlock—she screamed it in her thoughts, as if she could make the tight bands of plastic other than they were. Ariadne had mentioned Map. Was Lantern here to? Where were they when Eric needed them so badly?

Then Eric explosively gasped in a breath, another, coughed. Ariadne stared at him, lips parted in apparent shock. "Hound?" She snatched the sunglasses from his eyes and flung them aside to clatter against concrete. The blackness of his pupils shrank as if in a supreme effort of will, then flooded right back. "I hardly believed it when I felt it. How—?"

Eric stepped back and she pressed in on him, snarling. "The baby. Of course. Whose was it, your sister's?"

"Cousin." Eric wheezed the word more than spoke it. Key urged him silently to run, but he only stumbled back single step by single step. Disorientation, or stubbornness? Either would get him just as dead. She could free herself. He needed to get out of Ariadne's reach.

"I'll know just the family tree to look for Hound in this time, then." Ariadne was right in front of him, and his hand lifted once more, instinctively clutching at his throat.

"Breath!" Key shouted, even though Ariadne was right there, couldn't help but hear her. Nothing to unlock, she couldn't reach, all she had left were words. She wasn't good at this like Eric, had failed with Ethan, but words would have to do anyway. "I won't lie to you. I don't love you. I don't know if I ever can, even with time. But I will never—never—love you if you kill Eric now."

Ariadne twisted to look at Key directly, and in her inattention, Eric breathed again. He rocked back a step from her as his chest hitched up, down, up again. Another couple of steps back as he panted. Ariadne shook her head at Key. "You'll have Hound back before you know it. I'll put her in an older child this time, for you."

"Eric. Not Hound." Panic kept the words flowing. Please, let each one be another breath for Eric. "You of all people should understand that there's a difference. If it's always the same Key, why ask her the same question hundreds of times and expect a different answer?" That assumed the logic of a sane person, of course, but that wasn't the point.

The point was Eric's next breath.

Recent: Breath, going, returning. Uncrossed. Even as Eric drew the overwhelming sweetness of oxygen into his lungs, the trail beat at his senses. Ariadne had paused, saying something he couldn't hear, but it wouldn't last. Any moment now, she'd take up her grip again, and this time he wouldn't survive. Not the Eric part of him.

And if he used the powers, wouldn't the Eric part be subsumed anyway? Lose/lose, nothing left of himself. But that was a secondary concern now, when the instinctive part of himself wanted to *live,* no matter who he lived as when this fight ended. He let the trail in.

"So if we were to start again, in this new life, it would have to be on a different foundation. One without killing. No virus, no more targeting." Key's voice was raw, fear stripping it down to the most basic tones of desperate persuasion.

Ariadne's emotions through her trail hit him like a slap. *Did it matter what foolish conditions Key imposed? Love was worth a few conditions. To finally be with her Key again—*

Eric dared a step toward Ariadne. If only he could knock her out physically . . . But he could feel it in the trail as her attention swung toward him. Key jerked that attention back, but only just. "And what we have in each life is each other, isn't it? Don't hurt Eric."

Always Eric, or Hound, or the others. This was about just her and Key.

Eric tightened his attention on the trail. Key had tried, but Eric knew the next moment, Ariadne would decide the solution to her problems would be to get rid of him. He had to use the power. He couldn't, but he had to. Lose himself either way.

But was that right? Eric drowned when Hound's memories poured in, but was the power really part of the memories? If it was like a skill instead, he could incorporate it into Eric, same as his magic, same as any skill. He held the trail now, only needed to concentrate harder. Make that skill part of himself, part of the Eric self, and kill Ariadne.

Because he had to kill her, or die himself. If it wasn't really killing, it wasn't really dying either, and he didn't believe that. However much he managed to keep of himself, that would change; he'd be someone who'd killed. But Ariadne had murdered others, many others, and he'd already helped with that, if ignorantly. Willfully ignorantly. It wasn't about weighing her crimes. It was simple enough. He had to do it for the others. For Key, or Map, Lantern, Lantern's family, and even the memory of the Hound who had preceded him.

Eric concentrated, and the worst happened, what he'd been afraid of all along. Rather than bringing him closer to the feel of her emotions, his effort made them recede. He was working in the wrong direction, and he couldn't find the right one. He didn't know how to do this.

But he did, he realized. He *remembered* how. He had to relinquish that last barrier to live.

"You might need it someday to defend yourself," Key said, her turn to teach Map around the fire in the evenings because they were the two newest in their bodies. Hound listened, eyes closed to doze. "Breath says it's like crushing people so tight, they can't breathe, but it's not really. You have to open something deep in

them, so their life escapes." Hound thought of correcting her, but was too sleepy to bother. You had to follow their trail into the core of them, right down until you found the part so fragile, it disintegrated at a touch.

Eric held Breath's trail in his mind, followed it deep, deeper. She felt it, of course. He sensed the snap of her attention to him, her rage—not fear yet—and the heavy press of her power against him in return. But he had a head start, and he couldn't lose it.

Then she felt fear. It brushed against the edge of his attention, the same way his heartbeat did, growing heavier as the air remaining in his lungs grew thin. But he left all that behind, and followed, followed until he found a shivering spark of life that vibrated beneath the weight of his attention.

Vibrated until it slowed and stilled and without motion, nothing was left.

Ariadne fell. Boneless, inelegant.

Eric could hardly see her, the brightness of the light washed out his vision. He had done it. Ariadne was gone.

29

Key hadn't thought Eric could target yet. She swayed herself, light-headed with relief. She got a good grip on the bars and let herself down to kneeling to get a closer view of Ariadne. Having seen Ethan lie sleeping, she couldn't mistake that total stillness for sleep, but she examined Ariadne anyway, once, again. Centuries, finally ended. Had it really been necessary? She'd stopped killing him, when Key asked her. Maybe they could have reasoned with her.

Too late now.

"Eric? There are scissors in the middle drawer in the kitchen—" Key hadn't looked over to him before speaking, but she did quickly when she heard him retching. She'd cried on and off for nearly twenty-four hours when she killed Maeve, then saw the funeral on TV. She remembered feeling so raw, she might have been turned inside out. "Eric, it'll be all right. Please. Let me out first." Either his name or her tone got his head up, and she saw enough hazel ring of iris to think he might have heard her. "The scissors—"

"Got a knife," he muttered, pulled a modest utility knife from his pocket, and unfolded the blade. His hands shook so badly, he could hardly get it into place and even then only the path between the two tied bars guided the knife onto the tie. When it popped through, he slashed his opposite thumb shallowly.

"Eric, give me that." Key got the knife away from him and set it down on the boards first. She clasped his hands through the bars, both of them, ignoring the blood. "The worst of it ends."

Eric examined her face. "Truth," he said, soft but heavy, like he really believed it. Key didn't know what trail of hers he might have in the cage or around it, but if he was targeting her enough to get her emotions, he knew *she* believed it. Or maybe he was simply reminding himself what he already knew about grief. He'd been the one to tell her that.

Key released his hands and wiped a smear of blood on her jeans to keep her grip on the knife from slipping. It took a frustratingly long time to saw through the rest of the ties, but maybe it only felt that way because she wanted out of the cage so badly. When she kicked it open, she dropped the knife and tumbled out to hold him. "You did what you thought had to do."

Trust Eric to catch her slightly too-honest slip in phrasing. He tried to pull away from her. "Thought? No, if I'd *thought*, I wouldn't have been in that situation. I had to kill her to save myself because I'd put myself in danger with my own stupidity."

"Eric, no." What was done was done. Her reservations crumbled in the face of his pain. She could cast no stones in her glass house of murders. Key tightened her arms around Eric, determined he shouldn't have to collapse into himself again. "It's over. Clive's tied up around here somewhere. We can make him to destroy all of the virus."

"It's over until she settles into whatever body she's in now, and comes looking for us." Eric's next breath hitched on the way in, Key felt it against her body, but he finally brought up his arms to hold her too. "Lantern and his family are safe, but I know I've only delayed most of our other problems."

"It's all right." A new, female voice, one Key didn't recognize.

Key twisted to face the newcomer, but didn't let Eric go. The woman reminded her of Ariadne in some indefinable, worrisome way, though she was taller and slightly darker of skin. It was her poise, Key decided, though that poise lacked both the sternness she'd grown up with and the glittering edges Ariadne had just exposed underneath it.

"She's the youngest of the gods, apparently." Eric laughed suddenly, a note of hysteria in it. "Lantern enlisted her help. What do you mean, it's all right? I didn't just kill Ariadne for good, did I?" Key couldn't be sure, but she thought he was starting to shake.

"Youngest of the gods, like in the story?" Key immediately wished she hadn't said anything so stupid, but the Youngest smiled at her, and Key started to feel like maybe things were almost all right. Getting there.

"Like in the story. And I merely made sure Breath returned in an infant. One generation as a pure-state child will do her good, I think, after how warped she had become in this one." Sadness tinted the Youngest's expression. "Thinking beings are not made for such a timescale—even the gods have their own cycle of rebirth."

"She's been stealing people's . . . lives, I guess, for centuries. Who knows when she last died and passed to someone new," Key explained to Eric. She shivered. Saying it out loud made it seem real all over again. Six or seven hundred years. The Youngest nodded in apparent solemn agreement with Key's reaction, then slipped away.

"Fuck," Eric said, voice low, and for once Key agreed with the bad language. "All right." He said it as though the next thing would be what he planned to do next. All right, I'll . . . But nothing followed.

"I need to go talk to Ethan. Convince him to leave and not to tell anyone about Ariadne's power." Key twisted in Eric's arms, trying to see if Ethan had stopped playing asleep yet. "And then let Clive free, I guess."

"Yes," Eric said. "And Lantern and Map. I think they should be all right, I haven't heard any shots, but we need to tell the guards their boss isn't going to need their services any longer." He drew a sharp breath. Had a plan been jarred loose? Apparently, because he let go of Key and knelt beside Ariadne. He tugged her until she lay on her back. Key wasn't going to interfere, but Ariadne's ponytail was slipping and a lock of hair flopped across her forehead and into her eyes, and Key couldn't stand it. She leaned down and smoothed Ariadne's hair then jerked back upright.

Eric ignored her movement and laced his hands together,

one on top of the other. He placed the heel of his bottom one on Ariadne's chest then leaned up on his arms. He slammed his weight down, then again.

Key grabbed at his shoulder. "Eric, stop! What—?" But then she recognized the CPR. It was such a violent attack of a movement, seen in person. "You can't . . . " Could he start her heart again? Was that even possible?

Eric sat back on his heels and shoved his phone at her. "Ariadne's too rich to assume no one will ask questions when she turns up dead. We've got to call this in to the authorities now. She told us to meet her back here, and then she collapsed—no, we found her already on the ground. They'll be able to tell CPR was done. I'm still officially her employee; that should help. We should get the guards back here, to see this."

"You don't have to start the CPR now." Key doubted Eric was entirely rational at the moment, and the way he shook his head too fast supported the idea.

"I don't trust myself not to miss something. If we play it straight as possible from here on out, it will look right in the details." He shoved the phone at her again. "Call 911."

"I can't call anyone." That definitely wouldn't be playing it straight. Key had no idea what a normal person said to the 911 operator. They never showed that conversation on TV. "You call, and I'll go tell the guards the story, all panicked." She presumed none of them would raise objections to the story as told by Key, who'd been restrained earlier by the woman who was now dead, given that they weren't the types to raise objections to that restraint in the first place.

"Then I can get Map and Lantern to help me grab the virus and deal with Ethan and Clive. And get rid of the cage." Surely there would be a dark corner in the back that paramedics wouldn't look at. It certainly didn't fit with any sort of Ariadne-collapsing idea.

Eric nodded in a jerk. Then, instead of going back to the violence of CPR, he hesitated before smoothing the same lock of hair Key had. "She really did love you, you know. Long, long ago."

"I know." Key looked at Ariadne's still, beautiful face for as long as she could stand, then turned away. Love wasn't enough. If Ariadne had let that love drive her to the right actions, instead of the wrong ones, they'd be in a different place now.

She heard Eric speaking into the phone behind her. "Yes, my boss, she must have collapsed, I think it might be heart attack—"

Key jogged toward the front of the hangar. Ariadne gone. Breath caught in a pure-state child. Key was free to go where she wanted in the outside world.

And she had no clue what she was doing.

30

Lizbeth York @lizyorkauthor

July is fairy tale month for #TwitterReenactors, and I'll be doing #HandoftheGods! @handmap kicks us off! #YOLOverandOver

Key stirred beside Eric, but was clearly not yet fully awake. She snuggled deeper into all the covers she'd stolen, and he flipped back the blanket he'd brought in solely for himself, swung his feet to the floor—and wondered when he'd gotten so used to sleeping in someone else's bed, he'd started automatically making that kind of accommodation.

Light outlined the curtains, of a tone that told him it was shaping up to be one of those quintessentially Northwest days when the sky was overcast but still bright enough to need sunglasses. Under the habitual trails of Key's movements and more sparse ones of the cleaner, the guest room was relatively restrained on the scale of some in Ariadne's mansion, though the impeccable match of headboard to chair back to Greek key motif on the curtains spoke of professional design. Among the matching elements, Key's basket shelf of keys marked her territory quite effectively, lighting the personality of the space.

Eric scrubbed at hair mussed from sleep. He *had* a room of his own. He'd chosen it, and Key was a dragon about guarding the whole wing on that floor against anyone else, leaving it to slowly fade to a state blessedly free of trails for him. He did take refuge there occasionally during the day when the walls of Ariadne's office started to close in. But somehow every night for the two weeks or so since Ariadne's death, after pulling out his hair trying to wrap up Ariadne's complicated financial affairs late into the evening, he'd wander by Key's room and the door would be open in invitation. And sometimes they'd have sex or sometimes just cuddle, but he'd always sleep over.

And yet. And yet he could remember loving Map so keenly.

Key's weight shifted on the bed behind him. Then a touch brushed at the gauze taped to the back of his right shoulder. "What happened to you?" she asked, concern banishing sleepiness from her tone. He'd forgotten she'd see it right away if he slept shirtless as usual.

"It's a tattoo. You can look if you're careful and stick it back down when you're done." Eric braced so he didn't wince as she did so. He imagined the design as sketched out by the artist as he listened for her reaction: a hunting hound, running, with the rich colors and background of an illuminated medieval manuscript, or perhaps a stained glass window.

"After all, it's not like my power's ever going to go away either," he joked. Or it was supposed to be a joke, but it came out harsher than he'd intended. He turned, one knee tucked up on the bed, to face her and reassure her if necessary. "It's meant to be a way to embrace it."

"It's stunning. I want one from the same artist." Key pulled up the hem of her pajama tank and examined her hip then contorted to extend the examination onto her lower back. "Where do you think I should put it?" She grinned and straightened out, released her black locks from the elastic so she could finger-comb them. "I could get a background with lots of *red.*"

Eric wasn't sure he missed her red hair, but it was certainly bound up with how he thought of her. He managed a grin of his own for a moment before hovering worries resettled. "Don't feel like you need to get one just to support me or something," he said cautiously.

Key leaned impulsively forward, kissed him with hands in his hair, then settled back again, sweetness of the touch all too brief. "Eric, much as I love you, do you really think you could guilt me into doing anything I didn't want to do?"

Maybe she was just using the expression, and it didn't mean anything, but Eric had been thinking too hard and too long about love not to react when he heard it out loud. From Key, not Map. What the hell was he doing here, leading her on when he didn't know his own mind? And in a second, Key's face would fall because he'd just made things awkward, and he had no idea what to *say.*

Instead, Key's expression tightened with resolution, and she spoke first. "Map." When he made an inarticulate noise that was probably agreement, she took his hands and drew in a deep breath. "I'd hoped since you were, you know, *here* . . . but okay. It's early yet, but this feels like it's love on my side. But what do I know? I've never been in love before. No matter what Ariadne said, I have no memory of it. But you probably remember exactly what it feels like."

"I—" Eric did remember. And when he allowed the memories to link in that way, through "love," not "love with Map," the strength of the epiphany was like a physical breath after too long underwater. The remembered love hadn't all been with Map. It hadn't all lasted. Some of the memories with it were sharp enough to cut, some were so soft, barely any details remained besides the contentment.

But they were all *memories*. Useful only in how they illuminated how he felt *now*. What he felt was for Key; what he had for Map was memories. "You know what? I'm a moron. I love you, Key."

She laughed, and smiled such a smile, but when she tried to throw her arms around his neck, they were both seated wrong for the hug, and Eric tumbled them sideways onto the mounded covers instead. It felt right, to take what could have turned saccharine to something playful, and with just a light brush of his power against her trail, wrapped around them both, he felt Key's delight for certain.

"Here, I have something for you." Key climbed over him to get to the nightstand, and he sat up behind her. She pulled out a necklace chain, on it strung a tiny key, barely two inches long, but in the same brass, ornate style as the one she'd once told him was the key to his heart. Back at the beginning of it all.

"Oh, Key. Thank you." He reached for it, but she lifted a hand for him to hang on. With great concentration, she displayed it, then appeared to snap the key free of the chain. She showed him the key, the chain, closed them together in her hand, blew on them, then revealed the key strung once more with a curl of her fingers.

"Brava!" Eric took it from her, but had trouble with the tiny clasp where he couldn't see it at the back of his neck. She took over, fingers over his, and fastened it for him, smoothed it down against his chest.

A symbol of power and sleight of hand, magic and magic. Perfect.

While Key showered, Eric decided coffee was of higher priority for him and padded down to get it started brewing in the more human-sized of the house's two full kitchens. The other was all stainless steel on a scale ready to cater entire dinner parties twice a week, and he'd noticed none of the others used it either.

Lantern joined him first, comfortable in nonverbal coffee drinking as they looked out at the lake. From this window, the view was merely beautiful rather than breathtaking, the glow of gray clouds over the shine of gray water against the slashes of green along the shores.

Surveying the day ahead of him, the contentment Eric had attained in sorting out his feelings was quickly eroding. Their immediate battles were won: Clive had destroyed all the virus while they watched, and been suitably threatened into absolute silence. Breath was in a pure-state child. But they didn't know where that child was, as the Youngest had disappeared, and while she took Lantern's calls, he reported she was evasive when it came to questions like when she'd be back. They none of them knew or could predict what the gods might do next, in fact.

Not that the short-term deluge of details left him much space to worry about the gods. Probate was happy to consume every hour he fed to it, with researchers and household staff to fire or pay and properties like the cottages and hangar to keep or try to sell.

"New tattoo?" Lantern asked. His timing rather suggested he thought Eric needed breaking out of his thoughts. Eric was willing enough to be broken out, and he presented his back to Lantern's curiosity, as he had to Key's. That left him facing the doorway as Map entered, dressed and groomed for the day.

"This is some good work. Want to see?" Lantern nudged Eric's shoulder, but Map was staring at Eric's chest instead. It took Eric a beat to realize what he was reacting to. The key pendant. He was still holding his coffee mug, but his free hand came up instinctively to touch it.

"It's all settled, then?" Map's voice walked the link between sarcasm and hurt, uncaring and caring far too much. If he'd had an uncrossed trail, Eric supposed he could have discovered which, or what proportions of each, but that seemed rude.

"Yes," Eric said, because he needed to stand up for this, even if Key wasn't here. "I'm sorry."

Lantern craned his neck to check what they were talking about. "Different lives are different lives, Map. I suppose you don't remember in Mongolia, when you two ended up with such opposing personalities, you barely spoke for an entire winter."

Rather than answer, Map banged a pan down on the stove. "How does everyone want their eggs?"

Eric figured he'd best take his coffee and come back for breakfast later, but Map's "wait" stopped him in the doorway. Map was still glowering into the pan, but he blew out a sigh, and seemed to set his bad mood aside. "You've been doing all this stuff with the estate; the least I can do is cook you breakfast."

Eric's mug was almost empty anyway. He came back into the kitchen, and matched the conversational olive branch with one of his own. "Before you go out today, if you can come by Ariadne's office and sign your Social Security card, that would be helpful. When I started going through Ariadne's documents, I discovered you and Key are both perfectly legal. We can probably start on getting your driver's license and all that soon as well."

Map shook his head, and turned to the fridge for eggs. "What name am I even signing?"

"Martin Respiros. Key's Kerry," Eric said. Key's paperwork to get on the grid in the modern world was farther along, but while not precisely avoiding each other, he and Map hadn't really been talking to each other much, so it had been easy to let other things push that aside.

Coffee refilled, Eric leaned a hip against the counter. "In her will, Ariadne left the two of you trusts, to last your lifetimes. And the former Hound, too, but we also found a death certificate for him for an accidental death, so that's taken care of. No idea how she swung that." Eric grimaced. "More than enough for you two to live on, anyway. The rest goes to her closest nonadopted—since that's what you two are, legally—relative, once he or she is found. The executor, or personal representative, as the lawyer keeps calling it for some reason, gets a trust to make sure the genealogy data doesn't get lost or deteriorate, and any properties get kept up while he searches. All very neat, assuming she'd passed normally."

"Who's the personal representative, then?" Map cracked the eggs one-handed without looking, leaving Eric quietly impressed.

"Me." Eric gave a bark of ironic laughter. "And your trustee. She only had a few days between when I stopped being the loyal family friend and when she died. She didn't change the will." He laughed again, turned away to pull out plates and cutlery. "There's a provision in the will that I continue getting my former salary until the heir is found, too. I'm hoping maybe I can hire Taylor with money from the estate so we all have some kind of income."

Map looked confused, mouthing the name, but he seemed to work it out even before Lantern had lifted his fingertips and given them a little wiggle. Eric had asked for his legal name at the start, but Map must not have thought to be curious. Or he hadn't been talking to anyone very much, not just Eric.

Eric shook his head. "Anyway. So there will be plenty of money for you two after probate's finished, but we have to get there first. As soon as I can—and the lawyer thinks I probably can—I'm going to try to sell all the properties except for this one. It costs a lot in upkeep, but moving all the servers and such with the genealogy data would be a pain in the ass. If we make it that long without being smited—smote?—by lightning, I'll see if I can find some dedicated head of the project so we can forget the damn thing and just get our money."

"Hello?" A female voice, and footsteps zeroed in on the kitchen quickly enough to suggest she'd waited to call out until she'd actually located them. The Youngest entered, having apparently just let herself into the house. Hadn't the front door been locked? But no, the cleaners would be leaving around now, she must have charmed her way in, much as Eric would have.

Her black hair was braided more simply today, she was smiling cheerfully, and she was also carrying a baby. The screwed-up face and tiny, intricately shaped hands visible outside the swaddling were a soft, medium-brown shade. "I don't know how any of you find anyone in this place if you're not Hound." The Youngest tried to give the baby to Eric, who couldn't help a stutter-step back in surprise. Baby, what?

Lantern swooped in and cuddled it up and cooed to it. Eric finally caught up. "That's Breath." The Youngest nodded.

Really, he should have wondered about this long before now, but— "And the baby came from . . . where? They had a special, nine-ninety-nine a pound at Safeway?"

"No, we have relationships with several adoption agencies." The Youngest cast a parental sort of look of disappointment at Eric. Apparently that kind of humor didn't appeal to her. "I sent her to a baby I'd looked up ahead of time. And now I've got the paperwork squared away for you all."

Eric held up his hands to fend off the very idea. Not that he had any particular objection to kids in abstract, but fuck, he didn't want one more legal responsibility at the moment.

"Chill," Lantern said, falling into steady rocking of the probably a bit unnaturally silent baby. "It's probably under my name, since that's the one she actually knows."

"Oh, we looked you all up immediately," the Youngest said, cheer not distracting Eric from the fact that that "we" was probably the gods. "But I figured Lantern wouldn't mind, and I didn't know about the rest of you." She nodded at Eric.

"And what else is that 'we' going to do about us?" Eric crossed his arms and tried to look as confident as he could shirtless, in pajamas.

"Nothing for the moment." The Youngest grew solemn and clasped her hands loosely in front of her. "With one of you so recently passed and another a pure-state infant, you're nearly useless." Her smile stole back. "Or so I assured my siblings. It won't last forever, even if I continue to downplay your level of ability, but as long as you live your lives and generally keep results of your powers from making it to the Internet, you should have something on the level of years of peace, if not a decade or more."

She dipped her head in a formal nod of farewell and turned to go. Eric took a step after her. If she was telling the truth, that would be a great gift, not one he'd have expected from one of those gods. she was telling the truth. "Why are you helping us?"

Lantern made an annoyed noise, but the Youngest waved him away. "It's a fair question. I'm helping you because I owe you. Had I not made a foolish mistake and put myself in danger with my wanderlust, you would not be as you are. The least I can do is make sure 'as you are' brings you as little pain as possible."

Her body language was truthful enough. Eric decided he had no wish to feel a god, through an uncrossed trail. He gave her a formal nod of his own. "Thank you."

"Would that I could do more." The Youngest slipped out, leaving them alone. With additional baby. Map plated two sunny-side-up eggs and came over to examine it, poked a forefinger at it, and his face softened into delight when he was caught by the grip reflex.

Seeing Lantern with the baby reminded Eric of something he'd been meaning to bring up ever since Lantern had settled in with the rest of them rather than disappearing off to whatever life Taylor had been living before. "I have Laura's current number, you know, if you ever want to contact her."

"Laura?" Lantern's tone was breezy, but Eric could see in the tightening of muscles around his eyes it was an act.

He treated the question like it was serious anyway. "You know, your daughter?"

"When we inherit children from our . . . former selves when the power passes, it's not really quite the same as 'our' children." Lantern bent his head over the baby, hiding his expression, but Eric watched the muscles in his arms, holding the child close, thought about how Laura had talked about her childhood, and made an educated guess.

"But that wasn't the case this time."

"It doesn't matter. The Hand doesn't visit people we knew before." Lantern turned away to start opening and closing cupboards. "We need to buy some formula. And a bunch of other stuff."

That was a no, then, on contacting his daughter. For now, at least. Eric knew the answer he could have given, had he wanted to push: undoubtedly the Hand hadn't killed each other, imprisoned each other, right up until Breath had. But Eric didn't push, because heaven knew there were things he was avoiding himself at the moment.

Key broke the moment by wandering in, with a sock-skid on the hardwood that took Eric so powerfully back to when they'd first met that he had to smile. She claimed the as-yet unclaimed eggs, and listened with dawning relief as he relayed what the Youngest had told them.

When he was finished, she bounced up and pushed at his back, angling him for the door. "You have no excuse not to come along, then. Go hurry up and get dressed."

"Come along where?" Eric barely had time to set his mug down on the counter before Key was propelling him in earnest. Lantern laughed, and when Eric checked on Map, he looked more amused by a younger sibling than anything.

"Diane said she'd take me to the zoo." Key pronounced the word with glee. "They have snow leopards!"

Those words provoked an association, and Eric had to smile, once the memory played out completely. "You had a plan to capture and raise a cub, at one point. I found you a den, but at the last minute, you didn't want to deprive the mother." He braced a little, waiting for Key to demand more details. But while her eyes widened, she only laughed, nodded her thanks.

"There's no guarantee they'll be out where you can see them, anyway." Eric turned, took her hands, squeezed them to make it clear he was teasing, then tried to drop them. "I don't think I should come. You have fun."

Key hung on and tried towing rather than pushing. "Why

not? I listened at least the first sixteen times that you told me that probate lasts for months at the very shortest. You have time for a break."

"You may also recall a remark I made about Grand Central Station." Eric tried to peel her fingers off, but with both hands entangled, he had no leverage. "It's not raining so there will be at least seventeen million small children running in every direction."

"It'll be good for you." Key beamed when Eric gave up on resisting her pull. "You'll need to get used to that if you want to work up to magic shows again, right? It'll build character, as your sister says." She sobered for a beat. "You brood."

Eric had to laugh. "I do not!"

"You do." All three of them said it, overlapping. If they'd been free, Eric would have thrown up his hands. All right. Maybe he had been. Only a little.

Key dropped one of his hands, but kept her fingers firmly laced with his on the other. "Come enjoy the zoo. Make fun of me gawking like a child. Take a break from brooding. If you zone out, I've got your back."

Eric realized he could think of worse ways to spend the day than going along with Key, while she was having fun, wherever that was. He pressed a quick peck to her lips, then slipped out of the kitchen to go get dressed, as directed.

ACKNOWLEDGMENTS

As ever, I owe a great debt to those who helped me with the revising and the publishing of this novel, the former even more so than usual as I embarked on a novel in a new world after four in a world I had grown practiced and comfortable with. From the perspective of several new worlds later, it seems easy, but I remember my trepidation at the time. Corry Lee-Boehm and Kate Marshall helped with the first draft; my agent, Cameron McClure, offered suggestions on the next, and Kevin Jewell, Harold Gross, Paul Dixon, and Dave Hendrickson helped at later stages. I have probably forgotten someone, so if you've critiqued any of my projects, thank you!

In the course of production, Kate Marshall was invaluable as ever, creating the cover and doing layout as well as acting as a second set of eyes on the whole process with patience and wisdom. Andrea Howe of Blue Falcon Editing took time from her busy schedule to provide meticulous copy editing. My critique group ladies not already mentioned, Shanna Germain, Erin Evans, and Susan Morris, helped with cover and advertising copy and provided key support in the last push to getting this book into your hands. Duane Wilkins at the University Bookstore and Peter Honigstock at Powell's generously offered me a signing and shelf space, even as a self-published author. The writing and reading community of the Northwest is lucky to have them.

This book as a product of an imagination nurtured by the communities that surround it. Online gamers, choristers, Northwest writers, archaeologists, and my family: I owe you more than I can say.

READ ON

for a short story from the world of

Read more about the SILVER series and get updates on
new books and stories at www.rhiannonheld.com

LADY CEREMONY

A Short Story From the World of *SILVER*

By Rhiannon Held

Lady Ceremony

Ginnie's anger at her father kept her running along the rural highway until her back was plastered with sweat. The late evening sun striped the much-mended pavement and she stomped hard on each shadow. She was nearly thirteen, for Lady's sake. Why couldn't she go visit Tom and her other friends in Boston for the summer, instead of being stuck up here in Quebec because her father had screwed—no, fucked—up and got himself exiled? And let himself stay exiled because he was too proud to apologize.

Ginnie heard a car in the distance and slowed to pick her way onto the shoulder without tumbling into a ditch. Sometime in the run, restlessness had relaxed its teeth from her neck. Fine. Maybe she'd sneak off. Take the bus to Boston. If she could get onto another pack's territory fast enough, then her father's pride would be working for her because he wouldn't be able to follow unless he apologized and asked for permission. She clambered up the slope on the other side of the weedy ditch and into the bushes between the trees there, to cut back to the house.

When Ginnie looped around to approach the house from the back, she crossed her father's outgoing trail. She should be grateful he'd left, she supposed, because she'd avoid punishment for their earlier shouting match a little longer. But he'd left in wolf, since it was nearly the full, and that suddenly made her even angrier. She wasn't sure why. She should be having her Lady Ceremony soon enough, but the first shift itself seemed slightly scary to her. What if it hurt more than people said? But her father was off running and having fun in wolf and she was stuck here hot, sticky, and in human.

At least her mom was still home. Her voice drifted through an open window as Ginnie approached the back door. Her mom must be on the phone. Ginnie probably should have gone up and opened the door noisily rather than eavesdropping, but Ginnie couldn't not. What if her mom was angry with her too? You could never tell with her mom, she was so quiet and nice.

"—both of them screaming at each other, and Ginnie didn't even eat her dinner. I'm afraid it's turning out like you warned me, Boston." A pause. "You know I don't have any status anymore. . ." Ginnie's mom sighed. "Yes, all right. Like you warned me, *Benjamin*. Two alphas squaring off without even other pack members to distract them. He's gone a lot for his job, guiding the hunting and fishing trips, but he doesn't have as many overnights scheduled this year. It's not enough to give them space."

Alpha? Ginnie looked at her hands, like it would be written on her skin somewhere. She didn't feel much like an alpha. And there was no one around who would listen to her if she told them what to do, so how would she even know?

"I'm afraid she pushed him. She wants out as well, now school's finished for the summer." Ginnie's mom laughed, low, and Ginnie relaxed a little. Things couldn't be *that* bad, then. "None of you alphas know how to persuade someone subtly, do you?" She listened for a few seconds. "Well, I'm glad you agree, anyway. I'll see what I can do to convince him slowly."

Convince her father of what? Ginnie crept closer to the house, making sure to keep at least one tree between her and the window, but then a breeze trickled in from behind her. Her mom would smell her in a minute, so Ginnie gave up on eavesdropping and jogged up to the back door as loudly as possible like she'd just gotten there.

Her mom was off the phone when Ginnie opened the door. She sat at the kitchen table where Ginnie's plate of food still waited for her. Probably a little cold by now, but she didn't really mind at this point. Her stomach had remembered it was really hungry. She checked her mom's face and scent. She seemed worried, but better than she must have been while Ginnie and her father were yelling and not paying attention to her at all.

Ginnie felt really bad about that, now she thought about it. So when her mom held out her arms in invitation, she ignored the food to sit on her lap. It was a little silly now she was as old as she was. She was still a little shorter than her mom when standing, but sitting on her lap, she could practically rest her chin on the top of her mom's head. She curled down to at least get her cheek on her mom's shoulder. "Sorry," she muttered. She hoped her mom wouldn't tell her to apologize to her father too. He was still wrong.

"You do have to learn diplomacy, puppy. You can't be disrespectful like that." Her mom hesitated for a moment, then leaned her head so her hair tickled Ginnie's nose. "But maybe not during the full. Your friend Alouette, didn't she invite you to go with her and her family to Montreal this weekend?"

Ginnie sat up straight, pulling away from her mom. Alouette had, and Ginnie hadn't bothered mentioning it to her father, because she hadn't wanted to waste any good mood he had—which apparently wasn't any—on Montreal when she could put it toward Boston. Apparently her mom thought it would be good for her and her father to stay away from each other for a few days.

And how much easier would it be to catch a bus from Montreal? If her mom was suggesting the trip, Ginnie assumed she'd stop her father from showing up and dragging her home immediately, so she wouldn't have to worry about that. She could go to Montreal and have Alouette's family take her to the bus station. And maybe Tom could pick her up at a closer bus stop than Boston—he had his truck to roam in, and they'd only talked about meeting in Boston when Ginnie thought her mom could take her straight there.

She'd love to be able to drive part of the way with Tom. He was *fun*, and she'd missed having him around to act like a big brother, after he moved so far away and then her father got exiled. He could drive her into Boston's territory, and once they were there, her father wouldn't be able to do anything about it, no matter how long she stayed. If he tried to show up to get her without asking for permission, he'd get his ass beaten. And he'd never ask for permission in a million years.

Ginnie felt like jumping off her mom's lap and dancing around in victory. "Thanks, Mom." She hugged her mom tight instead. Maybe she shouldn't seem too happy, so it wasn't suspicious, though. "Maybe when it's not the full, I could ask Dad—"

Her mom squeezed tight in return, then let go so Ginnie could see her grimace. "We'll see, puppy."

"Okay," Ginnie said, focusing on her disappointment from earlier so hopefully her mom wouldn't smell that it had disappeared now. She was going to get to see Tom after all!

It seemed later to Ginnie that things went wrong right about when she started feeling smug about having gotten away with her plan. She and Alouette had a such great time running around Montreal and shopping and staying up half—well, nearly all—the night, Ginnie almost wanted to stay one more day. But she'd told Alouette's mother that the plan was for her to get the Sunday morning bus to Albany, and she'd texted Tom to meet her at the station there. When she called Boston to get her permission to visit his territory, he didn't ask her any questions, just told her she'd be welcome.

So she took her backpack and got on the bus that stank of humans, but not as bad as she remembered the Metro doing, back when her family still lived in Virginia, and congratulated herself. Her excitement made it hard to sit still, and her stomach felt a little weird too. Maybe all the restaurant food she'd had yesterday. But she really hadn't slept much last night so she finally dozed, secure in the knowledge that by the time her parents would be expecting Alouette's family to drop her off tonight, she'd already be with Tom.

She woke when they went through customs, then again when the bus pulled into the first stop in New York. The first thing she smelled on waking was blood.

That was a little scary, but not that weird, except that it was really close. Ginnie scrubbed at her nose as everyone filed off to go into the station and use the bathroom and buy snacks or whatever if this wasn't their stop.

The smell of blood didn't move, and that was when she realized it was her. She wasted a little time checking her arms and hands for where she'd been scratched, but she knew better than that. As soon as she admitted it to herself, she stood up quickly and checked her pants and the seat. No blood on the seat, thank the Lady, and she couldn't see anything on her jeans either. She'd better get inside to the bathroom before that changed.

In the hurry of digging out quarters and getting the handle to turn on the ancient metal dispenser to get a pad, Ginnie almost managed not to gag at the smell of the bathroom. Public ones were never great, but this was down at the very bottom of ones she'd ever had the misfortune to have to use. And she had to *stand* on the *floor* with her stockinged feet for a couple seconds while she changed to a clean pair of underwear.

But then it was done, and she actually felt a bit proud of

herself. She wasn't a child anymore. She could handle getting her period when she was on her own, no sweat. The pad was thick and gross when she sat back down on the bus, just in time, and she smelled blood too much to nap now, but she'd deal with it.

As they pulled away, she started to ache. Not in her belly, like it was cramps, but all over her body. She wished she had a shade to block the sunlight spearing her through the window like an ant under a magnifying glass. She hunched down as far in the seat as she could, leaned against the wall, and tried not to think about running. If she could only work these aches out, stretch and twist and unkink her muscles and run—

That was when she got it. First shift happened after your period, at the next full, or the one after that, but what about if your period was *on* the full? Shouldn't that mean you had a whole month to wait until the next one? But it was supposed to happen faster for high-ranked Were, and her mom had called her an alpha. Was she going to have her first shift *today*?

That couldn't be right. Ginnie was just worrying too much. But when they got to the next stop, an hour later, she could no longer deny it. She hurt, really bad, and she wanted to—to something. Her mind kept suggesting "stretch," but that wasn't right at all. She wanted to be home and with her mom and dad and not here stuck on a bus full of humans who'd all see her if she shifted. She absolutely couldn't shift here.

What should she do? She didn't know. The moment the bus was empty, she called her father. She almost sobbed when it went to voicemail. That wasn't really that strange. Even if he and her mom weren't in wolf, he was probably out of range.

The voicemail beeped and she hadn't even heard it telling her to leave a message. "Daddy—I'm sorry, I'm so sorry, I'm on the bus to Albany and I feel like I'm going to shift—I got my period—and I don't know what to do, should I keep going to meet Tom, or . . . ?" There must be so many other things she should say and she couldn't think of a single one of them, so she ended the message and scrubbed at her tears before they could fall on the phone. She typed a quick text to tell him to check his voicemail, then called Tom.

He did pick up, and that made Ginnie cry so hard she couldn't get any understandable words out. "Ginnie Gin? What's wrong? Did your father change his mind?"

Ginnie choked into something trying to be a laugh. Her father didn't even know she was here. "Tom, I don't know what to do—" A woman with two children clattered noisily up the stairs and Ginnie ended the call in a panic. She'd have to text him so no one would hear. Her fingers were shaking now, and she had to pause to ride out a wave of aching, so she sent the text as the bus was pulling away again.

Tom didn't take long to type his answers, full of typos probably because of his hurry: *get of the bus.* Then, *now. find someway private and text me where you are okay?*

Ginnie stared out the window at the buildings sliding by, getting farther apart and giving over to trees as they headed out of town. She'd made the wrong choice, then. Again. Lady damn it. She clenched up into the smallest ball she could for a minute. She couldn't shift here. She'd have to wait. Wait two hours. She remembered this next stop was farther away. When she could breathe again, even if she still hurt, she typed carefully, putting all her focus into the task. *Can't. Have to wait until the next stop.* She sent that and hung onto her phone like that was her lifeline.

Okay, came back. *I have to drive now, I can't text, but hang on. I'm coming.*

Ginnie clutched her phone to her chest. She thought about checking the map on it, to see how far the next stop was from Albany—or from wherever Tom was now since he hadn't expected to pick her up yet. But she didn't really want to know. She wanted to focus on not letting the ache take over her whole body until she shifted in front of humans. And on praying to the Lady. She'd made some bad choices, but maybe the Lady would still help her get through this. She'd never try to trick her parents again. Ever. She promised with her whole voice.

Ginnie gave a great gasping sob of relief when the bus pulled away from the next little station, a modern brick building that still kind of fit with the old brick buildings in the little downtown. It was bigger than the downtown where she lived now, but nothing compared to where they'd lived in Virginia. Some of the other passengers who'd gotten off here were still loading luggage into their cars so she wasn't alone yet, but she was getting close.

She clenched her hands on the straps of her backpack and the next problem occurred to her. Where was she supposed to be private in a strange town? Not in a bathroom, and someone could always come out to the Dumpster if she tried to hide behind a store or something. She needed woods, but everything here was single trees and decorative plantings.

She took one step, then another, with no thought beyond "away." But it didn't really matter which direction she went, did it? As long as she headed out of town. Walking helped the ache a very little bit, and forward movement was better than nothing, so she moved forward. She'd follow the sidewalk in a straight line until it ran out and then she'd smell for woods because hopefully there would be less car exhaust in the air by then.

She wasn't sure how long she walked. The sun got hotter, but not unbearably so and she did have a water bottle in her backpack. She was probably healing a sunburn, too. But this town was surrounded by *fields* and she couldn't shift in those, someone would be sure to see her. She felt so tired of fighting against the all-consuming need to do something that she didn't even properly understand. Maybe if she got exhausted enough, she wouldn't have to shift yet.

Cars passed her regularly, some giving her plenty of room along the shoulder since the sidewalk had long run out by now, some whooshing right past. She was too miserable to be angry at them. One slowed and she started to get worried, because maybe she was going to get in trouble with the humans for being a girl walking alone, but then it pulled up behind her and the door opened and she smelled Tom.

She ran for him and he grabbed her up in a hug and lifted her feet off the ground to carry her, backpack and all, to the back of his pickup. He set her down to open the canopy and lower the tailgate, so she scrambled up on her own.

"You left a good trail," Tom said, in that voice adults used when they didn't want her to think they were angry at *her*, rather than her situation. He seemed more than a little scared, mixed with the angry. "I could follow it pretty well even from the truck, with the windows open. I'm sorry we couldn't get here sooner."

Ginnie missed the "we" until the passenger door of the truck opened and shut. Felicia set her hand on the side of the canopy and leaned around to give Ginnie a tentative smile. "Hello," she said. Ginnie hadn't seen her in a long time, and now she looked so *adult*. And glamorous, with her long, wavy black hair and big chest. Why did *she* have to be here, and see Ginnie such an aching mess and smelling of humans and that bathroom and blood?

But she was Tom's girlfriend now, wasn't she? Ginnie had heard that, though she'd thought she'd also heard they broke up. Why wouldn't he want to go roaming with his own girlfriend? Ginnie wished she didn't have to be here now, though. "I have to shift," she told Felicia, and climbed farther back into the bed. Felicia made a noise of sympathy—like Ginnie was a pathetic injured child or something—and boosted up to join her.

"I'll keep watch," Tom said, and closed the tailgate and leaned against it. Even not fully enclosed, the space was uncomfortably warm and the light was dimmed by the grime on the windows in the canopy. Ginnie tossed her backpack to the corner to join a spare pair of boots and an old sleeping bag and pointedly ignored Felicia.

Now. Now she could shift. But she didn't . . . know what she was doing. Should she clench up her muscles? Try to relax and let something happen? She didn't think she could relax right now. It felt like she should be doing something, but she still didn't know what.

She wiggled out of her clothes, she knew to do at least that much, but then she leaned her weight on her hands and panted and nothing happened. "How do I do it, Tom?"

Tom glanced back, then grimaced and returned his attention to the road. He scraped his sandy hair out of his face. "You . . . kinda fall into it? It's not really something there are really words for."

"Silver talks about—" Felicia's Spanish accent threaded through her words. "Wild selves. She says kids keep their wild selves behind their eyes. So I guess you have to set it free?" She sounded as confused and worried as Tom, which actually made Ginnie feel a little better. She might be eighteen or nineteen, but she didn't know the right answer to everything either. Ginnie looked at her, kneeling on the plastic of the pickup bed, and noticed the sweat starting to stick down her shirt under her arms and the crinkle where she'd had her hair in a ponytail earlier. Maybe not so glamorous after all. Just normal.

Ginnie tried to fall. Or set something free. She really did. But she had no idea where she was falling to or falling from. Or what she was freeing.

"I could show you?" Tom rolled his shoulders like he was pretty itchy in the full too, but then he'd had ten years or more to learn to control it. "Do it with you."

"I've seen it before," Ginnie snapped, suddenly angry and then it *hurt* again and she dropped her head to get through it. She'd had twelve years of being around shifts and watching them happen. It wasn't particularly helping.

Tom straightened away from the tailgate with a noise of surprise. "Are you allowed to be—?"

"Move." Her father's voice. Tom did move, and her father stepped into view and opened the tailgate. Felicia knelt up taller, not quite bristling yet, but definitely keeping an eye on him. Ginnie hugged her arms around herself. She hoped he wouldn't be angry right now. She couldn't deal with him being angry right now. If he could wait, for when she'd shifted and they were home . . .

But he was in another pack's territory. She'd never thought he'd unbend enough to apologize and get permission for that. He must be even more angry about having to do that. "I'm sorry," she tried to say, but it came out as a sob. "I'm tired."

"I know, puppy." His voice was gentle. Her father, big and strong and broad-shouldered, climbed up to sit on the open tailgate and opened his arms. When she crawled into them, he embraced her and stroked her hair. "Should have known you'd be a strong one. Surprise us all by shifting early." She hadn't heard him speak so softly since he'd been exiled and became angry all the time.

Though maybe Ginnie had spent so much of that time arguing with him, she hadn't really given him an opportunity for that either. He pulled back to catch her eyes. "Let it take you, all right? Don't fight it. My father used to have a lullaby he'd sing to the cubs in his pack…" He hummed, low and sweet. "Listen to the song. Let it carry the Lady's light through you, until you're floating." He measured dominance through their gaze, and she let him be the stronger, protective one this time. "Relax." That last was an order, an alpha's order. Ginnie knew he was trying to help her, so she tried to follow the order, instead of opposing it because he was so often wrong, like she usually would have.

And he sang, voice deep. If the Lady's light moved through her, it was because the song settled low into her skin first. When she stopped holding on so hard, everything changed. It was hard getting there, but her muscles twisted and settled and then that was right, too.

She was on her side now, four legs stretched out, and her dad ruffled her ears. Tom, leaning in to see her properly, laughed in slightly giddy relief. "You're almost white! Throw on a little flour and you could be Virginia Dare for Halloween."

Ginnie wanted to grumble at Tom for dredging up that bit of childishness—she hadn't wanted to be white like Virginia Dare for years now—but the words came out as a yip instead. She examined her flank and found it to be the lightest of grays, but peppered with flecks of black on the guard hairs. It wasn't really white at all and it felt exactly right. Felicia grinned at her and smoothed the fur along her flank. "Lady welcomed," she said, solemnly.

Tom's phone beeped and he pulled it out and typed a reply to what was probably a text message. "Boston ended up not being that far behind me."

Ginnie's dad tried to get his arms under her belly, but she wiggled away from him. She wanted to stay here and rest for at least a few more minutes before she walked anywhere, and she wasn't going to let him carry her. She wasn't a baby now. She'd had her first shift.

Ginnie's dad growled. "We have to go, Virginia."

A car pulled up behind them. Tom didn't look surprised

this time, so he must have recognized it, but Ginnie didn't relax until Boston got out. He always made her feel centered, somehow, dark-brown skinned and deeply grave. When she looked at her father again, he'd jumped to the ground and was backed up against the tailgate, smelling of fear turning quickly to anger.

He hadn't asked for permission, Ginnie realized with a jolt. When he'd gotten her message, he'd just come straight to her. Maybe he'd hoped he could take her home before he got caught. But now he had been caught. Would the Roanokes have him beat up before he got dragged back to Quebec?

"Rory," Boston said. He stopped about two meters away and waited.

Her dad closed his hands over the edge of the tailgate, barely-suppressed violence seeping into his scent. He couldn't possibly be planning to fight Boston, could he? Her dad was in the wrong here and everyone knew it. He knew it, she could smell that too with her nose newly sharpened.

And if he did hurt Boston, that was so much worse than territory trespass. The Roanokes would have to give him a similarly worse punishment. Would they decide they had to exile him to somewhere different—and terrible—like among all the hostile packs in Europe? He could move to somewhere without many Were instead, like South America, Ginnie supposed, but that seemed worse in another way. At least from Quebec she could visit other packs within a day's drive.

If she went with him. She knew her mom would. Would she have to see her parents only once a year, or even less? Ginnie didn't want *any* of those possibilities.

So she couldn't sit back and let this happen. She had to talk to them, and to talk she had to be in human. She didn't know if going back would be like falling as well, but she did know trying too hard probably wouldn't help. She tried to search for the feeling of herself that had twelve years of weight behind it instead of a few minutes. This was her too, now, but that her was more familiar.

This time, it did feel like stretching. Stretch and then she was back to herself. She didn't really feel any different in human than before she'd been able to shift, which was odd. She would have expected to. "Daddy, please. Can you ask for permission to be on his territory now? Better late than never, right?" It came out breathy, making her realize that she was still so *tired*. She leaned on her palms again.

Her father ignored her completely and pushed away from the tailgate. He flexed his fingers, then they settled into fists.

"You're not allowed to be here, Rory," Boston said, tone sharpening, though he didn't get any louder. Ginnie didn't know how he managed to sound so dangerous while still being so soft.

"What are you going to do, drag me home all by yourself, old man?" Her father's voice was plenty loud, in comparison, laid over a growl. "None of Dare's eager bootlickers are here to help you."

Boston settled into frightening stillness. At least, it frightened Ginnie. It didn't seem to change her father's plans. "I can cause you more pain than you think, Rory. Little as I want to. And greater pain than that will come later, when the Roanokes hear."

Ginnie took a deep breath, but swallowed anything she might have said. Her father was wrong again and she wanted to shout at him. Apparently nothing had changed with her first shift. Nothing at all. He wasn't even listening to her to shout back this time, he was so focused on Boston.

She groped after her clothes. She had to at least get between him and Boston. She didn't want her dad to get beat up and have to move to South America. She didn't. She got her pants on herself, without underwear, and then Felicia was handing over her shirt and helping her pull it on. "Stop him before he says something worse I can't 'forget' to mention to my father," Felicia whispered.

Ginnie's legs were unsteady, so she didn't make it to the narrowing space between her father and his chosen opponent. Instead, she caught herself against his back, fingers clenched around a handful of fabric. He started like he'd forgotten she was there.

Ginnie should say something, now she finally had his attention, but she had no idea what. He *had* come to help her. He wouldn't swallow his pride now, but he could have let that make him stay home and let Tom and Boston help her instead.

So maybe she could be the one to make a change—she could be happy he'd do that for her, and let go of the fact that he couldn't set his pride aside. If she admitted it to herself, something in her knew that he'd never change that much, at least not anytime soon. She loosened her grip on his shirt to press her hand against his back and made sure not to shout at all. "Would you be willing to go now, Dad? If Boston could pretend not to have seen you . . . "

"I can't do that, I'm afraid." Boston offered Ginnie the smallest of smiles, and grew a little less still. "But I'm sure, if I advise them to, the Roanokes will grant your father a certain latitude due to the extenuating circumstances." Boston turned his attention to her father, gaze tight. "Ginnie deserves better than to have you make this rather traumatic experience worse for her."

Her father twisted to hold her and Ginnie felt like some kind of contest between him and Boston had snapped, so it would no longer escalate. Now it was Boston he pointedly ignored. "We can leave once you feel ready to travel," he allowed. He ushered her back to the truck and she climbed up to get dressed properly.

Ginnie tried to dress as fast as possible, but she ached all over. "I think you have to go *now.*"

"Not without you." Her father leaned in to grab her shoes and socks, and she sat on the tailgate and allowed him to put them on for her.

Another shout bubbled up. *If this is for me, then ask for permission, for my sake!* Ginnie swallowed it too. "Boston, may we have a little more time—" She got tangled up in her words, trying to phrase it diplomatically, like her mom had said. "To let Dad get out of here because he'd too stubborn to give in" wasn't diplomatic.

Boston sighed and rocked his weight back on his heels. "If you promise, as you grow up, to not shield him from the consequences of choices he makes only on his own behalf," he said solemnly.

"Oh, for Lady's sake," her father snarled under his breath.

"Okay," Ginnie agreed, over top of him. She wasn't sure she completely understood what Boston meant, but she'd gotten the gist. Her father was here because he was helping her this time. That might not be true other times.

When her shoes were on, Ginnie pulled on her backpack and held out her arms for her dad. Maybe she was a little bit okay with being carried. This time. "Dad, I want to come back to Boston for the summer in a couple weeks, after we have my Lady Ceremony at home."

Her father considered her, face set. "Why should I reward you for disobeying me and getting yourself into a lot of trouble because of it?"

Ginnie bit her lip. Because he frustrated her but he was a good dad and she wanted this so badly? But she supposed good parents didn't give their kids everything they wanted. They gave their kids what was good for them. But why would he believe her opinion about what was good for her? "Because two alphas yelling at each is making Mom upset," she said finally. "Only until school starts again. Please?"

"I suspect Ginnie has fully reaped the consequences of her actions in this case," Boston put in.

Her father was silent for one more beat. "Fine." He boosted her up and held her tight, head on his shoulder like she was much younger, his touch protective, not angry.

"Thank you, Daddy," she said, because that seemed right. He'd helped her. She did love him.

"Sorry, puppy," he said, so low she wasn't sure she'd heard it. Was he actually apologizing for—no. She wasn't going to prod at it.

She let her head rest on her father's shoulder. Viewed sideways as she climbed out of the truck, Felicia gave Ginnie a nod like maybe she was a little impressed, which felt pretty good. And Tom caught her eye and grinned. He dropped his head over his phone, then hers buzzed. She could guess the message: *See you soon.*

She closed her eyes. So that was her first shift. If she felt different now, it wasn't really due to having a wolf form. And she'd think more about that later when she wasn't so Lady-damned tired.

CPSIA information can be obtained at www.ICGtesting.com
Printed in the USA
LVOW11s1550201016

509596LV00005B/824/P